SPACE GADGET

The reporters at the press conference were persistent. An unknown nation had launched a satellite, which was now orbiting through space.

"Mr Secretary," one reporter demanded, "what intelligence do you have about this satellite—who launched it and why?"

This was the question the Secretary of Defense had been anticipating, and he was ready for it. "Ladies and gentlemen, I find it difficult to get excited over a harmless gadget that will sit out in space doing nothing. I abhor the sensationalism with which this story is being treated, and I'm counting on you to help me put the matter to rest once and for all."

He smiled benignly at the audience and the cameras, not realizing that with each reassuring word he was helping to seal the doom of the world.

We will send you a free catalog on request. Any titles not in your local bookstore can be purchased by mail. Send the price of the book plus 50¢ shipping charge to Leisure Books, P. O. Box 511, Murray Hill Station, New York, N. Y. 10156.

Titles currently in print are available for industrial and sales promotion at reduced rates. Address inquiries to Nordon Publications, Inc., Two Park Avenue, New York, N. Y. 10016, Attention: Premium Sales Department.

NOONBLAZE

Milan Chiba

LEISURE BOOKS ∞ NEW YORK CITY

**To the Pentagon press corps—
for its four-decade pursuit of truth in government.**

A LEISURE BOOK

Published by

Nordon Publications, Inc.
Two Park Avenue
New York, N. Y. 10016

Copyright © 1981 by Nordon Publications, Inc.

All rights reserved
Printed in the United States

1

An urgent call from the London bureau of the International Press roused Quentin Ross out of bed. He tiptoed past his mumbling wife and dressed in darkness. Unshaven and without breakfast he drove hurriedly from Georgetown across the Potomac to the Pentagon and parked his rusted '49 Ford coupe in the spot reserved for senior reporters. At the Mall entrance a civilian guard waved him through with a grunt. He took the short walk up a bilious green corridor, halting at the cavernous Defense Department newsroom where he found Lt. Colonel Terry Stewart sitting alone, hunched over the phone in guarded conversation. Ross waited a long minute, staring at endless rows of empty desks and padlocked filing cabinets, then tapped Stewart on the shoulder.

"Colonel, I hate to interrupt—"

Startled, Stewart cupped his hand over the receiver.

"Colonel, I've got a hot query for you."

Shrugging, Stewart begged off the phone, fingered the hack watch on his wrist and studied it in disbelief. "Good God, Mr. Ross! It's only six o'clock!"

"Colonel, I know damned well what time it is."

"But no self-respecting reporter hits this newsroom before ten."

Ross lit his pipe, propping himself up on a corner of Stewart's cluttered desk. "I'll do anything to protect a scoop, Colonel. I hope you're the night duty officer."

"Sorry."

"Where is he?"

"In the can or slurping coffee at the cafeteria. I guess I've relieved him by showing up early. I'm just trying to beat D.C. traffic."

"A real eager beaver, the last one in Washington!"

"I find Pentagon duty not half as bad as Strategic Air Command alerts."

Ross said through a cloud of acrid smoke, "You must've screwed up at SAC to get transferred to the Pentagon, and worse yet, to the Defense Department itself! If you're that incompetent, Colonel, I'll wait around for another spokesman."

Stewart laughed. "I'm afraid you're stuck with me for at least two hours, Mr. Ross, so you got up for nothing. Relax."

"Hell! I can't relax! I must get the scoop confirmed as soon as possible. I'm first in with the query and I better be the first out with the answer. London's all over me to meet its European deadline: noon, our time."

"Well, good luck, Mr. Ross. And speaking of incompetence, I admit I majored in journalism."

"You've just explained it, Colonel. Air Force computers scanned SAC's personnel tapes and you fell out."

Stewart snickered. "You sure know the system."

But Ross suspected Stewart as a general's protege at SAC who had been shipped off to Washington for broadening and promotion since the Pentagon was the Vatican of the armed forces. Ross asked, "Are you still on flying status?"

Stewart touched his command pilot's wings. "Yes, thank God."

"I hope you know the Defense Department civilians look down their noses at flyboys, especially flyboys in public affairs."

"That doesn't make sense, Mr. Ross. I think a solid background in aviation and missiles would help a spokesman talk convincingly about space defense. Don't you agree?"

"Not in Washington. Everybody's an expert in Washington. But I'm on your side, Colonel. I've watched flyboys go in and out of the Pentagon since the day it opened in '43. Guys who fly are my kind of guys. I'm sure I would've been one, except for polio." Ross tapped the orthopedic shoe on his left foot. "But enough of this chitchat, Colonel. Let's get on with the damned query."

"Righto!" Stewart said, imitating London. He inserted a mimeographed news query sheet into the typewriter, then with surprising speed typed in the obligatory information regarding time and date, the reporter's name and media affiliation, followed with his own name, grade, office symbol and telephone extension. He initialed the signature block and asked Ross to do the same.

Sighing, Ross complied with the inane bureaucratic procedure for at least the thousandth time. Stewart reinserted the form into the typewriter and sat with fingers poised over the keyboard. Ross slid off the desk, cleared his throat and said, "Okay, Colonel, quote me as follows:

> LONDON IP ADVISED BY SYMONDS OBSERVATORY THAT A SATELLITE OF UNKNOWN ORIGIN WAS LAUNCHED EARLY TODAY FROM THE SOUTHERN HEMISPHERE. SATELLITE IS DISCLAIMED BY THE U.S.S.R., FRANCE, AUSTRALIA, SOUTH AFRICA, ISRAEL, CHINA, AND INDIA. QUERY ONE: DID THE U.S. LAUNCH A YET UNANNOUNCED SATELLITE DURING THE PAST 24 HOURS? QUERY TWO: IF NOT, DOES THE U.S. KNOW WHO LAUNCHED THE SATELLITE? QUERY THREE: IS THE SATELLITE CURRENTLY TRACKED BY THE NORTH

AMERICAN AEROSPACE DEFENSE COMMAND AT COLORADO SPRINGS? QUERY FOUR: CAN THE DEFENSE DEPARTMENT ASCERTAIN THE NATURE OR PURPOSE OF THE UNIDENTIFIED SATELLITE? END QUERY. NOTE FOR THE ASSISTANT SECRETARY OF DEFENSE FOR PUBLIC AFFAIRS:AN EARLY ANSWER IS REQUESTED DUE TO LONDON IP'S NOON DEADLINE FOR EUROPEAN NIGHT ROUNDUP OF WORLD NEWS.

"A blockbuster!" Stewart said as he time-stamped the query sheet. "I wish I knew something about that satellite, but nothing's been passed on to me."

"Yet, Symonds has never been wrong in its findings, whether reporting on Russian, U.S., or anybody else's space shots. The British are most fastidious in their scientific efforts, and a thorn in the side of the superpowers."

"Mr. Ross, I'm puzzled that the launch took place south of the equator. I know there isn't a single launching pad in the bottom half of the world."

"Don't kill a lot of time puzzling over the pad, Colonel. It's only part of the query."

"What if the administration delays, or refuses to answer?"

"Ho ho!" Ross rasped through a cloud of acrid smoke. "There are many ways to skin a cat. I'll go outside of government channels for the answer, to industry sources, or to academic and scientific friends. They all have bits and pieces of the space program. I might contact certain embassy officials on Connecticut Avenue since London IP paved my way by calling their capitals. But I first deserve a decent response from my own government."

Steward bolted from his desk, then grabbed the query sheet.

"Where the hell are you going?" Ross demanded.

"Relax, Mr. Ross! My civilian boss is rattling dishes behind the filing cabinets. He's making breakfast on a bootleg hot plate."

"The cheap bastard! But have at him, Colonel," Ross muttered as he departed for the adjoining ticker room. Teletypes of the three competing wire services clattered with early morning news roundups, features for afternoon papers, sports schedules, weather reports and obituaries on the prominent dead. Two wirephoto machines had spewed out so many sepia-toned photographs that Ross was forced to kick the evil-smelling paper into the corridor. He scanned the opposition teletypes, and to his relief found not a word on Symonds. Yet time was the real enemy. The Symonds sighting was too big not to seep. The European opposition would sniff it out, ending his scoop unless he filed a dissecting Pentagon analysis of the satellite discovery for London IP.

Stewart could be trusted to get the query moving, a mandatory first step. Ross had great faith in the integrity of the uniform and believed Stewart would neither leak the query nor the answer to the competition, a nasty habit of the Pentagon's civilian hierarchy.

With a sense of mounting anticipation, Ross crossed the corridor to the deserted bullpen, a badly lit rectangular room holding forty-six desks for reporters accredited by the bureaucracy to cover the Pentagon. Three major wars had been reported out of the bullpen and the scars on its walls and furniture were permanent. Years earlier, Ross had found sanctuary in the farthest corner at a window, and then had let Pentagon press releases, photographs and industry handouts accumulate on his desk top until they formed three-foot-high obelisks. He called the towers of paper his instant memory, but the barricade screened him from unwanted visitors, other reporters, officialdom and commotion, an impregnable, psychological wall.

Ross sat down behind his fortress and glanced at a

dozen or more Pentagon press releases that had been printed during the night by public affairs elves. Silent messengers then slapped the sheaves of propaganda on the exact center of his desk, covering the one clean spot at which he functioned. Ruffling through the blue-bannered tout sheets, he read that the Army had promoted a lieutenant general to the grade of general, the Navy had mothballed still another flotilla of fighting ships, the Air Force bravely computerized another combat function, and the Marines still sought a few good men. He saved a fact sheet on the development of yet another tactical air-to-ground missile, placing it precariously on top of the current year's obelisk. It was a clear day, almost shimmering, and he stared out of his prized window at the Washington Monument a mere mile away.

Ted Harris, the absolutely bald, wizened GS-14 stooge for the assistant secretary of defense for public affairs, suddenly appeared in the bullpen and announced in a barker's voice that a press conference was scheduled at ten o'clock on the Army's enlistment problem. The Army's chief of personnel would brief on the draft to bring attention to the perennial manpower plight, a trial balloon more for Congress than the reporters. Ross silently shook his head at the ineptness of the senior service, knowing that Scotus Olney, assistant defense secretary for public affairs, would not be caught dead at the briefing, although it fell under his purview. And Harris dared not peek behind the barricade to see if Ross were present, since Ross threw large and lethal press kits at intruders, hoping to maim them with propaganda.

Ross looked at the wall clock and decided there was time to type a two hundred worder on Defense Secretary Browning Whitley's impending cancellation of the supersonic tanker for the Air Force and Navy. The prototype Mach 3-7 tanker would have paid most development costs for a first-cousin civilian airliner wanted desperately by NASA, the aviation industry and U.S.

airlines, a custom followed faithfully by all previous administrations. But Ross's ears had been filled for weeks with bitching by industry marketeers over the impending cancellation, and so the time had come to file. The story would call the secretary's hand. Odds of the secretary reversing himself at the last moment were almost nonexistent. Emboldened by this, Ross calculated that the speculation would prove correct, although earning the secretary's wrath. For certain, cancellation would gladden the hearts of Europe's shaky aerospace competition and the exclusive story would enhance IP's position in the capitals of Europe and the Orient.

Instinct dictated that he file the tanker cancellation before the Symonds query preempted his attention. He phoned his new Washington bureau chief, Merle Ivorson, to advise that the incoming tanker story be accorded priority on the European and Far East circuits. But Ivorson had only the Symonds query in mind, saying he wouldn't let the tanker story clutter the wire, then demanded that Ross extract a Symonds statement from the Pentagon within the hour and move it to London. Ross put him off until noon, explaining that the query was deep in the bureaucratic mill and further pressure would only bog it down. Ivorson slammed down the phone.

At nine o'clock Ross's coffee-drinking buddies descended on the barricade to match quarters in the King Bee game. They flipped first to find the odd man to buy the round of coffee. He then matched everyone for the round, sometimes pocketing several dollars in the noisy process. Although rarely instigating King Bee, Ross enjoyed phenomenal luck, often winning two or three matches during the day. At the moment, Milo "The Mustache" Karayn of *World Report* became King Bee but failed incredibly to match any player, a loss resulting in joyous hoots and hollers in the bullpen.

They straggled up the escalator to a third-floor coffee bar. Eric "Shrimp" Loveridge of the *Baltimore Telegram* led the way, followed by Cary Clapham of the New York Sun Syndicate, then Karayn and Ross at the rear. One of a dozen coffee bars scattered throughout the Pentagon, the horseshoe-shaped, stand-up facility was designed to accommodate at least fifty customers. Huge urns and twin cashier registers were positioned at the room's center, while the shelflike bar lined three walls and circled each post. Hard news rarely surfaced at the coffee klatches, but the raucous meetings proved mutually supportive, especially when one or more of the group felt manipulated or brutalized by Washington's political maniacs. Notes were compared to search out hidden administration motives, obfuscation of the truth and official acts of duplicity. They weren't a club, but called themselves "The Despicables," self-willed knights riding white chargers up the Hill, the White House and the Pentagon. Jousting daily with elected and appointed politicians, they brought down the invulnerable enemies just often enough to make combat worthwhile. It pleased editors but made publishers wince.

As the eldest and most experienced, and historian through survival, Ross believed that an innovative, conceptual solution to Washington's ills was impossible because all decisions were the results of committee action, which at best only improved on the obvious. And Shrimp, a generation younger, ranted beyond his years about the world's do-gooders, claiming all ills were caused by tinkerers, whether Communist, Liberal or Democrat. But Clapham and Karayn scoffed. Ross thought Shrimp more right than wrong and said they argued only about degrees of excess.

"Look who's coming through the door," Shrimp said in a stage whisper.

Resplendent in ribbons and tailored uniforms, Major General Noel Glasscock, public affairs director of the Air Force, and his counterpart, Rear Admiral Paul "Ape" Gibbon of the Navy, strode into the coffee bar and flipped coins methodically. Ape won, then staked out a place at the bar while Glasscock stood in line to pay the cashier.

"That's a pair to draw to!" Clapham exclaimed.

"They're aces, not deuces," Ross said. "I'd give my eyeteeth to know what drew them together. I'd guess they're ganging up on the Army or some civilian turkey to serve their common interest. Tomorrow they'll square off at each other."

"A shrewd analysis, Quent," Karayn said sarcastically, twirling the tips of his handlebar mustache. "Whatever the deal, Ape won't stray too far from the dictates of the chief of naval operations, no matter what his civilian secretary wants. Ape is a Green Bowler, to boot. I'm amazed the Navy sacrificed him for the crappy public affairs job."

"You don't understand that it's the new Navy look, Milo," Ross said. "Nowadays, you've got to be savvy in public affairs to get ahead in the service."

"Yeah, I did a big piece on that subject," Shrimp said.

"On the other hand," Karayn continued, "Noel is a West Pointer, but you'd never know it. He's shown no loyalty to the Army or the Air Force or anything else except machines: Mach-busting airplanes, megaton missiles and killer satellites."

"C'mon, Milo! What would you expect from an ex-fighter jockey?" Ross asked. "Once upon a time the cavalry was forced to transfer its love from the horse to the tank, then to antitank missiles, and now to laser weapons."

Shrimp agreed with Ross's analogy, but Karayn scoffed. "Apples and oranges!"

Ross shrugged and sipped his coffee as he watched Glasscock and Ape huddled over the bar, faces to the wall, shoulders touching. He prayed they weren't kicking his Symonds query around, although he didn't understand just what the Navy could contribute to the answer. Still, the services ranged far and wide in their interests. Glasscock often operated outside of his boss, the Air Force secretary, and was known to ignore the chief of staff even for courtesy backgrounding. When he had taken the Air Force's key public affairs job, Glasscock knew he was dead insofar as public relations motion was concerned, pointing this out to Ross whenever his motives were impugned. He had absolutely nothing to gain and could be his own man. One day the Air Force would quietly place him on the retired list, marking the moment he had outlived his usefulness. On the other hand, Ape was younger, vying for three stars and would make it with the slightest bit of luck.

Louise Shaw, harridan newshen for the *Tampa Herald*, loomed up in the doorway, searched for and found the quartet, then bought a cup of coffee and waddled toward them so eagerly that she spilled it over her hand and dress. Clapham cursed softly at her presence, but moved his burly frame to make room for her at the bar.

Ross offered a handkerchief to stem the spill. Lu muttered, "Hello, you bastards," and got a chorus of moans in response. "Quent!" she said imperiously, cigarette hanging off a snaggled eyetooth, "I hear you've got a hot query working."

"Do I?" Ross asked, missing a heartbeat.

"Something about four squadrons of cheap F-25 fighters being foisted off on one of our unsuspecting allies."

Ross smiled. "That's about right, Lu."

She swirled the remains of the coffee in the paper cup, then said for all to hear, "I've got all the facts on the F-25's, but I don't have the date it's to be announced. Any help?"

"It has to be on any Friday after the stock market closes in New York."

"I know that better than you do, Quent. Which Friday?"

"This Friday, Lu," Ross volunteered with relief that she hadn't stumbled across Symonds.

"Thanks, Quent. And I'll tell you guys this sale saves

Consolidated Aircraft Industries from going down the tube financially. As usual, the domestic economy dictates military decisions, not military worth of the equipment."

"Lu, it was ever thus," Shrimp said, "although the F-25 isn't the worst bird in the world."

"Buy Consolidated F-25's and save NATO," Lu grumbled. "It's worth five points on the market if you call your broker immediately, boys. And I'm sure the administration's all loaded up on Consolidated if Quent's right."

Ross bowed to Lu. "Now that the story's out at my expense, thanks to Lu, what do I get in return?"

"Lu will give you a big fat kiss for all of us," Clapham said with zest as he and the others eased out of the bar.

Lu reddened. Ross saved her pride with a hug and a peck on the cheek. In spite of her arrogance and ragged appearance, she was smart as a whip, extracting more respect from the Pentagon's leaders than all of the male reporters put together. More than once Ross had prevailed on her good nature to interview a balky official who had made himself inaccessible to any reporter. She never failed to get the interview, then shared the story with Ross as a gesture of professional kinship.

All smiles, Ape and Noel departed suddenly, each to his propaganda machine numbering hundreds of military and civilian subordinates scattered on the third and fourth floors of the Pentagon. Ross wanted out of the coffee bar also, but Lu held him back. "Quent," she whispered, "there's something big brewing. I feel it in my bones. I've heard a rumor that the Strategic Air Command is on yellow alert."

"Hell! SAC goes on yellow alert every time Russia's dictator gets gas pains, to put it politely."

Mollified, Lu clutched his arm and propelled him to the escalator. He was sorely tempted to alert her to the Symonds query, but couldn't quite bring himself to betray London IP's confidence. In times past Lu had also held out on him. At the moment he would have preferred joining the Despicables on their daily stroll through the Pentagon's parklike central mall for a breath of fresh air. Many of the building's ten thousand secretaries were similarly inclined, so the sport of girl-watching had no peer in Washington.

Parting in the bullpen, Lu dove into her typewriter to file a financial analysis of the F-25 sale for a confidential weekly newsletter. Ross found a fresh batch of neatly stacked press releases and skimmed through the pile, hoping to discover something of value, but the Pentagon's public affairs office rarely put out hard news. Scotus Olney yipped frequently at the Pentagon reporters that they were spoiled with unnecessary attention and spoon-fed with information, yet any reporter writing stories based on Olney's puffery would soon find himself fired. Ross heaved all of the Defense flak into the wastebasket, then wandered into the ticker room. He searched for word of Symonds on the opposition teletypes, saw nothing and felt a tingle of satisfaction that he still held a scoop.

Gladdened by good fortune, he trailed a trim airline captain into the bullpen. Airline people were seldom seen in the Pentagon, but the gold-braided captain knew exactly where he was going and without hesitation approached Lu's desk. He caught her unawares with a kiss on the nape of the neck, causing the ever-present cigarette to fall from her lip as he sat down on a broken swivel chair. Amused, Ross retreated to his barricade. Lu prattled with elation and moments later called Ross across the bullpen to join them. Driven by curiosity, Ross abandoned the barricade.

With a smile reserved for men, Lu said, "I want you to meet Captain Tim Quarles of Transatlantic Air Services, and this is Quentin Ross of International Press. Believe it or not, Quent, Tim's my source on the F-25 sale."

Ross chuckled, shaking Quarles's hand. "Round-the-barn information, Captain?"

Quarles's mouth tightened.

Lu added quickly, "Quent is true-blue."

"God, I hope so!" Quarles said. "I could get canned."

Lu said, "Tim played an interesting role as a courier for Consolidated. He relayed information between Los Angeles and Athens while the sales agreement was being worked out in Washington and Wall Street. If the Greeks bought the F-25, the Turks would follow, and then the Italians and Spaniards would fall in line."

Quarles explained defensively, "All I really do is fly 747's from Los Angeles to Athens for TAS."

"But I'm damned if I understand the mickey-mousing," Ross said. "What's wrong with Consolidated using the State Department's diplomatic pouch, or better yet, State's commercial desk to relay information to and from the sales force in Athens?"

"Quent, you're naïve!" Lu said. "Let's start with commercial cable. Even coded information sent commercially is intercepted by Consolidated's competitors, as well as by the Greeks, Turks, not to mention the Russians. Airmail takes forever—a week or more—and absolutely worthless for that reason. Anything put into State's diplomatic pouch is illegal and therefore leaked to British and French competition. Anything transmitted through State's commercial desk is instantly betrayed to Consolidated's American competitors. Okay?"

Ross laughed. "Okay."

"So," Lu said after lighting a fresh cigarette, "Consolidated had but one choice: find a secret conduit. Bill Drake, chairman of Consolidated's board of directors, called me in a twit. I suggested using TAS, with Tim in mind, to pass instructions back and forth. My suggestion worked, as we now know."

"Would you do it again, Captain Quarles?" Ross asked.

"I made an extra thousand bucks a week while it lasted—in cash, of course," Quarles said disarmingly. "I had one reliable contact on the Athens end, but he wasn't exactly waiting for me at the end of the runway.

Missed connections always were a worry. There was so much at stake that I got caught up in the excitement, especially when I discovered the competition would stop at nothing to put Consolidated out of the running. That's another story."

"Save it," Lu warned. "Quent or I will pick it up after the dust settles."

Ross was impressed. "It's obvious Consolidated would've perished without you. And Lu's reward is an exclusive story for the financial and aerospace trade publications. Fair enough."

"You're damned right," Lu said.

"Leave it to a woman to arrange something clever and cozy," Ross said.

She loved the flattery. "Quent, I'm sorry I sandbagged you at the coffee bar, but I panicked after bird-dogging the F-25 sale for such a long time. The date was terribly crucial. And, Tim, by way of explanation, although Quent and I are in the same business, our readership is mutually exclusive. I do in-depth story treatment and Quent's copy is limited to two hundred and fifty words. His is an instant, worldwide audience; mine slanted to Central Florida, also to special financial interests on a weekly basis. See the difference?"

Quarles nodded. "I'm amazed at the specialization."

"Captain, you didn't answer my question," Ross said. "Would you do another courier job?"

"One restriction. No packages."

Ross and Lu laughed over the narcotics implication.

"One last point, Quent," Lu said. "Who was your source on the F-25 date?"

"That's a naughty question, but I'll tell you it's someone on the Military Assistance Program desk. Captain Quarles, MAP is the halfway house between the Pentagon and State. It's rarely contacted by reporters and for that reason neither gun shy nor dishonest."

Quarles threw up his hands. "And I thought the airlines were all screwed up!"

Lu flicked an ash on the floor. "Quent, it never occurred to me to work the MAP people. May I lean on you for that contact?"

"Anytime. My source is a girl, unmentionable, of course."

Lu grimaced as she pulled a carbon of her story and handed it to Ross. "Whatever you want to salvage out of my newsletter is okay."

"Thanks," Ross said, then shook Quarles's hand. "Good luck, Captain Conduit," he added with an exaggerated wink and returned to his barricade. Staring out of the window he thought about the complexities of the State Department and recalled Jack Kennedy's words about firing all but fifty of State's employees to save U.S. foreign relations. A moment later the phone rang. Marge wanted to know if all was well, since he had leaped out of bed without a word. He explained the Symonds scoop rather tersely and she countered with the suggestion that he pick up lamb chops for dinner. He found grocery shopping a willing chore because Marge had difficulty getting around on certain days, a victim of glaucoma. A frail woman, she spoke softly with a Tidewater accent and possessed the innate grace of Virginia's wellborn. Their only child, Judy, produced two sets of twins in three years of marriage, all girls, all hellions. Ross reveled in the grandfather's role, feeling very much in step with the times because women outnumbered men and therefore ruled the country. He insisted that the civilization was a de facto matriarchate.

Turning to the typewriter, he banged out fast words on the F-25 sale, developing his own lead but using background pulled out of Lu's newsletter. As always, her research was complete, her facts incontrovertible. He spent several minutes editing the draft, walked quickly to the ticker room, sat down at the IP teletype and filed the story, compulsively adding a five o'clock hold on its release, not only to protect Lu's copy, but to leave himself open for a kill in the event of an official denial of the sale. It would follow the Symonds story, certain to please Ivorson. Returning to the bullpen, he told Lu he had filed with a hold. She nodded perfunctorily while digging through a mound of Congressional Records, GSA regulations and contract announcements for suspected fraud in GI blanket and uniform procurement. He smiled, remembering she was a good Back Bay Boston lawyer above all else.

Time neared for action on the satellite query. If the answer was in the affirmative, Stewart would rush across the corridor to hand him the completed query sheet. If the answer was in the negative or particularly stupid, Stewart would sit back and wait for him to come and get it.

Reporters straggled into the bullpen to check mail, to scan press and photo releases, and to horse around in almost adolescent behavior while waiting for freebie lunches. Invitations by phone came through in flurries, raising din and confusion as names were paged and conversations brought to shouting levels. A handful of reporters typed stories off the press releases or conducted quickie phone interviews, oblivious of the tumult. Ross hated the hour and was not at his best declining the freebies. He knew he was a special prize for the defense industry's public relations and marketing men. They tried hard to expose him to their pitch, which they hoped would be reflected in what he wrote. His name on an expense account gladdened the hearts of their employers whether he had lunch at an expensive restaurant or ate a sandwich alone at the Pentagon coffee bar.

At a quarter past twelve he left the barricade, crossed the corridor and walked through the Defense newsroom to Stewart's desk, fearful for the worst. His instinct proved correct. Stewart was nowhere in sight. Ross cursed aloud, turning several clerical heads as he stomped out. In the corridor his imagination pictured Scotus Olney coaching Stewart in a recitation of official lies regarding the Symonds query. Ross decided to beard Scotus in his den, but detoured for a moment to the men's room. While standing at the urinal he was jostled by a person who offered no apology. Furious, he stepped back only to recognize Stewart.

"I'm glad I bumped into you, Mr. Ross," Stewart said with a smirk and handed him the query sheet across the urinal partition.

With his free hand Ross read the Defense Department's answer:

> "No evidence exists regarding the launch of an alleged satellite from the southern hemisphere. Neither the Defense Department nor NASA has launched a satellite during the past 72 hours."
> /s/ Scotus Olney, ASD/PA.

"I must say you've caught me in the right place with your answer, Colonel," Ross said with disgust, shoving the query sheet into his pocket. He moved to the sink and washed his hands.

After examining the stalls for feet, Stewart joined him. "Mr. Ross, we're alone. I can background you on the satellite, but it's not for publication."

"Is that Scotus Olney's idea, Colonel?"

"No. It's my idea."

Ross leaned against the sink. "Colonel, I know you're trying to dampen my frustration with a backgrounding, but it ties my hands. Apparently you've learned something since we came in this morning. If what you tell me is not for publication, then I'm forced to sit back. Even though I get a clearer picture of what's going on, I just can't print it. The administration thus gets the upper hand and pursues one of two routes, either of which destroys my story. It makes a general press release on the satellite, thus killing my scoop, or worse, leaks only what it wants the public to know through one of its captive media outlets. Do you follow me?"

"Sure, Mr. Ross. It's fascinating the way the government works."

"So I can't accept your backgrounding, Colonel. Remember, if I were to listen to what was not for publication and then violated your confidence by printing, your bosses will find you out because you possess the information, yet are too green to cover your tracks, especially during an inquisition. They'll have your ass!"

Stewart blanched.

"I apologize for the diatribe, Colonel. I'm not attacking you personally for the Administration's tactics. I don't want to see you wounded. You're a clean-cut kid, a straight arrow, and all that. Of course, I could let you background me and then murder you by printing what you said. Half of Washington's news corps would do it and lose no sleep. If that happens, goodbye career, Colonel. The civilians in this building love to chew up guys in uniform—a display of power. So you have enemies in your camp as well as out of it. Okay?"

"Okay. I understand, Mr. Ross."

"Call me Quent, and I must take you to lunch or dinner to finish the briefing, a place that isn't bugged."

"How about dinner at my house?"

"No thanks," Ross said abruptly. "We try not to drag our wives into the jungle we work in."

"Good God!"

"Colonel, you're not in the attaché service or in Legislative Liaison up on the Hill. Wives are important there, but not here. If anything, we try to shelter our families from the effects of daily combat in the news business and so we take little or nothing home. Phone calls are bad enough. If you don't find the guts to swing a super-large, super-sharp machete in the Defense newsroom, let alone in my bullpen, get out before you're hacked to death."

"Quent, I've been in Vietnam and been hacked at. I don't run scared. By the way, my friends don't call me colonel. I'm Terry."

Ross smiled at Stewart's unbending. "Fair enough, Terry. Maybe we can walk two-abreast on the long, hard road ahead of us."

2

In a blue mood, Ross phoned the bureau chief, Merle Ivorson, to say that the Pentagon had shafted him with its inane answer to the satellite query. Ivorson wanted the Pentagon's exact words so he could protest directly to Phil Fairly, the White House press secretary. Ross refused on the grounds that the answer had been coordinated with Fairly before release, although he couldn't prove it. Ivorson pressed the issue and Ross finally told him to get out of the act. Ivorson remained silent for a long minute, then spluttered, "Quent, you're the highest paid hack covering the Pentagon. You're supposed to get results. We've got a clear jump on the whole damned world because of IP's friends at Symonds, but if you dick around much longer, playing games with friends and foes, we'll get scooped for sure!"

Ross sucked hard on his pipe to control his temper, then said hoarsely, "Damn it, Merle! The Pentagon hasn't changed. It takes time to unearth anything of value. If worse comes to worse, I'll file the satellite story as part of the usual military news roundup for the late evening and early morning editions." While talking, Ross reminded himself that Ivorson was the fourth Washington bureau chief to come aboard since the

Pentagon was built. Of the two assignments, his versus the one downtown, running the bureau was child's play, a role like that of a traffic cop, channeling local and regional news, moving national and international stories on the proper circuits to member newspapers, magazines and radio-television networks. Little news was edited by the bureau chief because of the caliber of copy written by the reporters. Wirephotos were a matter of simplistic judgement. Insofar as Ross could tell, Ivorson saw that the office was swept up and the reporters and office help paid punctually. More than enough time was left over to swill with the other bureau chiefs at the bar of the National Press Club.

"I must send London an update on the Pentagon's official satellite position within the next half hour, Quent."

"Dear God!" Ross groaned. "The Pentagon isn't the world's sole source of satellite wisdom."

"But it sure as hell is the most likely source of satellite information. Just think of the billions of dollars spent by your Pentagon wizards on space defense in the past ten years. Today, Quent, you can't seem to get a friggin' dime's worth of information out of them!"

"It means I may be forced to speculate, but using a Washington dateline will make it more believable. Please keep London open to me for any late data out of Symonds."

"And what are you doing while Symonds does your legwork for you?"

Ross ignored the sarcasm, explaining patiently, "I'm forced to go one of two routes in shaping the story. I can play up the huge mystery behind the Symonds sighting, using the Pentagon's crappy statement as a simple footnote. Better yet, I can speculate that the Symonds sighting of the unidentified or orphan satellite presents a real threat to one or more nations, stressing that the satellite's very existence is something far beyond the Pentagon's ability to verify, let alone assess and cope

25

with. This angle will shake up the White House, the Hill, NATO and assorted allies."

"Sounds great, but the administration will put the heat on me."

"Only to muzzle me. It's not the first time, Merle, nor the last."

Ivorson swore with frustration and Ross could hear his heavy breathing for a minute afterward. Finally, Ivorson asked, "Any leaks yet?"

Ross half-stifled a laugh. Ivorson hated heat and was praying for a way out. "No," Ross said. "I'm convinced the administration doesn't know what to do with the query. That's the only reason they haven't leaked the answer to their captive media boys. And I suspect they're beating the hell out of the Air Force at Bright Lake to lock onto the satellite. The Air Force got caught flat-footed because of the southern hemisphere launch and I'll bet defense center at Colorado Springs is on full alert and sweating. Not too many of their detection satellites are turned on while orbiting the bottom of the world. I remember that's how they cut down on critical battery drain."

"You ought to be writing science fiction, Quent."

"A compliment, of course. Getting back to the heat, I don't give a damn if IP is a source of embarrassment to the administration. We're both eager for front page coverage of a mysterious sighting, an unidentified satellite launched from the wrong place, an evasive denial from the administration, a new kind of Sputnik streaking around the sky for God knows what reason. Take your pick, Merle. Back off and be popular at the White House, or be a bum with me."

"Don't lecture me, Quent!"

"I just want you to declare yourself before the heat's put on. Are you Mr. Nice Guy or your true self?"

"Either way I'll ride your ass. If you quit, I must know your Symonds contact."

Ross clenched the phone, reminding himself he had to

26

outlast Ivorson because the next bureau chief couldn't be worse. He answered, "Whether I quit or not, my contact is a newly assigned colonel on the press desk, Terry Stewart. He's legal and official and the one that handed me Defense's stupid answer."

"Why a colonel?"

"It's a ploy the civilian hotshots use to give credibility to their handling of the press. After all, the Pentagon is supposed to be headquarters for the military establishment."

"So the colonel's a dummy?"

"Well, yes and no."

"How much does he know beyond the answer to the query?"

"I suspect some."

"Are you going to work on him?"

Ross hesitated, then said, "Merle, you know goddamn well the phones are bugged."

"Okay! Okay! I'll stall London and I won't go home until you file."

"Suit yourself," Ross said, hanging up in disgust.

Stewart rounded the barricade and whispered, "Coffee at the upstairs bar?"

"Why not, Terry? Let's leave the bullpen separately."

Stewart nodded and strode out.

Ross rode the escalator alone, wondering whether Stewart had been ordered by Noel to toss him a tidbit, or whether Stewart was acting in Scotus Olney's behalf.

Buying coffee separately, Ross met Stewart at the wall bar and huddled in much the same manner as Noel and Ape had earlier in the day.

"Who prompted this?" Ross asked.

Stewart looked chagrined. "No one."

"What's up?"

"You're sure suspicious, Quent. I just wanted to pass along an item that's obviously escaped you. What I'm going to say is clearly in the public domain, but only the aerospace press, one technical daily, and a weekly magazine reported the item."

Ross guffawed. "Nothing escapes my eagle eye!"

"Well, this did, or you would've pounced on it by now."

"Go on."

Stewart's face broke into a conspiratorial smile and Ross was thankful that they faced the wall. "I suggest you sip and stare into your coffee when passing a confidence, Terry," Ross instructed, "because you're telegraphing your intentions all over the place."

"Roger," Stewart said reflexively in Air Force jargon, then with downcast eyes began in a barely audible voice so soft that Ross muttered, "For God's sake, Terry, now I can't hear you at all! You are overreacting! Be a bit more natural. I'm not running a school for spies."

Stewart cleared his throat, but it was apparent Ross's criticism had stung him. He sulked for a moment while Ross waited patiently. Then in a studied tone he said, "Some time ago the Air Force launched a Minuteman intercontinental ballistic missile successfully from a large cargo aircraft flying high over a test range in California. The missile was yanked out of the rear of the cargo hold by huge parachutes. When it had slid clear of the plane's tail and stabilized itself in a vertical position, the booster stage fired and the inertial guidance system took over, theoretically steering the warhead to a target many thousands of miles away. The point is that the warhead could have been a satellite to be lofted high into space. The principle of injecting either a warhead or a satellite into space with an ICBM booster is the same. The guidance system simply maneuvers the payload either down to an earth target, into an earth orbit, or on a flight into deep space—whatever is desired."

"Aha!" Ross said excitedly.

"So the Air Force proved its point," Stewart continued, "that long-range missiles need not be fired only from massive, concrete launching pads using giant gantries and other ponderous support equipment. Unfortunately for the Air Force, Congress didn't give a damn about airborne missile launch technology and refused to put up any additional money for further developmental work. The Air Force quietly wrapped up the program with a low-key press release that simply announced a successful airborne missile launch, including a couple of technical photographs. All U.S. interest died right then and there."

"By God!" Ross said, rubbing the bowl of his pipe, "I do have a vague, fleeting impression of that press release. I think we all gave it the ho-hum treatment. Never would I have made the quantum jump from that airborne test to what's happening today. What you're implying is that any nation with large cargo aircraft and possessing a missile or booster can easily fire a satellite into space from almost anywhere on the face of the earth."

"Well, there are minor complications in celestial mechanics, but nothing that can't be solved easily by any nation that wants to put its mind to it. Quent, you've got the hang of it," Stewart said, pleased with Ross's instant grasp.

Touching Stewart's arm, Ross said, "I won't press you any further, Terry. You've given me enough background information to file a damned strong speculation story on the possibility of a southern hemispheric air launch, for whatever purpose. I hope I have time to dig that press release out of the mountain of stuff piled up on my desk. Although it's not that critical for my wire story, a few technical facts will serve as long nails for Scotus Olney's coffin."

"Why bear down so hard on my boss?"

"Terry, he's no different from the other eight or ten assistant secretaries of defense for public affairs that have waltzed through this building since I've come aboard. They come in fairly clean, prejudiced only in their party's interest. Within a year they begin tinkering with the facts—with the hard news—partly because some of the information is embarrassing to their administration, and partly because they've discovered personal power. So they manage the news to please the administration and their own egos. Guys like me keep them in line. After all, they're charged with the release of information on a one hundred billion dollar defense budget each year, and more importantly, on the facts relating to our country's ability to defend itself."

"Your own ego enters into this fray, doesn't it?"

"Of course. I'm a willful man. Most reporters in this bullpen are self-appointed custodians of the public good, of the public's right to know the facts. I'm one of them. In fact, I'm a member of a most despicable inner group that prides itself that it was and is cursed by five successive administrations. What drives your bosses up the wall is that nobody appointed or elected us. We appointed ourselves. For that reason we're invulnerable to political pressures."

"You can't always be right in your reporting, can you?"

"I must be more right than wrong, Terry."

"Still, there must be flaws in your reporting."

"Damned right. Some of the information—facts and figures on defense that we report out of the bullpen—are killed by bureau chiefs, editors, and by publishers themselves."

Stewart shook his head. "That's hard to believe."

"Sometimes our stories are preempted by other stories: assassinations, catastrophes, national and international crises. But more often they're killed or shortened and gutted because of a lack of space in newspapers, or by time or lousy camerawork on network TV. Once in a while a story is killed outright because a publisher caves in under pressure from the administration—actually under any administration."

"Your stories have been killed?"

Ross groaned. "Countless times, Terry. Better that than to have them shredded into nonsense under your byline. That's what really hurts. Watch what happens to this one."

Stewart's eyes widened and after a lapse he said, "What will happen to this story?"

"Damned if I know. Nothing good, probably. But since it has international origins and implications, Washington's control is that much less."

Gulping the dregs of his coffee, Stewart then scored a bull's-eye with the paper cup, tossing it exactly into the center of a tiny trash can at the door. Ross stalled for a moment after Stewart's departure, stoking his pipe with satisfaction, then walked slowly to a window facing the inner mall. He puffed on the smoldering pipe and watched Pentagon idlers lolling along the grass perimeter in the late spring's afternoon warmth. He envied their alienation from all about them. Choosing the broad, gently sloping ramp to the second floor, he began drafting the lead sentences of his developing story. It was to be a great mental jigsaw puzzle.

Back at his desk, he knocked apart one towering mound of press releases. Shrimp yelled from across the bullpen that the walls of Jericho were coming down. Someone else volunteered that the Pentagon's last defenses were now destroyed. Ross ignored the remarks, hoping only that Shrimp, Clapham or Karayn wouldn't drift over to chat about the nature of his search. Lu growled something in praise of tidiness, her cigarette butt dangling, while pounding out captions for a high-school educational supplement. Meanwhile, Ross swept through a two-year accumulation of press handouts, then suddenly discovered the air-launch press release plus two launch photos. His pulse quickened as he folded the yellowing, mimeographed two-page release into the inner breast pocket of his seersucker jacket, dropped the photos into a catchall bottom drawer, then left the bullpen for the men's room. Choosing a far-end stall, he sat down on the toilet and quickly read the release's contents. It was almost a purely technical report with no editorializing. After absorbing its detailed technology, he debated tearing up the release and flushing it down the toilet to protect his source from other newsmen, but reconsidered since he might well need it as instant evidence if Scotus Olney started another probe.

He curbed a desire to whistle and then slackened his return to the bullpen to maintain an air of nonchalance. Fortunately, his typewriter faced the stacked wall of paper and bystanders were unable to read what rolled off the platen. This was not true in the ticker room where teletypes for sending and receiving copy were set flush against the wall. Anyone could look over the sender's shoulder. Shrimp practiced the nasty habit, although he didn't lift outgoing copy. But clues to stories being filed were fair game.

Ross inserted a sheet of fresh newsprint into the scarred Remington and started pounding out the story in draft form. Because his mind functioned visually, seeing the actual words helped organize his ignorance. After chopping the raw copy down to two hundred fifty words, he'd file the edited story on the IP teletype to the Washington bureau for transmittal over national and overseas circuits. Halfway through the first paragraph he realized it would be foolish to expose even one key word of his exclusive story in the Pentagon's ticker room. Instead, he seized the phone and called old Evelyn at the bureau and alerted her to take down his unedited copy, pointing out that the story was too hot to handle otherwise. As she sighed, he saw her in mind's eye putting on the headset and unlimbering her fingers for a fast typing job.

Ivorson cut in. "I'll take it, Quent," he said preemptively.

Ross laughed. "Are you ready, teddy?"

"Shoot!" Ivorson commanded.

Ross began methodically:

BULLETIN:

OVER 'A' CIRCUITS
BYLINE QUENTIN ROSS
DATELINE WASHINGTON THIS DATE

A MYSTERIOUS SATELLITE WAS LAUNCHED INTO SPACE EARLY TODAY BY AN UNKNOWN COUNTRY FROM AN UNDISCLOSED LOCATION IN THE SOUTHERN HEMISPHERE, ACCORDING TO SYMONDS OBSERVATORY IN GREAT BRITAIN. THE QUOTE ORPHAN UNQUOTE SATELLITE APPEARS TO WEIGH ABOUT A HALF-TON AND MARKS MAN'S FIRST SPACE LAUNCH SOUTH OF THE EQUATOR. THE UNANNOUNCED LAUNCH IS IN DIRECT VIOLATION OF SPACE COVENANTS SPONSORED BY THE UNITED NATIONS.

THE ORPHAN'S TRAJECTORY INDICATES A PROBABLE DEEP SPACE PROBE, ALTHOUGH SYMONDS OFFICIALS WILL NOT RULE OUT THE POSSIBILITY OF A POTENTIAL MILITARY SPACE THREAT DUE TO THE UNUSUAL CIRCUMSTANCES SURROUNDING THE LAUNCH.

INQUIRIES BY INTERNATIONAL PRESS TO ALL GOVERNMENTS POSSESSING SPACE CAPABILITIES HAVE BROUGHT IMMEDIATE DENIALS OF SPONSORSHIP OF THE ORPHAN LAUNCH. ADDITIONALLY, THE U.S. DEFENSE DEPARTMENT'S SPOKESMAN AT THE PENTAGON, ASSISTANT SECRETARY SCOTUS OLNEY SAID QUOTE NO EVIDENCE EXISTS HERE ON THE LAUNCH OF AN ALLEGED SATELLITE FROM THE SOUTHERN HEMISPHERE. NEITHER THE DEFENSE DEPARTMENT NOR NASA HAS LAUNCHED A SATELLITE WITHIN THE PAST 72 HOURS UNQUOTE. HOWEVER, SYMONDS OFFICIALS STAND FIRM NOT ONLY

ON SIGHTING THE ORPHAN SATELLITE, BUT ARE PLOTTING ITS PATH THROUGH SPACE AT THIS TIME. THEY SURMISE THE ORPHAN'S SOUTHERN HEMISPHERIC LAUNCH CAUGHT ALL OF THE WORLD'S TRACKING STATIONS OFF-GUARD. THE SATELLITE WAS LAUNCHED FROM THE BOTTOM HALF OF THE WORLD FOR SURPRISE EFFECT, OR IN THE HOPE IT WOULD ESCAPE DETECTION DURING ITS FLIGHT INTO SPACE.

ACCORDING TO EVIDENCE JUST UNCOVERED AT THE PENTAGON, IT IS TECHNICALLY POSSIBLE THAT THE ORPHAN SATELLITE WAS LAUNCHED BY A CARGO AIRCRAFT IN A MANNER DEMONSTRATED BY THE U.S. AIR FORCE IN A MINUTEMAN INTERCONTINENTAL BALLISTIC MISSILE TEST OVER CALIFORNIA TWO YEARS AGO. THE MINUTEMAN WAS AIR-LAUNCHED SUCCESSFULLY FROM A C-141 TRANSPORT AIRCRAFT AND PROVED IRREFUTABLY THAT WARHEADS OR SATELLITES CAN BE LAUNCHED ANYWHERE AT HIGH ALTITUDE ABOVE THE EARTH, RATHER THAN BEING RESTRICTED TO LAUNCH FROM MASSIVE CONCRETE PADS WITH ATTENDANT GANTRIES AND COMPLEX BLOCKHOUSES.

EXISTENCE OF THE ORPHAN SATELLITE WILL PROVE EMBARRASSING TO THE PENTAGON'S FAR-REACHING NORTH AMERICAN AIR DEFENSE COMMAND WHICH IS CHARGED WITH DETECTION AND TRACKING OF ALL MAN-MADE OBJECTS APPEARING IN SPACE. SYMONDS OFFICIALS FEAR THAT IF OTHER SATELLITES OR WARHEADS CAN EVADE DETECTION DURING LAUNCH OR WHILE IN FLIGHT, ANY TARGETED NATION CAN BE BLACKMAILED OR DESTROYED FROM SPACE.

THE OBSERVATORY AT THIS MOMENT IS ATTEMPTING TO RETRACE THE ORPHAN'S FLIGHT BACK TO ITS LAUNCHING POINT TO GAIN ADDITIONAL EVIDENCE REGARDING ITS ORIGIN. BULLETINS FROM THE OBSERVATORY ON FURTHER ORPHAN SATELLITE DEVELOPMENTS WILL BE TRANSMITTED BY INTERNATIONAL PRESS THROUGHOUT THE WORLD.

Ivorson muttered, "I thought you'd never stop, Quent."

"Hell! There's no private place to edit copy in this bullpen. You're the bureau chief. You wanted to take it down. You edit it!"

Ivorson hung up. Ross unlimbered his legs, kicked the chair out of the way and walked over to Lu. "I need some coffee," he said.

She finished a sentence, killed a cigarette, then joined him on the trek to the coffee bar. "What have you been up to, Quent?"

Standing on the escalator step directly behind her, he caught a trace of her honest perspiration, then whispered into her ear, "I've just busted a story on an unknown satellite, an orphan, whizzing over our heads."

Lu turned, beaming with a newsman's appreciation for a real scoop. "Congrats! When can I pick it up from you?"

"Not so fast, Lu! I'm sure there'll be solid facts breaking tomorrow morning—either here or at Symonds—certainly in time for your noon deadline in Tampa. I'll feed you whatever you need. Right now it's mostly speculation and gut feel, and you don't want that. By the way, I don't see any financial sidebar stories on this orphan."

Lu looked squarely into Ross's eyes. "Was your source in or out of the Pentagon?"

"Symonds Observatory in England," he said hoarsely, "and a clue here."

"That figures," Lu said with a wry smile. "The English are more open because they are more honest in their scientific work. We're as bad as the Russians."

Ross agreed. "Too many people milling around in our government, just like the Russians and Chinese. Everybody monitors everybody else for conformity, in order to prevent disclosures. And progress be damned!"

The coffee bar was deserted. Ross paid a vacuous cashier and they moved near the door, talking openly. Lu tumbled the tarlike coffee in an extralarge cup. "I hate to think what my kidneys look like, swilling this slop all day."

"An occupational hazard, Lu."

"Speaking of that," Lu said, "have you thought through the administration's reaction to what you've just filed?"

"Only to the extent that they'll throw another fit, but you and I have weathered other storms."

"It's wearing me down, and I look it."

Ross said nothing.

Shifting gears, she asked, "Any guesses who owns the satellite?"

"Now, I have thought long and hard about that," Ross said, knowing his confidence was inviolate. "It could be a simple space experiment pulled off by a beggar nation, duplicating what our Air Force tried several years ago, or it could be something really sinister, perpetrated by a major power. I just don't know, but thank God for Symonds! I can't trust the administration on any aspect of this story."

"You mean we could get clobbered and never know what hit us?"

"Well, Lu, we've talked about it before. The administration might try to shield the nation, even though it knows the true nature of the orphan. Panic in the streets could kill millions. Yet the administration may be as befuddled as I am at this very moment, in spite of all the detections systems at its command."

"What about our new Colonel Stewart? He's Air Force, a logical, disciplined, informed guy."

"He doesn't know much more than I do on this late-breaking story. And I don't think the administration would expose him to any vital information to help him cope with his job. He's a sacrificial lamb, at best."

"A pretty one for a change."

Ross shrugged. "Just like a woman, injecting sex into the job. But back to my story. I wish I knew whether Symonds Observatory was very lucky or very expert in its sighting of the orphan."

"As astronomers and mathematicians they'd hardly admit to chance."

"Professionalism does get in the way, Lu."

"What's your next move?"

"I'm going home to get some rest. London IP will be all over me before dawn."

"There's got to be a better way to make a living, Quent."

"Too late now, for both of us," Ross said, placing his arm around her. They walked the ramp in reverie to the second floor, neither inclined to say a word. Lu went back to her typing after Ross reminded her to watch the IP ticker. He picked up a freebie copy of Washington's evening newspaper from the center of his desk and tucked it under his arm to scan at home.

Ted Harris bumbled into the bullpen and loudly summoned Ross to Scotus Olney's office. Lu laughed hard while typing. Ross hesitated, looked at his watch, then reluctantly decided to follow Harris.

"Good luck!" Lu yelled witchlike, waving a pencil as if it were a wand.

Ross said irritably to Harris, "It's getting late," as they strode the quiet corridor. "What the hell does your boss want?"

"Dunno for sure," Harris said, "except that he just got

37

off the phone to Phil Fairly at the White House. They've read your byline on the IP ticker."

Ross whistled. "That quick?"

"Mr. Olney is furious you didn't give him a courtesy briefing on what you filed. After all, you live here."

Ross snorted. "I moved that goddamned story in spite of your boss!"

"He's embarrassed that the entire White House staff read the story before he did."

"Isn't that too bad."

"And I caught hell because I didn't flash the IP ticker story so he could track it while the White House bitched and moaned."

"But Scotus has his personal copy now, doesn't he? You pulled it off the ticker machine—"

"Damned right! Guess I'll have to live in the ticker room from now on, since you reporters won't give us a break," Harris said petulantly as they neared the assistant secretary's unmarked private door.

Scotus rated three immense windows on the coveted outside "E" ring of the second floor. He, too, had a clear view of the Washington Monument, but, when sitting, turned his back on it so that on sunny days a visitor was blinded, and on dark days the visitor's attention was drawn off to the blinking Washington skyline across the Potomac. Scotus practiced the clean desk philosophy, and as some wag observed, this was symptomatic of an empty head.

Ross trooped in behind Harris and dropped his long frame into a well-contoured leather chair while Scotus held forth obliviously on a red scrambler phone back to his counterpart at the White House. The conversation was cryptic and Ross felt too tired to follow it. Instead, he surveyed Harris, standing almost at attention as administrator to Scotus, a professional lackey, bald, shrunken, and garrulous when probed. Scotus, even behind his enormous, rococo desk, seemed squat and potbellied. His tie, always askew, somehow matched the stray wisps of gray hair pasted across his shiny pate. Harris and he were known as the Gold Dust Twins, except that Scotus never conversed with anyone. He just shouted.

Surreptitiously, Ross felt for the air-launch press release, then thanked God he hadn't removed it from his breast pocket. He crossed and recrossed his legs, stretched his game leg, lit his pipe and let it go out while Scotus disclaimed on the phone. It soon would be too late to stop off at the supermarket for Marge. They'd have to settle for a bucket of fried chicken. Poor Marge, the untimate victim of madmen like Scotus.

Ross was tempted to walk out. Then Scotus would have cause to harangue Ivorson. Another phone call came in, signaled by a flashing amber light at the corner of the desk. Scotus hung up quickly and went through another set of histrionics with the second caller. Fortunately, it proved of short duration. Still shouting, he turned his attention to Ross. "You put me in one hell of a bind, Quent!"

"How's that?"

"You know damned well what I mean. I just got my ass raked by Fairly for not knowing what you guys are doing right under my nose!"

"Oh, get off it!" Ross said, rising to Scotus's temper. "I'm pleading the First Amendment!"

"Sure, Quent, you can file anything you want, but when it comes to a story of this magnitude, don't you think you ought to alert me, perhaps wave your copy at me, just out of courtesy?"

"And just what have you done for me lately?" Ross asked, fuming. "This morning I tossed you a damned legitimate query on that orphan satellite. So what happened? Let me refresh your memory, Scotus. You and your gang tried to screw me with a half-assed answer! Unfortunately, I must make a living reporting the news out of this crazy building. When you deny me legitimate answers to legitimate queries, you are taking bread out of my mouth."

Scotus pointed a gross finger at Ross. "You, sir, are guilty of a security violation! I'm going to lift your Pentagon accreditation for it!"

Ross slapped his knee and laughed. "Go right ahead, Mr. Secretary. You haven't got a case!"

"Where did you pick up the test data on the Minuteman air launch? I'm advised it is classified secret."

Ross said, "The Minuteman test might damned well been classified secret or top secret until the Air Force launched the missile into the bright blue sky. Scotus, you weren't even on board then, so how the hell would you know? Once a test is conducted in the open for all to see, then it must be declassified. That's just what the Air Force did, and here's the press release to prove it. Quit trying to intimidate me, Scotus, with fake security raps. Your advisors stink."

Scotus backed off under the rasping tirade. Ross tossed the press release at him. "Read it and weep."

Snatching the press release, Scotus scanned it in silence. When finished, it was obvious to Ross he was deflated but still had to protect his ego. "Who put you on to this release?" he demanded.

"Scotus, if you'd ever condescend to walk down to the bullpen, you'd discover piles of government propaganda stashed right on top of my desk. This press release has been sitting in one of the piles for two years. Look at those yellowed edges."

"And I still say somebody pointed you in the direction of that air test."

Ross scoffed. "Look, Scotus, I'm the living historian in this building, so don't tell me what I do or don't remember, what I do or don't save."

"Okay, Quent, so you're a living historian. We can't take that away from you, but we sure as hell can take away your informants."

"Like who?"

"Like Major General Noel Glasscock, for one."

"Why Noel?"

"Because the Air Force stands to look good in this caper, while the rest of us run around with egg on our face!"

"That's the craziest reason I've ever heard of, Scotus. Let's leave Noel out of this. I haven't exchanged a word with him for days."

"Then it's that colonel he shipped down to the newsroom."

"The kid's green."

"Maybe so, but he's a conduit!"

"It's getting late, Scotus. Let's get onto something else."

"Like what?"

"Like a followup to my query on the orphan satellite."

"Resubmit your query," Scotus shouted, slamming his fist on the desk and swiveling the back of his chair to Ross.

"Damned right I will, first thing in the morning! We're getting ourselves into another Mexican standoff, Scotus."

Turning his attention to the phone, Scotus dialed while Harris escorted Ross out of the office, this time past Suzy's desk in the reception room. Ross wondered why Sexy Suzy worked for the oaf, but where else could she snare a GS-9 salary?

Once in the corridor, Ross dragged himself to the nearest pay phone. He dialed in the privacy of the booth and was relieved when Stewart answered. "I'm glad you're still on board, Terry," he said quietly. "I must talk to you right away, but not here. How about dinner in town?"

"Great!" Stewart said enthusiastically. "It beats batching. My family left for Denver on summer vacation, now that school's out."

"Okay, then. I'll call Marge and apologize that I'll be home late. Meet me at Chambouard's on the river in an hour."

"Roger," Stewart said, but Ross detected a note of

hesitation, almost reluctance.

Leaving the phone booth, Ross wondered whether he was doing right by Stewart. He felt a moral compulsion to repay Stewart's unsolicited favor because the Minuteman air-launch information added substance and credibility to the scoop. Yet, any further involvement or professional intimacy was a form of entrapment. Once drawn into the Pentagon's inner circle of newsmen, sharing confidences and intrigues would strip Stewart of his strongest defense: innocence; that is, if he were charged with complicity and disloyalty by his civilian masters in the Defense Department. On the other hand, if Stewart was a principled man, if his combat experience in Vietnam was meaningful, then the tour in the newsroom would only strengthen his character and enhance his image in the eyes of his parent service, the Air Force.

Ross brooded walking down the long corridor, then dismissed his anxiety with the thought that neither Stewart nor he could really control any aspect of their private destinies, much less the nation's.

3

Chambouard's parking lot, long and narrow, fronted the muck-laden Potomac. Ross drove to the farthest end and parked in the lengthening shadows cast by an enormous willow. Stewart strode up laughing and pointed to the Old English lettering emblazoned on the right door of the coupe.

"Who named it Cuspidor?"

"Marge did when I wouldn't trade it for a new model. By the way, I didn't recognize you in mufti, Terry. You're one of the few the uniform doesn't do much for."

"A compliment?"

"Sort of," Ross said as he moved to the trunk and unlocked it.

Stewart peered at a mass of crumpled, yellow rubber. "What have you got stashed away in there, Quent?"

"An inflatable life raft."

"Are we going boating? I'm sure as hell not dressed for it."

"Exploring. Just relax, Terry."

"What happened to dinner?"

"A little later," Ross said irritably as he pulled out the deflated raft. "Help me set this damned thing up. I've got a CO_2 cartridge to inflate the raft quickly, but let's first untangle it."

43

Stewart got down on his knees and smoothed out the mass of rubber. Ross inserted the cartridge into the raft's valve and pulled the lanyard. The raft popped into shape with a loud bang that drove several nesting birds into the air. Ross threw two collapsible oars into the raft and then they carried it handily to the water's edge. He looked warily in all directions but the maneuver was unobserved.

"What's this all about?" Stewart demanded as if Ross were daft.

"You'll see soon enough. I won't drown you. Get into that thing, paddle to keep steerage way, then I'll hop aboard with this damned leg of mine. If we do it right we won't get wet, coming or going."

"Quent," Stewart said with a shake of his head, "it's been a long day. I never thought that there was enough time left to go boating, or an Inchon landing, or whatever the hell it is you have in mind. But it's a good thing I owned a dinghy as a kid."

"Indeed," Ross said, unimpressed. "You're supposed to be a many-talented guy, according to the Air Force. In fact, I can see the seaman in you. Just keep that damned raft steady while I get into it."

Ross grabbed a line strung along the raft's topside and crawled aboard without difficulty.

"Now what?" Stewart asked, pulling away from shore with his back to the direction of movement. Ross faced forward on his knees.

"Let's not get caught in the current," Ross warned. "It'll sweep us downstream. Hug the shore. We're going up to the pilings that Chambouard's is built on. I've got a little job to do there." He extracted a pair of wire clippers from a hip pocket as Stewart looked over his shoulder to maintain direction.

"Are you defusing a bomb?" Stewart asked. But before Ross could answer, the raft suddenly spun around and Stewart's oars made the motion worse.

"Let her drift for a second," Ross commanded, "and

she'll straighten out by herself."

"I know that," Stewart said, "but I've already lost fifty feet of hard rowing."

"Better that than to capsize, Terry. No one will rescue us. Know why?"

"Because nobody saw us."

"No! Because the Potomac's too polluted!"

Stewart groaned over the gallows humor as he regained headway. A bit of brisk rowing brought them to the pilings. Ross produced a powerful, space-age flashlight from another pocket, then said, "Terry, I'd like you to grab hold of a piling and hold us stationary while I flash the light on the underside of Chambouard's flooring."

"What are you looking for?"

"Wires, bugging wires."

"Just because we're having dinner here?"

"Partly, but more because I hate the government bugging every inch of our existence."

"Gad! It's that bad, really?"

"Sure. But this caper tonight is as much for revenge and spite as it is for anything else."

"Quent, you're a madman!"

"Probably."

"I'd think the buggers would use directional eavesdropping antennas. It'd be a helluva lot easier than wiring the restaurant."

Ross lowered his voice to a low rasp. "Not at all, Terry. Electronic gear picks up all of the extraneous noise and chatter that can't be filtered out. This drives the buggers crazy. They prefer to wire a place like this after business hours, and the gear functions for a long, long time."

"Then why Chambouard's for dinner?"

"They're all bugged, but Chambouard's more fun for me because I can get back at the buggers."

"Does the management know about the bugging?"

"Probably not. And if they did know, they wouldn't care. I doubt any restaurateur could stop it. Publicity would scare off business and the buggers would come right back with more and better microphones."

"How can the buggers monitor all conversations? It's impossible."

"They listen in at selected tables and locations when they're tagging someone or a sensitive situation. Mostly, conversations are monitored at random, just like the Pentagon's phone system. But we've talked enough, Terry. I've got to get to work."

Stewart held the raft steady while Ross played the intense light over a large section of the underside flooring without success. The river sloshed, gurgled, thumped and slurped in the man-made grotto. After much fruitless neckstraining, Ross motioned Stewart to row upstream to the very edge of the restaurant's overhang. Suddenly Ross stood bolt-upright, balancing himself with the flashlight in one hand and clippers in the other, then reached up and missed his mark, cursing the low tide. But on the next swell he fairly leaped, grabbed two slender black wires tacked to a rotting beam, pulled them downward, and with a deft snip severed the strands. Another yank brought them trailing down into the water. He doused the light and signaled Stewart to row back.

Once cleared of the pilings he lit his pipe and said, "There may be more wires, but I don't want to press my luck."

Stewart nodded and with the help of tide and current they quickly beached the raft at the willow, collapsed and folded it, then pushed it back into the trunk. Ross looked about in the darkness and was certain they had not been noticed. "Well done!" he said with pride.

Gleeful as a child over the deviltry, Stewart strode toward Chambouard's marquee, then stopped abruptly for Ross to catch up. "Sorry, Quent," he said solicitously.

"Not at all. I should tell you my slow going is due to this paralytic left leg—polio as a kid—it also accounts for my rotten, perverse personality."

Stewart waved his hand in protest. "Not true! You're sympathetic, honest and gutsy."

"Thanks for the kind words," Ross said, touched, "but I'm afraid this is degenerating into a mutual admiration society." He looked closely at his watch, pleased that they were within minutes of his phoned reservation. "We should be commandos with this kind of timing."

The maitre d' recognized Ross instantly, then led them to a smallish table directly over the spot where Ross had snipped the wires. Stewart laughed aloud, but Ross shut him up with a steely glare.

They studied the menu delivered by a waitress with extraordinary decolletage, then studied her while she waited for their orders. Stewart impulsively ordered Shrimp Norfolk, which pleased Ross, but for himself chose the season's last twenty-four Chincoteague oysters on the halfshell. Stewart whistled.

Ross said, "I don't know what I'll do when Chincoteagues no longer exist."

"You're doing a damned good job depleting them right now, but I've never tasted the slimy things."

They enjoyed a moment of fascinated silence as the buxom waitress bowed low serving Ross's enormous trayful of shucked oysters, then presented Stewart with a long-handled pan of shrimp floating in simmering butter. Her every movement was followed with four lecherous eyes and after she flounced off Ross recovered first.

"Here, have one," Ross said, handing a Chincoteague across the table. "Garnish it with hot sauce or a touch of horseradish, but don't let it stick in your gullet!"

Stewart wolfed it down, made an indifferent face, then attacked the shrimp. "Absolutely marvelous!" he said after several mouthfuls.

"Good! Make up your mind to sample most of Washington's better things while you're stationed here, Terry. It's what you'll remember best after leaving this traumatic town. Which reminds me. I'd like to give you a bit of guidance on personal survival in the Pentagon."

Stewart leaned forward to catch Ross's low-pitched voice after the waitress brought coffee. Ross lit his pipe, blew several smoke rings into the dead air, then said, "Drew Pearson brought the technique of reporting on the shenanigans of the government to a height never before or since achieved by any other newsman."

"What about yourself?"

Ross laughed heartily. "Sorry, I'm not even in his ballpark. Pearson reported as if he were the conscience of the taxpayer, crying in anguish at the excesses of the White House, the Congress, and the Executive Branch of government. He confirmed what others had suspected, that you could buy anything and everything in Washington."

"That bad?"

"Well, Pearson didn't print ninety-nine percent of the information thrust at him by disgruntled, dissatisfied government employees, or by losers of government contracts. Not that he didn't believe such information to be valid, but he simply didn't have the staff to run down all the facts behind the allegations. So in most instances he dug up his own exclusive stuff, researched it to his own satisfaction and had it published according to his own sweet schedule. Now why is all this background important to you?"

"It's interesting, to say the least," Stewart said, "but I wouldn't know what to do with it."

"Of course," Ross agreed, "but there's a message buried in all that. It proves that cold, hard facts are silver bullets that kill bad guys. Presidents, senators, cabinet officers and the like tried to get Pearson put out of circulation. Publishers tried hard not to print him. He survived them all because he had facts at his fingertips and most of the time his facts were more complete and more germane to the issue at hand than the people whose very careers depended on knowing the facts. He could separate fact from fiction, right from wrong, better than most officials."

"How does that relate to me? I don't make decisions, Quent."

"The lesson to be learned is never to enter the newsmaking arena without facts to serve you and to serve the press. Never speculate without labeling it as such. Never pass on anything you know is half-assed, half-true. And I'll bet you don't know your largest, single source of pure facts."

"That's easy," Stewart said brightly. "Operations, Logistics, Research, Communications—those groups have all the facts."

"Ha! I knew you'd miss it!"

Stewart thought for a minute, then said skeptically, "I give up."

"Plans, my boy, Plans. Each service has people in Plans, usually the brightest people. This is true, by the way, in the largest corporations. Sometimes the planning function is called by other names or labels, but Plans determine the future of the organization or service, how it will survive, whether in combat or up on the Hill. Every contingency, real or imagined, is anticipated, thought out, and then the proposed action spelled out and placed in folders for instant use by the leadership when the need arises. So what I am saying is that the Plans folders are the key to everything in the future, from today forward. The folders contain every fact known to the service on any given subject within its purview, and the course of action to be taken, including the gains and losses incurred by the action, if the issue or subject surfaces. What makes the folders even more significant is that they are constantly updated, always current." Ross paused to draw his breath.

"Are you suggesting I pass the folders on to the press, to you?"

"No, you damned fool! The press would print the contents verbatim. You'd get your ass burned in a minute since you signed for the folder."

"What the hell am I supposed to do?"

"You set up routine requests. I repeat. Routine requests of the Plans people to review certain subjects each week. They're delighted that someone cares to read their hard-thought-out work. They can't deny you the folders, except for the top secret stuff, which you don't want anyway. You take time out each week, speed-read the folders, and I guarantee you that at the end of the first year you will be almost as informed as General Glasscock, the secretary or the chief of staff. You're supposed to be informed if you are a press officer. But there are several pitfalls. You may not discipline your mind sufficiently to keep the truly sensitive stuff separated from the unclassified information. If you blur it in your mind you'll find yourself in deep trouble, if only as a patriotic American and a professional soldier."

"What else?"

"Gad, you're a glutton!" Ross said, pleased with Stewart's attitude. "It turns out that the unclassified information in the folder is a nice, tidy package of vital background and if you don't use it judiciously you will upstage your superiors with the free flow of facts. No one can stand competition and they will toss you out of the arena with a less than favorable effectiveness report."

"Nobody loves a smart-ass is what you're saying."

"Right, Terry. Then we have another twist in this news business. Drew Pearson rarely printed a fact, except as the result of a tradeoff for another fact extracted from him by his reliable informants. What that says to you is that if you leak a fact, you get one in return, or don't leak at all. Usually, the fact you get back is embarrassing to one of the services or to the Defense Department. When you've collected enough facts, you own a kitty of damaging, tradeable information, lessening your personal vulnerability by a helluva sight."

"What about investigations? I hear the guys in the

newsroom are under constant surveillance and investigation."

"Of course. The government always does the obvious. If you talk and work with newsmen, you are guilty of leaks through association. You'll be visited, I guarantee you, by the OSI, Army and Navy counterintelligence, the FBI and CIA under various covers, all trying to pin you down on one rap or another. I get the same visitations. You may find a plant sitting at the desk next to yours. In spite of the limitations imposed by the Congress, these people have run wild since the start of World War II. There's no stopping them, you simply learn to live with them."

"I don't know that I can wrestle with all that."

"It's easier than it seems. Volunteer nothing to your colleagues until you know them as well as your brother. Be a good listener, not a wise guy. Beware of people working with you who tell you they are on temporary duty. Be supersensitive about your phone calls and your correspondence. Pick places of your own choosing when backgrounding, like halfway between the ventilators in Pentagon corridors, or, better yet, the back seat of a public bus going to the District, or the Freer Gallery or the Smithsonian. When you're on the hot spot, answer specific questions with specific answers. More often than not, the interrogators have the right guy for the wrong leak. Don't betray your relief when you discover they're on the trail of a leak you didn't make! They'll remember that and come back at you later."

"Is the damned job worth all the risks?"

"Sure. You'll become one of the most informed persons on defense matters in the whole damned world. You can't rightfully walk away from the challenge. Not every Tom, Dick and Harry gets that chance. Who knows, it might make you general."

Stewart scoffed, fell silent as Ross watched him closely, then said, "Quent, I guess I'm on board now with this fantastic briefing of yours. Obviously, you must think I can hack it or we wouldn't be here tonight."

"That's essentially correct. Every younger man needs an older man to kick him in the ass every so often, and that's what I'm doing now in my own strange way. Which reminds me. I can't end this session without a word about the encounter I had with Scotus just before calling you for dinner. Let me say he suspects that you put me onto the Minuteman air launch."

Stewart flushed. "Oh, no!"

"Oh, yes. But don't panic. Technically, you did not hand me the press release on the Minuteman air launch. I already had it in my possession. He then called you a conduit. Technically, you did not pass information from someone through yourself on to me. But this was a close call, Terry. What saved the situation was that I referred to you as a green kid. Your innocence protected you just this one time. Tomorrow's events, whatever they are, will distract Scotus from barking up the tree you're in. But now he's discovered your presence and will finger you the next chance he gets. Deep down, he hates the military because he is afraid of their professionalism, whether it be handling hardware or their life style."

"I suppose you're right about my boss," Stewart said. "I hate to hear it. I want to be loyal as hell to my superiors, but you're disillusioning me."

"I should add that my only alternative was to lay the onus on another person, another service, another agency. This, too, was fraught with danger because of the inevitable backlash. But I've talked long enough for one evening, so let's get the hell out here," Ross said, paying the bill despite Stewart's protest.

They huddled for a moment under Chambouard's marquee, reluctant to make a dash to their cars in the worsening drizzle. Ignoring the parking attendant, they indulged in a bit of last-minute chitchat, Stewart complaining about going home to an empty house, Ross stating it was even more callous to have abandoned

Marge, who probably ate a peanut butter sandwich for dinner. Then as if on signal they shook hands, scrunched their shoulders and ran into the rain.

At six in the morning, Marge shook Ross, pushed the ringing phone in his face, then went back to sleep through sheer reflex. He knocked the phone cradle off the night stand trying to reach a pencil and pad, somehow retrieved it all, then took down enough information from London IP to file another Symonds exclusive. London reminded him the orphan satellite now was "T plus 31 hours" since the launch and that the unpredictable was inevitable.

He showered, shaved and dressed, then started up Cuspidor and drove downhill from Georgetown. Crossing Memorial Bridge he had his daily laugh at the positioning of two enormous, sculptured horses that flanked the bridge, heads facing the Lincoln Memorial and tails directed at the Pentagon. Wheeling Cuspidor into his parking spot, he formed queries in his mind to address to Scotus Olney through Terry. Bones aching and a bit winded, he dragged himself through the Pentagon corridor to the Defense newsroom and was pleasantly surprised to see Stewart at his desk.

"Thank God we don't have hangovers!" Stewart said in greeting.

"Indeed. I find my head clear but the body unwilling," Ross said, "yet I must press on with the day's business. I've got a new batch of queries for you, Terry."

Stewart turned methodically to his typewriter with a query sheet in hand, rolled it in, then looked up, feigning fear. "I'm unready, Quent."

"Quote me as follows," Ross said:

> SYMONDS OBSERVATORY REPORTS THIS DATE THAT ORPHAN SATELLITE WAS LAUNCHED AT 0400 HOURS ZEBRA MONDAY AT HIGH ALTITUDE SOMEWHERE IN THE SOUTH ATLANTIC OCEAN BETWEEN ASCEN-

CION AND ST. HELENA ISLANDS. QUERY ONE: REQUEST DEFENSE DEPARTMENT CONFIRMATION AND/OR COMMENT ON SYMONDS LAUNCH REPORT.

SYMONDS PREDICTS ORPHAN SATELLITE ON TRAJECTORY INDICATING PROBABLE GEOSYNCHRONOUS OR STATIONARY ORBIT ABOVE EARTH AT ABOUT 66,000 MILES. QUERY TWO: REQUEST CONFIRMATION OR COMMENT ON PREDICTED TRAJECTORY. SYMONDS OFFICIALS EXPRESS CONCERN THAT THE ORPHAN SATELLITE CAN TWO DAYS HENCE CAST AN ELECTRONIC SHADOW OVER A SUBSTANTIAL PORTION OF THE EARTH AND FOR THAT REASON IT IS IMPERATIVE THAT THE SATELLITE'S NATIONAL IDENTITY AND CAPABILITIES BE ASCERTAINED SOONEST. QUERY THREE: HAS THE DEFENSE DEPARTMENT DETERMINED THE NATIONAL ORIGIN OF THE ORPHAN SATELLITE?

QUERY FOUR: HAS THE DEFENSE DEPARTMENT ASCERTAINED THE TECHNICAL CAPABILITIES OF THE ORPHAN SATELLITE BASED ON SIGNALS EMITTED AND GENERAL PHYSICAL CHARACTERISTICS? IF SO, WHAT ARE THE CAPABILITIES? NOTE: INTERNATIONAL PRESS REQUESTS ANSWERS TO QUERIES NOT LATER THAN NOON TODAY.

"Well, here we go again," Stewart said, getting up from his desk.

"Damned right! The plot thickens."

"I'll make certain calls before Mr. Olney arrives."

"Be careful, Terry."

Stewart laughed as they parted in the corridor. Ross went to the bullpen, checked the overnight press handouts on his desk and was relieved that the administration hadn't busted his exclusive with a general news release on the orphan. He then examined the opposition wires in the ticker room. Again nothing, not even pickups off his original story. He guessed they were afraid of it, in spite of his byline.

Ivorson called to advise that the story had gone front page among all subscribers in Europe and the Orient.

"It's Symonds's clout everywhere but here," Ross said. "Symonds is unknown in the U.S., except to a handful of astronomers."

"Did London call?"

"Yes, at six. I've put in four new queries against a noon deadline."

"Why not earlier? It's almost too late for Europe."

"Let's not go through that drill again," Ross said, hanging up.

Lu arrived, wanting to spirit him off for a private cup of coffee, but he held out for the Despicables.

"Scotus is at the White House," she volunteered.

"Doing what?" he asked skeptically.

"Catching hell, for one thing."

"He was catching it but good from Phil Fairly late yesterday."

"Well, your story's a beaut, Quent."

"And there's more to come, Lu."

"Any queries in the hopper?"

"Four."

She laughed. "The administration's getting its act together, so you'll get screwed for sure, Quent. Have you coached the boy?"

"I took him to Chambouard's."

"You should've invited me along."

"Next time," Ross said, smiling inwardly at her improbable presence.

"I can help the boy, too, you know."

"No doubt about it, but right now I need him more, as he does me. By the way, I think you have a crush on him."

The color rose in her face. "Wish I were thirty years

younger."

"Not me," he said. "I live upon expectation as if that bud would surely blossom, to quote Thoreau."

"Ha! We have a poet amongst us. Very nice, Quent, but I don't buy it."

Shrimp, Clapham and Karayn arrived within seconds of each other and the decibel level rose accordingly. Ross joined them and promptly lost the King Bee match just as Ted Harris burst into the bullpen, announcing an immediate press conference in the Defense briefing room.

"A trick to catch everyone off-guard," Shrimp muttered, "but at least the electronic media won't get a chance to cover it. It's too early for those bastards. They'll be forced to use Defense footage. It'll take at least six hours for the Defense motion picture unit to process the handouts."

"Quit worrying about the electronickers," Clapham said. "The only break we get as print media is that we're instantly available to cover whatever crap Defense wants to shovel out."

"I wouldn't call it crap this morning," Lu said. "I'll bet the press conference is in response to Quent's latest satellite queries."

Ross winced. "I hope not!"

"That's how Scotus hopes to keep it in low-key, Quent," she said with a note of finality.

Walking the corridor, they were soon caught in a tangle of cables, dollies and cameras wheeled awkwardly by Signal Corps soldiers to the briefing room.

"Boy, the networks will scream at Scotus about this end run," Shrimp persisted.

"Knock it off about the electronickers," Clapham growled. "What have they done for you lately?"

"Somebody's always getting set up around here. I just hate to see it go on," Shrimp said.

"So what?" Lu said as they approached the swinging doors of the miniamphitheater. They filed in and took front row seats as two radio tapers hooked up microphones to the lectern. The usual coterie of Defense underlings, Stewart among them, walked to the farthest corner of the room but still outnumbered the working press by five to one.

Scotus Olney fussed at the lectern, testing the public address system and the baby spotlights as anguished technicians looked on. He then flipped through the contents of a large, looseleaf notebook under the hooded reading light. He checked his wristwatch repeatedly, waiting for a magic moment. Suddenly, he summoned Harris to hold the fort at the lectern while he fetched the briefer.

Lu groaned out loud that it would be the vote-getting, but inarticulate Philippe Mondragon, deputy secretary of defense, rather than his boss, Secretary Browning Whitley. She had recently disclosed in the newsletter that both bought substantial blocks of stock—in their wives' names—in a defense company subsequently awarded an eight hundred million dollar contract. She'd fire the other barrel if they dropped their guard and filed joint income tax returns. Ross deeply admired her tenacious memory, yet knew if they were ever found guilty, it would be long after they were out of office and very rich nobodies.

The Defense group came to attention as Scotus escorted Whitley into the room. Seconds later Scotus nodded at them to sit down, then stepped to the lectern and introduced Whitley to the reporters. With a broad smile and a wave of the hand at the grinding Signal Corps cameras, Whitley acknowledged the audience as he moved directly behind the lectern and Scotus slid off camera. It was a parrot dance performed a thousand times by various players before Ross's eyes.

While Whitley flicked through the pages of the prompter, Ross studied the formidable adversary, a Wall Street banker and bag man for the administration, an articulate Princeton product, tall and prepossessing, wavy gray hair and black, piercing eyes. Lu sighed with pleasure. "Isn't he gorgeous?" she whispered in Ross's ear.

"An eighteen-karat bastard, you said so yourself."

"Whitley's pretty to look at. That's my prerogative as a widow."

Ross nudged her. "Every male you meet is pretty, except me. But thank God you don't call them cute!"

"You're the cute one."

Ross flinched, then lit his pipe, sending up an acrid cloud of smoke.

Whitley opened the press conference with the comment that pressures of other business regrettably limited the session to twenty minutes. It brought forth muffled protests. Ignoring the hostile reaction, he accepted a blue-bannered press release from Scotus and displayed it for camera and audience.

"This is the Defense Department's statement regarding a fast-breaking story that we believe merits more attention than an exclusive answer to one reporter's inquiry. I will summarize Defense's position on an unidentified satellite now coursing its way through space. The full text is releasable at the end of this briefing."

Lu kicked Ross, who glared at Whitley.

After donning massive, black-rimmed glasses and with practiced resonance, Whitley said, "An unidentified nation yesterday launched an unannounced satellite somewhere over the South Atlantic Ocean in direct violation of the space covenant signed by all members of the United Nations. At this time the satellite is apparently destined for a geosynchronous orbit over earth. I now should like to mention that several nations in the past have launched unannounced satellites, which gave rise to the United Nations covenant to prevent such surprises in the future. As a signatory to the UN covenant dedicating space to peaceful uses, the United States deplores any infraction of the covenant's spirit and intentions. It is my view that a satellite in geosynchronous orbit is a passive instrument used by the U.S. and many other nations to relay digital and voice communications, television pictures and weather information.

"Ladies and gentlemen, I find it difficult to get excited over the matter of a harmless gadget that will sit out in space about a quarter of the distance to the moon. I abhor the sensationalism with which this satellite story was treated in Europe and I trust it will not reach such ridiculous proportions here. With the advice of my public affairs staff, I decided to hold this brief press conference to put the matter to rest once and for all." Whitley took off his glasses and smiled benignly at the audience and cameras.

Karayn jumped up first, usurping Ross's prerogative to ask the first question. "Mr. Secretary," Karayn demanded, "what intelligence do you possess that would explain a nation's mysterious air-launching of a satellite, then to remain silent during the satellite's flight into space?"

"None. We can only speculate—"

"Then speculate!" Karayn insisted.

"My position and responsibilities forbid speculation. You, sir, would seize on it as the truth."

"I might and then I might not," Karayn continued. "But I'll tell you one thing, Mr. Secretary, speaking for the rest of the reporters assembled here, we will not sit by idly while you try to unravel the satellite mystery in your own sweet time, and then tell it in your own sweet way!"

Whitley's face hardened. Scotus moved so close that their shoulders touched, then tapped his wristwatch and whispered into Whitley's ear.

Ross finally got Whitley's attention. "Mr. Secretary," he said hoarsely, "aside from having aced me out of a scoop, tell me why Defense and NASA permit Symonds Observatory in Great Britain to speak alone to the world on the orphan?"

"Why not? It's a gadget."

Shrimp cut Ross off. "Eisenhower called Russia's Sputnik a bauble. You're calling this orphan satellite a gadget. Has it crossed your mind that it could be an ill-fated comparison?"

"No. There is no comparison."

Ross pointed his pipe stem at Whitley. "We have your press release now on the orphan's existence, but what are your experts at NORAD saying? What do your space defense wizards think about the orphan?"

"That's classified!" Scotus yelled. Whitley stepped off the lectern.

"Bullshit!" Ross yelled back, regretting it instantly, if only that the segment would get blipped in editing. The expletive also made him unnecessarily vulnerable. He let the anxious Clapham take over as Scotus gripped the lectern.

"What's secret about the actions of other countries? Who are you protecting, Scotus? Russians? Chinese?" Clapham shouted.

Scotus yelled, "Because the technical findings and analyses at Bright Lake and Colorado Springs are classified. Period!"

"Why?" Clapham demanded.

"Such techniques would divulge state-of-the-art assessments. Also, other sources must be protected."

"You're crazy, Scotus," Clapham said, sitting down with a thump. Whitley walked off the podium. Before Scotus could call off the press conference, Lu rose and asked in a strident voice, "Mr. Secretary, before you leave, has the Defense Department asked the UN for help in identifying the orphan's nationality?"

Whitley returned to the lectern, smiled directly at her. "Yes, Lu. We have requested our ambassador to the UN, through the State Department, to ask UN assistance in identifying the violator of the space covenant."

"How long will that procedure take?"

"I have no idea. It rests with State."

"Give a guess. This we won't hold against you, Mr. Secretary."

"One week, two weeks, maybe three weeks. I simply don't know, Lu."

"Meanwhile, anything can happen."

"I doubt that," Whitley said with finality.

Ross rose. Scotus glared and tried to wave him back down into his seat. Preemptively, Ross said, "Mr. Secretary, for myself I've found this press conference highly unsatisfactory. I must apologize for the unfortunate expletive on my part. But I must protest that my press queries were preempted by the conference, which cunningly ignored my queries. I find I still must depend on Symonds Observatory for progress on the quote gadget unquote. This morning you protected and defended the strange actions of an unidentified country by playing its game of divulging nothing of value to anyone in this room. I am forced to use the findings of a foreign astronomical observatory while billions of tax dollars spent by the United States on its space defenses are publicly unaccounted for. This is disgraceful stewardship on your part, and those who serve you."

Whitley backed away and Scotus led him out of the room.

Lu broke the silence. "You're going to catch hell, Quent!"

"Bah!" he said, stoking his pipe. "It's T plus 34 hours and maybe later than we think."

4

Second time around, Ross won the King Bee game. The other players then demanded that the game prior to the press conference count instead. Ross protested, but was forced to compromise by flipping again. Shrimp called the toss, matched everyone and lost to all. As usual, Lu wanted in the game, but King Bee remained inviolate to women. She tagged along to the coffee bar and bought her own, while Shrimp reluctantly stood for the rest. Ross welcomed the game. He played it daily since the Pentagon's erection because it brought the reporters together and broke tensions and sometimes averted outright fighting.

Still nettled over the encounter with Scotus and Whitley, Ross drew on his pipe in silence. He debated filing the press conference proceedings out of sheer spite, which wouldn't get past Ivorson, then decided to let the encounter roll off his back. Bureau chiefs, editors and publishers wanted definitive packages written instantly on every defense and space issue. Even the president, his cabinet and his generals suffered under the neat, complete-package illusion. Only the Hill, arena of buyoffs, ripoffs, tradeoffs and moral compromises, knew better. The House and Senate press galleries were a far more practical world. Reporters simply covered the actions of adversaries in a free society and secrecy was merely a matter of protecting the taxpayer from the truths of advocacy. Ross made a mental note to caution Stewart that nothing ever really succeeded in Washington because of all of the diverse forces at play at any given moment.

Karayn broke his musing. "Quent," he said with a puzzled look, "I don't know what you're going to do now, but for myself, I'm damned if I touch this story and I'm damned if I don't. So I think I'll file a safe think-piece on space hardware. Thank God I'm not on deadline."

"But I am," Shrimp said.

"Me too," Clapham joined in.

"It's very simple," Lu cackled. "Let's ignore the ethics of competitive reporting. After all, it was a press conference of sorts. We were at the common trough, and since the working press is faced with a noon deadline, I suggest one of us attack Whitley for his crack about the space gadget. It Whitley's right, the story will be forgotten. If not, he'll come out of it as a bum, even if he is pretty."

"You do that one, Shrimp," Ross said. "Remember, you set Whitley up for it."

Lu nodded. "And Clapham should pursue his line of questioning on U.S. secrecy constraints."

"Sure," Clapham said, "but I expected Quent to follow it up."

"No," Ross said. "I've got another angle."

"Oh? What's that?" Lu asked.

"First, let's find out what you're going to file, Lu, then I'll settle for what's left."

"That's a helluva angle!" she said suspiciously. "I'm going to write a wrapup of the press conference, just about the way it happened. Knowing my editor in Tampa, the story'll wind up next to the hernia ads, but at least he'll know I'm alive. I'm okay, timewise, for the newsletter. That's three days off."

Ross said, "Obviously, I'm going to check London IP

63

before I file a word. That's my one advantage over the rest of you on this particular story. If London extracts some late-breaking data out of Symonds, that'll be my angle for sure."

"Remember to get your filing done on time," Lu warned, "because tomorrow's a holiday."

"What holiday?" Ross asked, blanching.

"Memorial Day."

"Cripes! I forgot!"

"Do you like your work that much?" Lu demanded.

"Quent loves to flagellate himself," Shrimp said.

"Wow! I didn't realize you knew the word," Ross retorted, "because your Baltimore readership doesn't."

"Ha, ha," Lu laughed, butt dangling off her lip. "We sorely need a jest or two this morning."

"That's right, Lu," Clapham said. "It's been a bad day for reporters, especially for our friend Quent. Things go along pretty bad for awhile, then they get worse in this friggin' place. But let's be of good cheer, ladies and gentlemen, for tomorrow is a holiday. We honor the dead, just next door at Arlington Cemetery."

"What's so funny about that?" Karayn asked.

"It wasn't supposed to be funny," Shrimp explained for Clapham. "He simply made a statement about the geographical proximity of the two places. Even I understand that. By the way, the *Baltimore Tribune* will want pix of the wreath laying at the Tomb of the Unknown Soldier, and preferably not from IP's jaundiced wire-photo service."

"Get your own," Ross growled.

"Who's laying the wreath? The President?" Karayn asked.

"The President delegated it to Browning Whitley, our fearless secretary of defense," Lu volunteered.

"Oh, shit!" Shrimp muttered. "That dirty, rotten bag man!"

"Now, that is funny," Ross said, "and as our second jest it meets Lu's quota for the day."

No one laughed as Ross gimped out of the coffee bar. Lu caught up with him on the escalator and they again descended in silence. Then in the bullpen she touched his arm, turned to her desk, plopped down at the typewriter and began churning out copy as if possessed.

He sat limp behind his barricade and stared out at the Washington Monument. It stood sharp and pristine-white against the low, green skyline. He glanced at his watch, reminded himself it was T plus 36 hours since the orphan's launch and hoped the damned thing would just keep on flying through Memorial Day. In a matter of hours official Washington would come to a screeching halt as its employees indulged in a mass evacuation for the holiday. Unfortunately for Ross, European papers, TV and radio expected Washington coverage as usual, although they guarded their own holidays vengefully. It crossed his mind that Marge might have holiday plans but they hadn't seen enough of each other to discuss it. She loved rides out to the old tree and horse country at Middleburg and Upperville, yet they seemed to do less and less each year. A telephone in Cuspidor would have freed him from anxiety, missed calls and telephone-bound duty at home, but he couldn't bring himself to put a phone antenna on top of the rusted hulk. During holidays Ivorson reduced the bureau staff to a sole switchboard operator. Defense and space business was shunted automatically to Ross's home. Tomorrow London IP might relay Symonds information instantly to him and demand in minutes a Washington-datelined story for European consumption.

He puzzled how best to keep a channel open to Stewart over the holiday, just in case the Air Force developed significant data on the orphan and Stewart was willing to pass it on. But the government buggers never quit on holidays. In fact, their monitoring jobs actually were made easier because of lessened phone traffic, unfettered mobility and greater target visibility, assuming, of course, the subject of their attention had

65

not fled the city too.

Running short of tobacco, Ross walked down the ramp to the concourse, loitered at one of several newsstands and scanned the headlines, then entered the drugstore and bought the rankest, roughest cut. Unable to resist the adjacent bookstore, he stepped into Brentano's and to his delight found Stewart speed-reading a bestseller.

"You cheap bastard!" Ross said. "Buy the book!"

Startled, Stewart almost dropped the book. "It's not worth it, Quent. The sex scenes are infantile."

"Too bad," Ross said. "Let's go separately to the bus loading area. Tyson's Corners is as good as any."

"Okay," Stewart murmured and turned on his heels.

Ross refueled his pipe, lit it and reentered the cavernous concourse, only to get caught up in a rush of girls charging six-abreast down the ramp to the stairwells of the bus-loading platforms. They fanned out by the dozens under signs marked for the District, Bethesda, Silver Spring, Fairfax, Alexandria, Prince Georges County and other suburban destinations. He marveled how well the herd instinct worked. Smitten with holiday fever at some magic moment, the Pentagon's secretarial and clerical help of every race and persuasion decided to desert desks and flee. After the stampede subsided, Ross found Stewart sitting on a bench near a group of unhappy girls milling around under the Tyson's Corners sign. The next bus wasn't scheduled for another half hour.

"Cripes! I thought war was declared when those girls came flying down the stairs," Stewart whispered.

"Memorial Day fever," Ross explained. "You'll notice the prettier girls carry overnight bags or large makeup kits."

Stewart thought for a moment. "Don't tell me! Are they going somewhere to shack up?"

"You're catching on, Terry. This is Washington. Every holiday, including weekends, is shack-up time, especially for those who come prepared."

"I'm green with envy."

"You've had yours, I'll bet. Saigon, Tokyo, Paris."

"Yeah, but I can't remember what they looked like."

"So much the better. You might hate yourself if you did."

"Ha, ha. The French may like anonymous sex, but I'm not that sophisticated."

"You are in Washington. It's either a sex sewer or a banquet."

"Nobody mentioned it during my first-day orientation."

Ross grinned. "Don't be a smart-ass. Nobody talks about sex at the seat of government. But why are we standing here? I sure picked the wrong place. Let's take the bus to Twelfth and Pennsylvania. It's just across the river in the District and we can ride the same bus right back. It departs every ten minutes."

Stewart agreed. They changed loading platforms and got on a District bus jammed with black secretaries and clerks talking up a happy storm. Worming their way to the rear, Ross said, "These gals couldn't care less about our conversation. We're safe here."

Swinging precariously with each lurch of the mammoth vehicle, Stewart nodded, almost asphyxiated by the diesel fumes.

"What I have in mind," Ross said unperturbed, "is to keep a clear channel open between us in the event something important develops tomorrow."

"I've thought about it too. For some strange reason I escaped the holiday duty roster. Perhaps Mr. Olney doesn't want me to serve as spokesman for the Defense Department, even on holidays. So I guess I'll be in civilian clothes and not doing much. If need be, I can come to your house at some set hour to check notes."

"Normally," Ross said, "I'd discourage it, but under the circumstances it's not such a bad idea. If my house is under surveillance, you'll probably fool them out of uniform. It's a hell of a note to worry this way in a quote free society. Modern government can't resist the temptation to toy with instruments of advanced technology, and the moral consequences of spying are conveniently relegated to the waiting courts. But to answer your point, yes, I'd be pleased to see you about four o'clock. I think I'll take Marge to Middleburg for lunch with the horsey set. Whatever we do, we'll be back at four. By the way, Terry," Ross added, "be sure to park several blocks down the street in Georgetown. The walk will do you good."

Stewart scoffed, then stopped and whispered, "Guess who's riding at the front of the bus."

"Tell me."

"Our bald friend, Ted Harris!"

"Oh, damn it! Let's not be seen together. Has he spotted us?"

"I doubt it. Too many people."

"He's twice as dangerous as his boss," Ross said contemptuously. "Let's split up and stay split. I'll meet you back at the fifth-floor coffee bar at three o'clock. Is that okay?"

"Sure," Stewart said. "A close call, eh?"

"You better believe it, Terry."

After crossing the Potomac the bus driver pulled adroitly into a passenger offloading lane on Pennsylvania Avenue, opposite the red-bricked, old Post Office Building in the heart of downtown Washington. Voices of the departing girls reached crescendos of pleasure as they jived through front and rear bus doors. Ross kept himself within the larger, rearward group, far behind Harris, while Stewart, the one remaining passenger, moved forward and sat behind the driver for the empty ride back to the Pentagon.

Ross walked several blocks of a slight rise to the National Press Building, then rode the elevator to the twelfth-floor offices of IP's Washington bureau, his head full of events and people in the reality of time long past. He turned it off as he opened the door to the three-oom suite decorated in red, black, and period English furniture. International Press was known as the most elegantly furnished newspaper office in the well-worn building, the legacy of an otherwise forgotten bureau chief, who shortly after the war brought the suite up to Continental standards.

Dawn Kelly, switchboard operator in the anteroom, greeted him with a cheery Irish smile while manipulating the PBX. Between plug-ins she said, "How nice to see you, stranger." Her violet eyes, framed in a jet-black bob, flashed with warmth.

"Coming here was an accident, Dawn," he said, then decided not to pursue the thought.

"Whatever," she said. "Merle is tied up for the moment. Care to wait?"

"Might as well. I've come this far." He was glad for the stall. It helped gather his wits and he swore never again to blunder into the bureau without a valid reason. The subject of surveillance deserved discussion. He could talk an hour on the subject without drawing an extra breath.

Dawn's attention was held to the PBX, shunting calls from one end of the world to the other, but he managed to ask in a fleeting pause, "Where's Evelyn?"

"Poor thing's ill. Merle hasn't been very nice to her."

"That figures," Ross said with a wince. "We were hired within a week of each other. She married the job. Don't you do that, Dawn."

"I prefer men, Quent."

"I believe it, I believe it," he said, sitting down at Evelyn's desk and staring out of the window that once was his. In that spot he had gotten his own byline writing national news at age twenty-three. He had dreamed of the ultimate assignment as a war correspondent while watching the Pentagon spring up along the banks of the Potomac. To his horror and before the monolithic concrete walls of the five-sided monster had set, he was ordered into the bullpen as IP's youngest-ever military analyst.

Ivorson's light went out on the PBX and Dawn buzze automatically. He opened the door. "Quent? What th hell brings you to town?"

"Thought we should chat for a minute, Merle."

"Okay," he said, looking at the wall clock. "Not fo long, I hope. Virginia and I are flying up to Boston for th holiday to visit her folks."

Ross followed him into the executive office and othe than Ivorson's personal photographs on the desk, noth ing in the room had changed from that of his man predecessors. A blond, rawboned Swede with a cow college education, Ivorson was unimaginative and ner vous for his job, and as soon as the door was closed h spun around at Ross and asked apprehensively "What's up?"

Hating to lie, Ross cleared his throat. "Just happene to come downtown on a personal errand, got side tracked and thought I'd drop by before I went back to th desk."

"Oh? Nothing hot?"

"Well, the orphan's still on the front burner."

"You mean you can add nothing to what's alread printed?"

"Damned right. The Pentagon's a tighter prison than ever was. No one will sing, Merle."

"That's your job, to break down the resistance."

"And a good reason to talk to you at this moment. W had a disastrous press conference on the orphan thi morning. It was doubly disastrous for me because I los my temper. You may hear about it from your golfin buddies in the administration, but on the other hand thi present administration is worse than—"

"Quent! For Christ's sake, quit complaining!" Ivorso shouted and batted down the subject with a wave o his arm.

"That's where you're wrong, Merle. I cannot single handedly make the administration open up. Nor can singlehandedly demand the administration call off its buggers. I'm sick and tired of the whole damned system. It's impossible to do a normal reporting job with all official channels sealed up tight. Every action and every word that I say or write is instantly scrutinized by a mullet in the government who then disclaims what I've filed, or worse, threatens and removes the few people who have answers and who will communicate."

"And what magic trick am I supposed to pull off to change all that?"

"Merle, you're bureau chief, you get IP's political reporters, Gene Hildebrandt and Joe Cranmer, to complain in the House and Senate about the bugging going on in the Pentagon. I can cite a hundred specific cases. If petitioned convincingly, a joint committee will be formed to investigate the Pentagon under the Freedom of Information Act."

"Bah!" Ivorson spat. "It's not an election year."

"But some things do get done in off-years."

"Name one."

"Merle, if you won't turn Gene and Joe loose on this officially, do you mind if I talk to them informally? I need help. I admit it. I need help."

"Help, my ass! Stay away from the Hill. That's final. Stay in your own backyard. Do the best you can. Things change and I'm not going to start a ruckus with the administration over your personal problems."

"Oh, crap! How can you reduce this to the personal? It's political."

"Quent, you know the rule: Political reporters don't report on Defense matters, and vice versa. Don't let me catch you playing games on the Hill."

Ross stood up. Ivorson ignored him, picked up an attache case and stuffed it full of freebie magazines.

"Okay, I won't go to the Hill, but the problem's bigger than the Pentagon or the White House," Ross said hoarsely and walked out.

Dawn called after him, "Have a good holiday, Quent.

My best to Marge."

With a wan smile he waved his pipe, then entering the elevator he swore silently he would never set foot in the bureau so long as Ivorson remained on board.

On the street the usual horde of Washington's work force was absent due to the upcoming holiday, but Gold Star mothers drifted aimlessly in their overseas caps, waiting out the hours for the next day's Arlington services. Ross first viewed them with indifference, then remembered that through seniority he had become curator of the niche in the bullpen where faded photos and brass mementos lined the wall, a gallery of reporters long dead, covering World War II, Korea and Vietnam. He had known them all. Sadly he caught a bus and soon found himself on the Pentagon concourse. He window-shopped at Brentano's and gazed at a three-inch bust of Nefertiti—only thirty dollars—which would delight him in the sanctuary, but he resisted the temptation to buy the glorious female, for some thieving bastard would surely lift her off his desk.

The Defense newsroom was as deserted as the bullpen, with the exception of the duty officer, a navy commander who had no news to offer other than a hearty bitch about being called four hours early to man the holiday roster. Retreating to his desk, Ross had an inspiration and dialed Marge, proposing that they abandon Washington for Ocean City. They'd stay the night and in the morning he would do a bit of surf fishing, followed by a picnic in the sand dunes. She agreed but in the next breath asked, "What about London?"

"To hell with London and Ivorson. Get my fishing gear ready so we can leap off without delay. God knows what the outbound traffic will be like over the one-hundred-thirty-mile stretch. Hopefully, we'll be behind it."

"Should I answer the phone?"

"Let it fall off the hook!"

"Quent, I hope you know what you're doing," she said, hanging up.

He left the Pentagon lighthearted, revved up Cuspidor and headed for Georgetown. He stopped off at a supermarket for picnic supplies and remembered dog food for his daughter's royal poodle, Lupe, whom they were babysitting while Judy and the twins vacationed in Maine. He maintained a love-hate relationship with the apricot-colored, almond-eyed bitch who at one moment struggled to get into his lap and then stole up to the bedroom and shredded his slippers.

Marge was ready and at the door when he arrived, along with Lupe, wagging her tail at the sight of the eleven-foot surf rod. They packed Cuspidor and were backing out of the driveway when a Western Union messenger arrived. Ross almost ran him down but Marge foiled the escape by opening her door.

"Stop! I bet it's from Judy."

"Judy, my foot!" Ross said, opening the telegram after dismissing the messenger without a tip. "It's from Dawn. Couldn't get me on the phone so she's sending telegrams."

"What does it say?"

"London and Paris IP are holding space for wirephotos of the wreath laying at Arlington."

"What's so unusual about that?"

"I let the photographer off for the holiday and by now he's fishing at Ocracoke or Cape Hatteras. Another fishing nut."

"Why did you do that?"

"Lots of reasons. If the President doesn't lay the wreath, anyone less isn't international news. I hate his pinch hitter, Browning Whitley, who gave me a hard time at the press conference this morning. Why should I give Whitley publicity?"

"You're thinking small, Quent, and now you're stuck with it."

"I sure am," Ross said, turning off the engine. "Let's unpack."

Marge sighed with both compassion and relief. Ross

left the fishing gear in the driveway, then spent several hours replacing fishing lines, oiling and adjusting three huge surf-casting reels, and in continued disgust during and after dinner fell asleep on the living room sofa allegedly watching TV. In the morning he had to solve the wirephoto dilemma. He was damned if he'd pay homage to Whitley by fighting the Arlington crowds and elbowing his way to the press area to snap a few shots of the ceremony with Whitley at stage center. A sudden inspiration provided the answer. To Marge's disbelief he brought the TV out from the wall, put the instant-picture camera on a tripod, and took several test shots which proved adequate for wirephoto transmission. Then when the ceremony unfolded on the screen he snapped several photos and chose one with Whitley's back to the camera, although the wreath and honor guard were plainly visible.

"I gotcha! I gotcha!" he shouted with glee and commanded Marge to go downtown with him. She obeyed, marveling at his adolescence. He chortled all the way to the National Press Club building, and after slapping the captioned photo on the sending machine, he insisted on a leisurely, expensive lunch at Rive Gauche.

Homeward bound, he dragged Marge through areas of the District unseen for years, all the while humming and beating a rhythm on the steering wheel. She finally stayed his hand.

"I worry about your ups and downs, Quent."

"Let me have my fun, dammit."

She pursed her lips, sensing another shift in mood and said nothing more as they drove the last mile along the Potomac. She welcomed the spire of Georgetown University, sharply visible on the bluff against the very hazy sky. Their neighborhood, rows of exclusive Federal houses set on slanting, narrow, brick-paved streets, was deserted of cars and people. Ross pulled into the garage to find Stewart sitting on a barrel, leafing through piles of old *Life* magazines.

"Hallelujah!" Ross yelled with sheer delight, having forgotten about Stewart, then introduced him to Marge.

Stewart explained he had parked his car several blocks away, as instructed, and finding no one at home, hid out in the garage.

Appalled at Ross's cavalier treatment, Marge took Stewart by the hand and led him into the kitchen through the rear entrance, seating him at the well-worn dinette.

Ross was amused. "Terry, we've never had a son and Marge has been trying to make up for it ever since. Her son-in-law sometimes escapes her clutches, maternal, I hope."

"You're fortunate to have such an attractive wife," Stewart blurted out, "even though it is presumptuous of me to say so."

"Yes, it is," Ross answered before Marge could get in a word, "but the Air Force has long been famous for having no manners. However, that's still a cut above bad manners."

"You should know, Quent," she said, "because your bad manners are showing."

Wryly, Ross said, "My apologies to everybody," then turned to Stewart. "I can't tell if this is a social call with a heavy accent on manners, or if there's something else we should pursue."

"It's something else, Quent."

At that point Marge summarily excused herself.

Stewart said, "General Glasscock isn't long for this world, but that's not why I came, Quent."

"What happened?"

"You know the Air Force is madder than hell over the President's cancellation of the proton gun. It accelerates particles out of a barrel at the speed of light, a hell of a weapon when perfected."

"Okay, but what did Glasscock do?"

"He phoned what I'd describe as a tightly reasoned

and persuasive editorial to the *Financial Journal* in New York, which they're printing tomorrow. It spares no facts. It makes an ass out of Whitley and a fool out of the President for ordering the cancellation."

"So what? It's happened before."

"He phoned it to Wall Street from his office. The whole conversation was bugged and Whitley played the tape for the President."

Ross waved his hands. "Noel knows better than that. I wonder what caused him to drop his guard. Must be the old Air Force death wish. What else? He knows his office is bugged. I'll bet it's the first tape they play back every day." Still incredulous, he got up suddenly, went to the kitchen's wall phone and dialed London IP. His jaw dropped after a moment's conversation, then hanging up, he turned to Stewart. "Here's the second bombshell. Symonds is out of business, down for repairs. What a hell of a time for that to happen!"

"But I've got new poop—"

Ross didn't hear. "I wonder if the Symonds breakdown was an accident or sabotage."

"Quent," Stewart said firmly, "it doesn't matter that much. I've got new poop."

"Oh, poop it out your butt!" Ross said, then caught himself as Stewart's jaw tightened perceptibly. "Terry, you don't understand. I've lost my cover with Symonds out of the picture. I could've laid anything at Symonds's feet with no one a damn bit wiser. Now that's gone. I don't want to hear what you've got to say until I get—or dream up—a new cover. That's as much for your protection as mine. The administration will kill you and kill me unless we can lay red herrings across the trail. Let me think for one damned minute."

Marge returned and brewed tea. They sat in silence, Stewart bewildered, Ross casting about for a solution. After agonizing minutes, Ross jumped up, thinking aloud. "I must use a dateline and an attributable source other than Washington. So I'm forced to set NASA up for this ploy. Yes, it must be NASA. It can't be Air Force or Defense. And it must be NASA far removed from here. NASA Goldstone? No, that's California and a relay station at best. Ah! NASA Houston, of course! IP has a stringer there. I'll lay the story at his feet. Now—" Ross turned to Stewart—"let's go back to the garage and hear what you've got to say. If that garage is bugged, the administration deserves all that it will get! Let's go, Terry."

They walked back to the garage and as in the bullpen, Ross sought refuge behind the piles of magazines and asked, "Terry, do you think an electronic directional eavesdropper can penetrate *Life?*"

"Never!"

"Good," Ross said with satisfaction. "Reminds me of talking about dirty things in the garage when I was a wee kid. Now, what's up, Terry?"

"The Air Force at Bright Lake finally got a positive lock on your orphan. According to a friend of mine in Space Defense Operations, the orphan's flight has been slowed down almost to a stop by the controlling country so that it can be maneuvered into a stationary position over earth. We'll know for sure at T plus 66 hours."

"Tell me again in local time so there's no confusion in my mind, Terry."

Stewart looked at his hack watch, then counted off, "It's four fifteen here at this moment, so it's T plus 63 and fifteen minutes since launch. The orphan's retro-rocket was fired not long ago to stop its forward flight and we estimate that at T plus 72 hours, or one AM, it will be in geosynchronous orbit over earth, that is, in a stationary position over our planet. The controlling country achieves this by firing small vernier rockets attached to the orphan to maneuver it exactly where they want it to be in space."

"And that's at an altitude of sixty-six thousand miles above the earth?"

"Right," Stewart said. "In other words, the orphan

spins at exactly the same speed in space as the earth, or in other words, it stays put, it doesn't zoom off anywhere."

Ross frowned. "What worries me is that I've helped create a monster that doesn't exist. The Russians, the European consortium, and the U.S. have for years placed satellites into orbit over earth without much fuss. Maybe Browning Whitley is right, satellites are space gadgets, satellites are passive electronic gadgets whirling around silently and harmlessly over our heads."

Stewart jumped up. "Except for one thing, Quent. Until yesterday all satellite launches were detected instantly and their purpose determined quickly by the space experts. You sure as hell can't say that about the orphan."

Staring off into the darkness of the garage, Ross asked in a whisper, "What else?"

"The orphan is being positioned so it will cast an electronic shadow exactly over the western hemisphere. Its shadow will cover all of the United States and it will overlap the southern border of Canada and all of northern Mexico."

"Well, that's an interesting exercise in electronics, but what does it mean?"

"It means, Quent, that the controlling country has targeted the United States."

"Targeted for what?"

"We don't know."

"No clues?"

"Nothing, Quent."

"But I do have a story?"

"Damned right! Your instinct is as right as rain. The orphan is a threat, until proved otherwise."

"And it's just dawned on me that I must move the story before five if I'm to meet my deadline. That's less than an hour away. I'll place a Houston dateline on the copy, attributing the story to informed sources at NASA headquarters. The IP stringer will get a bonus for it."

"Won't that start a commotion at NASA?"

"Of course! It's the red herring I'm talking about. One more thing, Terry. Is NASA Houston kept informed by Bright Lake?"

"Absolutely, but through rigid channels through its innocuous Pentagon liaison office with the Defense Department."

"So the secret stuff is funneled through NASA's office at the Pentagon," Ross said, shining the bowl of his pipe. "That certainly makes sense and it's still another tree for the gumshoes to bark up! Terry, let me assure you that your flanks are protected. Also, I owe you one of those blue chips. Thanks."

Stewart emerged first from the gloom of the garage and walked directly downstreet to his parked car. Ross entered the kitchen mulling over the precise words of the bulletin he would call in to the relief switchboard operator at the bureau. She'd then punch it out for the national, European, and Far East circuits, thus beating his five o'clock deadline. But to his consternation she didn't answer. He called repeatedly with no success, then decided the damned girl had left the switchboard for dinner. Ivorson ran a loose shop but refused to give Ross or any other reporter a key to the bureau, thus barring him from its teletype. Phoning New York, London and Tokyo from his home was not only time consuming but exasperating and unreliable. He didn't dare take the chance of getting through to one and not the others, which always led to insurrection by IP's left-out subscribers.

Consumed with frustration, he realized that filing the story on deadline meant a mad drive to the Pentagon to get at the IP ticker and the loss of thirty minutes just getting there. He toyed with the idea of not succumbing to the compulsion of meeting the deadline. No other profession was as self-disciplined with so few rewards. Yet he couldn't imagine not filing. At the moment the Pentagon was the worst possible place in the world from which to send the story, but he had no choice. Discovered, the civilian hierarchy would view his action as sheer arrogance or sheer madness. He laughed that reputations were made and lost with behavior such as this.

Marge stood at the door with hands on hips as he gunned, then backed Cuspidor out of the driveway. He shouted that he was off for the Pentagon and hoped to be home before dark. She threw up her hands.

En route, he brooded over the possibility of being scooped by a Defense or White House disclosure to a favorite newsman, by a calculated NASA leak, or by an astronomer who just happened to be gazing at the heavens in the right spot at the right moment.

At the Mall entrance the civilian guard puzzled at his haste and even after personal recognition examined his press pass with considerable care. Then admitted with a kind of studied, slow contempt, Ross trudged down the silent corridor, peeked into the Defense newsroom to find the duty officer absent from his desk, walked through the empty bullpen to the ticker room, sat down at the teletype and began filing:

BULLETIN: OVER "A" CIRCUITS
FLAG LONDON
DATELINE HOUSTON, TEXAS THIS DATE
MYSTERIOUS SATELLITE POSES ELECTRONIC THREAT TO UNITED STATES AND BORDERS OF CANADA AND MEXICO.

AN UNIDENTIFIED SATELLITE LAUNCHED 66 HOURS AGO (HOUSTON TIME) MAY DISRUPT MILITARY AND CIVILIAN COMMUNICATIONS BECAUSE OF ITS UNIQUE POSITION IN SPACE TO CAST AN ELECTRONIC SHADOW OVER MUCH OF THE WESTERN HEMISPHERE, ACCORDING TO SCIENTISTS AT THE NATIONAL SPACE CENTER.

THE ORPHAN SATELLITE WAS FIRST DIS-

COVERED BY SYMONDS OBSERVATORY OF GREAT BRITAIN, ALTHOUGH U.S. OFFICIALS LATER DISMISSED ITS EXISTENCE. SYMONDS SUBSEQUENTLY SUFFERED A MALFUNCTION OF ITS TRACKING APPARATUS, BUT THE U.S. SPACE CENTER EVENTUALLY LOCKED ONTO THE STREAKING SATELLITE AND NOW REPORTS THE SATELLITE HAS BEEN SLOWED DOWN BY THE CONTROLLING NATION FOR A MANEUVER INTO GEOSYNCHRONOUS OR FIXED ORBIT EXACTLY OVER THE UNITED STATES. THIS PRECISE MANEUVER SHOULD BE COMPLETED IN FOUR HOURS (MIDNIGHT HOUSTON TIME).

BECAUSE OF THE EXTREME SECRECY USED BY THE COUNTRY CONTROLLING THE ORPHAN'S LAUNCH AND FLIGHT, SPACE OFFICIALS FEAR THAT THE ORPHAN'S GEOSYNCHRONOUS ORBIT OVER THE U.S. MUST BE VIEWED WITH CONCERN, IF NOT WITH ALARM. THEY EXPLAINED THAT ONCE IN POSITION, THE ORPHAN'S SIMPLEST TASK WOULD BE TO CAST AN ELECTRONIC SHADOW OVER THE UNITED STATES AND BORDER REGIONS, THUS DISRUPTING VOICE, DIGITAL, TELEVISION AND WEATHER TRANSMISSIONS. THEY ADDED THAT SUCCESSFUL DISRUPTION OF VITAL U.S. COMMUNICATIONS MAY ENCOURAGE LESS PASSIVE SPACE ACTIONS BY THE UNKNOWN COUNTRY.

AT A HASTILY CALLED PRESS CONFERENCE YESTERDAY IN THE PENTAGON, DEFENSE SECRETARY BROWNING WHITLEY DOWNPLAYED THE PRESENCE OF THE ORPHAN SATELLITE AS A QUOTE HARMLESS SPACE GADGET UNQUOTE, RECALLING PRESIDENT EISENHOWER'S CONTEMPT FOR THE RUSSIAN SPUTNIK AS A BAUBLE. EXPERTS IN

CELESTIAL MECHANICS STATE THAT THE ORPHAN SATELLITE, ALTHOUGH IN FIXED POSITION AT AN ALTITUDE OF 66,000 MILES ABOVE THE UNITED STATES, IS PROBABLY INVULNERABLE TO ALL KNOWN MEANS OF ATTACK AND DESTRUCTION.
END.
END BULLETIN.

Ross turned off the sending machine and dearly hoped the administration would fall for the phoney Houston dateline. Ivorson was still another problem. Under pressure, the son of a bitch would surely cave in and admit the Houston stringer didn't file the bulletin. But that possibility had to be chanced.

It now was T plus 64:15, according to Stewart's calculations, and Ross relit his pipe, not knowing quite what to do next. Instinct dictated he get the hell out of the Pentagon, yet rationally staying at his post made a lot more sense. The bulletin would get picked up by radio, then TV, and finally the morning papers. He wished there were a way to block the IP ticker sitting in the White House press room; the duty officer would quickly sound off the alarm at the highest level of government if anything was attempted.

A terrible sense of loneliness befell him. Here I am, he thought, again wearing the mantle of conscience for the government. Yet, at this moment nobody else gives a fig. Hope I can suffer the onslaughts. They'll all come pouring in here, half after my scalp and the rest furious they didn't get a piece of the story. Then an awful thought struck him: What if Stewart were wrong? He laughed aloud at the consequences. The story would rank as the biggest blooper of the century, drop IP to its knees, and probably put it out of business, along with his pension.

The desire to flee finally proved overwhelming and propelled him down the corridor. At the Mall door he was accosted by the guard, who now insisted he sign out. Chuckling in compliance, he signed the departure register with a flourish. If the administration examined the roster, they'd deduce he had remained inside the building for the past twenty-four hours and that would screw up the buggers for sure.

He rapped Cuspidor's rusty roof as he got in, then drove aimlessly on the George Washington Parkway, listening for the first radio break. It came as a jolt—as alien as if he had never heard the words before—from a disc jockey mouthing the words and phrases so badly that the bulletin was rendered unintelligible. Instead of irritation, Ross found he was pleased with the breakdown in communications, a fractional delay in an inexorable march toward the showdown.

An image of the Washington Golf and Country Club flashed through his mind, and at first he puzzled over the incongruity, then realized what beckoned was its bar. He spun off the Parkway and in a matter of minutes ordered a double Scotch on the rocks in the staid Wasp bastion. He downed it in a hurry and left as quickly as he had arrived, feeling a bit foolish over the caper. Yet the liquor sloshing through his belly reinforced his spirit, steeling him for the unknown.

He avoided the Parkway in order to drag out the return journey down Military Road and Lorcom Lane through Arlington's loveliest tree section over to Rosslyn's glass and brick housing. He then drove past the bronze Marine assault on Mount Suribachi, then past quiescent Ft. Myer, and finally to Mall parking where he found a number of cars scattered at random. He spotted Scotus Olney's official black limousine, Lu's new Buick and Shrimp's red Jaguar roadster. Behind him came General Glasscock in a Model T Ford. So, he thought, the clan is gathering. They've gotten the word—my word—just as the orphan is being jockeyed into orbit over our heads. He stared into the darkish sky wishing he could see the damned thing.

In mufti, Glasscock caught up, grabbed him by the elbow and offered a fighter pilot's cheery greeting. "Good to see you looking up out of the cockpit, Quent. They'll never shoot you down that way." He then added, "First star I see tonight, I wish I may, I wish I might..."

"Have the wish I wish tonight," Ross concluded.

"And what would you wish?" Glasscock asked.

"I'm not supposed to tell, or it won't come true."

"Oh, come on," Glasscock pleaded, "I won't leak it."

They laughed like teenagers approaching the Mall entrance. The guard made them sign in and started to say something to Ross but Glasscock cut him off with a hearty salutation. Ross sighed with relief.

"Let's find a latrine," Glasscock suggested.

"Sure," Ross said, following him to the deserted NATO area where toilet facilities were certain to be unoccupied.

Flushing the urinal repeatedly, Glasscock said barely above the rush of water, "I'm glad you got the word."

Startled, Ross replied, "Thanks, Noel."

"It kills me the Air Force and the other services can't explain their hard work. We've gone balls-out for the administration, but the muzzle is on so tight we can't breathe. The taxpayer doesn't know what the hell's happening to his money, yet his very safety is at stake."

"I'm training the kid."

"I know and I'm obliged, Quent."

"How bad a threat is the orphan?"

Glasscock moved to the sink, turned on the faucets, then said while washing his hands, "Wish I knew. Disruptive at least, catastrophic at worst."

Ross whistled. "Damned glad I'm tracking it."

"So are we."

They broke up, Glasscock up to his fourth-floor office and Ross to the bullpen.

Shrimp spotted him first, jumped up from his desk and extended his hand. "Goddamned IP did it again!"

Ross shrugged, continued toward his desk as Lu

joined Shrimp. She boomed out, "Damn you, Quent! You've rousted us out of a quiet holiday."

"Tough!" Ross said, sitting down behind his barricade. "I didn't invent the orphan. My boy at Houston got on top of it. By the way, where did you characters hear it first?"

With her usual display of professional admiration, Lu said, "On TV. An off-camera newsbreak. Right in the middle of my favorite situation comedy."

"You're beating this scoop to death on the networks, Quent," Shrimp said.

"Don't you wish you could," Ross answered. "That's the beauty of being with an international wire service, and a hungry one at that."

Lu sidled over. "Quent, I don't believe you. That IP guy in Houston is phoney."

Ross forced a laugh. "There you go, Lu, your feminine intuition is running rampant again. You're wrong!" He bit his tongue.

She seemed to accept his judgment, then asked, "Tell me what I should know."

"Midnight's the witching hour, Lu."

"Should I stick around here?"

"Absolutely. We're just orchestrating. Wait till later tonight."

"Okay, Quent. I'll do as you say."

Clapham arrived in tennis clothes. Shrimp greeted him derisively. "All the way from New York City in that garb, Cary?"

Flushed, Clapham answered, "Playing tennis with an old friend. I raced down when I got the word."

"I'll bet you didn't go home."

Ross stepped in. "Let our superjock alone, Shrimp," he admonished. "I'm sure we've all been doing our own thing today, except for me. I covered the wreathlaying at Arlington, then sent the wirephoto to London." It was a good alibi.

"You a photographer? I don't believe you, Quent," Lu

85

said.

"Why don't you query London, Lu? For the first time in my life I wish the IP bug carried the photographer's credit, but of course IP's largely anonymous."

Hoots greeted Ross's self-deprecation as Scotus Olney appeared in the doorway flailing his arms.

"Everybody out for a press briefing in my office. Right now!" he bellowed.

Lu ran after Scotus but he was long gone by the time she waddled out into the corridor. Like a clucking mother hen she returned to the bullpen and yanked Ross up by the arm. "Quent, you started this. Lead us to the altar of truth!"

Ross grunted and stepped first into the corridor to head the ragtag procession. It was suddenly attacked from the rear by Karayn, utterly out of breath, mustache fluttering, for once unable to fire a broadside of questions. He pantomimed his curiosity. Shrimp said to shut up and just go along with the rest of them. A moment later they were intercepted by Ted Harris, who put a finger to his lips for silence, then led them into Scotus Olney's reception room. He plumped himself down at Sexy Suzy's desk and held them at bay.

"Scotus has a pigeon in there," Lu volunteered.

Harris answered, "No, he doesn't. It's Phil Fairly."

"So you're right, Lu," Shrimp said.

"Ah! Big guns tonight," Karayn gasped. "Your fault, Quent."

"I'm not controlling the goddamned satellite."

"Don't you wish you did?" Lu said.

"I'd aim it right at the Pentagon."

"With us in it?"

"Sure, Lu. This building's a millstone around the country's neck."

"And make my kids orphans?"

"We've got one floating around right this minute." Ross thought for a moment. "Sorry about the sick humor, Lu. This stinking job is finally getting to me."

goggles. She primped at a mirror but couldn't see a thing.

Ross examined his goggles closely. "How do these things work, Terry?"

"Officially, they're known as variable density goggles," Stewart said, hefting the thick, spongy rubber frames, inset with large, darkish lenses, and bound with a stout, expandable headstrap. "Bomber crews wear them immediately after dropping a nuclear bomb, otherwise the light from the bomb blast would blind them. If you'll notice, you can vary the density or opacity by turning the center wheel on the nosebridge between the lenses to suit the light conditions. A real nifty gadget."

"How did you get your hands on these goggles so quickly?" Ross asked.

Stewart smiled like a Cheshire cat. "It turns out that at the time I was transferred from the Strategic Air Command to the Pentagon, our radiological safety kits, including goggles, were declared surplus. All of the bomber crews got more sophisticated equipment, so I grabbed five surplus kits for my family. Since they're in Denver, I brought you two pairs of goggles for this emergency."

"Damned considerate, Terry," Ross said, "but why did you cache the kits in the first place?"

"I could give you a million words on the subject of survival, Quent, but in a nutshell I believe the head of the family is morally and physically responsible for its survival."

Marge interrupted. "Okay, breakfast's ready. Let's eat while it's hot. But I want to hear your thoughts, Terry—"

"And I am starved," Stewart said, seating himself at the chromed dinette table in the breakfast nook. The kitchen was bathed in eerie light that penetrated the chintz curtains like an incandescent light. Although diffused, the light produced an aura of uncomfortable artificiality, yet Stewart wolfed his eggs with passion, broke the toast, dunked the pieces in black coffee and

"Yes, it is," Clapham said. "You've been on first base too long. Your problem is that you've got the guts of an ox."

Cigarette dangling off her lip, Lu said, "Take a month off, Quent. Screw IP. That's the only way Ivorson will miss you. Take Marge around South America."

Ross shrugged. "You ought to take your own advice, Lu."

Olney's door burst open. "Okay. Mr. Fairly, the President's press secretary, has a few words for you."

Marching in obediently, they chose chairs at random. It was Fairly, Scotus and Harris on one side of the room against Lu, Shrimp, Clapham, Karayn and Ross on the other.

Squat, swarthy and brash, Fairly served as White House jester. Although he displayed a questionable grasp of news reporting techniques, in spite of a stint as reporter for the *Passaic Herald,* he possessed the uncanny ability to turn disasters into one-liners, destroying the opposition. The President loved him and what Fairly said always stuck.

Scotus led off. "We are convened here tonight to discuss whether Quent Ross's orphan is a monster in the sky."

Everyone laughed but Ross.

Scotus continued loudly, "I want to add for the record, and please reflect this in your copy, that the satellite is not a biological threat. It is not a chemical threat. It is not a FOBS threat. Let me explain the latter. It is not a *F*ractional *O*rbiting *B*omb *S*atellite that could rain a hydrogen bomb down on our heads."

"Then what the hell is it?" Ross demanded.

"Our interception of signals sent to the satellite indicate that it is in no way a threat or danger to the security of the United States, in spite of the IP bulletin out of Houston."

"Just a goddamned minute, Scotus!" Fairly shot up, shouting. "I've been thinking about what you've just said. Don't come out flat-footed that the satellite poses no danger, no threat whatever. The damned thing might fall out of orbit and hit somebody smack on the head. All available evidence indicates it is no more of a threat than the scores of satellites now whizzing around in orbit. That's all!"

"What about the fact that it will cast an electronic shadow over us?" Ross asked.

"Hell! There are dozens of satellites, communications and weather satellites, doing exactly that at this very moment. They've got you covered, so to speak," Fairly said with a grin.

Ross pressed on. "That's the White House position?"

"Damned right! I might add, off the record, the President is concerned that you, Mr. Ross, are inciting the press to follow you on the bogey. So to stop this pissing contest from continuing ad infinitum with the administration, he asked me to come over here to provide an overview."

"Do you think you have?" Ross asked.

"Sure."

Lu cut in. "How does the National Security Council view the orphan?"

"The same way they view all other unknowns, with a smidgen of concern until the intentions of friend or foe are established. Perhaps Mr. Ross can give us a hand in that department too."

"I thought you came here to cut off the water," Ross said amid laughs.

Fairly broke into a broad grin. "That was a good shot, Mr. Ross. One other thing. We're fascinated at the White House with your continuing scoop on this bogey. What's your magic?"

"No magic. It's simply International Press's working relationship with Symonds Observatory in Great Britain. God knows, no U.S. agency would level to that degree with the press."

"Balls!" Scotus yelled. "You've got a romance going

with the Air Force. There's nothing they wouldn't spill their guts to you about, especially through their chief leaker, General Glasscock. Let's get that son of a bitch down here to defend himself. I know he's upstairs!"

Lu jumped up. "General Glasscock is one of the few persons in the Pentagon with the facts, Scotus. He keeps the communications channels open between technical people and the reporters who must report the facts, not political crap, to the public. Phil, please don't make an arid desert out of the Pentagon. If you listen to Scotus, you'll destroy your administration!"

"Agreed," Fairly said. "Scotus, knock off that crap about Glasscock. Besides, I'm going to get his ass on another matter."

"Just what is the point of this press conference?" Karayn asked, utterly disgusted.

"The point," Fairly explained with labored patience, "is that the President has expressed great unhappiness over the scare stories filed on the bogey. He has asked me to help reinforce Defense Secretary Whitley's position that the satellites are passive electronic space mirrors or mechanisms, if you will, and of themselves are harmless space gadgets. On his behalf I am asking those of you who are responsible reporters not to panic the nation with irresponsible reporting. Thank you."

Scotus then escorted Fairly out the secret door to his limousine, with Harris bobbing behind at a discreet distance.

Lu turned to Ross. "How now, brown cow?"

"Well, as the most irresponsible reporter in these parts, I'm going over to the teletype machine and file an add about White House heat to downplay the space threat."

"And then what?"

"Then, sweetheart, I'm going home to bed and hide like a damned coward."

5

Lupe licked Ross's face, frantically wanting out for her morning romp, yet he sensed he had just fallen asleep. The clock on the night stand pulsed its red digits at twelve thirty, but daylight seeped through the curtains. No wonder the damned dog was antsy!

Ross crawled out of bed, careful not to awaken Marge, although Lupe's prancing would have raised the dead. The phone rang, jarring him out of his wits. Marge reached over with unerring reflex and answered on the first ring. Anticipating London, he stopped in his tracks, but it was Lu. Marge tossed him the receiver and then rolled over, face in pillow, never once opening her eyes.

Lu's voice was strident. "Quent, do you see what I see?"

"I'm not really awake, Lu."

"Dammit! Look outside! Tell me what you see!"

"Hold on," Ross said, dropping the phone on the bed. He parted the curtains while Lupe tugged at his pajama leg. Struck blind by the intense light, he backed off, feeling a searing effect on his retina. He groped for the bed, disoriented, then sat down on the floor, reminded of the time when as a child he had looked directly into the arc light of an advertising searchlight. He rubbed his eyes compulsively, thinking to call out to Marge for help, then decided against it as his vision returned, although badly blurred. He grappled for the phone and located it in the bedspread by tracing Lu's hysterical voice in the receiver.

"Shut up for one damned minute, Lu!" he demanded. "Let me talk! Where are you?"

"In the bullpen, where the hell else? I was filing late copy when we got blinded. The corridors and restrooms are the only places we can hide from the light. I'm calling from a pay phone. Tell me what's going on."

"Lu, how the hell would I know? The dog just woke me up and now you're bugging me. But you're right, I looked out the window and got blinded. Trees and houses have a God awful appearance, like infrared photographs." He shook his head violently. "Lu, the blinding is wearing off, thank God!"

She sighed. "What should I do?"

"Stay put, for Christ's sake. I'm still half asleep and still half blinded. Let me gather my wits."

"Quent, don't abandon me!"

"Of course I won't. Just stay put, please!"

Marge rose bolt upright in bed, leaned over and tugged at his sleeve, demanding to know what was going on.

Ross spurned Marge's attentions trying to calm Lu down. Lupe leaped over the bed, then tugged at the bedspread. Marge muttered in disgust, took the dog down to the kitchen and let her out, then returned to Ross's side, rubbing her eyes and crying. "Quent, it's daylight out there, bright, burning daylight! What's causing it, Quent?"

"For God's sake!" he groaned, putting the palm of his hand over the receiver. "I don't know, dammit!"

"Is it your orphan?"

"Marge, shut up! Let me get rid of Lu." He turned his attention to the phone. "Lu, don't try to drive home, okay?"

Lu demanded he escort her to Rockville.

Ross began an ugly oath, but caught himself and said instead, "Impossible! I'll be over as soon as I get dressed and find some dark glasses to drive through that damned light."

She agreed not to leave the Pentagon although she was frantic about her daughters. She added, "You were right, Quent. Your orphan is terrorizing us!"

Marge assailed him the moment he hung up. "Are you going to abandon me?"

"Dear God! I'm hemmed in by women! Everywhere I turn there's a shrike trying to impale me on a thorn!"

"This shrike will impale you for desertion. Are you going out in that blinding light?"

"I'm going to the Pentagon as usual, dear. That's not desertion. My chickens are coming home to roost and I'm going to count them all. And I'm goddamned if I don't file!"

She stroked the back of his neck while he sat on the edge of the bed struggling with his shoes. "Quent," she whispered, "I've shared you with the IP teletype since the day we married and I've never complained. Now I am afraid you will blind yourself in whatever's out there, or at least get caught in a terrible accident. Can't you go back to bed and just outwait the awful light?"

"No," he answered softly, touching her cheek with his lips. "I know what you're saying, Marge. All we've got in this world is each other. I'm worried most about the effect of that light on your glaucoma. That's number one priority. Secondly, I promise not to cause you any needless grief. I will be damned careful. And lastly, if you and I really believe God has touched us with His divinity, then we'll survive the orphan and all else. Okay?"

She threw her arms around him and at that moment he sensed her intution. Over the years he had developed grudging respect for that feminine power. Time and time again she had cut through the chaff to get right to the heart of a situation, then predicted its outcome.

"I don't think you'll be coming home for awhile,

Quent," she said dejectedly. "I think your orphan is a bad Halloween trick."

The phone rang before he could respond and Marge answered compulsively. "Yes, Terry," she said as her face lit up. "We're awake. Quent's just gotten dressed and at this very moment is sitting here beside me." She patted Ross on the head while handing him the receiver.

Stewart barked a military order: "Don't try to drive to the Pentagon before I arrive, Quent!"

"Why not? I've got sunglasses."

"Because they're not worth a damn in this light! I'm bringing density goggles that I stole out of the Air Force's radiological safety kits."

"Will the goggles do the trick?"

"If I show up, the goggles worked. Okay?"

"Okay," Ross said, then turned to Marge. "That's one bright boy, a godsend." As he finished dressing he asked himself aloud, "I wonder what else Terry knows about this weird light?" Symonds and Stewart were keeping his exclusive story very much alive and he marveled at the strange circumstances that had brought it all about.

Marge ran down to the kitchen to prepare breakfast, delighted that it would be for three. Lupe scratched at the door and staggered when let in.

"Lupe's blind!" Marge cried.

Ross captured the dog without a struggle, stroked her coiffured topknot, calming her down. Soon her pom-pomed tail began wagging and it became obvious she was regaining her sight.

Marge scooped her up in her arms. "I was afraid Lupe would never see again! Thank God she's coming out of it!"

"Terry's right about the goggles. How thoughtful of him to share the gadgets."

"I'll say a secret prayer to St. Francis to protect all the poor animals for the rest of the night," she said, turning to the stove to break eggs, lay strips of bacon in a skillet and put bread in the toaster.

"Hell, Marge," Ross snorted; "get St. Francis to protect a few humans tonight."

Marge turned. "You dolt! Have you thought of St. Christopher?"

"Okay. St. Francis for you and the traveler's guardian for me. And while we're at it, who's the patron saint of healing? I'm worried about the effect of the light on your glaucoma, sweetheart."

"I'll be careful," she said, turning on the radio to catch a disc jockey babbling about the sun returning at midnight because the earth's axis had tilted. Then another jockey explained the bright light as the result of a speedup in the earth's rotation, only to be contradicted by a listener who claimed it was caused by a slowdown in rotation. A medical doctor came on hurriedly, obviously just off the street, and advised all listeners to stay indoors at all costs, but if forced to travel to wear at least one pair of sunglasses, whether walking or driving. He recommended wearing a broadbrimmed hat and taping two pairs of eyeglasses together.

"And not one goddamned word yet out of Health, Education and Welfare," Ross shouted. "I wonder where the surgeon general is at this moment, or for that matter, the head of civil defense. In fact, Phil Fairly ought to get on mike and camera and shed some White House words of wisdom. That would be an earful! But I'll bet all our leaders are panicked and in hiding."

"Maybe you're anticipating too much too soon, Quent. The light might disappear in a minute."

"I'd like to think so," Ross said skeptically just as Stewart loomed up at the kitchen door.

Marge gasped. The density goggles covered most of his face.

"Our man from Mars!" Ross said, slapping his knee.

Stewart pushed the goggles high up on his forehead, then pulled two pairs out of a paper sack. "Don't go out without them!"

"What a crazy world!" Marge said, donning her

ate the bacon with his fingers. Then after a deep draught of coffee, he addressed himself to Marge.

"Do you really want to hear about disasters, Marge?"

She leaned toward him. "It couldn't be more pertinent, Terry."

"Well, then," he said. "If a disaster befalls the family, whether earthquake or atomic bomb, it's stupid to expect a mayor, governor or president to feed, clothe, shelter and water your family. They can't make water flow, food appear, or provide heat to fuel the furnace. All they do is push some other people around. Yet we seem to fall back on the political process to provide the basic necessities. That's a lot of crap—pardon me, Marge—but politicians can't produce one damned thing necessary for survival. They're not Jesus with seven loaves of bread. That's the job of the head of the family. I'm the head of my family. I'm in double jeopardy, providing for the basic survival needs of my family and providing for the defense of my country. I dearly hope I've trained my wife and kids to look to me, and as it now happens, to themselves for food, clothes and shelter, not to some flunky of the government for survival. End of speech, folks!"

"Well done!" Ross said.

"You're marvelous!" Marge exclaimed.

"But back to the orphan," Stewart said, turning to Ross. "I assume it's okay to talk frankly in front of Marge."

Ross laughed. "She's an accessory—willing or otherwise—to this crazy situation. And I suspect the buggers are just as scared and confused as the rest of us at this moment. Furthermore, no one in power will listen to their goddamned tapes for the time being."

Stewart dropped his voice, regardless. "Bright Lake has positively identified the orphan as the source of this blinding light. Their guess is that the light is a diffused laser beam covering at least all of the United States."

"Sounds impossible, Terry. I know a trifle about lasers

because I've been assaulted by laser propagandists for the past ten years. Every lab in the world has one. Lasers produce very narrow, concentrated beams of pure light traveling at 186,000 miles a second. The laser beam can be blocked by its own impact on a target and for that reason is pulsed to prevent the problem. And I remember that large lasers consume enormous amounts of energy—electrical or chemical—requiring expensive, cumbersome energy sources. So how in hell can all this gear be packed into a satellite no larger than a couple of fifty-gallon oil drums?"

Stewart threw up his hands. "Quent, all I can tell you is the orphan is sending out a diffused laserlike light, completely saturating the U.S. tonight. How the laser gets it power, how its light is diffused, how long it will continue to shine, or why are questions I can't answer. I don't know enough to speculate. But I see its results coming through that window in the dead of night. I've just driven through a nightmare. I know it's eye-damaging, temporarily, at least, and I know it's your orphan because its geosynchronous position tells us that it is. Okay?"

Ross bit his pipestem. "The orphan's light is the ultimate terror weapon, I must admit. Just listen to the disc jockeys. If you're not spooked out of your mind looking around this kitchen, listen to those babbling idiots."

Stewart said, "We can't dismiss the technical possibility that the orphan's laser light might well be a prelude to something else, something worse, something more devastating. On the other hand, Quent, it could be a partial failure, not having achieved its full potential. Yet it might prove to be far more effective than what its designers had anticipated. Who knows?"

Marge clapped her hands to her ears. "I've heard enough."

Ross frowned at her hysteria, then said, "Terry, I've got a million questions racing through my head. The trouble in the defense business is that I must know the answers before I ask the questions. All the government does is to confirm the facts I've dug up. In normal times it's a tough enough task, but in a crisis the government fully enforces its security controls, partly out of vindictive display of power and partly to cover up embarrassment over its gross ineptness. So I find it damned difficult to find and track the truth in Washington. Terry, if I ever needed help, it's right now."

"Count on me," Stewart said enthusiastically. "Let's charge at the Pentagon! You lead and I'll follow Cuspidor."

Ross rose slowly to Stewart's spirit. "On horse, I guess, for the madhouse," he said and bussed Marge on the cheek.

"Try to do something for the blinded, helpless animals," she pleaded.

With a tolerant smile Stewart adjusted the goggle strap on Ross's head, then satisfied with the fit, turned to Marge for approval.

"You look like zombies."

Ross waved his pipe, opened the kitchen door and let in a blast of blinding light that forced them to recoil against the far wall. Marge fled into the hallway as Stewart calmly slipped the goggles over his own eyes, took Ross's hand and led him to Cuspidor, but Ross stumbled badly and stopped in his tracks in the driveway.

Stewart said, "Quent, I must change the density setting on your goggles. Is it too dark or too light?"

"Too damned light, Terry. I'm being blinded—too much light through the lenses. Can you darken them?"

"Of course," Stewart said, flipping the center dial to increase opacity. "Tell me when to stop, but if it's too dark you won't see a damned thing. It has to be something less than maximum opacity. Okay?"

"Stop now," Ross said, turning his head in several directions. "That's about right. Let's go."

He got into Cuspidor, then found she wouldn't start, although he almost wore out the starter and battery. Stewart stood by during the grind, finally shook his head hopelessly. "Better give up, Quent. Be my guest and ride out with me."

"I've got no choice," Ross said in disgust. "I'll bet dollars to doughnuts the orphan caused the no-start."

Stewart laughed. "I doubt it very much. Cuspidor's a senior citizen and showing it. Let's not worry about her ailment right now."

Ross sighed and followed Stewart to the station wagon parked curbside. Even through goggles the intense light made every object seem pure white or black. There were no grays or shadows. Cursing Cuspidor's recalcitrance, Ross debated backtracking to tell Marge, then thought it just was well she didn't have wheels that worked. He'd be trapped at the Pentagon too, and unable to respond to an emergency call. Once in place, staying put was the answer.

Stewart headed cautiously down Georgetown's Thirty-fourth Street amid swarms of low-flying, wildly erratic birds—sparrows, Ross said—one of which struck the windshield with a sad thud. No pedestrians were visible, although the intersections were marked with several wrecked and abandoned vehicles. Crossing M Street, they drove onto the ghostly, high-spanned Key Bridge and over the chalk-white Potomac to Memorial Parkway on the Virginia side. Traffic remained nonexistent and it was obvious that drivers without very dense lenses were blinded instantly. The lucky ones had pulled off the thoroughfares and out of harm's way.

Ross insisted that Stewart park in his special slot on the Mall.

"I'll get ticketed," Stewart protested.

"Quit being such a self-righteous soldier. I'm not about to walk up from your peon parking place. Where do you rank in the fifteen thousand assigned spaces, Terry?"

"11,283. That's my parking number, according to my grade."

"And how long does it take to walk to the building?"

"About fifteen minutes."

"Well, density goggles or not, I'm not walking it."

"Okay, but they'll lift my parking privilege."

"It's not much to begin with, Terry."

"But it's a constant reminder where I fit in the Pentagon hierarchy."

"You're a masochist! Your rigid, conformist, military mind is past salvation. I'd rather worry about the orphan than a goddamn parking ticket."

Reluctantly, Stewart swung into Ross's slot and turned off the ignition. Ross put his hand on Stewart's arm. "Terry, we've got some unfinished business before we dash in the building."

"Oh?"

"Yes. We are walking into a crisis probably without parallel. By morning the Pentagon will be a sea of confusion. I've weathered lesser crises in there, but each crisis exacts its toll of men and careers. Of all the reporters in Washington at this moment, I'm alone on first base and I want very much to get hit home, perhaps with the last scoop of my life. I hope for your help, but what makes this ballgame trickier than any in the past is that if the orphan keeps functioning, the rule book will be chucked, umpires will call bad plays, line drives will knock out pitchers and spitballs will be the order of the day. Now, to the point of all this, you will be forced to go to bat, get into the box and hit homers for your country, your service and yourself. One reward is promotion. In the not too distant future you might make general, but only if you please your Air Force superiors. Your civilian bosses cannot help you with promotions, in fact, their recommendations are a kiss of death. If you strike out, you'll retire a few years hence in your present grade. That's not too bad in itself, but you can do better. What I'm saying with mixed metaphors, disjointed reasoning and much passion is that I need your help, but your first loyalty is to the flag. Okay?"

"Okay," Stewart said, a broad grin breaking out below his goggles. "The flag it is!"

On Ross's count of three they sprinted out of the car, dodged several scattered vehicles and made it to the Mall entrance to find all six doors locked and barred with chains. In frustration, Ross pounded and kicked at one door and Stewart rattled another. Their curses turned into a chant. A guard appeared and waved them away while trying to shield his eyes. Ross persisted with manic force and when he had almost shattered the door's glass with the heel of his shoe, the guard relented, fumbled with the chains, opened a door just wide enough to let them squeeze through, then demanded Ross's goggles.

"Hell, no!" Ross snarled.

"I want them to drive home," the guard yelled, lunging at Ross's forehead.

Stewart grabbed the guard's arms, spun him around, then shoved him away. "We need marines here," he said. "Imagine panicked old civilians guarding the Pentagon!"

They strode down the silent corridor, leaving the guard sprawled on the floor. Ross said, "I can't blame him if he's smart enough to know he needs density goggles."

"The old bastard should've checked our passes and made us sign the roster."

"Bah! Everything falls apart in an emergency, Terry. You're assigned to a civilian world here. It quickly comes down to personal priorities."

"Which reminds me," Stewart said slyly, "let's hide the goggles under our armpits. Otherwise they'll get stolen, or worse, we'll get ranked out of them."

"Terry, you're absolutely right. The damned things are passports to the great outdoors. I'll see you later."

Ross turned into the ticker room while Stewart

continued down the corridor to the Defense newsroom. The teletypes were strangely quiet. I'll fix that, he thought, flexing his fingers, then sat down to file. But for a fleeting moment his mind went blank, boggled over the enormity of the event he was about to file. He roused himself with effort and set his fingers to the keys.

BULLETIN:
OVER "A" CIRCUITS
DATELINE WASHINGTON THIS DATE
BYLINE QUENTIN ROSS, MILITARY ANALYST, THE PENTAGON
LASER ATTACKS UNITED STATES

THE UNITED STATES AND BORDERING AREAS OF CANADA AND MEXICO ARE UNDER A BLINDING SPACE LASER ATTACK THAT AT MIDNIGHT (EDT) TURNED NIGHT INTO EYE-SCORCHING DAYLIGHT. THE AGGRESSOR'S IDENTITY IS UNKNOWN, AS IS THE DURATION OF THE SNEAK ATTACK, UNPARALLELED IN THE HISTORY OF MANKIND. THE LASER WAS CARRIED ALOFT THREE DAYS AGO BY AN ORPHAN SATELLITE AND NOW IS IN A STATIONARY POSITION 66,000 MILES ABOVE THE UNITED STATES. MOST AMERICANS—STILL ASLEEP ACROSS ALL FOUR TIME ZONES—ARE UNAWARE OF THE UNPRECEDENTED LASER BOMBARDMENT RAGING SILENTLY ABOVE THEIR HEADS.

AN UNIDENTIFIED PHYSICIAN BROADCASTED MEDICAL ADVICE TO LATE LISTENERS OVER A LOCAL WASHINGTON RADIO STATION TO STAY INDOORS UNTIL THE LASER LIGHT IS DOUSED IN ORDER TO PREVENT EYE DAMAGE. LOOKING DIRECTLY AT THE LASER MAY DESTROY THE RETINA, HE WARNED. BUT FOR THOSE FORCED TO VENTURE OUTDOORS HE RECOMMENDS WEARING TWO PAIRS OF

DENSE SUNGLASSES. PERSONS TRAPPED OUTDOORS AND UNABLE TO FIND SHELTER SHOULD PLACE THE FACE AND NOSE IN THE CROOK OF THE ELBOW SO THAT THE ARM AND FOREARM SHIELD THE EYES UNTIL RESCUE. PERSONS POSSESSING WELDERS' MASKS OR RADIOLOGICAL SAFETY GOGGLES ARE URGED TO OFFER THEM TO LOCAL POLICE OR FIRE STATIONS.

NO IMMEDIATE ASSESSMENT IS AVAILABLE REGARDING TRAFFIC ACCIDENTS ON CITY STREETS AND THOROUGHFARES, RAILROADS, OR ON U.S. AIRLANES CAUSED BY LASER EYE DAMAGE.

SPACE SCIENTISTS AT HOUSTON CONFIRM PREVIOUS IP REPORTS THAT THE EYE-DAMAGING LASER LIGHT IS BEING EMITTED FROM THE ORPHAN SATELLITE UNDER THE CONTROL OF AN UNIDENTIFIED NATION. THE SCIENTISTS SAID THE ORPHAN SATELLITE REPRESENTS A QUANTUM JUMP IN SPACE TECHNOLOGY BECAUSE ENORMOUS QUANTITIES OF ENERGY, EITHER ELECTRICAL OR CHEMICAL, ARE STORED IN A SPACE PACKAGE NOT MUCH LARGER THAN A 50-GALLON OIL DRUM TO POWER THE LASER MECHANISM. ONE SCIENTIST ADDED THAT THE LASER WAS THE PRODUCT OF HUMAN FOLLY, NOT HUMAN WISDOM.

ALTHOUGH DESIGNED AS A TERROR WEAPON, SPACE SCIENTISTS REFUSED TO SPECULATE ON THE LASER'S FUNCTIONAL LIFE OR DURATION OF OPERATION BEFORE DECAY OR DELIBERATE QUENCHING. IT IS EXPECTED THAT BOTH CANADA AND MEXICO WILL JOIN THE U.S. IN PROTEST AT THE UNITED NATIONS REGARDING USE OF SPACE BY AN UNKNOWN AGGRESSOR TO INFLICT TERROR ON SOVER-

EIGN STATES AND WILL SURELY DEMAND IMMEDIATE NEUTRALIZATION OR DESTRUCTION OF THE ORPHAN SATELLITE.

IT IS ANTICIPATED THAT THE PRESIDENT WILL DIRECT NASA TO SUPPORT THE DEFENSE DEPARTMENT IN DESTROYING THE ORPHAN SATELLITE HOVERING OVER THE HEADS OF ALL AMERICANS.

IP FIRST REPORTED THE ORPHAN'S EXISTENCE WHEN DISCOVERED BY SYMONDS OBSERVATORY IN GREAT BRITAIN AND TRACKED AFTER A SURPRISE LAUNCH HIGH ABOVE THE SOUTH ATLANTIC OCEAN. THE ORPHAN'S THREE-DAY EXISTENCE WAS DENIED REPEATEDLY BY KEY ADMINISTRATION OFFICIALS, THEN DISCOUNTED AS A HARMLESS GADGET. THE WHITE HOUSE OR DEFENSE DEPARTMENT MAY CONFIRM IN THE MORNING THAT THE ORPHAN SATELLITE CARRIED THE LASER TERROR WEAPON WITH IMPUNITY. END.
END BULLETIN.

Well, that's a long two-hundred-fifty-word bulletin, Ross muttered to himself, but the subscribers will use it all. I never thought I'd file a word on laser sats!

Staggering stiffly from the teletype, he hit its off-switch and pushed the torn chair out of the way, then stretched long and hard and turned for the door to the corridor. Scotus barred his way. "What the hell did you file, Quent?" he yelled.

"Look for yourself," Ross said with contempt. "It's still on the machine. Nobody else in the whole friggin' country is filing a word." He stepped around Scotus into the corridor and it then dawned on him that he had just filed the greatest scoop of his life.

The bullpen presented a black and white shambles. Stark light streaked through the five uncurtained four-by-fifteen-foot windows, although Lu, Shrimp and Clapham had attempted to tack up newspapers to blot out the incandescence, or so they advised him. Lu added, "You might know, General Services Administration never once touched those crummy blinds since the day the damned building was built. Now that we need them, they disintegrate on the first yank. Give us a hand."

"Sure. What do you want?"

"You're taller than the rest of us. Climb up on the windowsill and tack up some more newspaper sheets over the windows. It'll help a lot. My desk is right in line with the worst of the light."

Ross did as he was bid, but first donned the radsafe goggles, which brought forth cries of admiration and a string of questions. "One thing at a time," he said, managing to get two sheets up on each window without much effort, then slid off the last sill and faced his questioners.

"How in hell did you make it back here?" Clapham demanded.

"With these goggles," Ross said, handing them out for inspection. "I'm not giving them away." He explained the goggles were part of surplus radiological safety kits, but in short supply. "By the way," he asked, "how did all of you get back?"

"We never left!" Lu shrilled. "We filed our stories on that stinking press conference, got into a bridge session, then found ourselves trapped by the light blitz. You, at least, went home."

"That going home bit was a Chinese fire drill," Ross said, moving to his barricade. He lit his pipe, still feeling the afterglow of the scoop. It steeled his resolve more than anything else in months.

Lu came around the barricade. "Have you filed anything since the press conference?"

"Yes. A minute ago, Lu. It's a first-class wrap-up, but I'm afraid there'll be lots of adds before this night's over."

"May I check your copy off the ticker?"

"Why not? Scotus beat you to it, and he'll bust a gut because I didn't let go of the quote harmless gadget crap."

Lu lit a cigarette, then said as she dangled it precariously in her mouth, "You're absolutely right in your approach, Quent. The administration loves lolling around in false security. It never expects to get its hand called."

"Go read the ticker," Ross urged, "and catch up with current events."

She nodded, shuffling toward the door, only to collide with Scotus, who snarled and shoved her aside in a surge at Ross's desk. Hearing the commotion, Ross peered over the barricade as Scotus came with windmilling arms. The sight was so grotesque it forced Ross to laugh, but Scotus swept the desk top clean with one gigantic push.

"You son of a bitch! I'm going to kill you!" Scotus screamed and lunged across the desk at Ross's throat.

Jumping backward, Ross found himself trapped against the wall as Scotus sped around the desk to press his advantage. With pounding heart Ross grabbed one of Scotus's arms, wrenched it with all his might, then twisted it behind Scotus's back in a classic hammerlock. Scotus went face-down in agony and Ross straddled him.

"You're a traitor, Ross!" he managed to babble out of the side of his mouth. "You and your goddamned orphan! Inciting the enemy! Egging them on!"

Ross held Scotus pinned on the littered floor. Lu, Shrimp and Clapham acted stupefied at the sight of Scotus brought to submission. Ross said nothing, but felt his temples throbbing.

Revulsed, Lu shouted, "Quent, let the bastard go!"

"You've got three witnesses, Quent," Shrimp assured him.

"Aw, hold him down for another minute," Clapham

said. "Make him say he's sorry."

Ross bent down and rasped into Scotus's ear, "Get lost!" and released his grip, then added, "Stay the hell out of the bullpen!"

Scotus got up on his knees, drew himself erect, patted the stray hairs on his pate and fled without a word.

"Good riddance," Clapham said, rubbing his hands in glee.

"Let's feel sorry for Scotus," Lu said. "This laser crisis finally broke him."

"How about my throat, if he'd gotten at it?" Ross asked.

"He's no match for you," Lu answered.

Ross shrugged and began reconstructing the barricade. They all fell to, but the piles of paper, though just as high, were no longer in chronological order. He thanked them profusely when they had finished, then said, "I think I know what Scotus was saying. He has a point, although it's a minor one."

"Impossible!" Shrimp shouted.

But Lu touched Ross's arm. "You're a saint to say that after Scotus tried to strangle you. You hate him physically, yet you try to understand."

"Scotus and much of the country believes that a free, unbridled, unchecked press plays into the hands of the enemy by printing anything and everything it gets its hands on. We've all been accused of irresponsible reporting, right?"

They agreed.

"So," Ross continued, "we must reinforce our position against the administration's next attack on us. But nothing we print—good or bad, right or wrong—will deter the enemy. I am sure this laser assault was planned at least a year ago in the coldest, most calculating manner. In no way can a bunch of words on the IP wire or in the *Tampa Herald* change the enemy's determination. Yet, Scotus and his ilk think that my tracking the orphan encouraged the enemy, committed the enemy to his irrevocable action. Sheer crap!"

Clapham said, "It's obvious Scotus took out after you through frustration and embarrassment."

"No doubt about it, Cary. That's why I would not back off, nor would you. Let me inject one thought about morality into this discussion. There is nothing more immoral than for the U.S. to perish at the hand of an enemy without a whimper, without a struggle. How dare the administration censor any information about the enemy's attempt to blind us? How dare any individual or government interpose itself between the facts and the enemy?"

"There's an easy answer to that," Clapham said. "Any centralized government, since it's centralized, believes it is all-knowing and therefore correct in all its actions."

Lu shook her head in disapproval. "You haven't dug deep enough, Cary. Morality and government are mutually exclusive. That's exactly what happened when church and state were separated."

"But I have dug into it," Clapham said. "The men who wrote the Declaration and the Constitution were so steeped in morality that it proved to be an irresistible force on government, a moral force from within. Two hundred years later the men in this administration are amoral, so the administration is amoral."

Lu said, "Quent's point is the bullpen must cry out whenever the administration lies to the country."

"Or attempts to strangle someone in the bullpen," Shrimp said.

"The price of advocacy," Lu said. "It's ridiculous to expect Quent, Cary, you or me to report facts and facts alone. We're not computers or tally sheets. Numbers and statistics alone are meaningless to the public. All of us report on the facts with whatever wisdom we can summon."

"Wisdom?" Clapham asked.

"I'll answer that," Ross said. "Cary, you're a willful man, and damned intelligent, or you wouldn't be holding down a key job with the Sun Syndicate. You're the sum of all your parts, wisdom included. Each day you also draw on the vast genetic pool within you, some of it spiritual, some of it superstition, and much of it instinct."

Clapham laughed. "You're such a wise old bastard, Quent. When I get sprung out of this bullpen, I'll miss your poking around in my genes!"

Ross looked toward Lu and shrugged.

Shrimp said, "I don't know what's more unbearable, amateur psychiatry or that damned light streaking into the bullpen. Why don't we get the hell out of here before we lose our minds and eyes?"

"Not back to the cafeteria," Lu groaned. "Who'll handle the phones?"

"To hell with the phones. It's past two AM."

"Shrimp's right," Ross said. "Let's go to the cafeteria. It's perfect for our purposes, tucked away in the bowels of the first floor's "A" ring, artificial light, food, coffee and conversation."

Shrimp guffawed and led the way. Glasscock and Stewart were seated off in a corner, slurping coffee as if they were navy men, according to Ross, who walked over and so advised them. It brought forth protests, and Glasscock then invited the foursome to share his table. Only a handful of guards and several nightshift kitchen employees milled around in the three-hundred-table arena, which felt like a morgue.

"I'm glad the bullpen is so well represented in this hour of crisis," Glasscock said with a twinkle when they were all seated. "That's more than I can say for the rest of the Pentagon, military or civilian. But then I know, with the exception of Quent, the rest of you were stranded after late filing when that damned laser went on. Quent was mad enough to hitchhike a ride back with Stewart. Both wore radsafe goggles, which I think will be in vogue for the next night or two."

Lu gasped. "That long?"

"I dearly hope I'm wrong," Glasscock said. "I'm guessing. I don't know a hell of a lot more about the laser than you, but I know we're trying to put Ross's satellite out of commission."

"Oh, you've named it after me?"

"To legitimatize the orphan."

"Gee, thanks," Ross said. "I had hoped someday a heavenly body would bear my name."

"Too bad. You'll have to settle for this," Glasscock said. "And unless I gulp my coffee I'll have to settle for a backyard press conference."

"On or off the record?" Clapham asked.

"On the record, of course. I don't waste my time or yours in a crisis."

"Wonderful!" Lu said, full of anticipation.

Glasscock grinned. He enjoyed the briefer's role. He used his hands expansively, befitting a fighter pilot, and his words, as in the cockpit, were precise and well-phrased. He tried to avoid Air Force jargon and apologized when it crept into his speech, but Ross welcomed it as a breath of fresh air in the bureaucratic swamp of Washington.

Looking for a fleeting second at each listener, then halting with Ross, Glasscock said ingratiatingly, "I must compliment Quent for his tenacity in tracking the orphan. His copy, based on Symonds data, finally got the Air Force on the stick after its own sources proved worthless. The power of the press prevailed and I must thank Symonds, IP and Quent for keeping the record straight. Now that I've tossed this well-deserved bouquet, let's get down to late-breaking facts in this crisis that is of interest to all of us."

Lu applauded.

"I should inform you that certain intercontinental ballistic missile boosters—ICBM boosters like Titan and Minuteman—now in place on launching pads at Canaveral in Florida and Vandenberg in California—are being diverted to a new role, which is to kill the laser satellite.

Unfortunately, killing this satellite is a lot more complicated than we might suspect. Under normal conditions, months of intensive effort are needed to ready a space shot. Celestial mechanics cranked into the on-board guidance system, the booster and its lesser booster stages, the little vernier engines to be fired for minor corrections in space, and most important, the payload itself, whether full of cameras, sensors, dynamite or an atomic bomb, are mated together to work in infallible sequence. Tonight, we're diverting the basic ingredient, the massive booster itself, to destroy this laser satellite in a matter of hours."

Ross asked, "I thought we had killer satellites on the ready."

"Let me answer your question this way, Quent. The enemy took seventy-two hours to get the orphan and its on-board laser satellite payload into a geosynchronous spot about sixty-six thousand miles over the U.S., entailing a series of tricky maneuvers that used lots of time and considerable technical finesse. We need twenty-four hours after launch for our booster to intercept the laser satellite. I'm not sure if you'd consider twenty-four hours of flight time as on the ready. Mind you, this twenty-four-hour flight takes place after we've glued all the components together."

"Please don't neglect to mention the political factors, General," Lu suggested.

Glasscock smirked. "Yes, let's not forget the political factors. A million words at least. Here is the bastion of military might, the country's best reporters tracking military affairs, seated with a general of the Air Force, all supersensitized by the political process! But I guess it was ever thus. Lincoln spent years seeking a competent general and when they found each other, Grant stayed out of the political process and Lincoln out of the mechanics of war. Never again did two men in a common cause so respect each other's abilities."

Stewart replenished his coffee from a huge urn near

the end of the steam table, then filled the other cups.

Shrimp laughed. "We have a noble waiter!"

"Indeed," Glasscock said with a hint of the Georgian in his voice. "But to finish my indulgence in this political diatribe. I've speculated whether Lincoln would've resisted the temptations presented to modern presidents. Kennedy, Johnson and Nixon come to mind. Availability of instant communications to and from the battlefield, instant transmission of photographs from the battlefield and instant battlefield advice by Harvard geopoliticians caused each president to succumb to personal direction of day-to-day military operations, whether in confrontation with Cuba or Vietnam. Stalemate and outright defeat is what those presidents presented the nation. The seeds of destruction lie in the presidency."

Clapham was first to react with a sardonic laugh. "You are pleading that the military run military operations."

"Because it hasn't been true since 1962, the year of the Cuban missile crisis."

"What about the Korean mess?" Clapham pressed.

"Glad you asked. Truman stayed too long with MacArthur's actions. MacArthur had outlived his military usefulness, but Truman feared Mac's popularity. There were a hundred other generals who would've fought the Korean war differently, in spite of the incredible political constraints. The Yalu sanctuary was military and moral madness, but no more so than acceding to the isolation of Berlin. The Free World is most permissive of aggression. Don't ask me why."

Ross said, "But back to the killer satellite problems. Hasn't the threat posed by satellites been with us for a long time?"

"Of course," Glasscock answered, "ever since the Russians put up Sputnik in 1957. Satellites violate the territorial integrity of every nation of the world during their ninety-minute orbit. Very little can be hidden from their eyes or lenses. That's why surprise attacks are almost impossible—" Glassock looked sharply at Ross—"except for air launches. Quent was wise to pick that point up and hang on to it."

"But aren't we talking about something else? Don't satellites do more than just take pictures?" Ross asked.

"Correct," Glasscock said. "There are three categories of satellites. The first category transmits pictures, digital data, voice, television, weather, agricultural and other passive information. This is what Secretary Whitley had in mind when he referred to Ross's orphan as a harmless space gadget. The second category is designed to carry things like X-ray and cosmic-ray counters, biological experiments and telescopes. The third category consists of satellites designed to kill or destroy other satellites in space. Now for your questions."

Ross asked, "So the orphan satellite falls into the second category?"

"Correct again."

"Carrying what?"

Glasscock laughed. "Obviously carrying a laser device. I'm confirming your speculation in the IP bulletin. It's not that brilliant a deduction. Were you a technical expert on lasers, you would've hesitated, agonized long and hard over the laser possibility."

"For God's sake," Ross retorted, "what else is out there? Why was I forced to wear radsafe goggles?"

"Agreed," Glasscock said calmly. "We're being irradiated with laser light, which as you correctly reported, is being generated by an incredible source of power in a package so small that it is incomprehensible to our energy experts, but not to a layman."

"Are the experts really conducting a thorough analysis?"

"From the very moment the damned thing went on, Quent. They've been forced to rule out chemical and electrical power sources because each would be at least the size of a truck, yet the total weight of the orphan can't possibly exceed a thousand pounds, a peewee compared to the colossal stuff that's being thrown into space today. But we must remember that both the satellite and its booster were air-launched, imposing considerable constraint on size and weight."

"General, we're not getting quotable quotes," Clapham protested.

Lu snarled, "Cary, you've got a hell of an attitude! Who else would risk briefing us?"

Glasscock seemed unperturbed.

Ross asked, "General, either on or off the record, what do you think is the laser's power source?"

Shrugging, Glasscock said, "We simply don't know—we're baffled—on or off the record."

Shrimp whistled. "So you don't know how long the power supply will last."

"Correct. We're frustrated psyching out Ross's satellite."

"Ask Ross," Shrimp quipped.

"A good point," Glasscock agreed. "But there's one saving grace. At dawn the laser will be turned off by the controlling country. If not, the sun will extinguish the laser's effect."

Cheers greeted the prediction.

"But will it come again tomorrow night?" Ross asked.

"I haven't the faintest idea, Quent. I suggest all of you catnap in the building and then dash home as soon as the sun rises. You may have another wild night ahead of you. God help us all."

Lu asked, "General, why did you choose to brief us? Tell us in all honesty. And why on the record?"

Stewart looked stricken, but Glasscock grinned. "There are several valid reasons," he said, then ticked them off on his fingers. "First, the Air Force has been busting its butt trying to unravel the mystery of Ross's satellite—singlehandedly, I might add—for the past few hours. Second, the ungarbled word has got to be put out, and frankly, based on its track record, the administration is incapable of simple, straightforward statements.

Third, and of least importance, I have nothing to risk, careerwise. I'm to get a reprimand tomorrow for another matter, either from Defense Secretary Whitley, from the President, or both. So what's one more reprimand?"

"We can write without attribution, General," Ross said quickly, "if it will help save you."

"Don't bother," Glasscock answered instantly. "I've been on the administration's shit list ever since it came into office. The question is when I'll be booted out and retired. I'm surprised I've lasted this long."

"Why don't you transfer out of Washington?" Clapham asked.

"I'd rather go down in this job. I've loved it. Power, manipulation, in on the inside of decisions. Frankly, I'm spoiled. There's nothing else like it in two-star assignments. Military public affairs officers serve two masters: their parent service and the administration. But as St. Matthew said, No man can serve two masters. That implies responding to one's conscience and mine refuses to serve Scotus and Secretary Whitley. I already serve the President as my commander in chief, but I find I cannot serve the contemptible characters between him and me. Because of my age and time in grade, I cannot wait for a new civilian crew to come on board. So I'm taking the shaft tomorrow. It's no big deal, really. I've been clobbered before for sillier reasons."

He rose abruptly, smiled a practiced smile and said, "I'm sorry I spilled my guts," and with Stewart tagging along, left the cafeteria.

Lu wiped her eyes. "It tears me up to see him go. I don't have to quote Major General Glasscock of the Air Force. I can quote a high Pentagon official. My readers in Tampa couldn't care less."

"Lu, it doesn't mean a damn whether you quote him or not," Ross said. "The civilians want him out because he's his own man, a rare breed in Washington. So he's to get canned and retired. Quote him while you can. It'll be a long time before another Glasscock shows up."

"It just occurred to me," Clapham said, "all that intense laser light is bound to damage crops."

"You're a military reporter, Cary," Lu advised him. "You can't go over to the Department of Agriculture for an estimate of crop damage. Tell your wife to race over to a supermarket first thing in the morning and stock up."

Clapham glared. "Let's get the hell out of the cafeteria. I've had it here with everyone and everything."

"Don't forget to file, Cary," Lu said, "and as for you, Quent, if you were ten years younger, we'd have a desktop affair till sunrise!"

"A fate worse than death," Shrimp said.

Convulsing visibly at the thought, Ross said, "Unfortunately, Lu, I have a prior assignation with the teletype."

"I am a woman scorned," she warned, dabbing her cheek theatrically.

Shrimp whispered, "Take cover, Quent, and I don't mean from the laser."

"I will, I will," Ross said as they headed for the ramp and the bullpen. He turned off at the ticker room, massaging his fingers for the teletype drill and as usual found his head empty at the moment of truth. For a fleeting second he toyed with the idea of returning to the paper barricade to search for Defense press releases on killer satellites. Inasmuch as space weapons were considered top secret, the releases contained little substance, but might trigger past rumors and industry proposals in his mind. Regrettably, Scotus had so messed up the obelisks that an hour's effort could well be wasted in the search. Cursing Scotus, Ross decided to ride his memory, then sat down to file, hoping to make few, if any, typos.

```
    OVER "A" CIRCUITS
    ADD ONE—LASER
    DATELINE WASHINGTON THIS DATE
    LASER TO FADE AT DAWN
```

HELPLESS SINCE MIDNIGHT UNDER A BLINDING LASER ATTACK, THE UNITED STATES WILL BE REPRIEVED AT DAWN, ACCORDING TO A PENTAGON GENERAL WHO BRIEFED NEWSMEN TRAPPED AT DEFENSE DEPARTMENT HEADQUARTERS SHORTLY AFTER THE LASER LIGHT FLOODED THE NATION.

AIR FORCE MAJOR GENERAL NOEL GLASSCOCK, REPRESENTING THE UNIFORMED SERVICES DURING THE HARROWING VIGIL, PREDICTED THE LASER LIGHT WOULD BE EXTINGUISHED AT DAYBREAK BY THE CONTROLLING NATION, IF NOT FIRST OBLITERATED BY THE SUN'S EARLY MORNING RAYS. IRONICALLY, MOST OF THE UNITED STATES SLEPT THROUGH THE ATTACK, ALTHOUGH OBSERVERS REPORTED ERRATIC BEHAVIOR BY DOGS, OTHER DOMESTIC ANIMALS AND THE CRAZED FLIGHT OF BIRDS.

BLINDING CONDITIONS ON THE GROUND AND IN THE AIR CAUSED NUMEROUS TRAFFIC AND OTHER ACCIDENTS BUT PREVENTED ACCURATE ESTIMATES OF INJURIES AND FATALITIES.

GENERAL GLASSCOCK SAID HE WAS UNABLE TO PREDICT WHETHER THE LASER SATELLITE'S EYE-DAMAGING LIGHT WOULD REAPPEAR THE FOLLOWING NIGHT, BUT INDICATED THAT MILITARY ATTEMPTS TO DESTROY THE LASER SATELLITE HOVERING 66,000 MILES OVER THE CONTINENT WERE INEVITABLE. QUOTE THIS LASER THREAT TO THE HEALTH AND SECURITY OF THE UNITED STATES MUST BE REMOVED IMMEDIATELY. THE ONLY KNOWN MEANS AVAILABLE TO THE DEFENSE DEPARTMENT IS THE KILLER SATELLITE WHICH MUST REACH UP UNER-

RINGLY IN SPACE FOR A DISTANCE THREE TIMES THAT OF OTHER GEOSYNCHRONOUS SATELLITES IN ORDER TO DESTROY THE LASER. THE CONTROLLING NATION HAS CUNNINGLY PLACED THE LASER ALMOST OUT OF REACH AND AT THE VERY LEAST IS PRESENTING A CONSIDERABLE CHALLENGE TO THE UNITED STATES IN CELESTIAL MECHANICS. UNQUOTE. HE REFUSED TO COMMENT ON THE AVAILABILTIY OF KILLER SATELLITES IN THE U.S. ARSENAL.
END ADD ONE.

Thanks, Noel, Ross thought, saying a silent prayer that the add wasn't a coup de grace. One thing for sure, the add would goad the competition and queries would soon flood the night duty officer's desk in the Defense newsroom. Ross knew he had to get over there and put in a few of his own.

Moving quickly down the hall, he couldn't help but believe it a miracle that he still held an exclusive on the laser story. It was sheer luck that the competition was caught off guard and had not recovered its wits. Yet the scoop had its price. He wished he could avoid the administration's wrath in the morning, as well as Ivorson's quarterbacking. Perhaps Stewart would drive him home and he'd then take the receiver off the hook for a few hours' sleep. Marge would provide sanctuary if her glaucoma were under control.

At the duty officer's desk the lines were all lit and winking on the silent phone console. Stewart stood behind the duty officer, hands on hips and laughing.

At the sight of Ross, the duty officer glared, then cupped the phone, turned and cursed at Stewart. "Goddammit! Give me a hand with these lines, Terry! Or take care of that walk-in query. Don't just stand there doing nothing!"

"Sorry, old man," Stewart said. "I'm not on duty for

another three hours. My turn's at seven. Period."

"C'mon, this is a national emergency!"

"And I'll bet you that nine out of ten of those calls are not from newsmen. Those calls don't have a damned thing to do with media queries, they're from panicked citizens."

"Terry, you're learning fast," Ross said.

"I'm an ex-bomber pilot, Quent. I have a high survival instinct."

"What the hell do I do?" the duty officer asked.

"Let them ring. If they ring long enough and if they're not newsmen, refer the caller to civil defense, the mayor, the governor or the police department. You're not running an information desk. You're paid to run a press desk. Right, Quent?"

"Damned right! You'll have your hands full enough when the media wake up."

The duty officer sprang out of his chair. "Okay, you guys. You convinced me. I'm going to the can at long last and on the way back I'll kill the switchboard operators for bouncing all those calls to me."

"A good solution," Stewart said happily, patting the duty officer on the head, then led Ross through a maze of empty desks to his own. His phone console was dead. He slapped it with the verbal command to stay quiet.

Ross laughed. "You've sure gotten your second wind, Terry. I hope you know we're in the eye of the storm."

Stewart crossed his eyes.

"At dawn look for a fantastic flurry of action, some military, most of it political recrimination, followed by retribution."

"Me too?"

"Perhaps. Remember, you're on first base with Glasscock. Guilty through association, I'd say."

Stewart looked heavenward.

"Terry, anything said or done during the first hours of a confused situation, a crisis, is dead wrong. Why? Because the words and deeds were not blessed with

119

prior political approval. Sounds crazy, doesn't it? A classic case of the cart before the horse. Catch-22! But prior political approval is Washington's First Commandment, endorsed if not demanded by all recent occupants of the Oval Office. Prior political approval means political correctness that verges on the Kremlin's concept of control, and it really says infallibility. This attitude is best demonstrated in military affairs, seeping right down through the political chain of command. For instance, the secretary of the treasury involved himself deeply in Eisenhower's U-2 spy-plane fiasco. As a retired general, Ike should have been least influenced by individuals whose claim to fame was procuring votes or financing political campaigns, but their counsel prevailed and resulted in his incredible vulnerability during the confrontation with Khrushchev."

"Fortunately, satellites soon replaced the U-2."

"A damned lucky break, Terry. But back to our own crisis. Let me say that our free society abhors the very idea of its military forces taking unilateral or preemptive action, even though the nation's existence may well be at stake. The perverted movie *Dr. Strangelove* put that issue to bed forever, and I'm not going to debate the merits of second-strike concepts, other than that we are living in a tricky world of instant technological surprises. I know that the President will not condone independent military action tonight and mere words to that effect will only inflame him. I'm just as sure he's already turned his back on his handpicked generals, choosing instead the advice of cronies scattered about in the National Committee, the Cabinet, and more hopefully, in the National Security Council."

"Gad! Was it possibly that bad a hundred years ago?"

"As you well know, the Army has an old creed that states, Duty, Honor, Country, which has been ignored by successive generations of political animals who understand less and less what professionalism, integrity and dedication are all about. But to answer your question, I'd speculate that by and large the professionalism of the service was less ignored, more respected in days gone by. Certainly the politicians then didn't seek out political surrogates to solve threats to the physical well-being of the nation, or we wouldn't be here today. How many men did Lincoln interpose between himself and Grant? Or Davis and Lee?"

Stewart laughed.

"One last point, Terry, there is so much power centralized in Washington that those at the top feel compelled to dispense it through surrogates. After all, a handful of men control the very lives of more than two-hundred twenty million people and an incredibly potent industrial base. But this business of wholesale surrogation bothers the hell out of me. Perhaps the seeds of our destruction lie within it. I can't help but think of medieval days when the king or duke led his troops into battle and took the consequences, physically as well as politically. Today's politician leads only with his mouth."

"You sure talk mean, Quent."

"Just overstating the case to make the point."

Stewart sat down to the typewriter. "I suppose you have a query?"

"You bet," Ross said. "Let me put several queries into the hopper. God only knows when Scotus will release the answers."

"Okay," Stewart said, poised over the keyboard.

QUERY ONE: DOES THE U.S. POSSESS KILLER SATELLITES?
QUERY TWO: IF SO, ARE THEY EXPERIMENTAL OR OPERATIONAL WEAPONS?
QUERY THREE: DOES ANY SOVIET-AMERICAN ARMS AGREEMENT EXIST THAT PREVENTS USE OF A KILLER SATELLITE?
QUERY FOUR: WILL THE U.S. USE A KILLER

	SATELLITE TO DESTROY THE LASER SATELLITE?
QUERY FIVE:	IF SO, WHEN WILL THE U.S. LAUNCH ITS KILLER SATELLITE AT THE LASER SATELLITE?
QUERY SIX:	HOW LONG IS THE TRAJECTORY OR TRAVEL TIME THROUGH SPACE FOR THE KILLER SATELLITE TO INTERCEPT AND DESTROY THE LASER?
QUERY SEVEN:	IF THE KILLER SATELLITE MALFUNCTIONS OR MISSES THE LASER SATELLITE, WHEN WILL OTHERS BE READIED AND FIRED?
QUERY EIGHT:	WHAT OTHER MILITARY MEANS ARE AVAILABLE TO DESTROY THE LASER?
QUERY NINE:	DOES THE ADMINISTRATION CONSIDER THE ATTEMPT TO DESTROY THE LASER AS SENSITIVE, SECURITY INFORMATION? END QUERIES.

Ross laughed. "Sorry, Terry. I got carried away."

"You sure as hell did."

"I must submit the queries—they've vital. I've been trained too long not to follow through. Who knows? The administration may have a change of heart. Ha, ha! And by the way, what are your plans for the next few hours? I don't want to collapse here."

"Quent," he said, expelling a pent-up sigh, "we're both under the gun to the general. I haven't the vaguest idea where he is: up in his office, down in the Defense communications center in the basement, or whether he gave up and sacked out in some secret nook."

"That's a wide choice of places, my friend."

"Well, I can't in all conscience stray too far away from him. He said nothing, but I know the breed. They want you around in the clutch or it's your ass."

"Agreed. You've read him right, Terry. All hell will break loose when the White House gathers its wits and discovers that there is a Space Defense Command. White House minions will then shout fifty orders at Bright Lake and Colorado Springs, followed by fifty-one countermands. I feel sorry for the poor bastards at those stations."

"I don't," Stewart said. "For every day of terror they sit around doing nothing for a month or two, playing at mock exercises to break up the monotony. It's a petty point of view, but that's how I feel."

"How about the pipeline to General Glasscock? Will it get shut off?"

"Never," Stewart said. "They're just as aware of a bad press as we are here. One way or another, they'll get through to him, or someone nearby."

Ross laughed. "Gotcha! The military have finally wised up, I see. They're going to beat the politicians to the press. Not that I love the military, but I like the politicians less."

"Okay! Okay!" Stewart said, raising his voice in obvious exasperation. "Quent, please let up! My mind is boggled over who hit John. My bones ache, but I'm going to sleep on top of this goddamned desk until seven, then man the goddmaned phone until nine, after which I won't give a good goddamn what happens!"

Ross backed off, realizing that Stewart had reached the limit of his endurance. "You're right, Terry," he said as gently as he could. "I guess I'm treating my job like a religion. I'll take your cue and head for the couch in the niche dedicated to the honored dead."

6

Ross catnapped under a tent of carefully puckered pages of the *Times* that he had peaked over his face. It helped baffle the strident ring of phones and the commotion of incoming reporters. He stirred to find less uncomfortable positions on the ripped leather couch and in those moments thought about calling Marge, then wondered which of Glasscock's predictions had come true. From the loud, excited conversations he learned his copy had been well-aired on radio and TV. One bright lad, not far from the niche, even paraphrased FDR with a vocal lead: This night will live in infamy.

He longed for breakfast but first had to see the sky. Swinging his body off the sofa, he found his leg stiff to the point of lameness, then staggered to his feet and managed to get to the door without being recognized. Marines were everywhere in the corridor, and a squad was stationed at the Mall entrance. A lot of good that would do, he thought, signing out at a sergeant's directions.

The blue, cloudless sky hurt his eyes and his heart beat faster looking for the orphan's light, but there was no glare, no pinpoint of incandescence, nothing to betray the laser's presence. For a moment he wanted to believe he had lived a nightmare, a figment of the imagination. But the sight of brownish burn on the lawn and curling leaves of nearby trees betrayed the laser's effects. Shattered by the reality, he walked back into the building, showed his credentials and signed in, then went directly to the cafeteria for eggs, scrapple and coffee. The noise and push of customers proved unbearable and worse, he was forced to share a table with two obese secretaries whose conversation, based on radio flashes, bemoaned the fact they had slept through the light show staged by the Laser Sun Bomb.

So some disc jockey had stuck the orphan with another label! Well, why not? It was better than what he'd come up with. Laser Sun Bomb, inaccurate as it was, would stick for sure. He made a mental note to include it in his next add. Europeans, as well as Japanese, would delight in the nickname. But then he groaned inwardly at the thought of filing such garbage on the "A" circuit. Rising self-consciously, he nodded politely to his tablemates who never even noticed his departure.

His clothes clung like a second skin to his body and he longed for a hot shower, but the only bathing facility in the Pentagon belonged to the athletic club catering to super jocks: generals, field grade officers and key civilians. An exception would have been made for him as the senior newsman aboard, but years earlier he had decided his game leg ruled him out.

Taking the ramp up to the bullpen, a longer but much easier route, he was aghast at the flurry of activity in the building which had been so desolate just a few hours earlier. Men in all imaginable uniforms and grades rushed hellbent to conferences, secretaries chatted excitedly, carrying trays of coffee, while civilians dressed in Wall Street fashion and appended attaché cases walked in measured stride and guarded conversation. Ross damned near laughed aloud. So this was the nation's notion of response! Then in mind's eye he saw some poor GI bastard crawling up the gantry of a windswept launching pad and shoving a programmed guidance package into a missile's nose. That's what would kill the Laser Sun Bomb, nothing less!

Marge's radiant face came to mind. He had to make his first call to her, then Ivorson, and Stewart as a third priority regarding the status of the killer satellite queries. He debated methods of getting home without Cuspidor and his thoughts drifted back to the laser. Would it come on again in the evening?

He sneaked to the barricade, but caught sight of Lu limp in the broken swivel chair, burning butt between her fingers. In twenty years she had crawled to the top of the profession at enormous physical cost and by adopting masculine coarseness in speech and mannerism. There were times when he wanted to help fend off the unrelenting pressures imposed on her, but she proved as durable as he and always a bit smarter.

Since the bullpen had no provisions for secretarial help, reporters were not confronted with "While You Were Out" messages when they arrived at their desks. The bullpen's function was based on the traditional editorial attitude that mere reporters never needed secretarial support, in or out of the Pentagon. Actually, Ross and others preferred the environment of immediacy. They were either in or they were out when the phone rang, and the unwitting visitor took his chances. Appointments were as often ignored as preempted.

To his amazement, Ross found no press releases plunked down at the center of the desk, and for the first time in years he had ample working space, thanks to Scotus's clean sweep, although the obelisks tottered at the corners.

Phil Fairly rounded the barricade. Ross sprang up as if shot, then laughed. "My God! War's been declared!"

"Not quite," Fairly said, putting a finger to his lip.

"I know," Ross said, smirking. "You came over personally to answer my killer satellite queries."

Fairly leaned heavily against the desk and dropped his

voice to a whisper. "Quent, if you do as I say, you'll answer the queries yourself."

"Oh?"

"The President and I want you to take Scotus Olney's job as assistant secretary of defense for public affairs."

"You're crazy!"

"Nobody turns down the President, Quent."

"What happened to Scotus?"

"He flipped. Guess the job finally got to him. After he attacked you he tried to bite a guard at the door and got arrested. The guard simply stopped Scotus from blinding himself in the parking lot. Anyway, Scotus is cooling off in the kook ward at Bethesda Naval Hospital. I have his resignation. Whitley and I have accepted it. So how about stepping in, Quent?"

Ross flushed, sat down and leaned back in the chair. Scratching his head, he said, "Gee, Phil, I've got to think about it."

"Quent, there's no time to think. We've got an eighteen-karat mess on our hands and you and I know it!"

"Damned right I do! But I've got forty years with IP and a pension coming up. IP has no replacements. I can't walk out on them in the clutch. If I do, I'll kill the wire's military coverage of this crazy crisis."

"But as assistant secretary of defense for public affairs, you'll draw damned near fifty megabucks, ruffles and flourishes, limousines, other amenities, and you can do IP a favor from time to time with an exclusive. You know all that, Quent! Say yes."

"Phil, I'll call my wife. She has to live with the decision, too." After a silence, Ross added, "But I doubt I'll cross the river."

Chagrined, Fairly said, "I must get your decision in an hour, Quent. The President needs you. I need you. The country needs you. Crank that into your decision. What the hell more can I say?"

Ross bowed his shoulders and cringed dramatically.

"You've said it all, Phil, the most flattering words I've ever heard."

"The President is calling a press conference at noon to deal with the Laser Sun Bomb, so you see my panic, Quent. That's less than two hours away. I shouldn't even be here, but I was afraid you'd slide off the hook with anything less than a personal visit and a personal plea. Here I am. And we all know that you more than anyone else can handle the media. Your techniques, your sources are as good as ours. Here's my card with an unlisted phone number. Call me within the hour with your answer. I want it to be yes."

"What about the hiring paperwork? Isn't it complicated? You know, the background check on character and loyalty, the equal opportunity and affirmative action considerations, veterans preference and God knows what else?"

Fairly laughed hard. "This is a presidential appointment, Quent. All gives way before it."

"Is your buddy, Browning Whitley, aware of this?"

"Of course, Quent. We need help right now and he'll need it for as long as he remains secretary of defense."

"I'll phone you after calling Marge."

Fairly smiled, glanced at his watch, and disappeared round the barricade.

Ross stared hard at the papered window, abstractly reading the headlines, then looked upward at the dirty ceiling and shook his head in disbelief at the turn of events. The idea of role reversal held enormous appeal, the chance to set things right. The position's power had been badly used in previous administrations, making a mockery of the trust that Forrestal and others had placed in the original Defense Department's structure. After all, the Defense spokesman ranked second only to the secretary of state in wielding influence over the nation. It was about time a good guy got the job. Ross was sure of one thing, killer satellite queries and others like them would get answered once he held the long end of the stick. Never would he hide behind executive privilege to evade truth.

Lu peered around the barricade with a wild look in her eyes. "You're not going to take it, are you?"

His fantasy broken, Ross jumped up. "How the hell did you know?"

"Fairly begged me to talk you into it."

"Christ!" Ross swore. "I haven't gathered my wits yet!" He stoked his pipe methodically. "Well, Lu, what do you think?"

"You'd be out of your mind to take it, Quent."

"Why do you say that?"

She snarled. "They'll use you to get them out of this mess and then they'll find a good reason to sack your ass."

"They didn't do it to Scotus. He did it to himself, Lu. I'm amazed you'd be so hostile to the idea."

"This is the administration's first big crisis. They're beginning to clean house, replacing the more obvious misfits and malcontents. But Quent, you're not on their team. I'd say you're a necessary evil. Do you want to play that role?"

"Obviously not in that light. But aren't you overdramatizing?"

"Bah! I'm underdramatizing, Quent. You're the relief pilot to keep them off the rocks. When they've sailed safely past the danger they'll fire you with or without cause. I can't bear the thought of you bending each and every day to the caprice of those sleazy bastards. You haven't yet, nor do I think you ever will. Meanwhile, you've kissed your IP seniority away, plus your pension. Never, Quent!"

Ross sighed, then asked coyly, "Sure you're not saying all this because you'll miss me?"

"Call your wife and tell her the offer. I'll bet my bottom dollar she'll give you better reasons than mine not to take Scotus's job."

Ross seized the phone, dialed Marge, and when she

answered he asked how she had gotten through the night. She said she thought he'd never call, then added that aside from Lupe's spooked behavior everything else had settled down. Before he could pose his question, she fired off a list of needed groceries. He agreed to shop on the way home, not troubling her with the fact that Cuspidor was stalled at home. When she finally drew a breath, he brought up the job offer.

She responded quickly. "It's your decision, Quent. But you know I don't like administration society. They're all carpetbaggers, whether for four or eight years in Washington. I detest their women."

Ross laughed, "I hadn't thought of that. Anything else?"

"It's your decision," she said again as Lu caught the drift and slapped him on the back. Marge continued, "I prefer embassy flower arranging. I do the flowers and then enjoy the teas. No kowtowing to senators' wives, and worse, to those White House women."

"You're saying you're not for it?"

"I'm saying it doesn't make sense to throw over the pension."

"I'd get a consultant's job or become a lobbyist afterward."

"Quent, it's too late in life to abandon your professional status."

"Okay," Ross said, feeling deflated. "I hear you, Marge. I won't take it."

They then talked simultaneously, Marge repeating it was his decision, Ross agreeing her judgment was correct. He ended on a feeble note of love.

Lu was elated. "Smartest thing you ever did, Quent," she said, pecking his cheek. "Now you're one of us again."

"I'm not so sure," he grunted. "I may get sacked by IP, since I've just made the top of the administration's shit list. I'll be a permanent fixture up there from now on out."

"Get off it, Quent! They're afraid of you, not only as a person, but because you're the press. You've got the last word, always."

Ross rubbed a moist brow. "Now I've got to call Fairly and give him the word. Then that damned Ivorson. I think I wanted Scotus's job just to give Ivorson a hard time."

"That's a real lousy reason," Lu said, pecking him again on the cheek. "See you later."

He dialed the White House number and Fairly answered on the first ring. Like a schoolboy, Ross blurted out his decision. Fairly slammed down the receiver. Unnerved, Ross fled to the men's room and caught himself washing his hands repeatedly. Shades of Shakespeare's Lady Macbeth, he thought. Guilty even before the crime was committed. He would find Stewart and bring him up to speed.

The Defense newsroom was awash in noise and people, but he soon found Stewart flipping through an F-15 maintenance manual, oblivious to the racket.

"Where the hell are my killer satellite answers, Colonel?" Ross demanded half seriously.

"I hear you're going to be my new boss," Stewart said, bowing with outstretched arms.

"Get up with the times," Ross commanded. "I turned it down."

"Hooray for you and too bad for us," Stewart said with genuine dejection. "God knows who will replace Scotus now. I shudder to think of the possibilities."

"Beats me too," Ross said with a shrug. "Of course, there's temporary salvation in that all press action for the next few hours will be handled at the White House. You and I are spared that commotion for the moment. But beware the very moment after the White House has skimmed all the cream off the top of the bottle, after the broad statements have been stated, the platitudes pronounced, the generalities generated, then it's the Pentagon's turn to explain, defend and rationalize for the hardcore press just exactly what was meant at the

White House. It's a nice, clever, deceptive transfer of responsibilities, eh? A handoff that would put any quarterback to shame, believe me, Terry!"

"Wow," Stewart exclaimed. "That was a mouthful."

"The truth, nothing but the truth. By the way, Terry, any sparks on the killer sats, on or off the record, let me know, soonest. Ivorson's going to crawl all over me to keep that story rolling."

"I hear you, Quent."

"I don't want to go near the ticker room. It's probably as mad as this newsroom or the bullpen."

"Fairly's going to have your ass for sure."

"Maybe yes and maybe no," Ross said as they parted.

The bullpen possessed an old black and white TV that some willing soul had adjusted to view the President's news conference. Ross detoured the waiting crowd to call Ivorson.

"I thought you'd left us, Quent," Ivorson said sarcastically.

"Sorry about that. I'm still on your payroll."

"Well, thank God for small favors."

"Merle, I've got a bunch of queries working on the killer satellites."

"Good boy! When do you file?"

"The President may handle it. I hope you've got a man in the White House press room."

"You bet I do, but leg it yourself for specifics, for facts, for military details."

"I know, goddammit."

"Will the laser come back on tonight?"

"I haven't thought about it."

"Then get on it!"

"One thing at a time, Merle."

"Let's not get scooped."

Ross slammed down the receiver. He had two stories to follow up, the killer sats as well as the laser's return. They were related stories and he could well wrap them up as one and then go home. Hopefully, Stewart would give him a ride. If not, he'd call a cab, stop at the market and get home to Marge.

Shrimp poked his nose around the barricade and asked loudly, "Quent, are you with us or against us?"

Ross motioned him to come close. "You goddamn loudmouth! Why don't you use a bullhorn?"

"Answer the question, Quent."

"I turned it down."

"Praise the Lord."

"Since you're so smart, Shrimp, who's the next nominee?"

"Nobody for a while. The heat's on the White House, then it'll shift to the Congress, especially if the laser comes back tonight. Finally, the Pentagon will take the rap for all of it. After the dust settles, Scotus's replacement will be announced."

"I'll buy that reasoning. He'll be a proved vote-getter, or better yet, a bag man who extorted the aerospace industry."

"This goddamned country," Shrimp said, "looks on every threat, whether it's a drought, flood, or a laser blitz, as a political crisis. We go through a drill in adversary politics, choosing sides based on political advantage, and only then get on with the task at hand, delegating all hard work to those least able to protest, not how well they perform."

"Yeah, yeah, we've heard all that before."

"But it's still true, Quent," Shrimp said, winding down. "Since you've declined Scotus's job, I predict it won't be filled today or tomorrow because the administration can't find time to finger a candidate to suit its purpose. But if the laser crisis lasts another night or two, the administration will be forced to draw on a military spokesman as surrogate, mind you, a surrogate, because any action to repel the laser must be military action. The surrogate must be believable to the press corps."

"Glasscock?"

"Sure, Quent, if all goes badly enough."

Ross laughed cynically. "Boy, I'm damned glad I turned down the job."

"But if you had taken it and the crisis proved short-lived, they'd be forced to blast you out of the slot."

"You're wrong about presidential appointments. They're at his pleasure."

"A decent guy could secure a favorable press against removal. That would be hilarious."

"Shrimp, am I supposed to change my mind?"

"Hell, no! I'm just laying down a case for a military spokesman for the Pentagon, now that you've turned it down. You're the one and only exception. I can work with any guy in uniform, not so with the friggin' civilians they've positioned in that job."

The phone rang and Shrimp disappeared. Ross answered to hear Hildebrandt and Cranmer at the House and Senate press galleries screaming in unison about congressional heat for inside IP information on the laser. Ross reminded them there were at least twenty congressional committees briefed constantly in closed, secret sessions by Air Force, Army, Navy, NORAD, Defense Intelligence, CIA, NASA and others on every conceivable aspect of national defense. He advised that administrative aides to frustrated senators and congressmen should be told to get off their dead asses and arrange emergency briefings, rather than look for spoon-fed background by the wires. As for himself, he wouldn't do it, adding that congressional committees, if not drunk or asleep, had more access to facts than any other segment of government. What they did with the information remained a mystery and Ross closed out the lecture with an observation that in forty years he had never once gotten one iota of information from IP on the Hill. A moment later he had second thoughts about his roughshod manner and debated calling back to apologize, then decided to hell with it. Ivorson was paid good money to keep all IP communication lines open.

Stewart phoned. "How about the NATO latrine?"

Ross roared. "You too?"

"Now or never," Stewart warned and got off the line.

Ross hurried to the NATO area, now swamped with brilliant uniforms of fourteen or so nations, suspecting that Glasscock had directed the meeting. The timing proved perfect and he joined Stewart at the urinals. Hitting the flushing valve, Ross asked above the rush of water, "Killer problems?"

"Good guess."

"Infighting?"

"Another good guess. NASA versus Air Force versus Navy."

"It never quits."

"The system won't let them. Fighting for the same space dollar. Which translates into hardware. Which translates into power."

"But there's a laser satellite hovering overhead, Terry."

Stewart winked mischievously, moving to the washbasins. He turned several faucets full force as a phalanx of Norwegians burst into the room and lined up at the urinals, emitting protracted groans and anguished chatter over an overlong staff meeting. Disgusted, Ross nodded toward the door and Stewart followed quickly down the NATO corridor. They halted midway between ventilators and stood face-to-face at the wall.

Stewart said, "The point is that the killer satellite travels for twenty-four hours from launch to intercept, so it's a long sweat for us, not knowing if it will miss or kill the laser. Then we must add the additional hours consumed in the countdown prior to launch. If problems develop in the booster missile or in the killer satellite payload during countdown, we're forced to shut down the whole damned operation, fix the problem, then restart the countdown. You see it's not a routine, whambang firing like sending a Minuteman missile and its nuclear warhead from the U.S. to a target inside Russia, taking all of twenty minutes from start to finish."

"Okay," Ross said, "but what about the infighting?"

"It takes weeks to ready a booster and its satellite package for space flight. They're launched only from Cape Canaveral in Florida or at Vandenberg in California. At this moment we are seeking a booster that is ready for space. All we'll do is switch payloads, that is change the scientific package to a warhead armed with conventional explosives or a nuclear bomb. The problem is that no agency of the government admits possessing a ready space booster. We'll have to find it on our own and then pry it out of the owner. That takes time too."

"Which warhead will be used, conventional explosives or a nuclear bomb?"

"Another dilemma. If we use conventional explosives, we've got to get pretty damned close to the laser satellite to destroy it. If we use a nuclear bomb, we'll destroy it even with considerable space flight miscalculations."

"But aren't nuclear bombs forbidden in space?"

Stewart laughed. "It depends on whose ox is getting gored. Which is worse, getting dosed with small amounts of radioactive debris floating down out of space, or getting blinded by a laser sat?"

"For once I almost feel sorry for the President. He's cursed either way."

"Well, our people are over at the National Security Council, waiting to brief if called on. Political factors determine the military action."

"You're turning into a savvy young man, Terry. I wish I knew whether to file before or after the President's news conference."

"Can't help you there, Quent. I feel this briefing is simplistic, but if I get into the nuts and bolts I bog down and so will you," Stewart said almost apologetically as they parted.

Ross was more tired in spirit than in body as he retraced his steps. Every sentence required an editorial decision. Wouldn't it be nice to write something straightforward for a change! He hesitated at the ticker room door. Should he file or not? The President might scoop him and then again might not. The second add might well get buried in a lot of White House nonsense if he waited. What if the laser was a one-shot deal and not turn on again? He stood wavering as Lu came along and trapped him.

"Are you loaded?" she asked.

"Yes."

"Care to share?"

Ross scratched his back on the door jamb. His mouth opened but he couldn't summon words.

"I've got a funny," she volunteered.

"I need it."

"Ted Harris is sitting in Scotus's chair. He's driving Sexy Suzy crazy with orders and directives."

Ross smiled.

"I thought you'd enjoy that," she said. "They won't fill the slot for some time, least of all with Ted. You know, Quent, it's to our advantage that it remains unfilled, a chink in the administration's armor, and at the best possible time."

Ross nodded.

"Now, what were you going to tell me?"

"Oh, there's a internecine war raging about whose booster will be used to fire a killer satellite at the laser."

"I'm not surprised. Boosters are so damned expensive, time and dollar wise. Our national priorities are wrong. It's bucks first and then the mission, survival notwithstanding."

"That could be your story, Lu."

"It is as of this minute."

"Good girl!" Ross said, hoping she'd go away.

"You know," she persisted, "this laser crisis is unique in that a Washington dateline for once doesn't mean a hell of a lot. The laser's damage is just as bad in San Francisco or Des Moines. So my news peg must be totally defense oriented like yours and national in scope.

It's important to me that we keep cross-pollinating, Quent."

"Sure," he said with a smirk, "I'm certain New York IP is catching hell from European and Far Eastern subscribers on what the laser's done to one of the world's largest cities. I haven't checked the "A" circuit for international queries or what's been filed regarding laser effects on two hundred twenty million people, nor do I intend to get involved. This military beat is tough enough."

"We're agreed on that," she said as they drifted down the corridor. Ross turned into the ticker room and seated himself at the teletype, drummed the base of the machine with his fingers with a rhythmic beat while trying to put his thoughts into gear. What came to mind was, Let's file and damn the consequences.

> OVER "A" CIRCUITS
> ADD TWO—LASER
> DATELINE WASHINGTON THIS DATE
> KILLER SATELLITE SQUABBLE
>
> INTERNAL SQUABBLING AMONG VARIOUS U.S. AGENCIES IS DELAYING SELECTION OF A BOOSTER TO CARRY KILLER SATELLITES INTO SPACE, ACCORDING TO OFFICIALS AT NASA'S GODDARD SPACE FLIGHT CENTER, MARYLAND. SPACE-RATED BOOSTERS PROVIDE THE NECESSARY THRUST TO LAUNCH KILLER SATELLITE PAYLOADS INTO PRECISE TRAJECTORIES TO INTERCEPT AND DESTROY THE LASER SUN BOMB NOW HOVERING OVER THE CONTINENTAL UNITED STATES. THOUSANDS OF BOOSTERS ARE IN THE MILITARY ARSENAL, BUT ONLY A HANDFUL ARE REDESIGNED FOR SPACE MISSIONS. FOR THIS REASON THE AGENCIES ARE RELUCTANT TO SURRENDER THEIR SPACE BOOSTERS FOR THE INTERCEPT MISSION.

ON THE SURFACE THE INTERAGENCY TUSSLE SEEMS INANE IN FACE OF THE LASER THREAT WHICH MAY CONTINUE TO BLIND THE UNITED STATES, YET EACH SPACE-RATED BOOSTER REPRESENTS MONTHS OF RESEARCH AND ENGINEERING EFFORT AND MILLIONS OF HARD-FOUGHT DOLLARS. FOR SUCH REASONS THE AIR FORCE, THE NAVY AND NASA ARE RELUCTANT TO HAND OVER THEIR READY SPACE BOOSTERS TO THE SPACE DEFENSE COMMAND, KNOWING THAT THE WITHDRAWAL WILL SERIOUSLY DELAY TIGHTLY SCHEDULED SCIENTIFIC SPACE TASKS.

GODDARD OFFICIALS EXPRESSED HOPE THE PRESIDENT AT HIS NOONDAY NEWS CONFERENCE WILL ANNOUNCE HIGHEST NATIONAL PRIORITY FOR THE KILLER SATELLITE BOOSTER TO BREAK THE IMPASSE. THE KILLER SATELLITE'S PAYLOAD IS TO BE DECIDED TODAY AT A NATIONAL SECURITY COUNCIL MEETING. THE CHOICE LIES BETWEEN HIGH EXPLOSIVES OR A NUCLEAR BOMB. HIGH EXPLOSIVES REQUIRE A VERY ACCURATE TRAJECTORY, WHILE A NUCLEAR BOMB CAN KILL THE LASER SATELLITE ON A FAR LESS THAN PERFECT TRAJECTORY. HOWEVER, NUCLEAR DEBRIS IS LONG-LIVED AND ALTHOUGH DIFFUSED, PRESENTS HAZARDS IN SPACE AS WELL AS IN THE EARTH'S ATMOSPHERE. IF THE NUCLEAR BOMB IS CHOSEN, AN OUTCRY BY NEUTRAL AND THIRD WORLD NATIONS AT THE UNITED NATIONS IS EXPECTED.

SINCE THE KILLER SATELLITE WILL TAKE 24 HOURS FROM LAUNCH TO INTERCEPTION OF THE LASER SUN BOMB, NO RELIEF FOR THE UNITED STATES AND ITS BORDER NEIGHBORS

IS POSSIBLE TONIGHT IF THE LASER IS TURNED ON AT SUNSET BY THE UNKNOWN, CONTROLLING COUNTRY. END.
END ADD TWO.
NOTE TO EDITORS: STAND BY FOR ADD THREE AT CONCLUSION OF PRESIDENT'S NEWS CONFERENCE.

It occurred to Ross that had he filed such an add a week earlier it would have been thought a conspiracy by Buck Rogers and H.G. Wells. He shook his head at the course of events and shut off the damned machine.

The bullpen was bedlam. The TV in the niche blared forth a studied, reasoned commentary by the nation's most respected reporter, whose trust was that all citizens comply with the President's wishes expressed during the conference. Ross wondered why the President didn't stage a fireside chat and eyeball the nation, rather than mince his way through a parrot dance. It was probably Fairly's fault. The White House staffers hadn't organized their ignorance, but God help the country when they did.

Damned if he would suffer through more of the preamble. He found that the concourse beckoned and he took the ramp down to the shops, debating whether or not he had filed truly sensitive information. Of the many security criteria established by the government, one related to information that would provide aid and comfort to the enemy. He laughed aloud at the thought. Certainly, there was no comfort to the enemy in his second addition. And of aid? Well, internal divisiveness might be construed as aid to the enemy, but it was of a highly transient nature, dissolved by presidential edict the moment he issued the booster priority. Did his second add expose the order of battle, the method and ability to respond to the enemy? The country's ability to cope was overwhelming once the culprit was identified. At this point in time the enemy was a phantom—a thing unheard of in military annals—but soon to be unmasked. The detection techniques and devices available to the White House were among the best. Insofar as the method of dealing with the Laser Sun Bomb was concerned, only the killer satellite technique seemed feasible, short of wresting away the phantom enemy's actual space control of the laser, which was hardly likely before nightfall.

Business was brisk on the concourse. The drugstore was wiped out of sunglasses. Ross was more surprised at the dress shop's trade, as well as the crowded gift stall offering scented candles and salacious greeting cards. His own desires ran more to stockpiling staples such as dehydrated vegetable soup, canned tuna and freeze-dried coffee. He thought that the psychology of crisis and uncertainty led to a craving for the frivolous.

In a line at the newsstand for the first time in his life, Ross bought the final edition of the morning paper, also the evening bulldog, and laughed that for once the morning final was not much more than a broadside, while the bulldog contained ten times as many pages. He was pleased both papers headlined his bulletin, although the story's timing built a fire under the White House. He prayed that through instinct, logic and good advice, the President would arrive at the right decisions for the sake of the nation.

Although the Pentagon lay less than two miles from the White House, the TV's sound and picture came through fuzzy and blurred. Ross recalled that a distant predecessor to Scotus had carried in his own spare set for the reporters on the day of Kennedy's assassination in Dallas. Newer TV sets were scattered around the building, but not for reporters' use.

Considerably taller than the mob milling around the TV, Ross could see the screen halfway across the bullpen. He moved backward, feeling no compulsion to concentrate on the President's face. Stewart and several military friends from the Defense newsroom joined him. He quipped, "I see your cohorts have deserted your posts. Who's answering the phones and massaging the queries?"

"The phones were put on hold and the President will take care of your queries, Quent," Stewart retorted.

Three well-intentioned reporters ran around the bullpen and took all forty-six phones off their cradles amid bravos and cries of well done. Then an inexplicable delay developed in the telecast and a TV commentator ad-libbed over frame, paraphrasing Ross's second add while the camera locked onto the Seal of the President emblazoned on the lectern.

Shrimp couldn't contain himself. "What a helluva start that is!" he shouted. "What's happened? Only the White House press corps knows! They're first class reporters! We're second class!"

Hoots greeted his comments, but Ross savored Shrimp's sarcastic outburst because it was the bitter truth. The White House press corps, chosen by publishers and senior editors, then accredited by Fairly to the administration, represented the elite of American journalism. For the most part they existed comfortably on Fairly's press releases and served as on-camera baubles of the reporting world—at least in the eyes of newsmen covering the Congress, State and the Pentagon—proving that the press in its accommodation to the government was fragmented exactly as the government itself. Ross knew that not one accredited reporter had the ability or the guts to pry apart another Watergate coverup.

Without explanation the President appeared on screen somewhat breathless and distraught. Handsome as ever, his face turned fiercely grave as he plunged into the laser crisis confronting the nation. He read a prepared statement sonorously, in which he declared a state of national emergency, taking to himself vast emergency powers, then cited a series of legislative proposals, including a huge supplemental budget to fund emergency actions. Responding to queries from the floor he stated he had already placed the armed forces on red alert. In answer to an obviously planted question, he made an impassioned plea to the unknown aggressor not to turn on the laser in the evening. Another query prompted him to say that in company with the U.S. ambassador to the United Nations he planned to address an extraordinary session of the UN at noon the next day to present a formal protest of violation of U.S. sovereignty. Incredibly, not one reporter brought up a query regarding military counteractions to destroy the laser. In an unprecedented closing statement he asked for the nation's prayers to convince the aggressor to turn off the laser satellite, which implied a state of national helplessness. Harriman, the senior reporter present, thanked the President and in a matter of twenty minutes the news conference was over.

The watching bullpen was stunned. A dozen reporters leaped up and converged on Ross, shouting questions.

"Just a goddamned minute!" Ross shouted back. "I'm not Fairly!"

"The President didn't say one word about knocking off the laser, the dumb son of a bitch!" someone yelled. "What a half-assed idiot!"

"Don't tell me your troubles," Ross said. "Apparently the President hasn't been advised that the laser can be knocked off, or worse, he thinks it's a big secret. Why don't you wise guys call up Harriman and give him hell for cutting off the news conference. He's playing footsie with Fairly."

"What can we do with the crap we just heard?" Shrimp asked.

"Nothing," Ross suggested. "The President's just beached you on the rocks. If you want to eat, you file what you can scrounge out of corridors, waste paper baskets, latrines, and from advocates and soreheads, or the Telegram will fire you and find someone else who will file military news, Shrimp."

Lu sidled up and muttered, "Where's Noel?"

"He'll surface when the climate's right," Ross said, but thought to himself that the President didn't give one clue on which to file another add. He realized he had to go on sheer invention or get a blatant leak.

Major General Don Whitehead, chief of army information, appeared with a huge carton in his arms. He reached in and started passing out radsafe goggles to all comers in the bullpen. Spotting Ross, he rummaged around the carton and offered an unused, unblemished pair.

"No thanks, General."

"You'll need them," Whitehead warned.

"I've got a pair."

"Impossible!"

"Courtesy of the Air Force."

Whitehead's face fell. "I'll be damned! Those flyboys screwed the Army again!"

"Don't take it to heart," Ross said solicitously. "No one else in the bullpen has goggles. Keep handing them out, General. They'll be needed to get home tonight, after what I've just heard on TV."

Grimacing, Whitehead said, "It'll take more than talking at a phantom to douse the laser, I'm afraid."

"But the President may get lucky. The laser has to burn out sometime, perhaps this evening."

Whitehead harrumphed. "I hear everybody's being let off at three o'clock to beat the laser home. Also, the Army's getting stuck again with civil defense."

"Oh?" Ross asked with interest.

Shrimp chimed in. "That's a pretty good trick civil service pulls off. When nothing's happening, the civil servants with their big, fat salaries dick around with civil defense projects. The moment things get rough around the country, civil service bows out, keeps its paychecks and the GI is forced to pick up the pieces and risk his eyes in the process."

"Exactly!" Whitehead said. "I'm glad you see through the civil service ploy. It works for them in every crisis.

But I can't bitch about it, publicly, at least."

"But I can," Shrimp said.

Ross smiled, feeling a scoop coming from Shrimp's direction. He asked Whitehead, "Did the President order the transfer?"

"He sure did, about an hour ago as an executive order."

Ross said, "I'm glad he's thinking about some aspect of the military for a change. He probably feels uncomfortable dealing with uniforms. It's obvious from what he just said, omitting any reference to military response, killer satellites or any other hardware, that he doesn't believe in military response, doesn't trust it and won't use it until geopolitics fail. The fact our enemy is a phantom helps him delay playing out his military aces in what is still a game of solitaire, not stud poker."

"I'm afraid you're right," Whitehead said as Shrimp returned to his desk with a pair of goggles and for laughs began filing while wearing them.

Ross compared his goggles with a pair that Whitehead handed him. "General, there's a difference between them, substantial, I'd say."

"Impossible!" Whitehead said. "They're all to the same specs."

"But mine say U.S. Air Force. Yours carry only the manufacturer's name. It's no goddamned wonder the Army can't fight its way out of a paper bag!"

"You sure know how to hurt a guy," Whitehead muttered. "Public relations is the Army's greatest downfall."

Ross laughed heartily at Whitehead's expense. "Without public relations, General, you'll never get a decent share of the defense budget, especially in this friggin' administration. If you're invisible, you will disappear."

Whitehead nodded dolefully.

"I'll give you a hand in the visibility department," Ross said, "but like everything else around here, it's not magnaminous. This crisis is a space-land war, the first of its kind. I'll need your inputs, if you're willing."

"I'll be in touch," Whitehead said. "Should've done it months ago."

Ross smiled and walked back to the barricade. Lu was sitting in his chair.

"I won't get up!" she announced.

"All right, Lu. I'm a gentleman. But what's the problem?"

"I want to cry."

"Then cry."

She actually wiped her eyes. "We're going to burn up, burn to death!"

"Lu, give the President some credit, please. He has more information available to him than you think."

"Are the killer satellites ready to go? Like Polaris and Minuteman?"

"If you mean sitting on alert in a launching tube or silo, the answer is no, Lu."

"Why not?"

Ross sighed at the thought of making a torturous explanation, but her eagerness impelled him to go on. "Killer satellites," he said, "must be tailored to the target in space. It's not like lobbing a warhead at a Russian city from a launching pad up into space and then down to the target. Killer sats must be carefully tailored to fly up to the space target and then explode up there with great precision."

"Is that why we and the Russians outlawed them?"

"Exactly. Nobody gave up a damned thing."

"Are you going to file?"

"I'm forced to, Lu. Europe and the Far East are standing on their ears."

"Won't your White House IP reporter carry the brunt of the President's message?"

"He'll report the political pap, but the Europeans and Japanese want blood—the military action—so I've got to file, come hell or high water."

"What peg?"

Ross flexed his fingers repeatedly. "I'll hang my story on civil defense, or the lack of it."

She whistled. "I never thought of that peg."

"Shrimp's doing civil defense too. Except that my coverage is for a wider readership, of course. The rest of the world is watching us, curious if the two-hundred-year-old noble experiment is about to fail."

"And you're the conduit."

"A self-appointed, self-willed reporter of human folly."

"True," she agreed.

"Folly begets folly. Who else would be handed radsafe goggles?"

She said with satisfaction, "I got four pairs from Whitehead, one for me and for each of my daughters so they can get out at night."

Ross laughed. "Rockville cruisers?"

"You bastard," she spluttered. "I mean emergencies, maybe evacuation. I must leave an avenue of escape for them. I'm a working mother, you know, and I can't hover over them like Mother Carey."

"Enough!" Ross protested.

Lu flounced off to her typewriter. Ross went to the ticker room to file add three and ran into Stewart, foaming with hatred.

"I want the hell out of the Pentagon!"

"Why would you want that?" Ross asked, irritated with the distraction.

"I've got to be a doer, not a talker. I want to be with hardware like the killer sat, I want to be on the pad, putting that son of a bitch together, then watch it blast off at the target in space. I don't want to rot between these walls."

"Too damned bad," Ross said. "You now have a face and a name in the Pentagon. On the pad you'd be just another light colonel with full bulls and buck generals breathing down your throat. Here you're a press officer, working directly for a two-star general, performing a vital function. A lot of facts come to a focus on your desk and that's why you earn the grudging respect of peer and superior, civilian and military. If you bug out of this job, Terry, you're a gutless wonder. Okay?"

"Okay," Stewart said sheepishly. "I had to get it out of my system."

Ross nodded, then asked, "What the hell else do you know?"

"The killer sat launch is scheduled at eight tonight at Canaveral, but I don't think you can file it yet."

"Why not?"

"It'll provoke the President. We're doing it on our own."

"That's high risk. What's the rationale?"

"The killer sat will probably miss the laser satellite with its conventional, high-explosive warhead. If it misses, no one will know. If it destroys the laser, who can fault success?"

"How long will this flight take?"

"About twenty-four hours."

"So then if it's launched tonight—the first killer satellite fired in anger—no measure of its success will be known until the laser does or does not light up the skies the following night?"

"Right. And don't get confused on this point, Quent. It took three days for the enemy to get its laser satellite into a functioning, geosynchronous position, but it only takes one full day for intercept."

"Still a long time."

"The best we can do, Quent. General Glasscock thought you should know the truth so you don't get off-base in your filing. He doesn't want you to print the specific facts, though."

"Okay. I appreciate and respect the backgrounding."

Stewart nodded, turned on his heels and disappeared.

Ross asked himself: What do I do now? The Air Force is clever in its killer satellite strategy. It has little to lose and much to gain. They're using me to keep the record straight, but I'm using them to stay alive. I guess we deserve each other.

Turning on the teletype, he wished he had first typed a rough draft at his desk, but that wish was impossible. Yet, composing cold on the live machine had its advantages. Somehow the juices were summoned up and somehow the juices flowed.

>   OVER "A" CIRCUITS
>   ADD THREE-LASER
>   DATELINE WASHINGTON THIS DATE
>   KILLER SATELLITE IGNORED
>   THE WHITE HOUSE NEWS CONFERENCE HELD TODAY AT ONE PM (EDT) PROVED NOTABLE ONLY IN THAT THE PRESIDENT DID NOT ANNOUNCE ANY MILITARY RESPONSE TO LAST NIGHT'S LASER SATELLITE ATTACK ON THE UNITED STATES. ALTHOUGH THE BLINDING SATELLITE SITS OVER HIS HEAD LIKE THE SWORD OF DAMOCLES, THE PRESIDENT DIVULGED NOTHING REGARDING LAUNCH OF A KILLER SATELLITE TO DESTROY THE SPACE LASER, NOR DID NEWSMEN AT THE CONFERENCE POSE QUERIES CONCERNING THE PRESIDENT'S INTENTIONS AS COMMANDER-IN-CHIEF TO USE THE NATION'S MILITARY MIGHT TO END THE ATTACK.
>   THE PRESIDENT'S SILENCE IS INTERPRETED AS PART OF BEHIND-THE-SCENES MANEUVERING TO GAIN SOVIET RUSSIA'S CONCURRENCE FOR U.S. LAUNCH OF A KILLER SATELLITE, ALTHOUGH SOME YEARS AGO BOTH GOVERNMENTS PLEDGED NOT TO PROCEED WITH EXPERIMENTS LEADING TO STOCKPILING AND DEPLOYMENT OF OPERATIONAL KILLER SATELLITES.
>   IF THE UNITED STATES CURRENTLY HOLDS

PERFECTED KILLER SATELLITES, IT MIGHT PROVE EMBARRASSING TO LAUNCH THE SPACE WEAPON FROM A READY ARSENAL, THUS A HOLDING PLOY MAY ACCOUNT FOR THE PRESENT INACTION. BUT INFORMED SOURCES STATE THE DELAY IS DUE INSTEAD TO THE DEFENSE DEPARTMENT'S FRANTIC ATTEMPT TO ASSEMBLE A PROTOTYPE KILLER SATELLITE TO BE DISPATCHED AT THE LASER THE MOMENT IT IS READY.

FURTHER NEGOTIATIONS SEEM INEVITABLE WITH THE SOVIETS AND THE UNITED NATIONS, ESPECIALLY IF THE KILLER SATELLITE IS TO BE ARMED WITH A NUCLEAR WARHEAD TO INSURE A FAR GREATER KILL PROBABILITY. A NUCLEAR EXPLOSION IN SPACE WILL CAUSE FURTHER INTERNATIONAL REPERCUSSIONS BECAUSE NUCLEAR DEBRIS WILL BE INJECTED INTO SPACE AS WELL AS THE EARTH'S ATMOSPHERE.

THE PRESIDENT ANNOUNCED TRANSFER OF THE CIVIL DEFENSE FUNCTION TO THE U.S. ARMY FROM A CIVIL SERVICE AGENCY AS HIS ONLY MILITARY DECISION TODAY. THE BATTERED CIVIL DEFENSE STEPCHILD, UNWANTED AND UNLOVED SINCE WORLD WAR II, WILL BE EXPECTED TO PROVIDE EMERGENCY SERVICES AND EQUIPMENT ON A NATIONAL SCALE TONIGHT IF THE LASER SUN BOMB REAPPEARS IN THE EVENING SKY, A TASK THE ARMY CONSIDERS FOLLY AND LOGISTICALLY IMPOSSIBLE. END.
END ADD THREE.

Before he could turn away from the machine, Lu tapped him on the shoulder. "I see you've done your duty, Quent."

"That I have," he said, "in fact, I've just put another

burr under the administration's saddle. I'm more right than wrong in what I've filed, but I'm pressing their patience. Trigger men will try to put me out of business on a security violation, now that the President has invoked wartime powers, one of which is to kill off the First Amendment."

"Hell, you're one of the oldest pros around, Quent! You'll beat them at their game. I'll help. Just holler."

"Thanks, sweetheart," he said, toying with the ticker's off-switch. "I've been through the drill with past administrations. When they charge you with a security rap, they first siphon off your attention from reporting to that of self-preservation, then while you function under that charge your credibility goes down in the eyes of your employer, and worse, your sources dry up because they're afraid of entrapment and guilt through association. So you lose all the way around."

"But no one's ever been hung in our business, Quent. You know that."

"Lu, I'm trying to tell you it's impossible to function when government terriers and pit bulls latch themselves onto your arms, legs and ass. Everyone then stands off, afraid of being bitten as the mad pack swirls about."

"Okay," she said. "I hear you, but I guess I've been lucky. They've backed off from me probably because I'm a woman."

"Damned right. They'd get a bad press attacking women. Meanwhile, pull a carbon off the teletype. It's a start for your cunning mind." He finally turned off the machine, flexed his stiffening fingers, got up and stretched, then said as an afterthought, "I've got to go home and get Cuspidor started before nightfall for a lot of reasons. Marge is trapped and I must do some grocery shopping en route."

"I'll hold the fort," she said. "Is Terry taking you home?"

"I hope."

151

"Good," she said, folding the carbon neatly in half, then tucked it in her cleavage. Ross leered as she left for the bullpen. He turned into the Defense newsroom and found Stewart, nose buried in the F-15 flight manual.

"Where the hell are the answers to my queries, Colonel?"

Stewart looked up, studiedly unimpressed. "You don't scare me anymore, Mr. IP Military Analyst. There's a war on. It'll be days before we hear a thing. Besides, we don't have a Scotus Olney to expedite queries for you."

Ross laughed. "Get off your dead ass, Colonel, and take me home. You're never going to fly again, so put away that F-15 crap."

"Absolutely right, Quent. The Pentagon is a pilot's graveyard. Let's go!"

They started down the corridor but were intercepted by a pert blonde in four-inch spikes. She threaded her hand inside Stewart's arm, looked up into his eyes and asked, "Terry, do you know a Mr. Ross? I can't find him in the correspondent press room."

Stewart drew her close with an affectionate hug. Ross stood off, puffing on his pipe. Stewart said, "Mr. Ross is the distinguished gentleman off to our side. Mr. Ross, meet Mrs. Charlene Biggs."

Ross stepped forward, grinning, and stole a glance at her ample bosom.

Indifferent to his gaze, she said, "I'm the defense general counsel's secretary, Mr. Ross. Mr. Trevelyan is anxious to see you. Will you follow me?"

Ross's face hardened. "I'm pressed for time, Mrs. Biggs."

"But it's not far," she said, "just up the escalator."

"A door or two away from Browning Whitley's, Mrs. Biggs," Ross added, shrugged and agreed to go.

"Good!" she said enthusiastically, flashing a set of perfect teeth. Stewart and Ross flanked her to the escalator.

Stewart said, "Lest Mr. Ross jumps to the wrong

conclusion, Charlene, I should tell him we've known each other for years. Charlene's husband is a JAG Major, a lawyer, and we've been stationed together at three different bases."

Ross smiled understandingly, but decided to press his point. "Mrs. Biggs," he said softly, "do you know why Mr. Trevelyan wants to see me?"

Stewart interrupted. "Charlene, it's okay to level with Quent. He's a godfather to me." He then turned to Ross and said in a confidential voice, "As you know, Quent, most service wives in Washington are forced to work to make ends meet. It's bad office politics if bosses are made aware of certain relationships or allegiances. Charlene and I don't usually flaunt the fact we know each other, although it's great to see her where she is. Now, back to Quent's question."

"It's about security regulations and violations, Mr. Ross. That's all I know."

Ross groaned. "Thanks. That's a headstart. I'll gather my wits in the next few seconds."

They walked in silence to the general counsel's door in the quietest corridor of the Pentagon. After arranging to meet Ross in the parking lot, Stewart kept walking along the sacrosanct "E" ring. Charlene escorted Ross into the inner office, introduced him to Trevelyan, a portly individual in his seventies, hard of eye and possessed of prominent, shaking wattles. A shock of white hair and a Southern drawl completed the portrait of a lawyer turned politician in pine country. Ross barely stifled a snicker at the sight of the living caricature.

After a simple introduction, Trevelyan said almost inaudibly, "The rules governing the press are being modified, Mr. Ross. Tomorrow morning you will have in hand an advance copy of the executive order on security safeguards regarding the release of information in the public domain. This order will remain in force only for the duration of the national emergency. I have addressed you because you are the most senior, most knowledgeable military reporter in Washington. Whether we like it or not, other reporters will emulate you in the manner that you report the present crisis. We beg your cooperation in observing the new order governing release of information affecting the security of the United States."

Ross said, "Those are great motherhood words, Mr. Trevelyan. Is the security guideline a takeoff on that imposed during Vietnam, Korea and World War II?"

"Let me correct you, Mr. Ross. We are not talking about a guideline. We are talking about security regulations, regulations which, as you know, are clearly codified and readily enforceable with the full authority of law."

"Then why hasn't a single newsman ever been successfully prosecuted for alleged violation of security regulations?"

"I haven't called you to debate enforceability, Mr. Ross, only to advise you that the new security regulations will be off the presses and enforced tomorrow. I suggest you familiarize yourself with the provisions soonest, or at least before you file another story."

Ross stood up. "I'm tempted to print your veiled threat now, Mr. Trevelyan, but I'm just too damned tired. If the laser doesn't reappear tonight, the administration's attack on the press as its first order of business is worth reporting on the IP wire."

Trevelyan's wattles shook convulsively. "You're a smart bastard, aren't you, Ross?"

"No. Just a worm, a lowly reporter."

"I've made my point, Ross. Good day." Trevelyan made no attempt to get up or shake hands, turning his attention to a sheaf of papers on his desk.

Ross let himself out and Charlene met him in the outer office. She asked, "How did it go?"

"Awful."

"I thought it would," she said, opening the door to the corridor. "I typed the draft regulation that was sent to the White House."

Descending the escalator, Ross thought that the cute wench could well serve as a Trojan horse.

Stewart's station wagon sat in Ross's slot in Mall parking, but Stewart was nowhere in sight. Ross leaned against a fender and after a fifteen minute wait wondered what misfortune had befallen the boy. Suddenly, on a dead run, Stewart appeared and jumped into the driver's seat.

"What happened?" Ross asked.

"You wouldn't believe it, Quent. I forgot where I parked! After searching North Parking for ten minutes, I remembered moving the damned car up here." He started the engine with a roar and they took off with a lurch.

Ross told him of the encounter with Trevelyan and ended asking, "How do you like them apples?"

"Charlene will keep me informed," Stewart said. "After the fact, of course, but better than nothing."

"Terry, I think you fit well in the Washington scene."

"I'd rather push an F-15 Eagle around at Mach 3 or 4."

"You'd get bored boring holes in the sky."

"Never."

"Okay," Ross said with secret envy. They crossed the Potomac in the mainstream of trucks and cars hellbent for a thousand destinations. Ross directed Stewart to a supermarket where they encountered the equal frenzy of panicked housewives stocking up on groceries. Ross filled a basket with staples, plus the items that Marge wanted in particular. Although checkout lines were long, waiting women waved the resplendent Stewart to the fore. Ross slipped him the cash and they made off for Georgetown.

Ross carried in the groceries while Stewart attacked Cuspidor's engine. Moments later, Stewart burst through the kitchen door shouting, "Eureka! Eureka!"

"What did you find?" Ross asked anxiously.

"The sparkplug wire on number eight cylinder slipped

off. I just pushed it back into place. Cusp runs fine now."

Marge exclaimed, "You're wonderful, Terry!"

"What have you heard from the kids?" Ross demanded.

"Judy called to say they're staying put."

"That's smart," Ross said.

"And I'd better get back to the Pentagon," Stewart said, "before I'm declared AWOL in the enemy's camp!"

After Stewart left Ivorson called, insisting on a fourth add to meet the five PM worldwide deadline. Ross said he wanted to hold off until after eight and argued that the laser's return or demise was a logical peg for the fourth add. Ivorson pressed for the fourth add. Ross swore and said he wasn't a robot spitting up endless tidbits of news. Ivorson swore back. Ross thrust the phone back onto its wall cradle as Marge accosted him with a picnic basket and bedroll.

"What's that for?" he snarled.

"The picnic basket is to tide you over your hunger pains," she said compassionately, "because I know you're going to stay in the bullpen until the bitter end, Quent. There's yesterday's salami, bread, instant soup and coffee, red wine and a surprise dessert. But you're not going to share the bedroll with Lu. It's too small!"

The thought dissolved him with laughter, and then he roared. "Marge, you're the most incredible person I know," he said with a passionate embrace, "although your apprehensions about Lu are unjustified. Sexy Suzy is another matter, but she'd demand nothing less than the Queen's Room at the White House before she'd bed down. So you see, all four of us are safe."

"At least I'll know where you are, Quent. Do you think that awful thing will come back on tonight?"

"Wish I knew."

"Why can't we shoot it down?" she asked, handing him a mug of coffee.

"It's not that easy, Marge. The President must come to terms with himself politically as well as commander in chief. When these bastards run for the highest office in the land, they never think of the latter, other than the Marine Band serenading them with 'Hail to the Chief.'

"I wish I could think of a better word, but is dichotomy his problem?"

"Dichotomy is the prelude, decisions are the problem. Nobody wants to make tough decisions, decisions that alienate large groups."

"But I remember he campaigned like mad for the presidency. He wanted to be leader."

"For the trappings and the listing in the *World Almanac*. But like his predecessors, he's got too many advisers, both chosen and self-appointed. He's being confused with all the options and all the consequences of each option. Neither he nor his secretary of state put a foreign policy into effect after inauguration. The country's run by opinion polls. He bends every which way, unscathed by vision."

"Are you going to bear down on him?"

"I don't look at it that way, honey. I'm supposed to be a cold-blooded military analyst. I really hate filing all of those adds. I'm not supposed to be a spot news reporter, but that's the way this crisis is breaking. I'd like to get a few hours of objectivity into my copy before I punch it bylined on the teletype. I hate myself later for over-reaction, for transparent anger, but mostly for having missed reporting the crux of the crisis because it's too obvious. I'd like to play a bit of Arnold Toynbee in my analyses. After all, objectivity is why IP pays me." His voice trailed off as he picked up the basket and bedroll and headed for the door.

"I won't bother you on the phone, Quent, unless it's a dire emergency," she said, touching his face and pecking both cheeks.

He clenched the pipe between his teeth. "Marge, call me if anything goes wrong, anything!"

"I will, I will."

Cuspidor started up as new. Pleased with Stewart's

instant repair, Ross hoped destiny would prove kind to the many-faceted young man who seemed to possess attributes of the complete gentleman, something more than Congress had ascribed.

At Mall parking, Ross found a car parked in his slot and was forced to summon the Park Police to shove the intruder out of the way. To cap it off, marine sentries at the door refused to admit him without thorough inspection of the picnic basket, bedroll and his personal credentials. After passing their scrutiny, interlarded with barracks banter, he was assailed with catcalls as he entered the bullpen. The harangue ranged from optimist to coward, and when he raised the picnic basket and bedroll for all to envy, he was pelted with press kits and paper clips, driving him behind the barricade. He emerged a moment later and saluted the tormentors with his middle digit, then sat down at the desk still uncluttered with Defense press releases and wondered what in the world he ought to do next.

A sudden commotion erupted in the bullpen and Ross's curiosity got the best of him. He peered over the barricade to see Stewart handing out mounds of GI-wrapped packages to the scrambling reporters.

"What are you passing out, Colonel?" he yelled at Stewart.

"Survival gear. Come and get it, Quent!"

Ross entered the melee and grabbed a large paper carton. Printing on the waterproofed wrapping declared that the contents were concentrated foods for arctic survival. Another carton contained space-age flight gear: a blanket, tent, mask and gloves, vest and jacket, all tissue-thin but designed to protect downed aircrews against the world's worst weather. Ski and radsafe goggles completed the package, to everyone's satisfaction.

Lu asked what the Navy would do for the bullpen.

Shrimp quipped, "The Navy will sneak a sub up the Potomac to rescue the Pentagon press corps from

Ross's laser sun bomb!"

Jeers met his comment.

Ross carried his cartons behind the barricade and stashed them under the desk, the first place a thief would look if he dared trespass into the enclave.

Moments later Stewart walked behind the barricade. "Well, that's done. I feel like Santa Claus."

Ross chuckled. "The Air Force doesn't miss a lick."

"I'm for sharing the survival gear," Stewart said. "There are tons of it up on the fifth floor to take care of more than five thousand Air Force people in the building. A lot of them are away on trips or vacation."

"Was it Glasscock's idea to pass the gear to the reporters?"

"Sure was."

"Make a note, Terry. He's one helluva good public relations man."

"He sends his regards."

"Anything else?"

"Meet me at Brentano's in five minutes for a quickie."

"Okay. Near Nefertiti," Ross said. After Stewart's departure he sauntered out, unnoticed by the reporters fiddling with their new toys.

He met Stewart as planned, but was struck by the fact Stewart looked strained for the first time. A man pawed through poor-selling novels on a remainder table, well within earshot. Stewart tossed his head in the man's direction, then whispered, "Let's go."

Ross followed discreetly as Stewart made a beeline for the Joint Travel Ticket Office, an arena unto itself at one end of the concourse. At least ten lines moved slowly toward the ticket counters. Stewart picked the longest and Ross fell in behind. Ahead were two hamstrung English women apparently fleeing back to Great Britain, totally engrossed in their booking problems.

Stewart turned sideways and whispered, "The general said we lobbed a Saturn killer satellite from Canaveral and a Titan killer satellite from Vandenberg."

Ross resisted the impulse to slap Stewart on the back. "Wonderful!" he chortled.

"He said you should know both blew up."

"My God! What do we do with that?"

"Nothing. Nothing at all, Quent. Both boosters were bootlegged, the Saturn from NASA and the Titan from the Strategic Air Command. We can shut up the SAC commander in chief, but stealing from NASA is another matter. Those civilian queens will run right to the President protesting the robbery, since the shot was a failure. The other reason for the protest is that the President has ordered nothing."

"What failed?"

"The general said the failures were almost inevitable. Technically, you can't mate multistage space missiles in less than twenty-four hours and expect high probability of success. The boosters, Saturn and Titan, are tried and true, but the upper stages are makeshift for this killer role."

"That tells me the U.S. honored its agreement with Russia. We have no killer satellite stockpile. Were the payloads conventional explosives or nuclear?"

"Thank God, just high explosives."

"I can't file the killer sat story using the high-explosives angle because I don't want to blow the whistle on the two misfires."

"The general thought you'd see it in that light."

"Anything else, Terry?"

"Yes."

Ross laughed. "You're doing a damned good job stringing me along, Terry. But cutting your teeth on me is okay," he said with a glint of admiration. "Through your backgrounding you've gotten your commitment out of me and I guess I'm stuck with it. You might as well tell me the rest of the story."

The line had not budged an inch in five minutes. Ross lit his pipe leisurely. Stewart placed his weight on one foot and then the other, with his arms at parade rest and said softly, "The Space and Missile Systems commander—he reports to the secretary of the Air Force as well as to the Air Force chief of staff—is going to keep stealing boosters and keep firing killer sats until he gets one that goes all the way and busts the laser."

"What happens if he's caught?"

"Oh, he's just a three-star, a technical type. At worst, he'll get a fast retirement. Besides, he can tell his conscience it's not really stealing. The taxpayer paid every last cent. It's basically a question of authority or power within the government."

"Aha!" Ross said. "You've just refreshed my memory, Terry. So in this dichotomy the Space and Missile Systems general reports to the Air Force secretary, who is the political animal appointed to that job by the President, and for that reason the administration is not unaware of the caper. True?"

"Yes and no," Stewart said as they moved one body's worth toward the ticket window. "According to the general, the Air Force secretary must be as responsive to his political party in the House and Senate as he is to the man who appointed him at the White House. Since the President has done nothing yet and the heat from individual senators and congressmen is getting unbearable on the Pentagon to do something, the secretary is reacting first to those pressures, and he will keep reacting until called off first base by the President or by Browning Whitley, which amounts to the same thing."

"You're an apt pupil, understanding the system."

"I've got two hellishly good mentors."

"What's the tradeoff, Terry?"

"The tradeoff is that you treat this poop only as background. The general says you'll know when to file it."

"That puts me on my honor. But I know what he's doing. He needs someone in the press corps, Terry, who knows the facts and will file for the widest possible readership, come hell or high water, when the timing's right."

"I'd guess that's it, Quent. Oh, I almost forgot. Whoever is controlling that laser satellite is airborne, which is a damned clever technique. We're picking him up all over the sky, here and there and everywhere. There are more than two airborne command posts that he's working out of. We thought at first the laser was being fed energy from the ground, but our scanners can find no known energy frequencies capable of it. Actually, we're not sure we understand his technique, so it's hard to identify, and a damned sight harder to stop or destroy. You can file on that if you wish."

"You're implying the laser will come back on tonight?"

"Not exactly, Quent. Baffling things happen in space to make gadgets unpredictable. Right now somebody is sending hundreds of commands to the laser and we don't know why. The laser might be dying and so this could be a desperate attempt to revive it, or on the other hand it is just being exercised to make damned sure it works tonight."

"God! To think we're on the receiving end of this madness! I'm beginning to understand how the Third World feels about technology."

Stewart smiled wanly, said nothing, then stepped abruptly out of the line and disappeared in the milling concourse crowd. A discreet minute later Ross also turned out and plodded up the ramp, haunted by the specter of a hostile satellite in the hostile environment of space bringing the world's most industrialized and powerful nation to its knees. The United States had freed itself of drudgery by harnessing technology to the nth degree, yet a determined foe using technical trickery could reduce the nation to political bondage. He asked himself if this were another David and Goliath contest, with David being cast as the bad guy.

In the bullpen he remembered a prized meerschaum

pipe that he had hidden in a bottom desk drawer. It lay untouched and he fondled its pure white, intricately carved bowl, long stem and mouthpiece of clearest amber. The meerschaum was noted for its long, cool smoke, but needed tender, loving care. He smoked it only on special occasions and hoped this wasn't the last.

The sound of ringing phones rolled over the barricade with a stridency unequalled in his memory, but he could turn it off in his mind better than the reporters' voices that seemed an octave higher in parrying demands from editors for information on the laser's return. A lesser number of queries related to military action and Ross thought that if Whitley ever needed a press secretary, it was now.

Fairly would be smart, Ross thought, to combine the bullpen and the White House press corps for the duration of the crisis, but since there was no precedent, Fairly would never think of it. Ross again suffered a pang of conscience, but his decision was irrevocable.

In several short hours the ticker room was reduced to as much turmoil as the bullpen. Everybody pressed into it to catch the latest news flashes. The wires, including his own, ran every rumor the mind could conjure up. Restraint and news judgment was tossed to the winds. The Russians were almost universally accused of having fathered the laser by all except official Washington. The Chinese, the East and West Germans, the French, even the Vietcong were nominated as the enemy. A thousand ideas were propounded to destroy the laser and even more imaginative techniques were suggested for defense against it. Members of Congress, through their favorite newsmen, called upon the President, the defense secretary, the joint chiefs, even the marines, to eradicate the threat. Governors and mayors begged citizens to remain calm. Ross was thankful he didn't have to file such crap.

Lu intercepted him in the corridor. "What do you think, Quent?"

"The laser coming on? Who the hell knows, Lu?" He decided not to draw her into Stewart's disclosure on the enemy's airborne command posts. Her readers in Tampa wouldn't know what to do with it. Instead, he said, "I've got a sterling angle for you. There's an earth resources satellite that whizzes overhead every ninety minutes or so, and its job is to report the condition of crops for the Department of Agriculture."

Her eyes widened. "I know what you're leading up to, Quent. Actually, I should've thought of it first."

"It doesn't matter who thought of it first. With your financial understanding you ought to latch onto that satellite data as it is spit out of D.A.'s computer."

"Of course! The laser is bound to damage crops and cause chaos in crop predictions. Even last night's exposure must be substantial. The commodity market will be thrown into turmoil in the morning. Futures trading will panic. Now, if I can get my hands on those satellite readouts on damage!"

"Exactly," said Ross. "The taxpayer is paying for every last bit of the data. I suppose potatoes will be less damaged by the laser than citrus hanging on branches. That's for you to find out and report. It'll help housewives, too, because I don't have any more faith in the Department of Agriculture's ability to release information than the Pentagon."

"Probably worse, if that's possible, Quent, since they're rarely under pressure and won't be able to cope with a crisis."

Smugly, Ross said, "If you horn into that D.A. loop, be sure to tell Marge what to hoard."

Lu laughed at the funny, then hurried to her desk to call the public affairs officer at the Department of Agriculture.

Ross stretched his legs in the corridor, then peered into the Defense newsroom, recalling the image of Scotus shouting, ranting and raving, then countermanding his very own orders in the next breath.

Actually, the newsroom functioned without direction because it was propelled by the dynamism of a one hundred billion dollar annual budget and the kinetics of two million men under arms. As the focal point for reporters, it responded to queries ranging from airbase closure to the reassignment of navy yeomen. Days, weeks and years it continued as a perpetual motion machine, its humanity apparent only when one face at a news desk was replaced by another. Ross envisioned a voice computer that would answer routine news queries on subjects as varied as contract awards, payrolls, manpower numbers, even biographical data on officers and senior enlisted men. Yet Ross knew that any query relating to national defense, the government's vaguest, most quoted and trickiest phrase, would evermore be forwarded from the newsroom upward, even to the White House itself for debate and turndown. The nation as a free society was forever preoccupied with secrecy and zeal in protecting state secrets and putting the paranoid Russians to shame. Time and again Ross filed stories that the nation's strength lay in its exploding technology which bloomed because of an incredibly broad industrial base and in spite of government interference. Rubber stamps marked Top Secret and eight-foot-high chainlink fences surrounding weapons installations were irrevelant when a weapon cycle from inception to obsolescence lasted about five years, driving the other side berserk in its attempt to catch up. He hoped the laser wouldn't prove him a liar.

Stewart wasn't to be found among the newsroom's seventy desks. Ross searched behind the high filing cabinets and in the print shop with its mammoth mimeographing machines to no avail, yet was impressed that Stewart as legman for Glasscock managed to spend more time and effort at his official job in the newsroom than any of his predecessors, all of whom quickly succumbed to the job's split allegiance, managing to play one end against the other and as a result did nothing of value during their three-year newsroom tour.

Back in the corridor, Ross caught sight of Rear Admiral "Ape" Gibbon rushing past under full steam. Ross waved his pipe, Gibbon came to a halt, then motioned that they meet midway between ventilators.

"Hi, Quent," Gibbon said in a low voice. "Have you heard about the Air Force busting a Saturn and Titan?"

"I know," Ross said with a wry face.

"The Navy's dedicating a Polaris booster to the noble effort, off the record, of course."

"When?"

"Before midnight, whether the laser comes on or not."

"Good luck, Ape."

"If it flies, we'll let you know, Quent."

"Thanks, Ape," Ross said gratefully and watched Gibbon scurry down the corridor to some sort of clandestine hold. By nature and training, men in uniform were free of artfulness and duplicity during their junior years, but one tour of duty at the seat of government soon demanded all of the cunning within the marrow. They first cut their teeth on interservice rivalry, fighting over roles and missions and a fair share of the defense dollar, then as seniors on second or third tours, fighting off administration attacks in the defense secretary's office, in the halls of Congress and sometimes at the White House itself. Unfortunately, whether by design or default, once arrived at the Joint Chiefs of Staff level, they were bereft of public-affairs officers to serve their interest. So when presenting or defending important military issues, the Staff's position, ill-served by Scotus and his kind, was inevitably submerged and rendered invisible by House and Senate press galleries, by the White House news staff, or both. Ross groaned in frustration that his voice alone could not surface and then rivet national attention to vital defense issues from the Staff's point of view. Every other year or so a desperate chairman of the Joint Chiefs of Staff would blow off steam to an indifferent press, putting his career on the line in the process, and the results were no better than when the same information was leaked to Ross. Only the Europeans and Asians cared about Staff attitudes.

Ross drifted back to the bullpen and toyed with the idea of filing a roundup story on boosters in the U.S. missile arsenal, but the Despicables confronted him for a game of King Bee.

"I see we're back to normal," he said, fishing in his pocket for a flippable coin. He won his toss and got his coffee free at the third-floor bar. Lu shuffled in on their heels, bought her own cup and joined them in a moment of silence, a welcome respite from the bullpen's racket.

Clapham broke the mood. "I'm staying till nightfall. Any takers?"

Lu burst out laughing. "Anyone leaving before the laser comes on?"

Silence answered the question.

"Good!" she said enthusiastically. "Let's throw a lawn party at sunset. There's a pretty, grassy spot near the Mall entrance. I'll get hot water and we'll nibble on Stewart's survival rations."

Clapham uttered a low oath. "Lu, you're a phoney Druid waiting for the rise of the laser sun bomb. You're sick!"

"Well said!" Karayn added.

Shrimp defended Lu's idea. "What the hell," he said with a shrug, "Lu's point is that we are reporters. So let's report on the laser with a touch of class. If the laser repeats its performance, we'll report on an incredible scientific achievement: a man-made sun rising every night and far more destructive than Ole Sol himself. Who knows, we may be filing our obituaries!"

Ross said nothing, puffing on the meerschaum.

Karayn waved his arms. "You're an insane bunch. I'm betting the laser was a one-shot deal. It decayed during the day—it died—it crapped out. The President knows this and is waiting for confirmation."

"So why not go out and enjoy a few minutes of twilight?" Lu asked with a pout.

"Sure. We've got nothing better to do, let's stargaze!"

Ross gave Karayn a look of contempt. "You're whistling 'Dixie,' Milo, but I hope you're right. Your government and you are thinking alike. You're concerned with the effects of the laser, not what caused it to be put into space in the first place. Let me tell you, Milo, that wearing radsafe goggles, pleading on the podium of the United Nations for the enemy to knock it off, or even destroying the laser with a killer satellite won't prevent another launch."

"Okay, you pontificating bastard, tell us how the laser came about."

"At least I'm thinking about it, Milo. My guess is that a cadre of scientific madmen, perhaps in a captive commie nation, or less likely, a Third World consortium of the same breed of scientific dissidents who have a thing against the United States, put up the laser. I fear the President is mostly mesmerized by the implied threat of blackmail. There's an angle, you see, the laser lends itself to blackmail. The President is a politician skilled in compromise and may at this moment be weighing the terms of our own surrender."

Karayn snorted. "As the first victims of the first space war, we're as befuddled as the French were at Agincourt."

"A lousy analogy," Clapham said. "The English longbow was no mystery."

"Nor is the laser," Lu added.

"Dammit! The laser is a mystery," Clapham insisted. "It's not a pulsating laser and it's supplied by an incredible energy source we can't comprehend. Ask Quent."

"Cary's right," Ross said. "It's no bauble. We must do our damnedest to pinpoint the country controlling the laser. Don't look outside of the building for help, in fact, don't look outside of yourselves for clues. We'll solve the mystery right in the bullpen!" With that, he pushed himself from the coffee bar and Clapham followed him to the ramp.

"Quent," he said, pursuing the point, "spy satellites, long-range detection devices, passive noise discriminators, the CIA—all of these detection systems are supposed to get the answers that you're asking of us. How in God's name can we possibly pit our puny efforts against such sophisticated systems?"

"I don't doubt I sound irrational," Ross said, "but what results have all those complicated systems produced thus far? Not one iota of information that I know of. As usual, our detection and collection systems have failed us. So it's back to the drawing board, back to basics, back to intuition. Okay?"

"Okay," Clapham said, still skeptical.

The bullpen's babble prevented further reasoned discussion. Ross watched Lu enlist Shrimp's aid in preparing snacks from the arctic survival kits. Chocolate bars, jelly, crackers and peanuts were sorted out and arranged artfully in wooden, in-basket trays. With a flourish, Shrimp produced an unopened quart of gin from a cleverly concealed cache in his desk. Karayn bitched playfully about the lack of vermouth.

Shrimp flared up and swung the bottle at Karayn's head. "I'm going to curl your mustache, Milo, you ungrateful son of a bitch!"

Karayn ducked in time and moved off, muttering about Shrimp's sudden short fuse. Lu and Clapham laughed at the scrimmage and departed for the cafeteria to scrounge paper cups and ice.

Ross called to Karayn. "You got what you deserved, Milo, wanting to bruise the gin. We're all prima donnas today."

Before Karayn could respond, Ross's phone rang behind the barricade. Ivorson repeated his demand for a story to meet the five PM worldwide deadline. Ross's hackles rose.

"Gaddammit, Merle, I'm not a spot news reporter!"

"I need military copy, Quent," Ivorson said evenly. "The wire's flooded with political, medical and human interest crap on the laser, but not one word on military action. That's your department."

"Nothing's surfaced. We've got a passive President as commander-in-chief."

"And I can't believe the Air Force and Navy are sitting idly by with their thumbs up their asses—"

"Merle, we're not dealing with conventional warfare. Aircraft carriers aren't racing out to sea, troops aren't marching off to battle, tanks aren't overrunning trenches, dogfights aren't filling the sky, bombers aren't spiraling down in flames over our heads. Do you want more?"

"Okay, okay. But something's got to be happening."

"You want me to report military action as we've known it for a thousand years. This is the first space war, the silence is deafening!"

"Don't be so goddammed dramatic, Quent."

"I'm trying to get through to you that in a space war nothing is as we've known war to be. All of the weapons are sent out of sight. Once a killer sat is launched, you never see it again. It's invisible forever, a phantom weapon in the phantom space war."

"File that!"

"You know damned well that's not hard news. Our science editor in London has filed dozens of space-war fantasies. For myself, I'll wait for facts."

"So you won't file?"

"Not this minute, Merle. I haven't heard one squawk about the troops getting blinded last night, although many must have suffered severe eye damage carrying out their duties. And ironically, only a small segment of the Air Force and Navy is aware of killer satellite technology because of the tight secrecy clamped on the project. A still smaller group knows whether such a retaliatory weapon exists in the arsenal, or whether its parts can be whipped into shape on short order and dispatched against the laser. I'm not about to file a lot of speculative crap."

"Why not? I have no military copy on the wire."

"Too many unanswered questions, Merle. Is there a specific killer satellite launch button tied to a dedicated pad? Who pushes the button? Does a killer satellite device contain conventional explosives or a nuclear bomb? Has the U.S. already lobbed a killer sat into space? Since it take twenty-four hours from launch to kill, has the President, his National Security Council or the commander of the Space and Missile Systems organization in Los Angeles ordered a launch, taking advantage of the twenty-four float time to play dumb? If the killer sat misses the laser with its nuclear bomb, who will know the difference, except for some lieutenants at Bright Lake? How long does it take nuclear debris to float down from space and be detected on earth? Merle, I won't file until I get answers to some of the questions."

"You're a determined bastard. Are you filing for posterity?"

"I'm not filing horseshit under my byline."

"Quent, your voice is getting so hoarse I can't understand you!"

"Good!" Ross exclaimed. "I'll hang up after this thought. In two hours the laser may relight the sky. If it does, I guarantee you the Congress will force the President to announce military action to destroy the laser. All hell will break out and you'll get enough killer sat copy to choke the 'A' circuit."

"And I'll be waiting—"

Ross dropped the receiver onto its battered cradle.

The Despicables and Lu tromped round the barricade. With fanfare Shrimp opened the gin—London's best—and Lu played barmaid. They hoisted one for the road.

Shrimp warned, "Let's not forget to take our goggles, all except Milo. He won't need his, since the laser's dead."

Karayn shot Shrimp a hostile look as Stewart arrived, swinging his goggles like a brakeman highballing a train. Lu handed him a cup which he smelled suspiciously, then imitating W.C. Fields said, "Ah! Juniper! My favorite fruit! It's a good thing I'm not flying tomorrow, or I'd be forced to decline this fine libation."

"Colonel," Shrimp said, "you'll be lucky to fly your desk tomorrow."

"Will gin or the laser do me in?"

"Both," Lu said, touching his arm.

Stewart embraced her with exaggerated affection.

"Enough of that," Ross warned. "This scene is right out of Fellini's *La Dolce Vita*."

"Fellini's too highbrow for this crowd," Shrimp said.

"True," Ross added, tamping a straight-stemmed pipe, then with goggles in one hand and cup in the other, he tagged behind the noisy, ragged group down the deserted corridor to the Mall doors. The Pentagon's civil servants had fled hours earlier.

Startled at first, the marine sentries ceremoniously opened the doors while regretting that duty forbade them to join the party. Ross and Stewart moved like pathfinders across the parking area to a large expanse of manicured grass. Shrimp carried a plastic ice bucket and his jacket sagged with the ill-concealed gin bottle. Lu struggled with her purse, goggles, drink and a carafe. Clapham balanced the trays of hors d'oeuvres and Karayn brought up the rear with a sizeable radio-TV set. The parklike area presented an unobstructed view of the horizon. Ross motioned that this was the place. Stewart spread several thermal blankets on the grass and said loudly he hoped the sky-watch exercise would prove poetic and nothing else. A chorus of amens seconded his remark and Ross smiled at the spontaneous use of the biblical term of approval by the hard-bitten bunch.

Shrimp served another round, filling each cup to the brim, obviously intent on killing the bottle. Lu followed with the trays. Karayn switched the set from TV to radio and back, but no last-minute revelations were being aired by Fairly.

The sun lowered imperceptibly. When it had set, Ross barely resisted going beyond one line of Gray's *Elegy*, "Now fades the glimmering landscape on the sight." No one heard his rasping voice.

Stewart stood up playfully and with the practiced exaggeration of a drill instructor began demonstrating the art of placing the radsafe goggles on his head. With a heavy accent on consonants and staccato delivery, he adjusted the headstrap so that the goggles snugly covered the eyes, causing laughter with his definition of snug. He then turned the control wheel on the nose bridge as if he were steering a ship. Satisfied with the lens density at the moment, he stooped to chugalug the last of his drink when the laser's incandescent light burst over their heads, blinding everyone but Stewart.

Lu let out a shriek. Others cursed, fumbling with goggles and head straps. Stewart leaped from one to another, adjusting straps and lens density, then helped Lu and the rest to their feet. They staggered about in blindman's buff, groping helplessly in the incandescence. Stewart nudged them quickly into line, knowing it would take about five minutes for their retinas to recover from the laser's blazing debut. He put Lu at the head of the procession and Ross at the rear, then placed the hand of each person on the shoulder of the one ahead in a kind of lockstep formation. Ross marveled at Stewart's persuasive powers. Counting cadence with himself at the fore, Stewart marched off, but Lu couldn't hold onto his shoulder. She fumbled for a moment, found a belt loop on his trousers, threaded a finger through it and held on for dear life. He led them across the grass and over the glowing concrete up the Mall steps. The marines helped them enter, torn between laughter and compassion over the spectacle. Stewart congratulated them with pats on the back, then dashed out of the building to retrieve Karayn's radio-TV over Shrimp's protest.

Ross removed his goggles, blinked for a long moment, then waited with the others to thank Stewart for being a good shepherd. In modesty, Stewart soon disappeared. Ross walked shakenly to the ticker room and found Glasscock standing at the teletype, arms folded like Patton.

7

Grinning, Glasscock said above the teletype's clatter, "So you got zapped by Ross's laser!"

"A stupid maneuver, thanks to Lu's enthusiasm," Ross said, still squinting. "But what brings you to the ticker room? No general officer has bothered to step in here since Forrestal glued the Defense Department together."

"Why, I'm in search of the truth, Quent."

"You left your lantern upstairs."

Glasscock chuckled, turned back to the battery of teletypes and watched the words roll off the platens. "There's no news coming off the wires, including yours, Quent. There's nothing there we don't already know: the laser's back on, people hiding, air and ground traffic at a standstill, medics and hospitals overwhelmed, looting in urban areas. The wires are reporting last night's scenario."

"Just what the hell do you want them to report?"

"Word out of the White House, State Department, or even the U.N. What's wrong with the reporters?"

"Not a damned thing, General. Tell me what words of wisdom are being issued out of the Pentagon."

"No one's at the helm here. Browning Whitley is drunk at the Cosmos Club. Scotus is at the funny farm.

175

Besides, the Pentagon is low man on the administration's totem pole."

"Meaning?"

"The President finally got off his dead ass and made a flurry of decisions when the laser lit up again. I got the flash from his Air Force aide. That's why I'm down here looking for the followups."

"You're ahead of the wires, Noel."

"The aide told me State is delivering an ultimatum to the laser attacker through the UN. If discovered, the attacker will be subject to punitive measures, including annihilation, but he's got until midnight tomorrow to turn it off because he may encounter trouble technically in dousing it. Secondly, rationing of all consumer goods will take effect as soon as the coupons are printed. Next, civil defense is the Defense Department's highest priority. And lastly, the laser satellite is to be destroyed by whatever means necessary, by wiping out its ground control stations or deploying killer satellites, but use of nuclear weapons in space is forbidden."

"He's got his priorities all screwed up!"

"No doubt, but be thankful that congressional pressure finally caved him in, along with strong voices in the National Security Council. Fortunately, some appointees at NSC are apolitical."

"But I think he recognizes the NSC is worthless to him in some respects," Ross said. "NSC pushes high technology to solve problems, whether they're CIA collection techniques, nuclear energy or killer sats. High technology is a high-risk business. No politician can stay in office gambling on high technology, high-risk solutions. The guys who advise him on high technology are self-serving, arrogant, insensitive scientists who never feel the heat in the kitchen. So a high-technology failure, wasting time and treasure, alienates the voter who then laughs the politician right out of office. After all, the politician can't make a living except at the public trough, so he simply can't gamble, can't lose the confidence of the electorate."

"Yeah, I've heard the refrain. The art of the possible, the give and the take, the great compromise. But in weaponry where I'm the expert, a ten percent compromise in technology will cost you men and maybe the battle, then the war. There's no excuse for compromising the optimum in weaponry with our incredible industrial might. But this happens at every session of Congress and at the White House itself."

"Okay," Ross said. "Politicians and generals are different kinds of cats. It would be nice for the country to find one guy with both attributes. By the way, what's Browning Whitley's role at the moment?"

"Whitley is rightfully in charge of the problem to knock out the laser. And speaking of compromises, he'll compromise the space killer satellite system so that we'll get lowest risk with the lowest success rate."

Ross laughed. "You're prejudging the bastard. Does he know the present success rate?"

"I hope not. Let's see. NASA's Saturn, the Air Force's Titan and the Navy's Polaris—three disasters in a row."

"The Navy too?"

"The damned fools insisted on firing it from a sub instead of a concrete pad. Better experience curve, they said. Must've scared the hell out of the fish."

"Why did they all fail? Tell me without miring me down in details."

"Random failures, Quent. They're the worst kind to find. When you mate an untried payload like the killer satellite to a booster, the payload is dependent on the booster and its stages for much of its existence. There is little time now to guarantee a perfect mating with the usual checks, rechecks and triple checks. The intricate circuitry is enough to boggle your mind, not to mention proper functioning of explosive bolts and rocket-engine cutoff devices. We know that all three boosters, Saturn, Titan and Polaris are basically reliable. The killer satellite checks out okay on the experimental test bench.

Then you put the satellite on top of the booster, shake it to death on blastoff, add large G-forces, send it at Mach 30 into a vacuum called space where the temperature is absolute zero and you expect it to work. Really, it's a tribute to aerospace designers that anything of such a precise nature works at all."

"Who knows about the three failures?"

"The operators, obviously. They won't snitch on themselves. Then a handful on command level who don't like to be found with egg on their face. And last, but not least, you."

"No politicians?"

"Not a one, Quent."

"Can it be held?"

"If you can."

Ross nodded. "What's the next step?"

"To announce that the three-star general at Los Angeles is in charge. Browning Whitley should do that. If not, you ought to prompt him. The military do have a hell of a lot at stake in the killer satellite. The public should know it and track it for better or worse, I might add."

"What about accountability on the first three firings?"

"Oh, for God's sake, Quent! Don't keep going back to it! Eventually, like five years from now, the General Accounting Office auditor will discover the shortage. You'll print it then and that'll be the end of it. Okay?"

Laughing, Ross said, "So my copy will be the obituary, if I live that long."

"I'm a lot more worried about getting reliability into the next shot. We should call in the think tanks—we have fourteen prima donnas to choose from—but those bastards will blab the failures among themselves in the sacrosanct scientific community and the very next day some half-assed science writer will expose the dismal failures as another military foul-up, never once citing the civilian contractors and their vendors, the university input, and the labs run by civil servants, all of whom made significant contributions to the failures."

"I hear venom in your words, Noel."

"Damned right. I get tired seeing the military made whipping boy for failures of scientists and industry."

"Well, what action is being taken right now?"

"The three-star got the word and the first thing he'll do is to throw a tiger team together—military, scientists, technicians—he'll steal everything and everybody that he can get his hands on to start assembling bona fide killer satellites."

Ross asked, "Will Whitley hover over the tiger team? Will he want the honor of pushing the launch button?"

Glasscock groaned. "I hope Whitley and his advisers stay the hell out of the nitty-gritty. He'll find it tough enough explaining progress to Congress and the White House."

"And I don't know how to begin filing. I guess I want to write the history of the killer sat, not spot news."

"Sort it all out in your mind, Quent. At best, you can file your story on only a piece of the President's many decisions. Some decisions will be beaten to death, like civil defense. Everybody's in that act and everybody's an expert and everybody's going to go for headlines. But when it comes to killer satellites and celestial mechanics, you stand all alone in the bullpen."

"Yet the trouble is that my two-hundred-fifty-word bulletins and stories are in highly stylized, teletype language. My copy tends to underwhelm the reader with its simplistic style."

"Well, that's what the wire services insist on, Quent. You learned to write the wire service way and you're reaching a lot more people, influencing a lot more voters than writing think pieces for the scholarly monthlies. If it's any comfort, I wouldn't be wasting my time and breath on you if you weren't reaching millions."

Ross smiled.

Glasscock asked, "Why don't you call Fairly if you need political backgrounding on the killer sat decision? I can't help you in that department."

"I'll do without it."

"Okay, suit yourself," Glasscock said with a shrug and departed.

Ross turned to his teletype, sat down and flipped the switch to send, then stared at the ceiling without a lead or phrase in his head. Several reporters burst into the room, having been held back by Glasscock's imperious presence. Ross hoped they would respect the unwritten rule that a man filing was not to be disturbed. He cracked his knuckles while dredging his mind on celestial or orbital mechanics. It was all there in the barricade as press releases and backgrounders issued by academia, but he wasn't about to get up and tear the paper wall apart again. The best way to file was to begin pounding because the words would flow to the machine's tempo.

BULLETIN:
OVER "A" CIRCUITS
DATELINE WASHINGTON THIS DATE
BY-LINE QUENTIN ROSS, MILITARY ANALYST, THE PENTAGON
PRESIDENT RETALIATES

MOMENTS AFTER THE DREADED LASER LIGHT REAPPEARED IN THIS EVENING'S WASHINGTON SKY, THE PRESIDENT ORDERED THE DEFENSE DEPARTMENT TO PREPARE KILLER SATELLITE MISSILES FOR LAUNCH AGAINST THE LASER, ACCORDING TO RELIABLE WHITE HOUSE SOURCES. SATURN, TITAN AND POLARIS BOOSTERS WILL BE READIED AS QUICKLY AS POSSIBLE TO CARRY NEWLY-FABRICATED KILLER SATELLITES ALOFT FROM CAPE CANAVERAL, FLORIDA, AND VANDENBERG AFB, CALIFORNIA. IN ADDITION TO THE INTERCEPT AND DESTROY MISSION, AIR- AND GROUND-BASED DETECTION DEVICES WILL BE USED TO FERRET OUT

THE LASER'S GROUND CONTROL STATION TO MARK IT FOR ANNIHILATION.

THE UNITED STATES DOES NOT POSSESS AN INVENTORY OF KILLER SATELLITES IN ACCORD WITH LONG-STANDING SPACE TREATY PROHIBITIONS AGAINST SUCH WEAPONS. LASER-DESTROYING SATELLITES MUST BE HANDBUILT, ASSEMBLED AND TAILORED TO THE BOOSTERS THAT WILL PUSH THEM WITH BRUTE FORCE ON A 24-HOUR, 66,000 MILE COLLISION COURSE WITH LASER-BORNE SATELLITE.

EXPERTS SAID ADDITIONAL TIME WILL BE LOST CARRYING OUT THE PRESIDENTIAL ORDER BECAUSE MATING SEQUENCES OFTEN TURN UP ELECTRICAL AND OTHER ANOMALIES IN THE COMMAND AND CONTROL, NAVIGATION, TERMINAL GUIDANCE AND TELEMETRY CIRCUITS. DELAYS WILL BE REFLECTED IN COUNTLESS HOLDS DURING COUNTDOWN ON THE LAUNCHING PADS. BECAUSE THE LASER SATELLITE IS AT WHAT SPECIALISTS IN ORBITAL MECHANICS CALL THREE-TIMES GEOSYNCHRONOUS ALTITUDE, THE TIME OF FLIGHT OF A KILLER SATELLITE IS EXTENDED THREEFOLD FROM 8 TO 24 HOURS, THUS DELAYING INTERCEPTION BY A LIKE PERIOD. EXPERTS ADDED THAT THE LASER'S 66,000 MILE ALTITUDE WAS A DELIBERATELY CALCULATED SPATIAL POSITION CHOSEN BY THE UNKNOWN ENEMY TO INCREASE THE LASER SATELLITE'S SURVIVABILITY. THE FASTEST INTERCEPTION, ACCORDING TO EXPERTS, USES BRUTE FORCE TO CROSS THE LASER'S ORBIT IN 24 HOURS AT THE INCREDIBLE SPEED OF 8,000 FEET PER SECOND. SINCE LARGE TRAJECTORY ERRORS ARE PROBABLE, A NUCLEAR BOMB

BURST IN THE VICINITY OF THE LASER SATELLITE IS THE ONLY SURE METHOD OF DESTRUCTION. USE OF CONVENTIONAL EXPLOSIVES WOULD REQUIRE EXTRAORDINARY ACCURACY, VERGING ON SHEER LUCK, TO ACHIEVE THE SAME RESULT. AN ALTERNATE METHOD OF INTERCEPTION REQUIRES AN EXTENDED 60-HOUR TIME OF FLIGHT FROM LAUNCH TO INTERCEPT BUT IS MUCH MORE ACCURATE BECAUSE CONTROLLERS OF THE KILLER SATELLITE CAN MATCH THE TWO ORBITS. THUS CONVENTIONAL EXPLOSIVES CAN DESTROY THE LASER SATELLITE. THE MATCHING TECHNIQUE REQUIRES ONLY SMALL SATELLITE THRUSTERS TO MAKE NOMINAL ORBITAL CORRECTIONS, WHILE THE BRUTE FORCE METHOD REQUIRES LARGE ROCKET THRUSTERS FOR LARGE CORRECTIONS, THUS IMPOSING ADDED PAYLOAD PROBLEMS. MORE IMPORTANTLY, SPACE EXPERTS PREDICT THE LASER SATELLITE WILL NOT BE ABLE TO EVADE THE INTERCEPTOR DURING THE MATCHED ORBIT TECHNIQUE, THEREBY INSURING ITS DESTRUCTION.

WHETHER THE POPULATION OF THE UNITED STATES CAN ENDURE THREE OR MORE NIGHTS OF THE LASER BLITZ IS A QUESTION FACING THE WHITE HOUSE AND THE DEFENSE DEPARTMENT TONIGHT.
END.
END BULLETIN.

Ross flicked off the machine and fled the ticker room before the bystanders buttonholed him. In the corridor Lu moved toward him like a dreadnaught.

"Pull a carbon," he said curtly and kept going for the barricade.

Moments later, Lu appeared and propped herself

against his desk. "Great copy, Quent!" she said with an admiring smile.

"Thanks, you're my only fan, Lu. By the way, you should know the ball's in Whitley's court. We've gone the brute force route three times and none of the killer sats achieved orbit. The brute force technique will be repeated officially, as well as the matched orbit. Meanwhile, I don't relish the thought of sleeping desk-top in the bedroll."

"Speaking of that, Quent, you're in bed with the Air Force. What's in the tradeoff for them?"

"First, much of the detail in my bulletin didn't come from the Air Force. I recalled it from handouts provided by industry and the technical societies. Of course, Glasscock provided the peg. But there's no doubt the Air Force is using me to get into print. There's a bit of the whore in the Air Force, and a bit in me."

Lu blinked at the analogy. "Whores with a bit of class," she added. "I guess I'll curl up in Stewart's thermal blanket.

"Since you're the only woman in the bullpen, take the couch in the niche. It'll be like old times," Ross said, nudging her onward.

Shrimp suddenly barred her way, wanting to get up a game of bridge to pass the night. Clapham said he was ready. Lu thought it a great idea, but Ross declined.

"I'll sit in only when somebody has to go to potty. Get Milo for your fourth."

"Damned if I won't get the Mustache," Shrimp said. "Bridge is more important than people. And Quent, your phone rang forever while you were filing."

Ross was struck with a pang of guilt, having neglected to call Marge. But before he could dial, Ivorson rang, demanding more copy.

"You've gone nuts, Merle," Ross said. "I've just filed the word count of three bulletins for the price of one. There's nothing more I can add. There's nothing coming out of the Defense newsroom. There's nothing on defense coming out of the White House. There's nothing coming out of anywhere in the whole goddamned administration. Okay?"

"But London, Paris, Rome and Tokyo—to name a few—are screaming for military copy."

"You forgot Moscow."

"Get up some words," Ivorson said and broke off the conversation.

Ross called Marge. All was well, except that Lupe hid under the bed one moment, then ran around in circles in the next. He suggested Marge placate her with a week's ration of yummies.

"Then she'll want out to relieve herself and the cycle will start all over again."

"Well, do what's best. How about giving her those old tranquilizers out of my medicine chest?"

She hesitated, then said, "Why not? I know I can't get through to a veterinarian anyway. Everybody with pets must be faced with the same problem."

"Try the tranquilizers on Lupe," he counseled. "Anything good enough for me is good enough for a dog. I'll see you in the early morning, mediante Dios!"

"Yes, God willing," she responded and hung up.

Ross put his feet up on the desk and stared at the thin shafts of laser light streaming through gaps in the papered windows. An amazing phenomenon, he realized, completely wrecking the day-night cycle of all life on the North American continent. How clever, how fiendish of the phantom enemy to maneuver the U.S. into a position where it could only react and not take the offensive. The country had lost its freedom of action and the President damned well knew it.

Ted Harris rounded the barricade with a stranger in tow. Deferentially, Ted pointed to the visitor's White House badge and then introduced him as the President's chief speechwriter, Tom Arundel.

Ross looked warily at the youngster. "Well, it's a good name around these parts, son, but what the hell do you want?"

"To pick you brains, sir."

"That's exactly what I need tonight," Ross said, laughing in spite of himself, and impressed that his brusqueness hadn't scared the towhead. "Tell me, Mr. Arundel, who suggested the cranial operation?"

Arundel winced at the cumbersome joke. "Phil Fairly sent me over in a presidential limousine, sir. It was a frightful trip, even though we used civil defense gear. Accidents, near-misses, sirens, chaos. It's impossible to see the traffic lights."

Ross asked brusquely, "What do I know that the White House staff doesn't already know? You're wasting your time and mine."

Harris interrupted to excuse himself.

Arundel ignored Ross's brushoff. "First of all, Mr. Ross, the President is mad at Phil. Said he was sick of Phil's face, always asking impossible questions on behalf of the media. I guess the President associates Phil with trouble, so he's turned to me, temporarily, I'm sure. The President said too much vital information is leaking out of the Pentagon and that he has to get ahead of it or lose clout with the public. He mentioned your bylined stories and added I should get my ass over here and talk to you about his nine AM speech to the nation."

"You've got a basketful of apples and oranges, my young friend. Are you trying to say that if I don't file military copy, the President will use my stuff?"

"Not exactly, sir. Just one aspect of the subject."

"I don't follow you, but should I be flattered by the approach?"

"I suppose so," Arundel answered, grinning.

Ross harrumphed, but took a liking to the youngster who didn't run scared. Arundel seemed to have fallen out of the same mold as Stewart. "How old are you?" Ross asked.

"Thirty."

"Where did you go to school?"

"Harvard. BA and MBA."

185

"That makes you a speechwriter?"

"Hardly. My father owns a newspaper. For the past seven years I've worked as a reporter and feature writer. Before he was elected, the President was impressed, I guess, with some of my features on his campaigning, so I got the call shortly after he took office."

"And do you like working for him?"

"I know his style, both thinking and speaking. He's got an orderly mind. He hates surprises."

"He sure as hell has one by the tail this minute!"

Arundel laughed. "The President loves to debate his options on any issue, then say yes or no to the decision before him. Phil can't do that for him with media queries."

"Can you?"

"Of course not. Every question turns into a moment of truth for the President. He doesn't have options. When he finds out I can't hack the job any better, he'll put Phil back into grace."

"I think you've psyched it out pretty well," Ross said. "Now, what the hell do you really want?"

"We need your thoughts on military posture, sir."

"Come on!" Ross growled. "You can talk plainer than that!"

Arundel flushed. "I mean I need an overview, the kind you punch out on the teletype."

"Hell, it's been nothing but spot news. I haven't had time to sit back and reflect on a damned thing."

"Regardless, Mr. Ross, it's more than anyone else has done. Let's just talk, please. I'll hear what I need."

Ross knew that flattery was his only reward, although any cooperation would not be lost on Fairly. He took his time lighting a Bavarian pipe with its foot-long, cherry-stemmed porcelain bowl, knowing that it lent to the appearance of a Black Forest burgomaster. Arundel sat fascinated and after several puffs Ross said, "There is no question in the mind of the military that the laser can be destroyed. The problem is time. Can the nation endure until the laser is put out of commission? This is the question to which the President should address himself tomorrow. Whether the laser is destroyed by killer satellites armed with conventional or nuclear warheads, whether it is destroyed by electronic ferrets wiping out its ground control, is a damned sight less important to the man in the street than eliminating the laser forever."

"What about civil defense?"

"Well, if it were functioning it might prove a positive morale factor. As it is, I'd say it'll take a month or more to get into gear, therefore its effect is demoralizing."

"Okay," Arundel said, tightening his lip. "Please go on, Mr. Ross."

"Above all, the President should speak the truth and eliminate the secrecy crap for a change. The threat to our lives is highly visible."

"I'd argue that point," Arundel said with surprising defiance.

Ross was amused. "Why play games, my young friend, when people are diving into dark places?"

"Because reporters are irresponsible. Reporters just can't back off. Their wants are insatiable. They can't let an issue mature. They shred it to ribbons from its very inception, forcing the President into hasty, often regrettable decisions. Vital issues must be guarded, protected, until the time is right to inform the public, Mr. Ross."

"Ho ho!" Ross exclaimed, waving the Bavarian pipe. "You've got the White House line down pat, my boy! Suppose I were to tell you that no issue is airtight, leakproof. The larger the issue, the more people and resources, the greater the cracks in the facade erected by the zealots of secrecy."

"But the Manhattan Project at Los Alamos, the bombing of Hiroshima and Nagasaki, the satellite overflights. These were massive programs never leaked to the press, Mr. Ross."

"You had to reach far into the past to get three notable

exceptions. Remember, you're talking about secrecy in a free society. I don't care what you say about invoking secrecy, on balance it just doesn't work. Suppose I were to tell you, a member of the inner sanctum at the White House, that three killer satellites have been fired at the laser and all three failed."

"I don't believe it!"

"That's not the point, Arundel. The point is I didn't file it for a variety of reasons. So don't peddle that crap in my earshot about all reporters being irresponsible. They behave the way they do when they suspect the administration is lying, concealing the truth from the public—which is most of the time!"

Arundel flushed. "I'm sorry, Mr. Ross, but in my judgment you are not the typical reporter."

"And for your amazement," Ross said, his voice cracking, "most reporters are decent, honest guys. It's the administration that brings out the worst in them. My contention is that reporters are put into an impossible adversary position when the administration lies. They are forced to lash back. I just can't let your comments go unanswered. Okay?"

Smiling faintly, Arundel said, "I appreciate your point of view, Mr. Ross. Can we get back to the President's speech?"

"Sure," Ross said. "The President should mention that our honest observance of the UN space treaty restrictions imposed in 1967 prevented the development of killer satellites to snuff out today's laser attack on the U.S. Space killer weapons are very complicated devices which take up to twenty-four hours to intercept a threat from space. A soul-searching debate might well rage over the use of conventional explosives versus nuclear warheads in space. The technical problems in counteracting a space threat are hellish: tricky space maneuvers, sophisticated guidance and mastery of orbital mechanics, the untried mating of boosters with payloads, etc. The public shouldn't be spared the problem. You can get the specifics out of the National Security Council people, if not here in the Pentagon from the Joint Chiefs or the Air Force. The President must promise disappointments as well as eventual victory. Okay?"

Writing in shorthand on a stenographer's pad, Arundel nodded that Ross should continue.

Clearing his throat, Ross said, "I'd suggest that the President admit, since any thinking citizen would deduce it for himself, that U.S. credibility to defend itself and its partners is decreasing with each additional night's laser attack, as is its vulnerability to ground, naval and air attack. However, coming to grips with a known enemy in conventional warfare is a task I'm sure our armed forces would eagerly undertake. He should assert that never again will he let the nation be caught unprepared, that military research and development programs will be accelerated, that total reliance on treaties and covenants is not enough. Lastly, he should promise relief because the assailant will be discovered, punitive measures will be announced and taken to forestall future attack, and that at the moment time itself is an enemy, but with God's help the U.S. will persevere. Okay?"

"Thanks," Arundel said, tucking the pad under his arm.

"By the way," Ross added, "I must caution you that my disclosure of the three killer satellite failures was a serious breach of confidence on my part. Even though you are on the White House staff, I still should not have divulged it. So, please treat what I've said as very sensitive information not to be passed on to anyone."

Arundel laughed hard. "That's rich! A reporter warns me to protect sensitive information!"

Ross aimed the pipestem at Arundel. "Son, that's the way it is around here. I'm asking you not to violate my confidence."

"I won't," Arundel said, summoning up conviction in

his face, then shook Ross's hand warmly and departed.

Lu rounded the barricade with a cackle. "I'm dummy for this hand. Quent, I see you're becoming a very important person. May I touch you?"

"Go straight to hell, Lu. Do you know the kid?"

"I know of him. He's bright and articulate and hand-picked by the President. He'd do anything for the boss, including a leap out of the White House window at the slightest presidential suggestion. What the hell did he want?"

Ross laughed. "You're right about the boy, damned bright but damned young. Everything in his head is black or white, good or bad, loyal, or disloyal. Everything carries a label that spells out the contents exactly. He'll be rudely shocked when he discovers all the gray areas. But to answer your question, Arundel wanted a military overview for the President's speech tomorrow morning."

Lu sighed. "I wish we had dog robbers around here to do our bidding."

"Then run for public office, sweetheart. And if you win you'll live well at the public trough with dog robbers at your beck and call to carry out your slightest whim. I'm amazed more women don't run for office because they're more involved with the human condition than men. After all, Lu, politics is the manipulation of human beings, getting people to see things your way, getting people to do things your way, getting people to do things for you."

"Okay, okay!" she shouted. "You sound like those German philosophers who explain everything that goes on in the world with just one fact at their fingertips."

"Well said," Ross admitted as the bridge players called loudly for her to sit in on the next hand.

She hurried forth and in a matter of seconds Shrimp arrived and accosted Ross with a sheaf of wire service clips.

"I thought you were playing bridge," Ross said.

"I'm dummy for this hand."

Ross groaned. "For Christ's sake, I feel like I'm running a confessional. What's your problem?"

"Listen to these crazy heads, Quent," Shrimp said, waving the long, yellow sheaves, "Airline Terminals Stormed By Evacuees, Subways Jammed With All-Night Riders, Hotels In Chaos, Docksides Swarm With Escapees, Patients Refuse To Leave Hospitals, Supermarkets Looted, Civil Defense Farce, Theaters Turned Into Shelters, Schools Closed, Borders In Shambles, Red Tide Dooms Fish, Crop Failures, Famine Forecast, Pets Misbehaving."

"I didn't need to hear them," Ross said, irritated. "Let's not forget this is exactly why the aggressor went to all that friggin' trouble air-launching the laser sat in the southern hemisphere. The rewards for pulling off this surprise attack make the Japanese assault on Pearl Harbor seem puny indeed."

Shrimp threw the clips into Ross's overfull wastepaper basket. "When will the attacker make his demands known?"

"Goddammit, Shrimp! You're thinking in the past. He may not say a word if we collapse from within. He'll just walk in and take over. That's what he's got in mind."

"A siege like Vicksburg," Shrimp said. "I hope to God we're sending up a barrage of killer satellites."

"Then wait days for the results, which might be misses. Bah! That laser sat's not self-contained. It's being fed signals from an earth control station, and maybe energy from still another source. The Air Force and Navy are capable of ferreting out those electrical impulses. They ought to sweep the face of the earth to find the control station, then bomb the bejeesus out of it, along with the country it belongs to, and after that's done, ask for permission from the commander in chief. Let's not forget, it's the President's ass also, not just the office, but the man's."

Shrimp's eyes flashed. "If the killer satellites fail, do you think the President will direct the space shuttle to do the job, that is, get it up into space with men aboard and knock out the laser?"

Ross was intrigued. He hadn't thought of the space shuttle. "Desperate measures for desperate times, right, Shrimp?"

With a manic look, Shrimp blurted, "By God, if they fire the space shuttle at the laser, I'm going to be on board!"

"C'mon, Shrimp, what in hell do you know about the space shuttle? What makes you think you can climb on board?"

"Plenty of reasons, Quent. The shuttle has been a pet project of mine for years. I've tracked it since it first appeared on the drawing board, followed it when it flew piggyback on the Boeing 747, and said prayers on its blastoff from Cape Canaveral. I've always been intrigued with the idea of putting a winged space ship on top of a booster, shooting it off into space and then having it fly like a bird to earth. The best of Jules Verne and Buck Rogers."

"Go on," Ross said.

"I've read every word published on the shuttle, even NASA's operating manuals. I have a commercial pilot's license in my wallet. I am accredited to the Defense Department as a military reporter. So I have all the tickets to climb on board the shuttle. Okay?"

"Okay."

"Quent, I'll need your muscle to get picked as pool reporter on the shuttle intercept."

"You're mad, Shrimp, to even think the thought! You're fantasizing! Defense hasn't even announced that the shuttle is going to intercept the laser. But if they did, I doubt they'd kick off a genuine astronaut to make room for a reporter, even for Shrimp with all his qualifications."

"They sure as hell will if you pressure Fairly."

"You're really serious?"

"Dead serious. Fairly will listen to you."

"Bah!"

"Remember, Quent, we don't have Scotus to trot the proposal over to the White House. It's got to be you as senior Pentagon reporter. Fairly has to listen."

"Shrimp, you know Fairly and I are not the best of friends, but I must admit I can find no fault with your idea if you're willing to risk your fool life." Ross then thought that Stewart or Glasscock would be needed to bless the proposal, although NASA could be bypassed since this would be a military mission in the strictest sense. By its charter, NASA's mission was directed only to peaceful uses of space.

"What are you thinking?" Shrimp asked apprehensively.

"I must bounce your idea around in the building before I go across the river with it. You're lucky we don't have to fight NASA's bureaucracy."

"So you are supporting me?"

"If you're all set to break your ass, only your mother can stop you."

"Great, absolutely great!" Shrimp shouted and dashed back to the bridge game.

Ross grinned at Shrimp's spirit, then decided to move on the shuttle idea before he got sidetracked. He found Stewart in the Defense newsroom and motioned they meet in the corridor. Stewart acknowledged the sign and moments later joined him between ventilators.

"Shrimp's got a noble idea, Terry," Ross said, projecting enthusiasm. "I'd like to get it flown past General Glasscock before we take another step."

"Sure," Stewart said. "The general's upstairs, running a conference call with Canaveral, Vandenberg and Bright Lake on the scrambler. It's an operational roundup on what's on the pads, what's scheduled, what the killer sat trajectories look like, and the health of the laser satellite itself."

Ross groaned. "How I wish he could brief the press afterward! Who is it for?"

"It's basically for the Air Force secretary, perhaps for

the chief of staff, although the chief has his own channels. He makes comparisons to fish out the technical truth. You just can't trust one evaluation."

"Then what?"

"I don't know, Quent. The chief probably transmits the information to the Joint Chiefs of Staff and the President's Air Force aide, while the secretary passes it to Browning Whitley and congressional committes, perhaps to the National Security Council—everybody but the news media and the taxpayers, I guess. But back to Shrimp. What's his noble idea?"

"He wants to put his ass in the space shuttle if it's to be used against the laser sat. I'm certain his is the first bid from the media. In fact, I'll make sure it is. Of course, he'd have to act and report on the ride on a pool basis. Honestly, Terry, I can't fault the idea if it doesn't botch up the flight from an operational basis."

"Christ! I'd like to get on board myself, Quent, but I guess the infighting would ace me out because I'm in uniform. I know I'm a damned well-qualified press officer, modesty aside, but I must control my ego. What can we say in Shrimp's behalf?"

Ross raised his hand and started ticking off points on his fingers. "He's a shrimp, which is an obvious advantage in the shuttle's cramped quarters. He's young and bright. He tells me he has read everything on the shuttle since its inception and I believe him. Also, it's better to send up a pool man who is in print media. The electronickers are tongue-tied. Their gear does the reporting. I doubt if all the cameras and recording devices can be fitted into the shuttle's cockpit and operated by just one electronicker. This problem might give the mission director an easy out in rejecting the whole concept of news coverage of the intercept. Do you agree?"

"Shrimp is the man," Stewart said with new-found enthusiasm. "He'll translate into layman's words what is going on during the intercept. What an opportunity! What a ride! Let's hope General Glasscock buys the idea."

"Go to it!" Ross said with a playful shove, then watched Stewart disappear down the corridor. Some things just seemed to fall into place, regardless of magnitude, and Ross sensed this was one. Turning on his heels he stole back into the bullpen, retrieved the bedroll, unfolded and laid it on the desk top so that it nestled against the barricade, then crawled up and covered his body and face with Stewart's blanket. Sleep struck instantly. Some time later the phone rang against his head. It was Ivorson inquiring into the state of his health and if it had prevented filing.

Groggy and with venom in his heart, Ross expelled several obscenities, adding he had no intention of speculating on the military content of the President's speech, only hours away. As Ross knew, the remark startled Ivorson, who pressed instantly for more detail, but Ross held his ground, suggesting that IP's White House leg man make a better effort to keep IP's Washington staffers informed, another left-handed slap at Ivorson as bureau chief. Ivorson felt the sting and hung up, suiting Ross's purpose.

But the nap had revived him. He slid off the desk, furled the bedroll and blanket, and wondered how long the laser attack would continue. He had to find time to go home for a few daylight hours after filing on the speech. Ivorson would lay in wait and cavil at the copy, although Ross had learned over the years that a presidential lead into his story required respectful treatment, else domestic IP subscribers would refuse to print it. The kid-glove handling always amplified and strengthened an administration's position, delighting the White House press secretary, but did nothing to discover truth.

The bridge game's cryptic bidding, overcalls and occasional renege surged over the barricade and proved amusing as he began typing a rough draft of the space shuttle program. Without references he recalled what he could of its peaceful uses in space, which the

Congress had funded generously for years, and of its tactic potential as a military countermeasure against space threats. But he hadn't gotten past the lead-in paragraph when Stewart rounded the corner and motioned him to follow.

Catching up in the corridor, Ross asked, "Where the hell are you taking me?"

"Glasscock," Stewart said, slowing to Ross's pace, but instead of mounting the escalator for the fourth floor he led Ross wordlessly down two flights of stairs to the Pentagon's basement level, then farther to an unmarked elevator which descended deeper into the building's bowels. Ross had never seen nor heard of the subbasement, obviously a well-kept secret and sanctuary.

"The general has a badge ready for you, Quent," Stewart explained as they neared a vaultlike guarded door. "Keep a low profile. Okay?"

"Okay," Ross said, knocking the ashes of his pipe against the palm of his hand while Stewart presented his own credentials to a pair of air policemen. They opened the blastproof door for Stewart, but barred Ross's way. Stewart disappeared behind a baffled inner structure. Seconds later Glasscock emerged and silently pinned a leather-encased VIP badge on Ross's lapel, then signed an authorization log for his admittance. The senior air policeman indicated that Ross countersign. This done, the vault door swung open and Glasscock ushered Ross inside.

With unbelieving eyes Ross realized he had just entered a vast planetarium, but instead of constellations of stars twinkling in the velvet-black dome, blinking alpha-numerics inched in arcs across the heavens. Ross deduced instantly that they were satellites in orbit. In the semidarkness Glasscock nudged him toward a series of consoles, each of which included several comfortably contoured chairs. Glasscock seated Ross between Stewart and himself. Stewart reached over and fitted him with a headset and lip microphone.

"The general, you and I are on a closed voice circuit, Quent," Stewart said with a metallic ring. "In this way we disturb no one at the other consoles. And to keep your mind at ease, I'm told the circuit is bugproof because some Air Force projects are sensitive."

Ross grinned.

Glasscock said, "Quent, let me first caution you about the overhead display. Don't speculate on what you see above your head. I can only tell you that it simulates a lot of our stuff and other stuff in orbit. If one of our killer satellite intercepts looks successful, I'll bring you back to observe it, but file nothing on this room for the time being." He looked questioningly at Ross in the eerie green light cast by the twin cathodes on the console.

"Fair enough," Ross answered.

"Okay. That's settled," Glasscock said while forming a church steeple with the tips of his fingers. He pointed the steeple at the large, twin TV screens imbedded in the console and explained, "The screen at the left is locked onto a launching pad at Cape Canaveral and the other on a pad at Vandenberg. Like our voice communications in this room, the TV is also closed-circuit and almost as inviolate. The booster that you see on each screen is a two-stage Titan and will soon launch a killer satellite payload with brute force at the laser. This is a balls-out Air Force effort and I thought you'd enjoy sharing the last few minutes of each countdown with us."

Ross smiled in appreciation.

Glasscock then manipulated several audio controls on the console, bringing in strident military voices that announced countdown and technical checkoff of critical items at both blockhouse command posts. The volume surged in Ross's ears and he suddenly shook his head in pain. Stewart laughed as Glasscock fumbled with the controls, then helped his boss meld the channels so that the countdowns remained audible only as background while they chatted.

Almost in unison, both launch commanders announced five-minute holds. Glasscock groaned.

Stewart turned to Ross and said, "Quent, this room is a miniaturized Bright Lake or Colorado Springs space defense command post. Its purpose is to inform, not make space defense decisions. That job takes place in Colorado Springs or in Omaha."

"But decisions could be made here?"

"Of course, Quent," Glasscock answered. "The President, the defense secretary or the chairman of the Joint Chiefs of Staff can waltz down into this room, assess the space defense situation, then order military action or countermand it. Sometime ago we worried about putting the display in here for that reason, since it could damn well destroy the authority of commanders appointed for the task, but we chanced it because the information is perishable and critically needed at the Pentagon too. I'm afraid before long all tactical ground, air and space decisions will be usurped from the field and made at the White House. As you know, Kennedy did exactly that during the Cuban missile crisis, directing ship's captains from the Oval Office, and managed only to stall off the confrontation. Johnson and Nixon meddled tactically every day in Vietnam and helped achieve total, abject defeat in Asia. Ford and Carter were caretakers, thank God, and didn't succumb to Hitlerian battlefield tactics—or didn't get the opportunity."

"And now?"

Glasscock debated answering, then said, "I don't know about this one. He's not aggressive by nature. He's more of a lover than a fighter. He's gotten where he has as a compromiser. Of course, Johnson was the great compromiser in the Senate, then the Vietnam war turned him into a blind tiger. What bothers me is this one has surrounded himself with the same sort of post-Harvard, Princeton and Yale wisdom in military affairs. Again, his advisers will never be held accountable for their disastrous advice. In fact, they'll publish books defending our military disasters and make fortunes."

"You sound bitter, Noel."

"Not really, Quent. I'm just getting the long look. That's why I've invited you here, someone with a nose for the truth, a third party, largely unprejudiced, but informed and skilled in getting the word out. Neither the military nor the civilian bureaucracy is capable of it."

Looking toward Stewart, Ross said, "Terry's learning fast. He can speak the truth as you speak the truth."

"Horse manure!" Glasscock exclaimed. "Terry's no more believable in uniform than I am, in fact, less. The uniform holds no credibility in a free society. Nobody listens, and if they did, they wouldn't believe a word because of the uniform. That's why I believe in the draft. Everybody in our republic deserves a two-year taste of military life."

"And don't forget," Ross said mockingly, "the bureaucracy our society set up to govern has so refined itself that only a handful of civil servants possess the authority to talk about the bureaucracy's functions, under the convenient restraints of policy, propriety and consistency of voice of course."

Glasscock nodded his head in agreement. "I know that without confidential sources the facts, the truth regarding government decisions and operations, would never surface, whether Watergate, CIA, Chile, Vietnam, the FBI or GSA. So for the sake of historical truth, and for better or worse, we are your laser pipeline, Quent."

Ross acknowledged the confidence with a conspirator's smile.

Stewart pointed to the Vandenberg TV. "They'll start the countdown now."

The Titan's vent furiously fumed liquid fuel, enveloping the gantry. The harsh voice of the announcer resumed the countdown. At zero the booster lifted off without a hitch and soon was lost to the tracking camera. At Canaveral the launch followed within minutes and seemed identical to Ross. Technical jargon swamped the audio channels.

"Let's wait for the range officers' signoff at both stations," Glasscock cautioned. "Then we'll know for sure the Titans are on their way to the intercept."

Ross said, "Those launches looked normal enough to me. Will they be announced?"

"That's up to the President," Glasscock said with a shrug. "They are not carrying nuclear payloads. That was our reluctant compromise, Quent. We're praying for a lucky trajectory, for a lucky intercept with these brute-force shots."

"I take it the President is aware of the intercept attempts."

Glasscock fiddled with his hack watch as he said, "Quent, the President's Air Force aide has the word. Whether he can get to the President is a matter of access and luck. We can't give either to the aide."

Ross whistled accidently into the lip mike and apologized. He thought about the speechwriter's visit and was about to mention it when Stewart raised the volume to hear the range officers' voices announcing that the ranges were clear and that Titan control was handed over to downrange stations.

Glasscock removed his headset and lip mike. Stewart and Ross followed suit, then trailed him out of the planetarium and signed out in the log. Once clear of the air police, Glasscock said, "We're out of sanctuary now, so let's break up and go our separate ways. Terry will take you to the first-floor stairs and I'd suggest you take a short walk on the concourse. Okay?"

Ross nodded.

Stewart pushed the elevator button and then as a stranger Ross got on without a word. They parted at the stairwell and Ross walked slowly to the concourse. He gazed lovingly at Nefertiti in Brentano's dimly lit window and made a mental note that if the Pentagon got looted, he'd make off with her. Meanwhile, he would covet her.

Behind the barricade he found his brain addled as he stared at the lead-in to the shuttle roundup stuck in his typewriter. Lu came by and asked if he'd play a couple of hands for her.

"Never!" he muttered. "The madness of the past two days is getting to me, Lu. I need sleep. If I'm lucky I won't wake up till dawn when that friggin' laser goes off."

"And where have you been?"

"Round and about," he said, pulling out the bedroll and blanket. "Care to join me, Lu?"

"You old goat! Shame on you! Not in front of all the children!"

Laughing hard at the absurdity, he tucked himself under the blanket as Lu ambled off.

At four he awoke, hating and fearing the hour. It was the time when most humans died. The bullpen had quieted down: no bridge, no chatter, no phones. He dozed intermittently, then propped himself up on an elbow and stared at the crack in the papered window which suddenly faded to the gray of dawn. A sense of relief overpowered him and he thought it odd that the bastards had synchronized the laser's light to Eastern Daylight Time. However, the bulk of the country's population was centered along the Atlantic seaboard and it was apparent the enemy had that target in mind, especially if the laser's energy was a critical factor. He reminded himself to pursue the laser energy point with a confidential source in the Department of Energy and then check those facts against Stewart's information.

The stubble on his face felt uncomfortable. He remembered the razor, soap and toothbrush in the Air Force survival kit and wondered how men in subzero conditions managed to fool with ablutions. Rousing himself into action, he walked with stiff joints to the men's room to clean up, swearing that desk-top sleeping was a bit much to expect of ancient bones. Laser or not, he promised himself to sleep at home henceforth.

Shrimp, Clapham and Karayn soon joined him, aching audibly as they washed up. Shrimp used Ross's comb, explaining he had given his to Lu, who had lost hers.

"A noble act," Ross said to the laughter of the men's room.

They waited impatiently for Lu near the ladies' room and were about to abandon her when she made an entrance utterly without makeup, hair still on end, cigarette smoldering on her lip, but absolutely ebullient. They groaned at her spirit, then headed for the cafeteria awash with incoming workers who had leaped on all forms of transportation the instant the laser's light had waned. The flag officers' and dozens of other executive dining rooms were closed for the duration, and Ross surveyed the hundreds and hundreds of military and civilian brass lining up at the steam table for hot breakfast. He thought it a damn good thing the brass was forced to exercise the common touch. Even among them very few were old enough to remember the battles of World War II when Western civilization was at stake, but then he hoped this was as close as the new generation would get to it.

Shrimp was first through the line and snared a far-off table for four. He removed a stack of soiled dishes as they crowded around with teeming trays. The noise level proved unbearable for all but Lu.

"I wonder if this laser crisis is managing the President, or if he's trying to manage it?" she asked, ever businesslike.

"We'll soon know," Karayn muttered.

Ross stayed silent, enjoying a double order of scrapple and fried eggs.

"Ask Quent about the President's speech to be delivered this morning," Lu volunteered. "The speechwriter visited Quent last night. Quent probably wrote the whole goddamned thing."

Shrimp picked up the cue. "Tell us when you're misquoted, Quent."

"Thanks a lot, folks," Ross said.

"That's okay," Lu answered. "I'm sure the President's speech is written, mimeographed and in the hands of the

202

White House press corps right now. Too damned bad we can't get a copy."

"And embargoed until he delivers it," Shrimp added. "But then he might make some changes just to keep some smart-ass from leaking it."

"Who, the President or Quent?" Clapham asked.

Even Karayn laughed.

Ross lit his pipe. "You've spoiled my breakfast," he said with a twinkle. "It's easy to be funny around here, we're all government reporters."

Shrimp suggested they give up the table to the waiting mob. Ross caught sight of Glasscock and Stewart, heads huddled, in what appeared to be an unhappy conversation, but he chose not to interrupt. On the ramp back to the bullpen, Lu told Ross she had written most of the copy for her Tampa paper and compiled a bunch of statistics on crop damage for the financial newsletter. Barring any real surprises in the President's speech, she intended to file immediately afterward and then go home to see how her daughters had fared during her long absence. It reminded Ross he had forgotten to phone Marge to hear how she and Lupe survived the night, but he consoled himself with the thought that if there was an emergency she would call. He ear had been within a foot of the phone most of the night.

He stopped off in the Defense newsroom as it bestirred itself, and filled out a query sheet for Stewart to complete on energy levels needed to operate a laser device. Yet he knew he would get evasive answers on fueling scaled-up lasers no matter how conscientiously Stewart would try to worm the information out of military experts. That is, unless it suited the military's need to expose the issue. He wished he had kept a copy of his query sheets over the years. What a remarkable autobiographical history that would have made! One solitary voice questioning the government for forty years. The flaw was that the government was not the people. The government was agencies, soulless, impersonal agencies. Ah, Voltaire! How right you were that the courts of law are the last refuge of human folly, Ross thought as he left the newsroom.

The bullpen's reporters had moved to the niche and tampered endlessly with the TV. Ross couldn't stand watching the adjustments. After all, it was the audio, not video, that was important. He fled down the corridor to the Mall entrance, stepped past the marine sentries and surveyed the squat, rusted form of Cuspidor sitting crowded in the parking area and wondered if the laser light would further corrode the metal and rot the rubber. He gazed over its roof toward the Washington Monument and knew exactly where the White House stood: just a bit to the left, shielded by a grove of trees, and hardly more than two miles away. For a fleeting moment in mind's eye he imagined himself staring at the President, prompting the old boy to do well, then turned on his heels and returned to the bullpen. Stewart stood as a beacon near the rear of the niche and they listened together.

Looking haggard even on the flickering, distorted screen, the President first stated he was giving the unknown attacker until midnight to turn off the laser as his final appeal. If the laser was extinguished by that deadline, he promised no punitive action, no reprisals, only confrontation at a peace table. This was greeted with boos by the reporters. If the laser remained lit past the midnight deadline, he would direct the launch of killer satellites and ground-ferreting aircraft to destroy the laser and its communications network. But, he added, no nuclear warheads would be used to destroy the laser because the United States firmly respected the international covenant to use space only for peaceful purposes, whatever the cost. Only conventional explosives would be used in killer satellites. This was met with sarcastic laughter, applause and more boos. He reiterated that the U.S. would never contaminate space with the debris of nuclear killer satellites, even if it meant suffering the laser light's blitz for several additional nights. He then appealed to the nation to observe law and order during the crisis, or martial law would be invoked and enforced by the National Guard, which was to be mobilized at noon in any event. Moving then to enabling legislation, he appealed to the Congress to fund a massive research and development effort for space defense, using proton particle guns, powerful ground laser beams and other beamed weapons to prevent similar attacks in the future. He expressed unhappiness with insubordination by certain elements of the armed forces and for that reason had asked the chairman of the Joint Chiefs of Staff to relieve and retire the commanders of strategic Air Force defense organizations. Ross and Stewart shuddered at the massacre. The President announced the physical move of the White House staff and cabinet to a secret headquarters in the Blue Ridge Mountains. Obscenities, catcalls and derision about cowardice drowned out the President's prayer for the nation to endure.

Ross stole out into the corridor wondering if his remarks to Arundel about the unauthorized killer sat launches had triggered the President's vengeance. Perhaps the massacre was simply an act of frustration, or possibly a demonstration to the armed forces that he indeed was the commander in chief.

Stewart intercepted him steps away from the ticker room and said, shaken, "God! That was a bloodletting!"

"As bad as I've seen," Ross agreed.

"The general passed it on to me at breakfast. Apparently some of the missile and satellite civilian contractors got together after the first killer sats were fired, and afraid they might not get paid for goods and services, queried some stooge at the White House whether they would disallow the unauthorized launch costs. This flak got to the President, later confirmed by the Air Force aide, and finally by his speechwriter. He blew a fuse over the launches and their failures and thought it time to show the soldiers who was boss, a la Truman. So three good guys out in the field bit the dust trying to knock out the laser before we all went blind."

"All that proves is there's merit nowadays in being a citizen of a small country," Ross said sarcastically. "His chances of being left alone and of survival are greater than as a citizen of a superpower."

"What are you filing?"

Damned if I know. It'll flow, somehow."

"Save me a carbon, please."

"You too? Well, why not?" Ross said, moving anxiously into the ticker room.

"By the way, Quent, the President is following in your footsteps."

"Oh?"

"At noon. I now doubt his visit here would be considered sensitive. He's demonstrating to the world he's getting with it."

Ross laughed. "Makes sense," he said as Stewart disappeared, then marveled at his good luck, having just heard the lead-in paragraph dictated to him. Turning on the teletype sending switch, he began filing with enthusiasm, freed from the guilt of betrayal to Arundel.

BULLETIN:
OVER "A" CIRCUITS
DATELINE WASHINGTON THIS DATE
BYLINE QUENTIN ROSS, MILITARY ANALYST, THE PENTAGON
LASER FORCES PRESIDENT'S HAND

THE PRESIDENT PUT POLITICS ASIDE IN THIS MORNING'S SPEECH TO HIS COUNTRYMEN TO DEVOTE ATTENTION TO THE POSTURE OF THE UNITED STATES IN FACE OF THE CONTINUING LASER BLITZ. SOURCES CLOSE TO THE WHITE HOUSE INDICATE HE WILL SOON VISIT ONE OR MORE SPACE DEFENSE PLANETARIUMS FOR FIRST-HAND ASSESS-

MENT OF THE LASER SPACE WAR AND U.S. CAPABILITIES TO END THE UNPROVOKED ATTACK. THE NEAREST MILITARY SPACE PLANETARIUM IS IN THE PENTAGON. MORE ELABORATE PLANETARIUMS ARE IN COLORADO AND CALIFORNIA, BUT THE FACILITY IN THE PENTAGON WILL PROBABLY ANSWER THE PRESIDENT'S QUESTIONS REGARDING FACTS, STRATEGY AND TACTICAL SPACE DEFENSE COUNTERMEASURES.

EXERCISING HIS PREROGATIVE AS COMMANDER IN CHIEF, THE PRESIDENT SACKED THREE SPACE DEFENSE GENERALS FOR ALLEGEDLY AUTHORIZING THE PREMATURE LAUNCH OF SATURN, TITAN AND POLARIS BOOSTERS ARMED WITH KILLER SATELLITES. ALL THREE LAUNCHES FAILED TO INTERCEPT THE LASER. FIRED AND RETIRED WERE THE FOUR-STAR GENERALS COMMANDING NORAD AND THE STRATEGIC AIR COMMAND. A THREE-STAR GENERAL DIRECTLY IN CHARGE OF SPACE WARFARE IN LOS ANGELES WAS ALSO SACKED. REPLACEMENTS WERE NOT ANNOUNCED BY MIDDAY EITHER AT THE WHITE HOUSE OR BY THE DEFENSE SECRETARY.

IN AN OVER-THE-SHOULDER GESTURE, THE PRESIDENT ASKED THE CONGRESS TO FUND A MASSIVE EMERGENCY RESEARCH AND DEVELOPMENT EFFORT FOR SPACE DEFENSE, CONCENTRATING ON DIRECTED ENERGY WEAPONS USING CHARGED PARTICLE BEAMS THAT WOULD IN THE NEAR FUTURE DESTROY TARGETS SUCH AS THE LASER SATELLITE WITH ELECTRON, PROTON OR HEAVY IONS TRAVELING NEAR THE SPEED OF LIGHT. INDISPENSABLE FOR BEAMED WEAPONS ARE LARGE POWER SOURCES—COM-

PENSATED PULSED ALTERNATORS—YET TO BE DEVELOPED BY THE U.S. IRONICALLY, THE PRESIDENT AND THE DEFENSE SECRETARY ONLY MONTHS EARLIER REFUSED TO SPEND MORE THAN A FRACTION OF CONGRESSIONAL APPROPRIATIONS EARMARKED FOR THE CHARGED PARTICLE BEAM PROGRAM, DESPITE DRAMATIC BREAKTHROUGHS BY THE RUSSIANS.

THE PRESIDENT AUTHORIZED THE LAUNCH OF KILLER SATELLITES ARMED ONLY WITH CONVENTIONAL EXPLOSIVES, ALSO GROUND-FERRETING AIRCRAFT TO SEARCH FOR AND DESTROY THE LASER SATELLITE AND ITS EARTH LINKS IF THE ATTACKING NATION DID NOT TURN OFF THE LASER PRIOR TO MIDNIGHT. NOT DISCLOSED BUT PROBABLY TO BE USED COLLATERALLY WITH THE KILLER SATELLITES ARE U.S. GROUND LASERS WHOSE NARROW BEAMS WILL BE AIMED AT THE LASER SATELLITE TO BURN OUT ITS INTERNAL LASER-PRODUCING DEVICE, IN EFFECT, ANTI-LASER LASERS.

ARMY HEADQUARTERS IN THE PENTAGON IS REELING UNDER TWIN PRESIDENTIAL EDICTS. THE FIRST IS TO BREATHE LIFE INTO THE TOTTERING CIVIL DEFENSE FUNCTION, ADMITTEDLY A MYTH. ARMY OFFICERS STATE PRIVATELY THAT NO CIVIL DEFENSE PROGRAM, ALTHOUGH CAPABLE OF SAVING LIVES IN THE SHORT TERM, CAN POSSIBLY SPARE THE LIVES OF MOST AMERICANS IN A CATASTROPHE. THE SECOND TASK TO MOBILIZE THE NATIONAL GUARD IS MORE TO THE ARMY'S LIKING, INASMUCH AS IT DRAWS ON HISTORICAL PRECEDENT AND LONG EXPERIENCE. HOWEVER, IF THE PRESIDENT PLACES THE NATION UNDER MARTIAL

LAW TO PREVENT LOSS OF LIFE AND PROPERTY, AND TO RESTORE LAW AND ORDER IN THE SEVERAL STATES, THE ARMY WILL FIND ITSELF IN AN UNTENABLE POSITION POLITICALLY DUE TO INEVITABLE SNIPING BETWEEN THE PRESIDENT AND STATE GOVERNORS REGARDING IMPLEMENTATION AND REVOCATION OF MARTIAL LAW.

HISTORIANS WILL LONG DEBATE THE PRESIDENT'S WISDOM IN RULING OUT THE USE OF NUCLEAR EXPLOSIVES IN SPACE TO DESTROY THE LASER SATELLITE, THUS LESSENING THE PROBABILITY OF A DIRECT HIT BUT PRECLUDING LITTERING SPACE WITH NUCLEAR DEBRIS.

ALTHOUGH THE PRESIDENT ASKED THE NATION TO ENDURE THE TERRORS OF THE LASER BLITZ, HE DIRECTED THE WHITE HOUSE STAFF AND KEY CABINET OFFICERS TO TRANSFER PERSONNEL AND FUNCTIONS TO A SECRET, HEAVILY GUARDED BASTION IN THE BLUE RIDGE MOUNTAINS SOME EIGHTY MILES WEST OF THE U.S. CAPITAL. THE EVACUATION IS VIEWED EITHER AS COWARDICE OR ASTUTENESS, DEPENDING ON PARTY AFFILIATION AND PERSONAL PREJUDICE.
END
END BULLETIN.

Well, that ought to hold London, Berlin and Tokyo for a couple of minutes, Ross thought, stretching to straighten out his back after the siege in the chair. In moments like this the hours spent reading academia's technical papers, contractor press kits, Defense news releases and other puffery were justified, although he had often questioned the seemingly irrelevant reading, the idle chatter with the military, other reporters, marketeers and public relations men. Recall was his ace in the hole.

A terrifying thunderclap struck something nearby as he entered the bullpen, illuminating the room with more intensity than the laser. A violent downpour followed, drawing everyone to the battened windows, and someone ripped off the paper on the window nearest the barricade, infuriating Ross. He'd have to struggle tacking it up again. Lu came over and they watched the lashing rain strip the trees of half-curled leaves.

Ross said, "I can't make up my mind whether this is a normal summer storm or something more violent induced by the laser."

"I've had the same thought," Lu said. "Maybe it's nature's way of compensating for the laser's damage."

"Could well be," he said.

Stewart arrived for a look at the torrent since the Defense newsroom had no windows. He stood fascinated by the fury of wind and water, then turned to Ross and said softly, "The twins died."

"Oh, no!"

"Upper stage separation problems on one and guidance failure in the other."

"Any more sacks?"

"Haven't heard, but it'll have a ripple effect."

"Now what?"

"We'll keep trying. The space shuttle is being readied at Vandenberg."

Ross asked eagerly, "Will General Glasscock help Shrimp?"

"He didn't turn down the idea."

"Good."

Lu moved in and murmured, "What's going on, Quent?" when Stewart departed.

"We're trying to get Shrimp loaded on the shuttle."

She crowed with delight. "Shrimp implied he was on the edge of something big, but I didn't suspect he was personally involved. How great!"

"Well, it's still a long way from being in the bag. Keep it to yourself for the moment. We may need your help later, Lu."

"Just whistle," she said and then stared out at the storm-rent scud.

Ross's phone rang and Lu left. Ivorson passed on Fairly's bitch that Ross's copy treated the President brutally, especially in the eyes of world capitals. In addition, references to charged particle beams, compensated pulsed alternators and the antilaser laser were top secret programs. Ross was guilty of flagrant security violations.

"Balls!" Ross said. "Merle, did you kill any of my copy?"

"No. Fairly called too late for me to censor it."

"You son of a bitch! You don't know enough to censor it."

"I'll respond to the White House anytime as a matter of policy."

"If you ever kill my copy, I'll fight it out with you in New York. London, too, if need be!"

"Call Fairly and tell him your sources. We don't need the FBI all over us today."

"Tell him your sources," Ross mimicked into the dead phone. No wonder most news coverage wasn't worth a damn. Finding Fairly's card, he dialed the White House. Fairly answered directly.

"This is Ross. What's all that crap about security violations?"

"Three of them."

"C'mon," Ross said. "Normally, I wouldn't divulge my sources till hell froze over, but in this case all three programs were spelled out in detail last fall in congressional hearings on research and development appropriations. If you want, I'll send you a copy, you dumb bastard!"

"You're sure?"

"Sure I'm sure! Don't embarrass yourself, Phil. Instead, kick your researchers in the butt for this one. They damned near set you up."

"Okay, I guess I'm wrong on this one, Quent. All hell's breaking out here because of the Blue Ridge move. But you could've been kinder to the President."

"I'll try. I'll try," Ross said with mounting sincerity. "By the way, while I've got you on, one of our brighter youngsters in the bullpen wants to ride the space shuttle on the laser intercept, on a pool basis, of course. I've checked him out and am putting his bid in for him now. I want him numero uno."

"Who is he?"

"Eric 'Shrimp' Loveridge of the *Baltimore Telegram*."

"Okay, Quent. I'll put him down as first. This is a large favor, you know, Quent."

"Damned right I know it's a large favor. You'll get it back as a bucket of blood and two pounds of IP flesh!"

Fairly laughed. "That I will, Quent!" he said, hanging up.

Ross felt pleased with the maneuver, but before he could gather his wits, Marge called. He promised to go home immediately.

Karayn appeared. "A nice wrap-up, Quent," he said. "I'd like to do a think piece on the informed layman level if I can quickly get my hands on some source material, those antilaser lasers, space-beamed weapons and the pulsed alternator programs that you cited in your copy. Anything handy?"

"Just so happens there is," Ross said, somewhat irritated. "It's in a brown-covered congressional hearing of last fall somewhere in this tall pile of stuff. Don't mess up the sequence worse than it is, Milo. Also, I've got to get it back as evidence because the administration's nervous as hell about not spending that portion of the research and development appropriation."

"Oh?"

"I've already had one threatening call from the White House about violating security on those programs. So be careful, Milo, and for Christ's sake don't lose the report! In our free society it'll take a month to get another. I'll be tried in absentia of documents. Okay?"

"Okay. Thanks for the backgrounding on the background."

Ross stepped away from the desk so Karayn could sort out the pile, then decided to get out of the bullpen during the dismantling. Shrimp intercepted him in the corridor.

"Guess what?" Shrimp demanded.

"What the hell is it now?" Ross asked with mock severity. "But make it quick because I'm going home for a change."

"Quent, I just called NASA Houston and a buddy there told me they just turned the space shuttle at Vandenberg over to the Air Force for a shot at the laser."

Ross smiled.

"Isn't that great news? The first real step in getting me up there!"

"You're behind the times, Shrimp. That's bad for a reporter."

"Meaning what?"

"You're number one to represent the news pool."

Shrimp slapped Ross on the back. "So you did it!"

"No, Shrimp. Your paper supports the administration."

8

Marge welcomed Ross affectionately but he grumped and rushed upstairs to shower and change clothes. She prepared eggs benedict and served coffee with a large wallop of brandy. It did him in and he dozed off on the couch. Later, he heard the phone but it seemed to stop in the middle of the first ring. He imagined Marge pouncing on it to protect him. Stirring, he crashed onto the coffee table. Marge rushed up, helped him to a sitting position and joined him on the floor. Laughing at his awkwardness, he pulled her into his arms and bit her on the nape of the neck. She howled in protest, escaped his clutches and ran into the kitchen. He followed, only to be fended off with a list of phone calls. Two were from Ivorson. Others included Stewart, Shrimp, Fairly and London IP.

He said, "Thank God Lu hasn't called! If the President visited the Pentagon and held a press conference with Browning Whitley, she would've covered for me as well as herself—I hope!"

"You're a naughty boy, abandoning your desk for several hours," Marge said sarcastically.

He called Fairly first. In his staccato voice Fairly said that Shrimp was "locked on board the shuttle" representing the news pool, then added he wanted Ross to lay off Browning Whitley because the President had put the drunk on probation. Ross readily agreed to the deal. Whitley deserved the silent treatment.

Stewart wasn't at his desk, nor Shrimp in the bullpen. Ross switched the call to Lu who said the President had come and gone without fanfare. No press conference, no visibility, no nothing other than a heavy guard. She barely caught a glimpse of him on his way to a classified briefing in the basement.

Ross laughed knowingly and thanked her for not calling. That left Ivorson and the London bureau. Gritting his teeth, Ross dialed Ivorson, but Dawn put him on hold and they chatted while he waited. She said she had read every bulletin. Even Ivorson had admitted to her that Ross's copy exceeded all of the opposition coverage rolled together.

"Thanks for the kind words, Dawn. I need all the moral support I can get when dealing with Merle."

"You've got the line, Quent," she said quickly, then switched him to Ivorson.

"Quent, where the hell were you when the President hit the Pentagon?"

"It was a secret visit. He granted no interviews, no press conference."

"You still should've written some copy on his presence."

"I'm not a protocol reporter, Merle. That's your leg man's job at the White House, goddammit! If the substance of the President's visit isn't releasable, the story takes on the tone of a protocol call, something best handled by someone other than a military analyst."

"You're one smart son of a bitch, Quent. Now sink your teeth into this one. London wants a wrap-up on killer satellite failures. They want to know what caused the failures, the effect on U.S. missile deterrent capabilities, and whether the space shuttle can redeem U.S. credibility in space. Okay?"

"Okay? My foot! Those Limeys get hung up on the damnest things at the strangest times! Credibility isn't the issue, Merle. It's survival under the laser blitz."

"Get up a response."

"I've got a shuttle wrap-up in the typewriter. It'll answer most of London's questions, Merle."

"Like for the five PM deadline, Quent."

Ross cursed and hung up. It meant going back to the bullpen. His facts were there and the story was too complicated, too full of space-age terminology to dictate.

He turned to Marge. "Duty calls, I guess. I can't walk away from the shuttle story because it paves the way for Shrimp. I don't want any hitches on his climbing aboard. It's first in space for a reporter, and what a first!"

Marge was crestfallen. "I hoped you'd spend the night at home."

"If I can get it all together, I may beat the laser home, sweetheart. If not, I can survive another night on top of the desk." He laughed. "But not much more unless Lu holds my hand!"

"You're a terrible tease," Marge sighed, pecking his cheek at the kitchen door.

Ross gunned Cuspidor down the driveway, saluted the gilt horses at Memorial Bridge, avoided shattered glass, auto bumpers and rubber strewn all over streets and parkway, then without incident parked Cuspidor so that she faced the exit for a fast getaway. The now-familiar marine sentries admitted him with a minimum of fuss. He found Lu and Stewart talking to an elated Shrimp in the bullpen doorway.

"Congratulations, Shrimp!" he said, extending his hand.

"Thanks, in more ways than one."

"And good luck," Ross added. "When do you leave?"

"Right now for Vandenberg. I'm traveling on White House orders. How about that?"

"Well, you won't get bumped," Lu said.

Stewart shook Shrimp's hand with obvious envy. "Lots of us will be up there riding along with you in spirit, Shrimp. I wish you a good intercept."

"And good copy," Lu said, kissing him.

Shrimp fled down the corridor.

Stewart said, "The only thing I don't envy him is the six-hour crash course on emergency procedures that he must master. An astronaut in six hours, how about that?"

"It can't be that hard," Ross objected. "Don't they have girl astronauts?"

Lu shot an elbow into Ross's ribs.

Stewart laughed as Ross winced. "They should've put the shuttle up before trying all that brute-force and matched-orbit killer satellite stuff," Stewart said philosophically.

"Why didn't they?" Lu asked.

"NASA would not release it to the Air Force without a direct White House order. Can't blame NASA. They had already lost an expensive, man-rated booster through some fast talk by the Air Force."

"Who cares about accountability when we're getting blinded by the laser?" Lu demanded.

"I can answer that," Ross said. "The system is based on accountability, not trust. It was just as true in the Civil War when the quartermaster at Fort Sumter telegraphed Lincon, protesting the destruction of supplies by Confederate bombardment."

"At any rate," Stewart said, "Shrimp's on his way, the shuttle's going up, the laser will be destroyed and we'll all return to normal."

Lu looked up into Stewart's eyes and said, "Terry, I hear the President privately tore the hide off Browning Whitley about his slurping and not being present on the job. Also, that too many press queries were being referred to the White House news staff, causing collapse under the workload. All of this resulted in General Glasscock being called up to replace Scotus. True or false?"

Stewart flushed and replied glibly, "No military man can serve in a high civilian position at the Defense

Department without special authorization from the Congress."

Lu said, "I know all about the administrative hassle, but you didn't answer my question, Terry."

Ross listened intently and threw an encouraging wink at Lu.

"For attribution or not?" Stewart parried.

"Aha!" Lu pounced on the statement. "I'm right. Glasscock is replacing Scotus!"

Ross raised his voice in warning. "Terry, that was a stupid remark. You gave yourself away."

"I know I did," Stewart said nervously. "I didn't know how to handle Lu's question."

Ross turned to Lu and said sternly, "Keep out of this for a minute," then spoke to Stewart. "Terry, there are times when a spokesman shouldn't speak. He should say nothing, nothing at all, not one syllable should come out of his mouth."

"Quent, I'd look like a fool!"

"You're absolutely right. There are times when you're paid to play the part of the fool, a dumb, silent, stupid fool."

"That's hard to do, Quent."

"Damned right! Your ego gets in the way. 'No comment,' and 'Is it for attribution?' have buried more official spokesmen than all other causes put together. There are times when a spokesman should look blank and stay blank on a subject he's trying to protect. Even a wisecrack won't get the dogs off the scent. So after an appropriate silence, one of two things will happen, Terry. Either the exasperated questioner will walk away with contempt for you, or someone else will butt in with an unrelated query and save your skin. That's because humans abhor a verbal vacuum. Okay?"

"Okay," Stewart said, still perplexed. "I should've walked away in silence?"

"Why not? It's the thing to do if you have no other defense. This relationship is not a popularity contest.

We'll face each other professionally tomorrow on still another crisis."

Lu asked, "Are you through, Quent?"

"I could talk another hour, it's my favorite subject."

"Well, don't!"

Stewart said softly, "If the general's appointment is leaked before Legislative Liaison can inform the Congress, and if Browning Whitley can't announce his own assistant secretary's appointment without being scooped, then it's damned embarrassing to the general because it looks like he leaked it to the Pentagon press to insure his own appointment, or that he's a bigmouth who can't keep anything to himself."

"Pretty well diagnosed, Terry," Ross said.

"Except that Quent and I would never betray your confidence," said Lu.

"Remember that Lu and I are the exception to what I've been preaching," Ross said. "The press is a hostile adversary to the uniform, and more so to the administration, because there seems to be no accommodation, only confrontation. Terry, you will get all scarred up if you are caught off-guard in this business. That's all I'm trying to get across. Okay?"

Lu nodded in agreement, then added, "In truth, nobody gives a damn about Glasscock's peculiar appointment except for those of us in the bullpen. If we report the appointment in normal fashion, it'll wind up next to the truss ads. I think it more important to nurture him so we can enjoy an honest pipeline into the Defense Department, especially during this laser attack. Terry, when do you think he'll move into Scotus's office?"

"He's ready."

"And you'll replace Ted Harris?" Ross asked.

"No. You can't get rid of civil servants. I heard him say he'll use both of us, that the workload will warrant it."

"Good luck, Terry," Ross said. Lu seconded the wish.

Stewart laughed. "I've got to get out of this corridor," and started off for the Defense newsroom.

"Leave with no fear," Lu called after him.

Ross tamped his pipe and left Lu for his barricade. Still no blue-bannered Defense news releases. Glasscock would change all that. Looking at his watch he realized he had less than an hour to file if he were to satisfy the five o'clock deadline, and so with reluctance he walked to the ticker room to put the shuttle story on the wire. He hated filing cold but it seemed more the rule than the exception for weeks on end. He moved the tattered chair to the teletype, drummed lightly on the base of the machine, turned on the sending switch and began filing.

BULLETIN:
OVER "A" CIRCUITS
DATELINE WASHINGTON THIS DATE
BYLINE QUENTIN ROSS, MILITARY ANALYST, THE PENTAGON
SPACE SHUTTLE TO STOP LASER

THE MANNED SPACE SHUTTLE, DESIGNED TO INJECT SATELLITES INTO ORBIT AND TO REPROVISION SPACE STATIONS, WAS DIVERTED AT NOON TODAY BY PRESIDENTIAL ORDER FROM NASA TO THE AIR FORCE TO INTERCEPT AND DESTROY THE LASER SPACE WEAPON BLITZING THE NATION EVERY NIGHT.

THE SHUTTLE WILL CARRY TWO AIR FORCE ASTRONAUT PILOTS AND ONE CIVILIAN POOL REPORTER ON THE 24-HOUR, 66,000 MILE OUTBOUND SPACE FLIGHT TO INTERCEPT AND DESTROY THE LASER. IF THE FIRST PASS PROVES UNSUCCESSFUL, THE CREW WILL MANEUVER THE SHUTTLE INTO MATCHED ORBIT WITH THE LASER SATELLITE, THUS GREATLY INCREASING THE KILL PROBABILITY BUT EXTENDING THE MISSION BY SEVERAL HOURS. BLASTOFF FROM VANDENBERG AFB IN CALIFORNIA IS SCHEDULED FOR MID-

MORNING TOMORROW, PROVIDED THAT CHECKOUT OF THE SHUTTLE'S THOUSANDS OF FLIGHT ITEMS IS SATIFACTORILY COMPLETED. RETURN TO EARTH AT EDWARDS AFB, ALSO IN CALIFORNIA, IS ESTIMATED AT 50 TO 60 HOURS AFTER BLASTOFF.

THE WHITE HOUSE DECISION TO USE THE SPACE SHUTTLE WAS UNDOUBTEDLY INFLUENCED BY REPEATED FAILURES INCURRED IN LAUNCHING MILITARY BOOSTERS WITH HASTILY MATED KILLER SATELLITE PAYLOADS. RANDOM FAILURES PLAGUED THE RETALIATORY LAUNCHES, BUT PENTAGON OFFICIALS SAID EMPHATICALLY THAT THE FAILURES MUST BE CONSIDERED EXPERIMENTAL TESTS OF AN UNTRIED KILLER SATELLITE SYSTEM. THEY SERVED NOTICE THAT THE RELIABILITY AND ACCURACY OF THOUSANDS OF TITAN, MINUTEMAN AND POLARIS MISSILES IN THE U.S. ARSENAL REMAINS INTACT.

THE PRESENCE OF HUMAN INTELLIGENCE ABOARD THE SPACE SHUTTLE WILL OVERRIDE GROUND-BASED PROGRAMMING IN THE EVENT OF SYSTEM MALFUNCTIONS AND WILL AID MATERIALLY IN THE ACCURATE INTERCEPT OR MATCHED ORBIT ENCOUNTER WITH THE LASER SATELLITE. THE SHUTTLE ASTRONAUTS MAY WELL BE ABLE TO SHOVE THE LASER SATELLITE OUT OF ITS GEOSYNCHRONOUS OR FIXED ORBIT, OR DISARM THE LASER MECHANISM, OR BOTH, WITHOUT RESORTING TO EXPLOSIVES TO DISABLE IT.

THE *BALTIMORE TELEGRAM*'S ERIC "SHRIMP" LOVERIDGE, 30, MILITARY REPORTER AT THE PENTAGON, WAS DRAWN AS POOL REPORTER BY THE WHITE HOUSE FOR THE SPACE SHUTTLE INTERCEPT, MARKING A

FIRST FOR THE MEDIA IN SPACE FLIGHT. HIS EYEWITNESS COVERAGE OF THE SPACE WAR WILL PROVIDE WORLDWIDE REPORTS ON THE THREE-DAY SEARCH AND DESTROY MISSION.
END
END BULLETIN.
NOTE TO EDITORS: CUTS OF SPACE SHUTTLE AVAILABLE THROUGH IP WIREPHOTO.
END.

Ross turned off the machine and sat for a minute wishing he had done more justice to the shuttle's technical features, but as it was, he had far overshot the ideal word wire limit. At least he had bothered to file before the five o'clock deadline, and there was time enough to get out of the building to beat the laser home.

Lu met him with purse in hand for the walk to the parking area, but Stewart arrived on the run and barred their way.

"Now what?" Ross asked apprehensively.

"Please don't leave," Stewart said. "General Glasscock is coming down to hold his first press conference."

Lu whistled. "That's great, Terry!"

"In the bullpen? I don't believe it!" Ross exclaimed.

"That's what he said, Quent."

"So we've traveled full circle. From the bullpen in the 40's to Scotus's office in the 50's to the conference room in the 60's to the auditorium in the 70's. Now back to the bullpen." Ross said, scratching his head.

Excitedly, Lu asked, "What's on his agenda?"

"Damned if I know, Lu. Probably wants to greet everyone. I've got to get back to him now," Stewart said with a broad smile.

It occurred to Ross that if Glasscock had anything substantive to say, it would require filing, what with more media openness and more competition. He groaned inwardly at the thought of getting trapped in the

Pentagon for another night. Turning to Lu, he asked, "Are you thinking what I'm thinking?"

"Yeah. There goes house, home and kids again! We're stuck tonight for sure, Quent."

"Goddammit! Let's call our respective families and get our apologies over with," Ross said, returning to the barricade.

Ted Harris came racing through the bullpen like the town crier, announcing an immediate press conference with General Glasscock. All reporters were to keep their places. Ross laughed long and hard.

Lu spun round the barricade. "Incredible! Incredible!"

"All we need is for Browning Whitley to introduce Glasscock."

"Too much to ask for in one day, Quent."

"I guess I won't see or hear a damned thing behind the barricade," Ross said, rising.

"Be my guest and share my desk," Lu said.

Amused, he followed her to the bullpen's battered central area, did as he was bid and sat down on a corner of the desk. He swung his legs while she primped again, her back ramrod straight on her ragged, armless, secretary's chair. Harris ushered Glasscock into the waiting bullpen with Stewart a discreet step to the rear. Glasscock went directly to Lu, kissed her on the cheek, then stood alongside her desk, forcing Ross to find refuge elsewhere. Two dozen reporters laughed at Ross's displacement. He moved to the very rear amid applause and lit his pipe.

"Sorry about that, Quent," Glasscock said with a grin, "but not really. A little distance can be a good thing."

"Absolutely right, General," Ross replied, raising more laughter. He was glad the press conference had gotten off on the right foot.

Glasscock turned serious. Twin stars glistened on the epaulets of his Air Force Blue blouse, silver command pilot's wings sat above seven rows of decorations, and below the rainbow-hued ribbons a circular, golden

223

badge of the Defense Department shone in contrast to his Air Force insignia. With a touch of exaggeration he pointed to the badge and said in a clear, loud voice, "I think I should start off with this badge. Although I am obviously Air Force, the badge reminds me and tells you that as of now I am assigned to the office of the secretary of defense and that is where my loyalty now must lie. The reason for this explanation is that I have been appointed assistant secretary of defense for public affairs. So until I am relieved, I will work with you to get the news out."

Lu clapped, interrupting him. Others picked it up and the room resounded with applause.

Glasscock put on a whimsical grin. "This assignment is illegal as hell. The Defense Department table of organization clearly lists the job as a civilian slot. It also requires—because of the level of responsibility—Senate confirmation, which is usually routine, but in this case I'm not so sure."

Someone asked, "But isn't it true that General Marshall was appointed secretary of state?"

"A different league entirely," Glasscock said, dismissing the question. "Let me go on and state my feelings, then we'll hold the usual quiz show. Okay?"

A chorus of okays greeted him.

"I intend to hold a twenty-minute news conference every afternoon at four o'clock here in the bullpen."

Harris looked appalled. Others murmured in disbelief.

Glasscock caught it and asked, "Why not? It'll be rough as a cob on me until we all get used to it. After all, you can't fire big-bore bullets at me all of the time. Everybody runs out of ammunition, even snipers. And I hope for an armistice from time to time."

It brought forth laughs.

Ross cleared his throat and called from the back of the bullpen, "General, will we get progress reports on the shuttle's journey, in addition to Shrimp's news flashes?"

"Blow by blow, probably through Colonel Stewart."

Karayn asked, "General, does that mean you will release all vital information on knocking down the laser?"

"Yes, or at least to the very limits of my authority. I'm not the whole damned government. Yet this crisis is our collective ass and win, lose or draw, we should know what's clobbering us. But to finish my little speech, I'm moving into Scotus Olney's office for better or worse. See me there if the Defense newsroom can't handle your query, but please give them a chance, give them first crack. As you know, I'll be battered to death from all sides, from the defense secretary on upward to the White House, laterally by the State Department, Congress, NATO, by a certain national committee, and of course, mostly by you."

Lu rose slowly to her feet. "For myself, and I'm sure for others in the bullpen, you're a breath of fresh air. I'm sorry it took the laser crisis to bring you on board, but thank God you're here, General!"

Then Clapham pulled his burly frame to full height and raised his hand incongruously. "Sir," he said with a sly smile, "I'm confused whether we should address you as Mr. Secretary General, or Mr. General Secretary?"

The question brought down the house. Several other titles were suggested, including general, Mr. Secretary, even a nasty Secretary Brittleprick.

Glasscock plowed into the question. "Unfortunately, presidential orders require me to wear the uniform at all times in the Military District of Washington while on active duty, so it would be silly to call me Mr. Secretary. On the other hand, it would be just as silly to call the assistant secretary of defense as general. Just call me by my first name, Noel. Okay?"

"Okay, Noel," came the response.

"Good," he said. "Tomorrow at this time here, God willing."

Harris jumped up and paved Glasscock's way through the well-wishers while Stewart covered the rear.

"Well!" Lu expelled the word over the cigarette butt on her lip. "This bullpen has seen some strange encounters, but this tops them all!"

"Don't be too optimistic," Ross warned. "The system will kill him." He then added, "Let's go to the cafeteria for a bit of dinner. Maybe the laser won't come on and we can then drive home on a full stomach, sparing our families the commotion of setting an extra plate for the stranger."

"I shudder to think what my kids are eating. It's always a contest of wills, but now without any supervision—"

"Which reminds me," Ross said as they walked the ramp, "I hope Shrimp lives up to expectation and files good copy on the shuttle rendezvous with the laser. I'm worried that because of his youth he'll get so taken up with the technical mystique he'll sit there wide-eyed and like a lump on a log. If he does, I'll kill the little son of a bitch the minute he lands."

"Quent, don't condemn him yet."

"But let's flag his copy as it comes in. He just might not transmit a damned word. The copy could get garbled. It could die en route for lack of priority. A thousand things could go wrong."

"You're a worry wart, Quent. The next generation will take care of itself."

As if not hearing, Ross continued, "But if no copy reaches us by the time he's halfway up there—twelve hours after launch—I'm going to send him a scorching reminder. Also, I must ask Stewart how to do that. I sure hope the Air Force has a good press officer stationed at Vandenberg."

"That's Terry's job," Lu scolded. "Don't try to mastermind everything, Quent!"

They found the cafeteria packed with early diners and since service had been singularly uninterrupted by the laser blitz, Ross wondered about the unsung hero who managed the concession. He thought it would be a nice sidebar on life in the Pentagon, but after the crisis he was sure it would read like the world's greatest anticlimax. Ivorson might take fiendish delight in killing it. London would laugh after what that city had endured in World War II. He recalled an admonition when he first sat at a teletype, Write only what you know, and then only half of that.

Lu chose a large dinner salad with zest and when they were seated at a small table in the farthest corner of the room she pointed to it and said, "I'm eating this not only because of my middle-age spread, but California's Salinas Valley reports a total loss of its lettuce crop. Laser burn! So this is the very last of the Mohicans, I'll have you know."

"What about liver?"

"I haven't got a good rundown yet on cattle losses. But your onions are safe."

Ross laughed. "What other happy chitchat do you have to pass on?"

"Well, for starters, you can't get near the airline terminals. Everybody with means is taking an early vacation in Europe, even South America. The laser's causing evaporation of water in our reservoirs. Air conditioners are taxing the utilities and other demands for water are exceeding supply. Rationing is almost with us. I read on the other wire that some shrink claims human copulation is down ninety percent. Do you want more?"

"Let's stay with the copulation topic, Lu. Did the shrink state how he got his numbers?"

"Quent, you're obtuse. Even I know the laser has wiped out ninety percent of darkness."

Ross guffawed.

Lu ignored the leer rising in his face. "Fishing is ruined on both coasts because the laser stimulated the growth of dinoflagellates—a red tide explosion—poisonous to all fish. The coastlines stink to high heaven!"

"Continue," Ross said, unable to resist the temptation to toy with her.

"Schools are in turmoil. Kids have unbounded imagination as it is, and when their parents can't explain the laser blitz, home and school become chaotic. Most schools were shut down today and I think rightfully so. About the only hope is prayer, regardless what you and government might think."

Lu's impassioned plea for the welfare of America's innocents unnerved Ross and he said a silent prayer for Shrimp and the shuttle mission. Nothing would succeed like success. It was apparent his mind had drifted elsewhere, so Lu brought him up short with a sharp question. "Do you know we're being picketed tomorrow morning?"

"You're kidding!"

"No, I'm not kidding, Quent. It's not the old Vietnam protesters, although an experienced handful might be involved in the demonstration. It's lots of kooks, freaks, fanatics, sickies. They're going to howl about the laser. They want to disrupt our futile military activities in order to get the laser turned off. By showing a pacifist attitude, by disarming the Pentagon, they are convinced the attacker will relent and douse the laser."

"Is your source reliable, Lu?"

"Absolutely."

"That's what we need tomorrow, a goddamned riot on the steps!" He played with his pipe, reliving for a few seconds the various Vietnam confrontations. "I doubt," he said slowly, "that the Park Police can cope with a massive demonstration. Their nerves are frayed after all-night sessions with the laser."

"It might well get violent and for that reason I decided not to file the story for fear of inciting an even larger crowd."

"Noble, Lu, noble. I'm not going to touch it either, but keep me up on it."

She smiled. Ross lit her drooping cigarette and then they sat silent in private worlds.

Clapham and Karayn arrived with overloaded trays

and stood over Lu and Ross.

She frowned. "Is this a hint to leave?"

"The nonverbal message, Lu," Karayn said cheerily.

She dumped her cigarette disgustedly into a full ashtray, nodded at Ross and lumbered to her feet, then with a look of contempt departed the cafeteria. Ross caught up and said, "The cafeteria was crowded at the time we finished eating, Lu."

"Don't apologize for those louts to me, Quent. Reporters have the worst manners in the world. I know, because I seem to have acquired most of them, or so my kids tell me."

They walked slowly up the ramp, Ross wondering how crude he was in the eyes of others. Profane, yes; crude, no. It fitted Lu also, but he decided not to get into it.

A distraught visitor waited for him in the bullpen.

"Who are you?" Ross asked, amazed at the man's appearance. He had a deathly pallor, beady eyes offset by thick, black eyebrows that spanned the width of his forehead, and he wore a white, broad-brimmed Borsolino, topped off with a Rudolph Valentino polo coat thrown over the shoulders of his squat frame.

"I am Dr. Victor Mansur, psychiatrist," he said offering a limp hand which to Ross felt warm and moist. "I want you to interview me, Mr. Ross."

Laughing, Ross asked, "Why?"

"Because military strategy is all wrong in fighting the laser. I have better solutions, Mr. Ross."

"Like what?" Ross asked, not inviting Mansur to sit down.

"I'll tell you if you quote me."

Suspiciously Ross asked, "Where's your badge?"

"I don't need one."

"Then how did you get in here?"

"I showed my medical credentials to the marines. I am on an emergency medical call."

"To see me?"

"Of course."

Ross groaned. It was true that medics had access anywhere. Was this a practical joke? He'd kill the bastard that set him up for this. But then he asked, "Doctor, why do you want to be quoted?"

"To put your lies at rest."

"What lies?"

"Military lies!"

Ross's ire rose as did his suspicion that the guy was flakey. "I don't write lies, military or otherwise. I suggest you get the hell out of here, Doctor!" he yelled, hoping he'd be heard over the barricade.

"Aggression is not the answer, Mr. Ross. There is a better way," Mansur yelled back.

Lu peered around the corner and motioned that she would call the guards. Mansur plopped himself into Ross's chair and refused to budge. He spluttered that the industrial-military conspiracy triggered the laser retaliation, that Wall Street reduced the rest of the world to have-nots, that the U.S. was exhausting the world's natural resources for its own pleasures, that retribution was inevitable, that the laser was a beacon of hope for the oppressed . . .

Ross made no physical move to oust him, praying that the son of a bitch was unarmed and that the guards would soon appear. Lu returned, winked at Ross, took on Mansur, pacifying him that there was truth in what he said and that she would print him. This brought down his adrenalin and moments later two burly marines appeared. Ross pointed at Mansur and without a word they picked him up by the elbows. As they maneuvered him past the barricade he bit one on the hand. The marine loosened Mansur's bite with a karate chop to the neck, then threw him violently to the floor. Mansur screamed obscenities while the marines pushed, dragged and shoved him out of the bullpen. A minute later one marine returned wearing a big grin, picked up the fallen Borsolino and polo coat and departed, shaking his head.

"Phew!" Ross exclaimed in relief, standing before the

barricade. "I'm glad the idiot didn't have a gun!"

Clapham and Karayn laughed until they convulsed.

Lu warned Ross. "If they don't lock him up, he'll be right out there in the morning."

"You know damned well the Park Police won't lock him up," Ross answered in disgust.

His phone rang and as feared it was Ivorson. "London's hollering for quotes from the defense secretary on credibility, military credibility, Polaris credibility, and most important, U.S. credibility with NATO."

Ross cursed. "I can't go to Whitley with that kind of query!"

"Why the hell not?"

"Would you expect him to admit to less credibility, for Christ's sake! Drunk or sober, he can only admit to strength. And insofar as credibility with NATO is concerned, why the hell doesn't London get its IP man in Brussels to query the NATO commander whether U.S. support is credible? Do you think he'll say anything less than yes? I'm getting goddamm tired of that friggin' word credible!"

"That's too bad, Quent. Go get some quotes for London."

"You're bugging the hell out of me, Merle!"

"Just do your damned job!" Ivorson shouted, slamming the phone in Ross's ear.

I ought to set him up for a fall, Ross thought, but not during the laser crisis.

The bullpen suddenly rose up in angry shouts as the laser came on. Ross cursed the blazing window and yelled for help to repaper it. Lu, Clapham and Karayn rushed over and lent him a hand after donning radsafe goggles. The job done, they insisted he sit in for several hands of bridge to get the game going.

"Okay," he said, "but I've got to work on an impossible query."

"Is Ivorson riding you in the middle of all this?" Lu asked.

231

"More than ever, Lu. I think the laser's touched his head."

"Who's been spared?" Karayn asked as he cleared a desk top.

Shuffling a worn deck of cards, Clapham said, "It just shows that man has learned how to release nature's energy, but he sure as hell isn't mature enough to control the energy. So we see the scientist on their side or ours—it makes no difference—unlock energy without the slightest regard for consequences. Why? Because the scientist is a moral midget."

"There's a quotable quote, Quent," Lu said.

"Be nice," Ross said, "or I won't be your partner."

Ross's first three hands were incredible. He was first dealt eleven hearts. He bid six and made seven. On the next hand he received an ace and king in all four suits, plus a queen and two jacks. He bid and made seven. His third hand fitted Lu's. She bid and made a grand slam that echoed off the walls.

Karayn went berserk as each score was tallied and Ross was afraid to quit. But his streak ended with the fourth hand and for the next two hours Lu and he lost every rubber. Depressed, he snared an eager kibitzer to take his place over Lu's protest, and walked to the NATO latrine to stretch his legs. He discovered Glasscock and Stewart talking across the urinal partition. Stepping alongside of Stewart, he cleared his throat and laughed loudly. Glasscock turned and repeated an old Air Force bromide, "Shorthorns stand close, the man behind you may be barefooted." Stewart and Ross hooted in derision.

Then at the washstand with the water running full force, Glasscock said, "We're discussing the shuttle mission."

"Why here?" Ross asked. "I thought we had a new regime."

Glasscock snorted. "Nobody has called off the gumshoes and the buggers. You can't kill a creature of the government, least of all something sub rosa like internal security. Besides, if we relaxed now, we'd get into bad habits. Okay?"

"Okay," Ross said, his leading question answered.

"I told Terry the shuttle will carry a nuclear device in the cargo hold. It's to be used only if all else fails in destroying the laser," Glasscock said softly.

"So it's not a clean mission?"

"Hardly. We're not about to spend time, muscle and money on the laser kill without succeeding. We're coppering all bets, Quent."

"Does the President know?"

"Someone in the National Security Council knows. He released the nuke. Whether or not he tells the President is his business."

Ross nodded, thinking of the layers of bodies in the decision-making process.

Glasscock continued. "The reason I've backgrounded Terry and now you is that I don't want an inadvertent link made between the shuttle and the nuke. If the query comes up, I will field it. At this point I don't know whether we'll deny it or not. Let's just hope nobody puts two and two together."

Ross read Glasscock's mind. What Glasscock didn't say was that if anyone else in the bullpen came to the shuttle-nuke conclusion, Ross should disabuse the reporter of that angle. After all, if he was constrained from filing, despite prior knowledge, why should another reporter file?

Ross turned to Stewart. "Your boss wants me to play censor."

"If you will," Glasscock answered quickly. Stewart stood silent.

"A fine web you've woven, Noel. I've been caught up in similar intrigues in the past. Can't say I've ever liked it, but do you know what has always saved the situation?"

Glasscock looked at Ross uncomfortably.

"Implausible as it may sound," Ross said, "another

233

crisis of an utterly unrelated origin will supersede this crisis."

"What could possibly top the laser crisis?" Stewart asked.

"Damned if I know, but let me assure you that one is waiting in the wings and it'll be stage center before the laser crisis gets off. The only way I can explain it is that we have a nation of a quarter-billion souls and trillions in material wealth. The dynamism of these forces drives one crisis after another across the Washington stage. What happens as a result of this dynamism? We seem only to transfer personal and professional anguish from one crisis to another as each passes before our eyes."

"Plato's cave?" Stewart asked.

"You take it from there, Terry," Ross said.

"You've put on a hellishly good latrine sermon, Quent," Glasscock stated with admiration.

"Speaking of latrine sermons," Ross added, "brings to mind my youth. I was brought up at the outskirts of New York City and I'd often meet with friends in vacant city lots to ritualistically piss in a circle at some hapless, drowning target—bug, worm, grasshopper, butterfly—reviling it with every obscene word that twelve-year-olds could think of, and then chanting the direst fate for it and all our human foes."

Glasscock recoiled in mock horror. "I'm damned glad I was raised on a cotton farm."

Stewart added, "I came from a small town, thank God."

"To hell with both of you lying, bugging, clean-cut country boys."

Stewart then said, "In a serious vain, Quent, we just got word on Shrimp from the Vandenberg public affairs office. They've thrown his butt into the shuttle simulator to learn emergency procedures. He'll be run ragged until blastoff."

"So there's no time for Shrimp to file," Ross said ruefully. "But while we're still together, I'd like to shift gears for a moment. I'm debating doing a post-mortem on the sacked commanders."

"Don't waste your time," Glasscock advised. "Their replacements are good men. I could write the story as part of an overview as the crisis ends."

"Okay," Ross said amenably. "One more query. My bureau chief is determined that I get quotes from Whitley on U.S. space defense credibility. London is hot on the credibility angle: tactical, strategic and space defense. Even if I got quotes, how can Whitley make anything but a motherhood statement about credible defense? What do you think?"

Glasscock pursed his lips, then said with deliberation, "I don't think we're reaching high enough, Quent, especially for the international press. I'd rather buck it up to Arundel and Fairly at the White House. Let them play with it."

"But then the answer will be tossed to IP's White House leg man, not me."

"So what? It's still in your family," Glasscock said, pushing the latrine door open. They parted in the corridor.

Frustrated, Ross walked slowly to the bullpen. He had to admit to Ivorson that the credibility crap would be enhanced by a White House response.

He found Admiral "Ape" Gibbon behind the barricade in his chair. Ape stood up but Ross nudged him down.

"What's up?" Ross asked.

"Quent, I'm worried spitless about the bad press the Polaris booster failure will get. It'll hurt the hell out of the Polaris family of missiles aboard our subs. Our credibility with Congress will be destroyed."

"Jesus! Not you too!" Ross exploded, but caught hold of himself and said, "Sorry, Ape. I've been involved in a credibility drill for the past hour. But have no fear. The Polaris booster is such a minor part of the overall killer sat fiasco that no one will pay any attention to it, no one will single it out, at least, I won't."

Gibbon jumped up, shook Ross's hand and said, "Quent, if you won't, then nobody will! We'll give you a VIP ride on a Trident sub."

"Thanks, but no thanks," Ross said. Ape disappeared.

Ross sat down and closed his eyes. What an odd handle on power he had. What a crazy position destiny had put him in!

He dialed Marge. As in *Hamlet* she said, "Not a mouse stirring," but reminded him that was in the first act.

"I now know why I married you," he said.

"Why? O why?" she asked.

"For all those curves, mental and physical, tossed at me out of left field."

"I love you too," she said, hanging up.

He called Ivorson to say that the White House leg man would get some sort of response to the credibility query since General Glasscock had tossed it at Fairly.

Ivorson begged off for another call.

Ross dropped the receiver onto its cradle like a bombardier, then saw Major General Don Whitehead of the Army standing alongside the barricade.

"Step into my parlor, Don," Ross said warmly. "You're the third of three two-star types to talk at me this past hour. It's a damned good thing this sudden show of brass doesn't turn my head."

Whitehead seated himself ramrod straight and said, "That's the Army's problem. We're lastest with the mostest, bailing out the Marines, the Navy, even the Air Force, and never a line in print."

"True," Ross answered, stoking a thin, needle-stemmed clay pipe. "But in your heart you know you're the best. So what's new?"

"I've got good news and bad news, Quent."

"Give me the bad news first. That's copy."

"The Army's desertion rate is the highest in our history."

"What's the good news?"

"Our recruiting offices are swamped with volunteers.

We can't process the recruits fast enough. It's broken every record for any week in war or peace."

"And how do we stand on balance?"

"Ten to one in favor of new enlistments."

"I'll file it as soon as I get some copy up and out of the way on the space shuttle, Don. The shuttle's due to blast off in the morning on a killer sat mission against the laser, as I'm sure you know. We have a pool reporter out of the bullpen aboard the shuttle and his copy is first priority. Meanwhile, get your statistics to me and I'll file soonest."

"Great!" Whitehead said, then added, "I hear Noel is reactivating Defense news release handouts. We may be forced to go his route with the recruiting information."

"No problem at all, Don," Ross said. "I'm alerted to your story and I'll move it. Just resign yourself that it's no shuttle flight and that it's upbeat to boot. Not page one. Page two, maybe."

Whitehead marched off with a smile. Ross was glad to accommodate him, if only that the Army rarely surfaced in the bullpen. Its role seemed to be that of underdog, janitor to the armed forces, catchall for all the non-combat crap the administration flung in its direction.

Lu surged around the barricade and snickered.

"Go to bed!" he barked.

"C'mon, Quent, I need a partner. The game's still going."

"Go find some other pigeon, if you can. It's time for me to fold up and get some sleep, even if you don't," he said, pulling out the bedroll and blanket.

"Play just one hand, please?"

He shook his head in disapproval.

She grabbed the bedroll and blanket, flung them high over the barricade, then laughed at the prank. Cheers rose from the other side.

"You're godawful!" he said, resigned to his fate.

To Lu's delight they won the first rubber handily. The

second dragged on and on because the cards were evenly divided and one hand after another was thrown in. Finally, out of fatigue, Ross made a psychic bid and went down seven tricks. Lu became apoplectic, unwittingly administering the coup de grace. Ross fled to the barricade, retrieved the bedroll and blanket and sacked out atop the desk.

Ivorson's call awakened him at dawn, after the laser and before the sun. Through sleepy reflex Ross agreed to file a shuttle bulletin and moments later tried to recall what he had said, but would not call Ivorson back. Under such circumstances Ivorson always embroidered the task.

Stewart shook him, whispering, "The general invites you to see the blastoff."

Ross rubbed his face. "I haven't washed, shaved or combed my hair."

"Who cares?" Stewart said, grabbing him by the arm. "It's dark in there. Let's go!"

Ross's left leg felt painfully stiff, but he kept at Stewart's pace down to the elevator. Although the air policemen imposed a short wait, Glasscock soon ushered him to the console for a closed-circuit look at the shuttle's departure. The countdown was in the final seconds and holds were minor. Ross again sat between them—favored seats—although the space planetarium was crowded with shadowy forms. Insignia glinted on every shoulder and almost every face was free of eyeglasses.

Glasscock leaned toward Ross and said quietly, "No need to put on the headset, Quent. Just watch and pray with us that the Air Force hacks its first space combat mission."

Ross riveted his eyes on the TV screen while the announcer's voice in the Vandenberg blockhouse rang out hypnotically with an unexpected five-minute hold. In the theaterlike darkness he glanced furtively at the moving alphanumerics above his head, then recognized the seven-man Air Council seated at a larger console below him, a group that rarely convened outside the chief of staff's office. Ross was amazed that Glasscock dared bring him into the planetarium, whether as hostage, friend, or as a prank. In any case, a low profile was desirable and he prepared himself to spring up and leave at the slightest signal, or to hold his place deferentially if the chief of staff elected to depart first in accord with military custom.

On the screen the shuttle, dwarfed by its two main launching tanks, looked like a white moth clinging halfway up the twin trunks of a massive, fog-shrouded tree.

Stewart whispered, "Imagine Shrimp lying on his back in that thing. Twenty-four hours ago he was racing around the bullpen. What a lucky guy!"

"Lucky guy, indeed," Ross said, hearing the ring of jealousy in his own ears.

Glasscock explained, "There's an on-board TV transmitter that monitors the shuttle's instruments for the experts down in ground control. After blastoff, we'll get a peek at all the dials and gauges and they'll tell us precisely whether all's well or not."

Because of the shuttle's exciting appearance and the unnerving fact that human beings were aboard, its departure from earth imparted an extra visual and emotional impact on observers. The planetarium was tense at blastoff, but the launch proved routine. The shuttle quickly cut through the earth's atmosphere and outdistanced the tracking cameras. Ross shuddered at the thought of the shuttle crashing at blastoff with the nuclear device aboard and wondered how many others in the planetarium shared the same concern. Glasscock's prediction materialized with a series of TV shots that locked onto the shuttle's flight instruments, then scanned and locked on others. Ross swore he saw Shrimp's small hands in several sequences. Minutes later the shuttle jettisoned its huge main tanks and then flew on three hydrogen-oxygen engines toward its rendezvous with the laser satellite some twenty hours away.

The chief of staff rose abruptly and departed with his entourage, full of happy technical chatter. Glasscock led Ross to the log which they countersigned wordlessly. Glasscock returned to the planetarium and Ross retraced his steps to the bullpen, unsure of what to file on the blastoff. Instead, he cleaned up at the NATO latrine, wishing for a shower and change of clothes. His feet felt wet, almost sloshing as he walked the ramp to the cafeteria for a solitary breakfast. Scrapple and fried eggs were the perennial pleasure, but while he ate he remembered he had to file without Shrimp's lead-in paragraph.

Nefertiti called. At Brentano's he found himself staring at her limestone bust. She was King Tut's aunt, the most beautiful woman of antiquity or of any other time. Then it occurred to him that Lu's nose closely resembled Nefertiti's, but all else ended there. Trudging up the ramp to seek out Stewart in the Defense newsroom, he speculated whether Nefertiti had surviving progeny, and if so, through what devious bloodline had Lu inherited that dominant nose gene. More was known about Lupe's poodle ancestry than of his or Lu's forebears.

In the newsroom Stewart gave Ross short shrift on shuttle information. "All the Vandenberg public affairs office will release is that a space shuttle launch took place successfully this morning, Quent. You can invent such words yourself. Vandenberg will not admit to a killer sat launch."

"Why not?"

"Policy, Quent. Defense insists that Canaveral and Vandenberg never divulge the nature or purpose of any space launch, other than it got off successfully, or it did not. Period."

"That's a helluva lot of help!"

"I thought you knew. NASA can brag all it wants to

about space shots, since their stuff is peaceful. Defense is prohibited from discussing space launches until after the fact. Unfortunately, this shuttle launch falls into that category."

"So with Shrimp up there, entranced by the drama, not filing a friggin' word, or with his hands full with knobs and switches and unable to transmit copy, we've got a news blackout on the flight."

"That's correct, Quent."

"I've been set up!"

"Not exactly. You pressed Fairly to put a man aboard the shuttle. The White House isn't about to scoop its pool reporter, nor will it let Defense do so. So you've got a double whammy working against you."

"If Shrimp files nothing until touchdown at Edwards AFB, there are no progress reports, no eyewitness accounts of the laser kill, nothing for forty-eight hours!"

"Nothing is quite right, Quent."

"I'll be a son of a bitch!" Ross spluttered. "And I'm boxed in on the other end. I can't print a goddamned word on the intercept displayed in the planetarium."

"Right again."

"I might as well be working for Fairly. I should've taken the job."

Stewart laughed. "Amazing how things work out, Quent."

Ross rubbed his brow. "I helped engineer this news blackout by putting Shrimp aboard, now I've got to find a way to unengineer the blackout."

Cursing, he turned out of the newsroom and walked directly to the ticker, flipped on the switch and the noise of the whirring motor prodded him into action. He cracked his knuckles and began filing.

BULLETIN:
OVER "A" CIRCUITS
DATELINE WASHINGTON THIS DATE
BYLINE QUENTIN ROSS, MILITARY ANALYST,

THE PENTAGON
SHUTTLE STREAKS TO RENDEZVOUS

EARLY THIS MORNING THE UNITED STATES THREW THE MANNED SPACE SHUTTLE, ITS ACE IN THE HOLE, AT THE LASER SATELLITE IN A BRILLIANT TECHNICAL COUNTERMEASURE TO END THE BLINDING BLITZ PARALYZING THE NATION FOR THE PAST THREE NIGHTS.

THE SHUTTLE BEGAN ITS KILLER SATELLITE JOURNEY INTO SPACE WITH NO PUBLIC NOTICE OR FANFARE, BLASTING OFF FROM CALIFORNIA'S VANDENBERG AIR FORCE BASE WITHOUT INCIDENT SHORTLY AFTER THE LASER WAS TURNED OFF BY THE UNKNOWN FOE.

THE THREE-MAN SHUTTLE CREW, INCLUDING A POOL REPORTER, IS TRAVELING 66,000 MILES THROUGH SPACE ON THE 24-HOUR INTERCEPT MISSION. BECAUSE OF THE PRESENCE OF HUMAN INTELLIGENCE ABOARD THE SHUTTLE, INFLIGHT EMERGENCIES AND COURSE CORRECTIONS CAN BE SOLVED WITHOUT TOTAL DEPENDENCE ON GROUND-BASED COMPUTERS AND OTHER SUPPORT EQUIPMENT. HOW THE SHUTTLE CREW WILL DISARM OR DESTROY THE LASER HAS NOT BEEN DIVULGED, BUT SPACE EXPERTS SPECULATE THAT THE LASER SATELLITE MAY BE SIMPLY NUDGED OUT OF GEOSYNCHRONOUS ORBIT OR INCAPACITATED BY SMASHING ITS RECEIVING ANTENNAS. OTHER POSSIBLE TECHNIQUES INCLUDE PLACING AN EXPLOSIVE CHARGE OF DYNAMITE ON OR NEAR THE SATELLITE ITSELF, OR ZAPPING THE LASER DEVICE ABOARD THE SATELLITE WITH AN ANTILASER LASER GUN CARRIED ABOARD THE SHUTTLE AND AIMED BY A CREW MEMBER. AN ADVANTAGE OF THE

LAST METHOD IS THAT THE SHUTTLE NEED NOT FLY ON A PRECISE COLLISION TRAJECTORY OR ENTER A MATCHED-ORBIT FLIGHT TO DESTROY THE LASER. SINCE MANY OPTIONS ARE AVAILABLE TO THE SHUTTLE CREW, IT IS UNLIKELY THAT THE LASER SATELLITE'S GROUND CONTROLLERS CAN SUCCESSFULLY MANEUVER IT TO EVADE THE SHUTTLE ATTACK.

DESPITE THE PRESENCE OF A POOL REPORTER, THE SPACE SHUTTLE IS TRAVELING IN A NEWS BLACKOUT, PRESUMABLY TO DENY THE ENEMY ANY LAST-MINUTE TACTICAL INFORMATION REGARDING DESTRUCT INTENTIONS. ADDITIONALLY, THE DEFENSE DEPARTMENT IS HOLDING FAST TO ITS LONG-STANDING POLICY OF RELEASING NO INFORMATION REGARDING SPACE DEFENSE MISSIONS UNTIL LONG AFTER THE FACT. IT IS ANTICIPATED, HOWEVER, THAT THE WHITE HOUSE MAY PREEMPT THE DEFENSE POSITION AND ANNOUNCE RESULTS OF THE ATTEMPTED LASER INTERCEPT EARLY TOMORROW. END.
END BULLETIN.

Well, oh, well, I've got my lick in, Ross thought, turning off the machine and steeling himself for whatever reprisals lay in store. The news is first, he again reassured himself, and all else must follow.

To his surprise he found the bullpen deserted, then discovered Lu's note on his desk: WE'RE WATCHING THE PROTEST—COME JOIN THE FRAY!

Curiosity got the best of him and he hurried down the corridor to the Mall entrance, ideally suited for demonstrations with its expanse of flat steps, a large, concrete apron, and endless acres of gently sloping lawn. Several platoons of marines at parade rest stood on the steps.

Park Police with bullhorns patrolled the very edge of the apron, apparently the physical boundary set for demonstrators. They had, however, the limitless area of grass on which to stage their protest and it lay within the shadow of the Pentagon's towering walls.

Ross indicated he wanted out and a marine made him sign the departure log. "I hope you know what you're doing, sir," the marine warned. "That's a damned ugly crowd out there."

"Can't be much worse than the Vietnam protests," Ross answered with a shrug, then threaded his way through the cordon of marines by showing his Pentagon press pass. He found Lu, Karayn and Clapham standing near the Park Police line, reading the placards waved by the shouting, chanting mob as they moved past their vantage point:

SAVE
OUR
CHILDREN'S
EYES

THINK
PEACE

MOTHERS
MARCHING
FOR
PEACE

PISS
ON
THE
PENTAGON

AMERICA
STOP WASTING
WORLD
RESOURCES!

TODAY
IS
JUDGMENT
DAY!

GODLESS
AMERICA
ASKS FOR
THE
LASER BLITZ!

PEACE
THRU
PRAYER

LOVE
THY
NEIGHBOR

NONVIOLENCE
IS
THE
ONLY
WAY

PRAY
THAT
NIGHT
WILL
FALL

"What a collection of garbage!" Lu exclaimed. "At least during Vietnam they were united on a single issue."

"This mob is just as vicious. I feel it!" Karayn said.

Ross stared at the ski masks, black hoods with peepholes, white hoods with no apparent eyeholes, saucer-sized sunglasses, welder's masks, white canes waved as cudgels and dogs in bizarre seeing-eye harnesses. Kids picked up clods of burned grass and flung it at the police. Broken branches with curled brown leaves came sailing toward the Pentagon, along with cries of "You caused it!

Lu said she didn't like the sound of the staccato chanting and urged they go to the cafeteria. She had seen enough, yet made no attempt to move.

"A terrible example of reverse psychology," Karayn said in disgust.

Lu pointed to a knot of demonstrators. "Look, they're standing right where we had our picnic. The nerve of those bastards!"

"It's park property," Clapham said. "We did our crazy thing and they're doing theirs. Okay?" He said more about Lu's inane remark but his voice was drowned out by the seething mob's shouting. Then on some sort of prearranged signal the mob surged at the police line, hurling placards, sticks, rocks and debris. Ross saw a brick flying directly at them, shoved Lu down the steps and ducked at the last moment. The brick hit Karayn square in the face.

Karayn bellowed and fell backward. Ross heard a second sickening thud as Karayn's head struck the steps. He moaned and writhed, one hand on bloodied eyes while the other flailed the air, then convulsed and lay deadly still. The police line held as Ross threw the brick back at the retreating mob. Clapham stooped, mesmerized, over Karayn's form. Lu sobbed uncontrollably. Ross ran up the steps and asked a marine to call an ambulance. He returned to Karayn's side only seconds before the marine corpsmen arrived with a stretcher. They carried him at a practiced trot to a GI ambulance parked near the steps but out of harm's way. Ross followed and talked himself into the seat next to the driver, who said his instructions were to take all civilian casualties to Doctors Hospital in the District, about five miles distant. During the fast but noiseless ride the corpsmen administered plasma and oxygen to the unconscious Karayn.

The staff in emergency barred Ross while a call was

made to the Park Police. He was instructed to fill out an eyewitness report in lieu of interrogation simply because the investigative units were overwhelmed. Afterward, he answered a questionnaire as best he could for the hospital's administrator, who quickly arranged for notification of Karayn's next of kin in New York.

He found a chair in the stark hall and prayed for Karayn. An hour later he called Lu and said there was no word and asked that she call Marge. Stewart arrived and paced silently while emergency processed a steady stream of laser-related accidents.

Later still, Ross jumped up, shaking his head. "Terry, Karayn's been in there over two hours!"

"Probably plastic surgery. It takes a lot of time."

An operating surgeon stuck his head into the hall and called for Ross, then motioned him near. Stewart followed. "It doesn't look good," the surgeon said bleakly. "Mr. Karayn suffered smashed cheekbones, among other massive facial injuries. A bloodclot formed and it's only a short distance to the brain. We're doing what we can surgically, and he'll be moved to intensive care after the operation. I suggest you wait there."

Ross nodded, then looked grimly at Stewart. "I'll stay until someone from the family arrives. I hope they beat the laser. I think Milo has a girlfriend hanging around in the area, but to hell with that problem right now."

"How are you getting back?" Stewart asked.

"Damned if I know, Terry, and damned if I care."

"If the shuttle makes news, shall I get word to you here?"

"Tell Lu. She'll cover for me. She'll save a carbon."

"Quent, please call General Glasscock when you get the medical report. He'll want to mention something current on Karayn's condition at his press briefing, I'm sure."

"And while we're at it," Ross said, "call Karayn's office even if you think they have all the facts. It will be a very proper gesture coming from the military at the Pentagon."

"Okay," Stewart said sadly as he left.

Ross sought out the intensive care waiting room. It proved chaotic because of the overload of patients. He wanted to avoid its tensions and anxieties, its mixture of age, race and language thrown together in common misery, but since smoking was forbidden in the halls, he remained and propped himself up against a wall, pipe ablaze at the peril of a near-empty tobacco pouch.

Later, he showed his press credentials to the duty nurse, a ploy that never failed to break the ice in starting conversations. He said he had a close, working relationship with Karayn and was standing by until the family came from New York. She said simply that Karayn's condition was poor and only a miracle would save his life. Ross thanked her, feeling the tears well up in his eyes, then dragged himself back to the waiting room.

Shortly before four o'clock he checked back with the nurse who said Karayn's condition was unchanged. Ross found a pay phone and advised Stewart, then asked if there were any word from Shrimp.

"Not directly," Stewart replied. "The flight is right on course with no major hitches. But a communications blackout is now in effect, and no further conversations or signals are allowed between the shuttle and the ground in order to keep the laser sat's ground controllers guessing about the shuttle's tactics."

"Guess I can't file that."

"I hope not, Quent. Stay put for as long as you want and if anything breaks, we'll call. Wait, here's Lu."

"How is he?" she asked in a breaking voice.

"Poor, Lu."

"Shall I come out?"

"I'd advise against it. Hospital waiting rooms are damned depressing. Tell Clapham he need not come. This intensive care waiting room is splitting at the seams. No one can help the patient anyway. I guess we're born alone to die alone."

"What can we do for you?"

"I'm running out of tobacco and change for the pay phone. If the laser traps me here, I may stay the night. Tell Marge. Meanwhile, let's say prayers."

Lu cried and Ross hung up gently. He then dialed Ivorson with the last of his change.

Ivorson said, "I hear you're at the hospital with Karayn."

"I'm waiting for his family to show up."

"Will he make it?"

"They removed a blood clot from his brain caused by the flying brick. His condition is poor."

"Are you wired into the Pentagon?"

"Merle, I know what's going on. A blackout has been laid on the shuttle flight, so there's no copy to be had until they hit or miss the laser."

"You'll move on that announcement?"

"I won't, but it doesn't matter."

"Why the hell not?"

"Because the announcement is bigger than Whitley and the Pentagon, especially if they destroy the laser. It's White House stuff for sure. Read my last bulletin again, for Christ's sake!"

"Don't drop the ball, Quent. It'll be your ass if you do!"

"Thanks, boss," Ross said as Ivorson got off the line.

Goddamned insensitive son of a bitch, Ross muttered to himself, then at the duty nurse's desk he volunteered blood in Karayn's behalf. She handed him a questionnaire and said blood was accepted only in the morning. He tossed the paper into a wastepaper basket and walked away.

The hospital's cafeteria food was several marks below that of the Pentagon, but the cashier rewarded him with enough change to phone for at least an hour. He checked with the newly arrived night-duty nurse, who with a wry mouth said Karayn's condition hadn't changed, but not to wander off too far. In turn, he tried to draw more out of her but she balked. At that moment the laser suddenly illuminated the hospital's interior. She ran off to draw blinds and to quiet patients. When she returned, Ross said, "Cheer up, nurse! This may be the last night of the laser blitz!"

"Why would you say that?" she asked as if he were a fool.

"There's a very serious attempt underway right now to kill it."

"Please go back to the waiting room, mister. We'll call you."

He retreated and it occurred to him that the laser had returned well before sunset. Was it to blind the approaching shuttle crew? Appalled at the thought, he rekindled the pipe just as the nurse opened the door and asked that he step ouside.

"Are you Mr. Karayn's next of kin?"

"No. I'm representing friends and his family until they arrive."

A waiting surgeon in an operating gown stepped forward and said, "Mr. Karayn died several minutes ago. He had the best medical attention we could provide, but under the circumstances, massive head injuries, it was impossible to save him. I'm very sorry."

Ross said, "I'm sorry too. It was a needless, senseless death."

The surgeon bowed and departed, but the nurse said, "When Mr. Karayn's relatives arrive, will you please tell them to ask for Dr. Millikin? It would be best if you met them in the main lobby. And I hope you're right about the laser. We can't take much more of it."

Ross stared at the ceiling as she returned to her station. What a lousy coincidence, he thought. Karayn died as the laser came on, and he was the only one so damned sure it would decay.

In the lobby he watched carefully for anyone approaching the information desk and then realized the laser was preventing night traffic. If Karayn's relatives hadn't made it before the blitz, the odds were it would be well in the morning before they arrived. Poor Karayn, ill-fated before and after death.

Ross called Stewart and asked, "Terry, can you rescue me? Karayn's relatives didn't show up. Nothing more can happen here till morning."

"Okay," Stewart replied, "but it might take some time. Do you have your radsafe goggles with you?"

"Hell, no! It was the last thing on my mind, Terry. Bring along an extra, if you will. Also, drive Cuspidor over. The keys are in it."

Stewart said he'd disentangle himself at the first possible minute. Ross settled down in a leather chair for the long wait.

His thoughts centered on Karayn, which he knew was quite natural. Though not close, their relationship was longstanding and genial, complementary in news coverage, each coveting the other's role. Karayn was either secretive in his personal life or Ross had never cared to know. It was odd that fate or destiny chose Karayn to be the first bullpen reporter to die in the laser blitz and that Ross was drawn for the deathwatch.

Head heavy, he dozed off, dreaming that Marge and he were on vacation along a craggy coast of Scotland and they had just caught a sea otter's ring of bright water. The otter surfaced and Marge was petting it when he was awakened by Stewart's gentle shaking.

"Ready?" Stewart asked, proffering the goggles.

Disoriented, Ross groped clumsily. Stewart laughed and fitted the headstrap to his head. "Now we're ready," Stewart said, guiding Ross to the door. At curbside, Ross adjusted the density wheel on the nosebridge and climbed into Cuspidor. Stewart drove off like a jack rabbit, crossed Memorial Bridge and in minutes entered Mall parking.

"Seems like I remember this goddamned place," Ross said.

"Hopefully never again under the laser blitz."

"Are you that sure, Terry?"

"Let me just say General Glasscock will invite you to see the intercept. He was pleased with the way you handled the last bulletin."

"I had qualms about Glasscock's reaction, but then, one never knows how people react to copy. Tell me, what time is this great moment of truth, the intercept?"

"They're ahead of schedule. It now looks like two o'clock, so don't run off somewhere."

"That's very funny, Terry," Ross said as they presented their Pentagon badges to the marines. After signing in, they parted, Stewart up to the fourth floor and Ross to the bullpen.

Lu, Clapham and others crowded him behind the barricade. He explained quickly that Karayn had suffered massive head and facial injuries and during the ambulance ride the medical corpsmen had indicated he had no chance of survival. But according to the operating surgeon, Karayn died of an embolism or blood clot that entered his brain. Ross guessed the initial injuries, plus radical brain surgery, were more than any mortal could take. None of Karayn's relatives had yet arrived, but he felt it was understandable. Besides, it was just as well that no one else saw Karayn during his last hours.

"What now, Quent?" Lu asked.

"Cary and I will clean out his desk and will box his personal belongings."

"I'll help," Lu said.

"No. Stay out of it."

"But a detective from homicide has already gone through his desk."

"So much the better, Lu. C'mon, Clapham, let's get on with it."

Stepping past Lu, Ross led Clapham to Karayn's desk, but before opening a drawer he said, "Cary, go to the print shop behind the Defense newsroom and bring back three cartons, the kind used to package mimeograph paper."

This gave Ross a chance to riffle through Karayn's correspondence, mementos, photos, travel vouchers, passport, checkbooks, bills and statements, and a mass of odds and ends. He wished he had gotten at Karayn's wallet to extract anything of questionable nature.

When Clapham returned with the cartons, Ross said one was for burning, another to be sent to the family, and the third to *World News*. Lu stood at a distance with hands on hips, consumed with curiosity and disappointment.

Correspondence took the longest to sort out and when in doubt Ross heaved it into burn. He finally found what he was seeking, a welter of letters and photographs from the back of a bottom drawer. Karayn had had several affairs and had sentimentally hung onto the evidence. Ross tossed it all into the carton and breathed a sigh of relief only after dumping the contents into a classified burn depository near the Defense newsroom.

One discovery brought joy, however. Clapham discovered a cigar box filled with two-ounce miniatures of Scotch, bourbon and gin left over from a Defense fact-finding junket to Bermuda's Kindley Field years earlier.

"This cache we'll appropriate and drink right now," Ross announced, waving a bottle. "Pass the cigar box to everyone in the bullpen," he told Clapham. "There are at least two dozen miniatures and that ought to go around."

Lu helped form a circle around Karayn's desk. She said, "Only Milo would have stashed such goodies away. I'm amazed that Shrimp, with his nose for booze, didn't discover the cache."

"That's not very kind, Lu," Clapham said.

"Just joking, Cary," Lu explained lamely.

"No matter," Ross said. "They're both very far away. I propose a toast and we must chug-a-lug the bottles like good reporters."

The bullpen raised its bottles.

"To the repose of Milo Karayn's soul. May he never

hurt in heaven!"

Cheers and amens greeted the toast.

Afterward, Ross said, "Please put the empties back into the cigar box. We don't have a fireplace in the Pentagon, so I'm going to toss them out of my window first thing in the morning."

Stewart came in and Ross admonished him for having missed a toast to the departed. Stewart looked crestfallen. Ross then reached into a pocket, produced a miniature of Scotch and said, "I filched it for you. Drink it now and wish the best for poor Karayn."

"To Milo, he went quick, the Air Force way."

"Well said," Ross agreed. "And what word on Shrimp?"

"They're chugging along on course and ahead of schedule."

"Still optimistic?"

"You bet!"

"I'm glad something's going right, Terry. Do you think the close encounter will give us clues to the laser's identity?"

"Well, we're hoping to establish its origin, but the enemy probably took a shuttle pass into account."

Ross said wearily, "I agree they're too smart technically to betray themselves. The answer is to psych them out, and I'm not going to quit trying."

"Meanwhile, get some rest," Stewart advised. "I'll wake you in time."

Ross agreed to the idea and Stewart helped him spread out the bedroll, then threw the thermal blanket over him and left.

Finding that he couldn't sleep on his face, Ross turned to the wall; but the laser patterns proved disturbing, so he lay on his back and scrutinized the long fingers of dirt that marked the ceiling ventilators. Sleep apparently was not to come.

Lu must have divined his problem for she crept around the barricade and broke into a smile that she had caught him awake.

"Quent," she whispered. "Are you awake? Really awake?"

"Dammit! I am now."

"Did homicide interview you?"

"Yes," he answered, startled by the subject.

"At the hospital?"

"What the hell is this, Lu? I filled out the eyewitness forms."

"Were you questioned?"

"No. The police are spread too thin."

"So the question of the brick never came up?"

"How could it? No." He sat up, yogalike, on the desk.

"They made a big thing of it here as a possible murder weapon."

Ross's heart thumped. "And what did you say?"

"Just that I lost sight of it. Clapham said the same thing."

"Thank God!" Ross said, relieved. "I did a dumb thing. I threw it back at the mob. I'm only sorry I didn't hit one of the bastards."

"You don't mean that!"

"I don't know what I mean, Lu. Why is the damned brick so important? There were at least three eyewitnesses to the fact that it came out of nowhere and clobbered Karayn, you, me and Clapham. And it could have been any one of us, you know!"

"I appreciate your pushing me out of the way, Quent."

"That's not the point! The whole goddamned incident was random. That's what mobs are all about."

"Homicide was looking for fingerprints on the brick."

Ross swore. "They should've disarmed the mob before they marched. It's not that easy to conceal a brick."

"You're absolutely right, Quent. I just wanted you to know the score. Now, go back to sleep. I'm going to the couch."

"I'm too tired to make love tonight, Lu."

He heard her cackle as she walked away.

Ross spread himself out and closed his eyes. Clapham roused him and asked if he knew about the brick. Ross raised up in a fury. "You too, you son of a bitch!"

Clapham drew off, visibly shaken.

Ross leaned against the barricade. "I'm sorry, Cary. I just got through explaining what I know to Lu. Talk to her about the goddamned brick."

"Okay," Clapham said deferentially and disappeared.

Ross rolled onto the bedroll, utterly agitated. Jesus! he thought, I made one friggin' mistake throwing the brick back at the bastards and I guess I'll never hear the end of it!

On impulse he jumped off the desk, ran over to the niche, shook Lu and demanded she get up a game of bridge.

"Are you crazy, Quent? Everybody's bedded down."

"I don't care. I want to play bridge until two o'clock. Then I've got an appointment."

"Who gets two AM appointments around here?"

"I do, dammit! I'll get Clapham and you wake up somebody else."

She looked at him as if he were possessed, but waddled off and found a victim, Vic Heslep of *Family News*.

Ross insisted on Lu as partner. Clapham and Heslep hit it off immediately, especially when Ross forced the bidding on the first three hands and went down in flames each time, doubled and redoubled. Lu got furious, but the next hand was hers without Ross's help. As dummy, he walked out into the corridor and then returned rather contrite.

But luck was not to be his. He turned cautious when Lu wanted to be bold and vice versa. They remained at cross-purposes for endless hands. Stewart finally rescued him, breaking up the game. Clapham and Heslep were elated over the score. Lu whispered to Ross that he owed her one large favor.

Stewart led him to Glasscock at the planetarium and after admittance he was placed at the now-familiar console. To his surprise the TV picture kept breaking up.

"The shuttle's video is strictly a bonus," Glasscock explained. "One TV transmitter is in the cockpit and we've seen its pictures. The other is locked looking forward into the nose of the shuttle and it sees what the pilot sees. We had it installed especially for this intercept and that is what you are looking at now. Okay?"

"Okay," Ross replied, "but why is the picture so bad?"

"I hope the interference is only temporary. While the technicians are trying to filter out the interference, Quent, let's look overhead." He pointed to two sets of green-flashing alphanumerics, SS-13 moving toward the stationary LS-1, on an obvious collision course against the black velvet of the space dome. Countdown was underway. Thirty minutes remained until intercept.

The shuttle pilot's voice rang cool and clear as he announced the time hacks, even though transmission came through a scrambling device. Ross put himself into Shrimp's place and decided that Shrimp need not file one damned word. A recap of his experience would suffice.

Glasscock said the shuttle's course toward the laser satellite was tangential to the diffuse light being shed over the United States for obvious reasons. Suddenly, the TV picture cleared and murmurs of approval rose in the planetarium.

At twenty minutes before intercept the pilot reported that the laser satellite had a twin, an object coupled to it, invisible on radar, yet just then picked up optically by the copilot.

Glasscock turned excitedly to Ross. "So that explains the laser's power source! I'll bet it's an electron ring accelerator pumping juice into the laser. But how did they ever miniaturize the accelerator, then cram it into a satellite?"

"And how did they disguise it?" Ross asked.

"That's the easiest part. An antiradar reflective paint. We've used it for years on special mission aircraft. They also managed to get this accelerator satellite into space without our detection. It had to be another air launch, probably before the laser."

"It sure got by Symonds Observatory!"

"Oh, well," Glasscock said, "there's so much crap zooming in and out of near-earth orbit that I'm amazed we can still sort it out."

Ross grimaced at the thought of space pollution of such magnitude.

Pointing then to the TV screen, Glasscock added, "Look closely now at the laser satellite. You'll find a faint outline of the accelerator satellite latched onto it. Together, they resemble a dumbbell. As the shuttle nears, their presence will become inescapable."

At ten minutes before intercept the shuttle made a pronounced course correction, maneuvering itself directly into the laser satellite's beam. The video suffered a whiteout. Ross asked, "How can the shuttle crew keep from being blinded?"

Glasscock roared. "Same radsafe goggles that you've got! This particular shuttle maneuver is the payoff. Let's hope it works!"

"What are they doing?"

"They're zapping the satellite's laser-emitting device with an on-board antilaser laser gun. The gun's pulses hopefully will burn out the satellite's laser. Fighting fire with fire, Quent. Our problem has been storing enough energy on the shuttle to make the antilaser laser gun work."

"How will they—or we—know if they were successful?"

Glasscock laughed. "You damned fool! The laser light will go out."

Ross laughed at himself, then looked at his watch—two AM—and prayed his favorite prayer for help.

"We got it!" the pilot's voice boomed over the audio system as the TV screen came back on. Ross saw the laser satellite and its twin accelerator outlined by the sun's rays, but the laser beam was gone. Wild cheers filled the planetarium.

Glasscock turned to Stewart. "Run outside, Terry, and make damned sure it's true. Then bring your ass back here and report to us."

Stewart sped off. Glasscock beamed and the planetarium quieted down. Ross looked up at the alphanumerics. SS-13 and LS-1 almost touched.

"Now what?" Ross asked.

"Now for the kill," Glasscock said jubilantly. "The shuttle will dump a small satellite loaded with high explosives to blow up the twins. We call our satellite *Remora*. It has a proximity fuse to detonate itself when it nears the target. We don't need a direct hit because all satellites are surprisingly fragile. After *Remora* leaves the shuttle's cargo hold, it will home in on the twins and destroy them. End of caper!"

"Won't we be accused of overkill?"

"Balls!" Glasscock said. "We want to stamp the goddamned laser sat to death. We don't want the other side to revive it and use it again in any way, shape or form. And I hope the United States learns a lesson that being noble and trusting is a sure road to national suicide. It's a naughty world out there, Quent. We lost the wars in Korea and Vietnam because we drafted men instead of drafting superior technology, and now we damned near lost this one because of the other side's technology and the will to use it. We've got to accept the fact whenever another nation gets the edge on us that somehow, someway, we will pay because envy and hatred go hand in hand against us."

At five minutes before intercept, Ross sat fascinated by the growth of the twin satellites on the TV screen. Glasscock said the shuttle crew was taking pictures with several kinds of cameras to help identify the satellites' origin, although he very much doubted the enemy had left telltale external evidence.

Stewart returned, took his place next to Ross and reported happily that the laser had been extinguished. Radio reports described mobs surging into the streets, some celebrating with a last-minute splurge of looting. Thousands simply basked in the darkness. Ross hoped Fairly was preparing a presidential statement. It would be needed for a lead-in to his bulletin, as much as he detested pronunciamentos. Now the problem was to get out of the planetarium gracefully.

"I must file a bulletin quickly for London and Tokyo," he advised Glasscock.

"Quent, you'll have to wait until the pass is completed. We're just minutes away."

Ross sat back and watched the screen while working the bulletin in his head. There was no doubt the shuttle was closing in on the dumbbell-shaped satellites at a furious rate of speed. The overhead alphanumerics fused into one blur and the TV screen overflowed with the satellite's image. Suddenly the TV picture shook violently. A gasp rose in the planetarium as the shuttle pilot called Vandenberg ground control.

"SS-13 to Van. We've collided with LS-1. Will assess damage, but first dumping *Remora* on schedule. Over."

"Roger, SS-13," Vandenberg control acknowledged without betraying concern.

Seconds later the pilot called in, "Van Control, *Remora* launched on schedule and looks good. New subject. SS-13 collided with antennas of LS-1. We suspect substantial damage to right wing's leading edge flap. Skin wrinkled at wing root. Hope spar is still intact. We now anticipate some lateral control problems during final descent. All emergency procedures will be reviewed during our twenty-hour letdown. Please provide contingency computer programs not later than five hours before touchdown. Will call back in one hour. Out."

"Roger, SS-13. Will advise."

Glasscock jumped up, almost violent. "One goddamned thing after another! Christ! We better not lose the shuttle!"

Ross's heart tripped. In mind's eye he couldn't stop the scenario of the shuttle screaming down to earth, out of control and red as a flaming meteor. Poor Shrimp!

"There's nothing more for us here," Glasscock said, visibly shattered. "I've got to cushion this fall politically, and you've got a bulletin to file, Quent."

"And no rest for the wicked," Ross said, attempting a faint touch of humor. "Thanks for letting me share in this experience. I'll do what I can to backstop the mission."

Glasscock ushered him to the log. "We've been a good team, Quent. There's more to come, so check with Terry or me before you go home. Okay?"

"Okay," Ross said automatically. Returning to the bullpen he thought *okay* was to adults what *mama* was to children, yet nothing was okay in Washington.

He wandered to the ticker room and found bulletins on the laser quench on every teletype, including his own. Nationwide civilian reaction had the play, but not a word on the shuttle. Who cared? he thought, entering the bullpen. The place was in an uproar, so he backed out and went to a pay phone.

Fairly answered and Ross put it bluntly. "I must have a presidential quote now, Phil. London and Tokyo will be all over my ass in another fifteen minutes."

Fairly was quick to unload his own problem. "Arundel hasn't prepositioned any words for the President to approve, Quent. I sure as hell am not going to do his homework for him."

"Where does that leave me?"

"Up shit creek without a paddle."

Ross scoffed at the analogy, then said, "Do you and I have the same picture, technically, of what happened up there?"

"You probably know more than I do, you bastard, so correct me if I'm wrong. The Air Force aide briefed the President just minutes ago. It went like this: The shuttle crew burned out the laser with an antilaser zap gun. Then they collided with the satellite's antennas, damaging the shuttle, but managed to eject a high-explosives package to blow up the laser satellite and its power source after traveling a safe distance away. Now all that's left is a hairy, possibly deadly landing, which in the President's words 'takes the frosting right off the cake' so he won't identify with the shuttle's precarious position. That's for Whitley to handle, regardless of what your bulletin alleged. In fact, the President's pissed off that the Air Force can't do anything right and is putting him through another *Perils of Pauline* routine. He wished it had been a NASA crew, and it would've been, except that NASA guys are good guys, dedicated only to peaceful missions in space. Okay?"

Ross swore. "Yeah, you've got all the facts, Phil, but with a perverted twist. I'm still hungry for presidential words because I'm filing as soon as I hang up."

"There's no way I can accommodate you, buddy. Make up some presidential words. You've done it before. London or Tokyo won't hang you for a misstatement."

"Thanks a lot," Ross said, then walked slowly to the ticker room. What a friggin' government! Why did it always bring out the worst in everyone?

Lu accosted him in the corridor. "Where the hell have you been?" she demanded. "What's up?"

"I can't talk. I've got to file, but don't stand over me. You'll get a carbon. Okay?"

"Okay," she said and moved off.

He cracked his knuckles over the teletype and began.

BULLETIN:
OVER "A" CIRCUITS
DATELINE WASHINGTON THIS DATE
BYLINE QUENTIN ROSS, MILITARY ANALYST,

THE PENTAGON
SHUTTLE KILLS LASER

THE UNITED STATES EMERGED VICTORIOUS IN THE FIRST SPACE WAR WHEN AN AIR FORCE SHUTTLE ATTACKED AND DESTROYED A LASER SATELLITE BLITZING THE NATION FOR FOUR SUCCESSIVE NIGHTS FROM AN ALMOST INVULNERABLE POSITION 66,000 MILES IN SPACE. THE KILL OCCURRED AT TWO A.M. TODAY, WASHINGTON TIME.

IN A BRILLIANT TACTICAL SWEEP WHILE TRAVELING AT 8,000 FEET PER SECOND, THE SHUTTLE CREW FIRST BURNED OUT THE LASER-EMITTING DEVICE ABOARD THE SATELLITE WITH AN ANTI-LASER GUN, THEN PHOTOGRAPHED THE DEAD SATELLITE FOR CLUES TO ITS ORIGIN. THE LASER SATELLITE'S DESTRUCTION WAS ASSURED WHEN THE SHUTTLE EJECTED A KILLER PACKAGE APTLY NAMED *REMORA* WHICH WAS ARMED WITH HIGH EXPLOSIVES, TIPPED WITH A PROXIMITY FUSE AND GUIDED TO ITS LASER TARGET BY AN UNERRING HOMING DEVICE.

THE SHUTTLE CREW DISCOVERED THROUGH OPTICAL MEANS ONLY MINUTES BEFORE THE ENCOUNTER THAT THE LASER SATELLITE HAD A TWIN SATELLITE ATTACHED TO IT. THE COMBINED SATELLITES RESEMBLED A DUMBBELL FLOATING IN SPACE. AIR FORCE EXPERTS IN GROUND CONTROL DEDUCED IMMEDIATELY THAT THE SECOND SATELLITE ACTUALLY WAS THE LASER'S SECRET POWER SOURCE, MOST PROBABLY A MINIATURIZED ELECTRON RING ACCELERATOR. ALTHOUGH IMPOSSIBLE UNDER MISSION CONSTRAINTS,

CAPTURE OF THE ELECTRON RING ACCELERATOR BY THE SHUTTLE CREW FOR TRANSPORT IN THE SHUTTLE'S CARGO BAY FOR RETURN TO EARTH WOULD HAVE BEEN PRIZED BECAUSE NO SUCH HIGH-ENERGY DEVICE OF SCALED-DOWN SIZE EXISTS IN WESTERN TECHNOLOGY TODAY. LAUNCH OF THE SECRET TWIN ELUDED DETECTION AND ITS PRESENCE REMAINED UNKNOWN UNTIL ACTUAL INTERCEPT. APPARENTLY COATED WITH ANTIRADAR REFLECTIVE PAINT, THE SECRET TWIN WAS SUCCESSFULLY MANEUVERED IN SPACE FOR PERFECT MATING WITH THE LASER SATELLITE, A DRAMATIC EXAMPLE OF ADVANCED SPACE TECHNOLOGY THAT STILL POSES A THREAT TO THE UNITED STATES.

SHORTLY AFTER INTERCEPTING THE LASER SATELLITE, THE SHUTTLE PILOT ADVISED VANDENBERG GROUND CONTROL IN CALIFORNIA THAT HE HAD COLLIDED WITH THE SATELLITES' ANTENNAS OR OTHER EXTERNAL GEAR, CAUSING STRUCTURAL DAMAGE TO THE SHUTTLE'S RIGHT WING. HE REPORTED THAT SPACE FLIGHT CHARACTERISTICS REMAINED UNCHANGED BUT SOME DIFFICULTY WAS TO BE EXPECTED WHEN THE SHUTTLE REENTERED THE EARTH'S ATOMSPHERE. WHETHER THE ACCIDENT WAS DUE TO PILOT ERROR, GUIDANCE INACCURACIES OR OTHER FACTORS IS YET UNKNOWN. HOWEVER, THE AIR FORCE, ALONG WITH THE SHUTTLE'S MANUFACTURER AND THE SHUTTLE CREW ITSELF, HAS NEARLY TWENTY HOURS IN WHICH TO ESTABLISH LETDOWN PROCEDURES COVERING ALL POSSIBLE CONTINGENCIES OF FLIGHT. BECAUSE OF PRIOR PLANNING BY THE AIR

FORCE AND NASA, THE SHUTTLE CREW MAY SELECT ONE OF SEVERAL WIDELY SEPARATED EMERGENCY AIRPORTS AT WHICH TO LAND, ALTHOUGH EDWARDS AIR FORCE BASE IN CALIFORNIA WITH ITS FIFTEEN-MILE, UNOBSTRUCTED DRY LAKE BED REMAINS THE MOST LIKELY CHOICE.

THE PRESIDENT WAS REPORTED PLEASED WITH THE DESTRUCTION OF THE LASER SATELLITE, THUS ENDING THE FOUR-NIGHT TERROR BLITZ THAT CAUSED UNTOLD DEATHS, INJURIES AND CHAOS, AS WELL AS HUGE LOSSES IN LIVESTOCK AND CROPS. IT IS ANTICIPATED HE WILL ISSUE A FORMAL STATEMENT BY MIDMORNING TO THE CONGRESS AND THE NATION ACKNOWLEDGING THE END OF THE LASER SIEGE. DEFENSE OFFICIALS EXPRESSED OPTIMISM THAT HE WILL PRESS A WORLDWIDE SEARCH TO DETERMINE THE LASER SATELLITE'S ORIGIN IN ORDER TO DETER FUTURE SPACE ATTACKS. SUCH EXECUTIVE ACTION WOULD MAINTAIN THE NATION'S ARMED FORCES ON EMERGENCY ALERT. BACK-UP SPACE SHUTTLES ARE AVAILABLE IN BOTH NASA AND AIR FORCE INVENTORIES.

THE CRIPPLED SHUTTLE'S HOMEWARD JOURNEY REMAINS UNDER THE PURVIEW OF DEFENSE SECRETARY BROWNING WHITLEY, ACCORDING TO WHITE HOUSE SOURCES. STATUS REPORTS ON THE SHUTTLE'S DESCENT WILL BE RELEASED TO MEDIA AND THE PUBLIC BY THE VANDENBERG AFB PUBLIC AFFAIRS OFFICE. THE SHUTTLE IS EXPECTED TO LAND AT APPROXIMATELY TEN P.M. TONIGHT (WASHINGTON TIME).
END.
END BULLETIN.

NOTE TO EDITORS: BE SURE TO SUPPORT YOUR OWN! PLAN TO ATTEND SHRIMP (ASTRONAUT) LOVERIDGE'S "WELCOME BACK" LUNCHEON AT THE WASHINGTON PRESS CLUB. DETAILS TO BE ANNOUNCED ASAP. END.

Still another mad two-hundred-fifty-plus worder, Ross thought, and yet not enough reported. When this bird lands and we've got Shrimp's bash over with, I'm going to get the hell out of here for a couple of weeks because I can't think anymore. They'll carry me out of here on a stretcher. I know that it takes a younger man to write spot news. There's no flow, no continuity to my copy. I'm surprised Ivorson hasn't jumped me on it. I'm surprised Marge hasn't jumped me over this insane life style. She's the silent victim. But I'll see her in a few minutes if Cuspidor survived the blitz and the riot. Like Karayn, I'm playing a role in this universe, but I'll be damned if I know what it is. Still bemused, he dragged himself off the tattered chair and toward the Mall doors.

Marine sentries greeted him with smiles, pointing to the darkness, then the platoon sergeant threw a smart salute which Ross acknowledged with a touch of grace. Human warmth arose from the most unexpected places, including the hearts of barrel-chested marines.

Cuspidor started up as if nothing had ever happened. He chose Key Bridge for its lofted spans above the Potomac and soon traveled its concrete length with his mind on the political consequences of the laser blitz. There was no doubt the blitz was international blackmail on the grandest scale. He recalled that the Germans, Italians, Japanese and Russians almost succeeded in taking the world down with them while trying to solve gross internal problems. Yet in this instance no one nation really qualified for the blackmailer's role. Was it a consortium? More likely. It was quite surprising the blackmailer had never tipped his hand, in spite of his monumental effort to intimidate the U.S. He never raised his head, never asked for a thing. His was a well-knit, tightly controlled, totally dedicated organization and that would rule out a gang of nations. Unless the President sorted out, found and then named the blackmailer, a think piece to end all think pieces was in order, which he would file on return from vacation. One angle would be the quality of military response to space-age blackmail. Another on preemptive space-war strikes. Still another on the kind of ground support, both military and civilian, needed to survive a space war. Perhaps the laser blitz was a good lesson. He found another consolation. The gutless administration had little chance of reelection in grass-roots America, but he asked himself if that was where the votes were.

He turned onto the defoliated, yet dark streets of Georgetown and except for a roving police car, nothing moved in the new night. He speculated that everyone had returned to bed to eke out what was left of the night. It reminded him to lay out a schedule to coincide with the shuttle's descent. There should be one last bulletin on the touchdown at Edwards, and perhaps a wrap-up on the killer mission, chiefly for international subscribers.

Lupe barked, then pranced and wagged her tail as Marge met and loved him at the kitchen door.

"Home for a while?" she asked happily.

"Yes and no," he said, seizing a fresh tobacco pouch. "I'm sorry to say the shuttle collided with the laser satellite's antennas, or something like that, and is coming down with a damaged wing. I hope it doesn't prove a crisis, Marge."

"What about Shrimp?"

"Obviously he's in it."

"Has he filed?"

"No, and I don't expect him to. He's a full-fledged crew member by now, not just along for the ride. I'm sure he's got his hands full sharing the shuttle's emergency procedures."

Marge bit her lip, then said, "First, Karayn . . ."

"Let's keep it at one," he retorted. "If there are two, then there will be three."

"You're right, Quent. Let's keep it at one."

"Shrimp lands at ten tonight in California and I've got to file that touchdown. Otherwise, I'm hoping the day remains rather loose," he said, pouring a healthy shot of Scotch. "Coffee might play hell with my sleep," he added with a wink as he headed for the shower.

Marge had neither drawn the bedroom blinds nor turned on the lights, but he discovered Lupe had preempted his place in bed. Shoving her off, he crawled in, only to have her follow. This went on until Marge called her off.

"Quent, you must admit she's funny."

"Call the kids in the morning and tell them to pick up their damned dog before they do another damned thing!" he growled, burying his face in the pillow.

Hours later Marge shook him. "It's Terry," she said. "He sounds terribly anxious."

Ross answered in the kitchen.

"We're in deep shit!" Stewart said. "The shuttle's headed for trouble."

"We suspected it, didn't we?"

"It's worse than we thought."

"How bad, Terry?"

"Based on the manufacturer's analysis, the shuttle has suffed no loss of control in pitch, the up and down movement. But lateral control is questionable due to leading flap damage and airfoil distortion of the right wing. This means the pilot's ability to steer the shuttle left or right is doubtful once he reenters the earth's atmosphere. What I'm saying is he doesn't know where he will land. We don't know where he will land. The computers can't tell us where he will land. His minimum touchdown speed is two hundred fifty miles per hour!"

Ross stood with mouth agape.

"Are you there or not?" Stewart demanded.

"Hell, yes!" Ross said. "I'm staggered by what you've said."

"I'll meet you down below in a half-hour. Okay?"

"Okay," Ross answered, shaking the specter of a fiery crash landing out of his head.

"What happened?" Marge asked.

"The shuttle's in trouble. We don't know where it will land."

She gasped. "They won't burn up like a meteor, will they?"

"I doubt that kind of horrible fate, but they might make one helluva groove in somebody's cornfield."

"Oh, dear," she sighed. "Poor Shrimp!"

"Guess I better get going," he said, grabbing Cuspidor's keys, then kissed her on both cheeks and drove off.

Bypassing the bullpen, he arrived at the planetarium on schedule. Stewart met him looking depressed and handed him over to Glasscock for the signing-in ritual.

"I've never seen anything like this," Glasscock said, ushering Ross to the console. "For each giant step forward, we take one giant step backward."

Ross looked overhead casually and was surprised to see the LS-1 alphanumeric still flashing in space, while the Shuttle's SS-13 had moved toward the horizon. "Why is the laser satellite still being shown?" he asked, wondering whether *Remora* had really done its job.

"The debris will take time to disperse. It's like flotsam resulting from a shipwreck," Glasscock explained. "That debris is the giant step forward."

Ross examined the TV screen. It was on but the picture showed only a faint outline of earth.

Glasscock said, "We've asked the shuttle pilot not to turn off the forward-looking video. Won't hurt and might even help on letdown. At this moment it's of no value, other than to prove the shuttle's still zinging along." He switched to the communications channel between the shuttle and Vandenberg ground control, which was loaded with technical gibberish. "Both sides are working the problem," Glasscock said, "and that's all we can ask. They've got several hours left, so let's get out of here for some of that cafeteria chow and then come back for the moment of truth. Okay?"

"Okay," Ross replied grimly as Glasscock led the way out.

The cafeteria was noiseless and strangely deserted. "Everyone's had a bellyful of this place," Stewart said as they served and seated themselves.

Glasscock groaned. "One more pun like that, Terry, and it'll cost you a promotion."

"Sorry, sir. I regret the unsavory, if not unpalatable, remark."

"That did it!" Glasscock said deadpan. "Off with his damned buttons!"

Stewart handed him a penny. "Sir, I'm buying my way out."

Ross guffawed at the prattle while digging into a heaping plateful of spaghetti and meatballs, a crusted leftover from the crisis. He secretly enjoyed the silly give-and-take of the two Air Force men whose worst hours, he suspected, still lay ahead.

When he had finished eating, Glasscock said, "Now that the laser is detroyed, I'm sure very few will care about the fate of the shuttle, unless it comes down on their heads. Quent, I'm between you and the White House on this particular business. We've got three possible scenarios. The first is that the shuttle lands safely at Edwards. I can high-key the dramatic mission from beginning to end and can charge up the Hill for research and development appropriations. The second scenario is that the shuttle lands out in the boondocks, but the crew is saved. This is low- to middle-key treatment and I wouldn't expect the White House to touch it. The third scenario reads that we lose the shuttle and its crew. I'd like to no-key it, but of course that is utterly impossible. I remember when Grissom and his space crew burned on the ground during the Apollo program, but that was caused by engineering boo-boos. The press and public jumped up and down for the best part of the week. Now we are faced with the aftermath of a collision. If scenario three is played out, then I'd better stress the heroism, the successful laser kill, the sacrifice of three for the safety and well-being of millions of fellow citizens. And, Terry, you ought to think about drafting the right words for Fairly to hand the President, even if they get bounced back to Whitley. What are your thoughts, Quent?"

Ross drew hard on his pipe. "Noel, there is no general public, only special publics with special interests and special prejudices. Take my international readership. They want everything personified and the more sensational the better. Obviously, the facts suffer and truth evaporates. Fortunately, in military analyses, I'm not in as bad a spot as those reporting on the White House, Congress or social affairs in Washington. What I'm saying, Noel, is there's no time left in which to establish a climate for any of the scenarios so that you can get prior understanding and support from your special publics. I would say to you to forget the public relations strategies and play the cards as they fall. To hell with the consequences. If your special publics get turned on and you reach them so that you have a commonality of interest, that's great. If not, tough titty. There's a point, Noel, beyond which the art of manipulation to capture a public becomes self-defeating."

Listening attentively, Stewart said, "After winning the first space war, I think it impossible to predict how the administration or the public will react to the shuttle's plight. The shuttle touched the life of everyone in the country. You can say that of almost nothing else."

"Well put," Glasscock said.

"You're following your painting numbers just like I thought you would," Ross said with what he then realized was an unnecessary touch of sarcasm. "Actually, Terry, you've made the leap to a conceptual grasp of the business and before long you'll be a real threat to colleague and press alike."

"That's a compliment coming from Quent," Glasscock explained.

"And who knows, Terry, you may turn out as another General Glasscock, the Sly Fox of Fairfax," Ross said.

"I've heard enough," Glasscock said with a wink. "Let's leave my sexual prowess out of this. On the other hand, I'm glad my reputation isn't petering out!"

Ross and Stewart snickered as they left the cafeteria for the equally deserted concourse. The shops were closed, including the huge newsstands. Ross stole a furtive look at Nefertiti while walking full circle and then Glasscock said they had stalled long enough. It was time to return to the vigil.

The planetarium was much as they had left it, although voice traffic increased from ground radar control stations at Christchurch and Christmas Island over which the shuttle would let down from final orbit toward Edwards in California.

Ross swore he recognized Shrimp's voice in the ongoing chatter, but it had nothing to do with copy.

He asked Stewart, "Has Vandenberg's public affairs office put anything out on the shuttle that I should have?"

"You won't get scooped, if that's what you're worried about, Quent. They must clear their copy with the Defense newsroom on this big a story before it is released. So, sitting here, you know all they know, and perhaps more. Okay?"

"Okay," Ross said, putting anxiety aside.

The planetarium filled quickly with silent observers as the shuttle entered its programmed letdown from final orbit. The TV transmitter scanned the ice mass of Antarctica, then over the equatorial Pacific Ocean the pilot said all systems were nominal. He squared the shuttle away for final approach to Edwards.

Stewart explained that in addition to the on-board computer, at least two other ground-based computers monitored the shuttle's position, course, altitude and speed. Real-time data come in from satellite and ground radar tracking stations. All of this information was digested and fed into the shuttle's autopilot. The human pilot's job was to override the autopilot and fly the shuttle manually in the event of catastrophic electrical, engine or aerodynamic failure, none of which had ever happened. Because of redundant electrical, hydraulic, motor and computer systems, chances of the shuttle misgauging its position, speed, altitude or course were considered infinitesimally small. However, if the shuttle's aerodynamic integrity were damaged or destroyed, then nothing other than pilot skill and Lady Luck would help.

Ross rasped into Stewart's ear, "Wish I could be filing minute-by-minute."

Stewart shrugged at the notion. "Look at the TV screen, the picture is starting to shake, Quent. That's due to the shuttle's passage through wispy fingers of the earth's atmosphere at eighty thousand feet. The picture will fall apart when the shuttle descends into the blanket of denser air, not only because of turbulence, but as the result of masive charges of friction-induced static electricity."

The pilot called out the letdown checklist, an array of items, but there were no malfunctions. Then at fifty thousand feet altitude he announced the sudden onset of buffeting and the loss of some lateral control.

Moments later, reporting four hundred miles west of Cabo San Lucas at the tip of Baja California, he advised Vandenberg of violent yawing. "I can't override it," he called in. "I've tried every power setting and control position, computer-programmed and my own feel. Nothing works!"

"Get out!" Vandenberg advised.

"Roger. We're tumbling. I hope the capsule jettisons."

"You'll blow clean. Get out!"

"That friggin' wing!" Ross heard Shrimp say.

"SS-13, you're four hundred miles north-northwest of Lucas. We'll be right there to pick you up. Keep the faith! Good luck!" Vandenberg said calmly.

"Roger, Van. We're blowing out now," the pilot said and then all communications went dead.

Ross looked in despair at Glasscock.

"Son of a bitch!" was all he said.

But Stewart added reassuringly, "We've got choppers stationed all along the shuttle's flight path, Quent. I'm optimistic they'll get picked up quicker than we think."

"What's the capsule like?" Ross asked.

"It's the crew compartment, completely self-contained, designed for emergencies just like this. It separates itself from the shuttle's fuselage with explosive bolts and then floats down on parachutes. They've got oxygen, food, medical supplies and survival gear on board."

"Will it sink?" Ross pressed.

"Not unless it's badly damaged."

"Do we know?"

"I'm sure the capsule's intact."

"Boy, will Shrimp have a story to file! What now?" Ross asked, turning to Glasscock.

"Damned if I know," Glasscock admitted. "This is the worst of all scenarios. It may take minutes, hours or days before they're found and fished out. If you sit in here, Quent, you'll be on top of it. If you leave, we'll have to come and get you. I hate to high-key the rescue and I can't low-key it."

Ross said, "I've got to file the fact that they are down in the drink, so I'd better move my butt to the ticker room, Noel."

"Sounds right," Glasscock said. "We'll escort you out. Terry will join me in my office for a bit of strategizing before we put out a Defense news release. On the other hand, we're glad you are an eyewitness to the truth.

We'll be in touch, Quent. The choppers should be hovering over them before long, as Terry says."

"God willing!" Ross exclaimed. At the teletype he found it harder than ever to file. Goddamned spot news stories. Would he ever be freed of them? When Shrimp returned they'd collaborate on a think piece to end all think pieces, using the first eyewitness to the first space war as a lead-in.

The machine skipped when he first turned it on. He waited for it to settle down, working stiffness out of his fingers by catching imaginary butterflies above his head, then began beating on the keyboard.

> BULLETIN:
> OVER "A" CIRCUITS
> DATELINE WASHINGTON THIS DATE
> BYLINE QUENTIN ROSS, MILITARY ANALYST, THE PENTAGON
> —BITTERSWEET VICTORY
> LESS THAN TWENTY HOURS AFTER DESTROYING THE LASER SATELLITE SOME 66,000 MILES IN SPACE, THE VICTORIOUS AMERICAN SHUTTLE CREW WAS FORCED TO ABANDON THE SPACECRAFT WHILE HOMEWARD BOUND ABOUT 400 MILES WEST OF CABO SAN LUCAS, MEXICO. THE THREE ASTRONAUTS EJECTED FROM THE COLLISION-CRIPPLED AND UNCONTROLLABLE SHUTTLE IN A SPECIALLY DESIGNED LIFE-SUPPORT CAPSULE THAT FLOATED THEM WITH PARACHUTES TO THE SURFACE OF THE SEA. THE DISABLED SHUTTLE IS PRESUMED TO HAVE CRASHED AND SUNK IN 300 FATHOMS OFF THE MEXICAN COAST.
> U.S. AIR FORCE HELICOPTERS STATIONED ALONG THE SHUTTLE'S FLIGHT PATH FLEW IMMEDIATELY TO THE PREDICTED POINT OF THE CAPSULE SPLASHDOWN. WORD ON

SUCCESS OF THE RESCUE WILL BE RELAYED VIA DEFENSE COMMUNICATIONS SATELLITES TO THE PENTAGON, THEN TO WAITING RELATIVES.

AN AIR FORCE BOARD OF INQUIRY WILL BE CONVENED IMMEDIATELY TO DETERMINE THE CAUSE OF THE FIRST SPACE WAR ACCIDENT. END.
END BULLETIN.
NOTE TO EDITORS: STAND BY FOR RESCUE ADD ONE. END.

Ross switched off the teletype and stared mindlessly at the wall. Then sensing someone behind him, he turned to see Stewart standing in the doorway.

"Well, Terry," he said, "what's new?"

"Quent, the escape capsule's parachutes failed to open. The capsule crashed into the ocean. The crew is dead."

9

A ten-day flu epidemic scourged the nation in the aftermath of the laser blitz. Ross was laid low but Marge provided an impregnable sanctuary until frustration and partial recovery drove him out of bed. He promised to work part time and to catch up on only the most pressing problems. Marge scoffed as she let him go.

The marine sentries were gone from the Mall doors, replaced by the same tired civilians stationed there before the blitz. And Lu accosted him the minute he appeared in the bullpen.

"Let me sit down first, if it's bad news," he said, moving behind the barricade. "What's up?"

"Plenty! The President demanded Noel's resignation with the accusation that he was running wild. So Noel retired overnight and flew to Santa Barbara. Would you believe it, he wants to open a poodle kennel! And guess who replaced him. Scotus!"

"No!"

"Yes! He got released from the nut house and Whitley had him reinstated. The rumor is he's moving over to the White House to replace Fairly!"

"Dear God! I'm sorry I came back."

"That's not all, Quent. Terry Stewart shipped out to Alaska as public affairs officer for the Alaskan Command."

"It breaks my heart, Lu. Was it by choice?"

"Sort of. He knew his days were numbered around here. Noel's retirement was the last straw. Oh, Terry left this envelope with me. He said it was for your eyes only."

Ross took the envelope and stuffed it in a pocket.

"Cary Clapham was transferred to New York as V.P. for his syndicate, a tremendous promotion."

"Good for him," Ross said enthusiastically. "It was inevitable. And what about yourself, Lu?"

"Quent, I hate to tell you this, but I'm leaving too."

"No!"

"I've bought into the newsletter. The board voted me in as publisher, an offer no decent girl could refuse."

"I'll bet!" Ross said with a pang, "but goddammit, I'll miss you!"

"Not as much as I. You'll never know. And while you were sick I took a minute to hang Karayn and Shrimp's photos in the niche."

Ross bit his lip.

"One last piece of bad news, Quent. It's obvious Dawn didn't tell you, but Ivorson has been transferred to Atlanta to head the IP bureau there."

"That's bad news? I would've recovered faster!"

"Hear me out. Your new boss came poking around yesterday. Strikes me as a very fussy kid. Looks thirtyish. Walked in circles shaking his head at your desk and barricade."

Ross swore. "Not that again!"

"Too bad, Quent! You just might lose your status symbol."

Ross uttered another expletive but stopped short as a stranger rounded the barricade. Lu winked knowledgeably and departed.

"Joe Watkins," the stranger said without a smile or handshake. "I'm your new bureau chief, Ross."

Taken aback, Ross watched Watkins straddle the

chair alongside the desk, unfolding a six-foot-six frame, spidery arms and legs, topped off by a burry pinhead.

"You've got an unbelievable mess here, Ross. I want to talk about it."

"Go right ahead," Ross said, taking a violent dislike to Watkins.

"Your desk is a disgrace to IP. Clean it up today, Ross."

"Oh? Will that improve my copy?"

"Sure as hell won't hurt it. I'm a great believer in the positive effects of a good image. It's simply good PR."

"Then hire me a goddamn secretary. Too much crap flows across this desk for me to take time to pretty it up for you. Maybe I should tie a whiskbroom to my ass to please you."

Watkins's jaw hardened. "I'm talking mostly about that towering wall of paper. Get rid of it. File it. Burn it. Eat it."

"That's my instant reference file, library, encyclopedia and font of knowledge. I can't function without this source material at my fingertips."

"Your problem," Watkins said, rising for what seemed minutes. "I want a neat and decent IP working area here when I return tomorrow. Remember, that desk represents IP to the Department of Defense."

Ross watched him stalk out, then muttered loudly, "You rotten son of a bitch!"

Lu returned, laughing. "I overheard most of it, Quent. My condolences."

"Go ahead and laugh, damn you, Lu. You're bugging out of this madhouse forever. What the hell is it about the Pentagon that brings out the worst in people?"

"You keep asking the same question, Quent," she said lightheartedly. "I'm amazed you didn't hit the smart-assed kid in the mouth. Resting up obviously did you some good."

"But not enough to cope with this."

"You should know the President took off for Maui for a well-earned rest," she said sarcastically. "And there are five congressional junkets flying off to every nook of the world to thank our allies for their loyalty and support during the laser blitz, not to mention the dozens of military inspection trips taken by the brass of all the armed forces."

"What else?" Ross moaned. "Human Services got its budget reinstated at the expense of space research and development. The hue and cry over malnutrition became unbearable."

"Have we identified the laser culprit?"

"Don't be a silly boy. The President tasked the head of CIA to follow through. That'll bury the investigation and the results, if any. Quent, everybody wants to forget the laser blitz. Washington's deserted. Wounded egos are being licked at Hilton Head and Acapulco. Only a few malcontents and hotheads are rabble-rousing the laser issue now. Are you going to be one of them, one of the dissidents?"

"You can bet your sweet petunia I'm not going to drop it, sweetheart."

She looked at her watch. "Well, good luck, Quent. I've got a board meeting I dare not miss," she said, shuffling past the barricade.

He didn't know whether to laugh or cry over the course of events, then remembered Stewart's letter. He tore it open but found no personal note. Instead, Stewart had enclosed a news photo of a giant Russian cargo aircraft, the Antonov 21, used by the Cubans to transport thousands of troops and supplies to Africa and other international hot spots. The other enclosure was a clipping from an electronics trade paper that cited successful Russian efforts to miniaturize the electron ring accelerator. Puzzled by Stewart's impersonal, cryptic message, he thrust the material back into his pocket, got up and walked almost aimlessly down the corridor, suppressing anger at Watkins's visit. Suddenly, the light dawned and Stewart's information fell into place. Ross felt his heart thump. He stopped, turned and raced to the ticker room, flipped on the teletype switch and began pounding with stiff fingers.

>BULLETIN:
>OVER "A" CIRCUITS
>DATELINE WASHINGTON THIS DATE
>BYLINE QUENTIN ROSS, MILITARY ANALYST, THE PENTAGON
>CAUTION: COPYRIGHT MATERIAL
>CUBANS GUILTY OF LASER BLITZ
>
>RUSSIAN-BUILT CARGO AIRCRAFT AND MISSILE BOOSTERS WERE DEPLOYED BY CUBAN ARMED FORCES TO LAUNCH THE LASER SATELLITE AND ITS HIGH-ENERGY TWIN TO TERRORIZE THE UNITED STATES, ACCORDING TO INFORMED PENTAGON SOURCES.
>
>THE FOUR-NIGHT LASER BLITZ WAS ENDED DRAMATICALLY WHEN THE U.S. SPACE SHUTTLE INTERCEPTED AND DESTROYED THE LASER SATELLITE, THUS WRECKING SOVIET-CUBAN PLANS TO BRING THE U.S. TO ITS KNEES FOR THE SECOND TIME IN RECENT HISTORY. IN 1962 A SOVIET-CUBAN THREAT TO ATTACK THE U.S. WITH SOVIET-BUILT, CUBAN-BASED NUCLEAR MISSILES WAS CHALLENGED BY PRESIDENT JOHN F. KENNEDY, RESULTING IN A KENNEDY-KHRUSCHEV AGREEMENT BANNING DEPLOYMENT OF OFFENSIVE WEAPONS AGAINST THE U.S. ON CUBAN SOIL.
>
>CITING CIRCUMSTANTIAL YET POSITIVE EVIDENCE, PENTAGON EXPERTS STATED THAT SOVIET-BUILT ANTONOV-21 CARGO AIRCRAFT, LARGEST TRANSPORTS IN THE WORLD, MANNED BY CUBAN AIRCREWS, CARRIED SOVIET MISSILE BOOSTERS TO THE VICINITY OF ASCENCION ISLAND IN THE

SOUTH ATLANTIC OCEAN. EMPLOYING U.S. AIR FORCE MUNUTEMAN AIR-LAUNCH TECHNIQUES, THE CUBAN AIRCREWS SECRETLY LAUNCHED TWO SATELLITES. THE FIRST SATELLITE CONTAINED A SOVIET-DEVELOPED ELECTRON RING ACCELERATOR (ERA) THAT HAD BEEN SUCCESSFULLY MINIATURIZED TO PROVIDE A HIGH ENERGY SOURCE FOR THE LASER DEVICE ABOARD THE SECOND SATELLITE. THE ERA LAUNCH WAS NEVER DETECTED. HOWEVER, THE SECOND LAUNCH WAS TRACKED BY SYMONDS OBSERVATORY OF GREAT BRITAIN AND PROVIDED FIRST WARNING WHICH WAS IGNORED BY THE ADMINISTRATION. BOTH SATELLITES WERE SUCCESSFULLY INJECTED INTO HIGH, GEOSYNCHCRONOUS ORBIT TO EVENTUALLY BLIND THE UNITED STATES. RESEMBLING A FLOATING DUMBBELL WHEN COUPLED TOGETHER, THE TWIN SATELLITES WERE UNDER CONSTANT CONTROL OF SOVIET-CUBAN TEAMS AIRBORNE IN SEVERAL OTHER AN-21 AIRCRAFT, THUS ESCAPING U.S. DETECTION. THIS MOBILE CONTROL TECHNIQUE PROVED HIGHLY SUCCESSFUL. BY MOVING THE ATTACK ON THE UNITED STATES FROM CUBAN SOIL TO A POINT OVER THE SOUTH ATLANTIC OCEAN, THE CUBAN AGGRESSORS TECHNICALLY DID NOT VIOLATE THE KENNEDY-KHRUSCHEV AGREEMENT, AND IN FACT DELUDED WASHINGTON.

THE COMMUNIST GOVERNMENT IN CUBA HAS BEEN REARMED IN STEALTH BY THE SOVIETS WITH THE MOST MODERN GROUND, AIR AND SPACE WEAPONS IN THE SOVIET ARSENAL. THE U.S. GOVERNMENT

HAS REPEATEDLY DOWNGRADED THE CUBAN TECHNOLOGICAL THREAT, OFTEN EXPLAINING AND APOLOGIZING FOR CUBAN EXPANSIONISM, THUS MAKING A MOCKERY OF THE ORGANIZATION OF AMERICAN STATES. WHETHER THE U.S. WILL IGNORE THE WARNINGS OF HISTORY AND MAKE ITSELF VULNERABLE FOR YET A THIRD TIME TO THE SOVIET-CUBAN ALLIANCE IS A QUESTION ONLY THE WHITE HOUSE CAN ANSWER.
END BULLETIN.

Ross turned off the teletype with a sense of satisfaction. He had just taken his ego trip, the self-appointed, willful watchdog barking at the White House to drive it out of its silence. But a moment's reflection told him the CIA quite possibly knew of the Soviet-Cuban role and had kept the information to itself, or had passed it on to the White House where the President or an aide stonewalled it. In any case, the IP scoop would force the issue into the open.

He relaxed behind the barricade, switching to a Sherlock Holmes pipe, and thought of visiting Nefertiti. On impulse he ran down to Brentano's, bought and pocketed her, and returned just in time to answer Watkins's call.

Watkins sounded savage, grossly unhappy with the Cuban copy.

"What's wrong with it?" Ross asked, feeling equal to the confrontation.

"Your last paragraph is editorialization, sheer opinion. I want spot news, Ross."

"Not from me, Watkins. I'm a military analyst. I signal the event and then flush out the facts so they can be acted on. I'm not a kid covering the police radio. Okay?"

"It's not okay. I'm bureau chief, Ross. I don't want your opinions. I want spot defense news from now on, or I'll kill every last word that you file. By the way, don't forget to clean up your pigsty."

Ross kept his mouth shut with difficulty.

London called direct to congratulate him on the Cuban scoop and said more words would be on the wire from other capitals. He asked that all bouquets be routed through New York as a personal favor. New York followed and Ross told the V.P. to be sure to relay the compliments to Watkins because that new broom was trying to sweep him out for all the wrong reasons.

Scotus phoned from the White House, enraged over Ross's speculation and the damage it had done to the President's image at home and abroad. He threatened to lift Ross's Defense Department accreditation. Ross suggested it would make a great story, especially if Scotus ordered it, adding that the whole damned bullpen should be disaccredited, thus leaving the administration with a friendly press. Scotus remained silent as he mulled it over, then snorted and hung up.

Glancing down at his desk, Ross discovered a stack of blue-bannered Defense news releases issued during Glasscock's short reign. He chose several and added them to the barricade, then retrieved Nefertiti from his pocket. He placed her gently on the desk and whispered, "If this wall falls, surely the rest of my life begins today."

THE TULPA
By J.N. Williamson

PRICE: $1.95   LB799
CATEGORY: Occult

Charlie Kavanagh felt all of his 73 years. He was worried about his aging mind, and his "spells," his dreams — or visions? No one would listen. No one except his son-in-law, who saw things coming, building, promising unheard of horror. Then it came. It rose from within, slowly at first, shuffling through shadows, learning of violence, developing a special hunger. Then it struck—and again. It grew, not quite quenching its thirst on blood and fear. And only one thing could hope to destroy the terrorizing appetite of...THE TULPA!

HEAR THE CHILDREN CRY
By R.J. Hendrickson

PRICE: $2.50 LB968
CATEGORY: Novel

A NOVEL OF UNRELENTING TERROR!

One...two...three small children have died hideously. Only their five-year-old brother, Danny, is left.
The only possible suspects are the parents–and, of course, little Danny himself.
One person knows the truth, and that evil someone is preparing the final, unspeakable atrocity!

POSITIONS By Bill Adler

PRICE: $2.75 LB966
CATEGORY: Novel

A SIZZLING NOVEL OF WHAT WOMEN CAN DO WHEN THEY REACH THE TOP "POSITIONS"

Three women changed the Hollywood scene. They had it all—beauty, brains and talent. Their stepping stones to the top were male egos, and they rose to rule the very men who desired them.
KELLEY LEE plunged into a career writing film scripts, and out-sold the best of her men.
DARLENE NORTH became a top talent agent, who bought and sold beautiful people—and most of her friends.
ANNA MANNERS fell prey to the worst in show business, and bounced back to become the biggest bitch of the silver screen.

AFTER SUCCESS, THEY WANTED LOVE —BUT CAN A MAN LOVE A WOMAN WHO CAN FIRE HIM?

SEND TO: LEISURE BOOKS
P.O. Box 511, Murry Hill Station
New York, N.Y. 10156-0511

Please send the titles:

Quantity	Book Number	Price
_____	_____	_____
_____	_____	_____
_____	_____	_____
_____	_____	_____
_____	_____	_____

In the event we are out of stock on any of your selections, please list alternate titles below.

_____	_____	_____
_____	_____	_____
_____	_____	_____
_____	_____	_____

Postage/Handling _____

I enclose _____

FOR U.S. ORDERS, add 75¢ for the first book and 25¢ for each additional book to cover cost of postage and handling. Buy five or more copies and we will pay for shipping. Sorry, no C.O.D.'s.

FOR ORDERS SENT OUTSIDE THE U.S.A., add $1.00 for the first book and 50¢ for each additional book. PAY BY foreign draft or money order drawn on a U.S. bank, payable in U.S. ($) dollars.

☐ Please send me a free catalog.

NAME _____
(Please print)
ADDRESS _____

CITY _____ STATE _____ ZIP _____

Allow Four Weeks for Delivery